JACK O' JUDGMENT

Colonel Dan Boundary runs a very efficient gang of London blackmailers. They find a business owner's weakness—clandestine lover's letters, compromising situations—and demand to buy him out for a pittance. It's all quite legal—money changes hands, a business moves from one name to another, and Boundary's gang continues to grow richer. Pinto Silva, Swell Crewe and Lollie Marsh—Boundary's trusted accomplices—do their jobs well. Until the apparent overdose of gang member Snow Gregory puts them in the spotlight. When the disappearance of Boundary's trusted partner, Solomon White, sparks the interest of Stafford King of Scotland Yard the mysterious Jack o' Judgment first makes his appearance, interrupting a Boundary meeting with fearless bravado. Who could this masked character be? A friend to the law, or a new foe, even more ruthless than the Boundary Gang?

CAPTAINS OF SOULS

Ambrose Sault has lived a rough life. He himself admits to being in a Caledonia jail for murder when he was rescued years ago by his partner, Moropulos. Despite his illiteracy, inside him resides the gentle soul of a poet and philosopher. This is what draws to him the disparate lives of Christina Colebrook, cynical invalid daughter of his landlady, and Beryl Merville, the esteemed doctor's daughter, now under the sway of the ruthless Jan Steppe. Moropulos works for Steppe, and so too the young cad, Ronald Morelle. Steppe's group has been manipulating the market, compromising Dr. Merville without his knowledge. When Christina's sister Evie comes to the dishonorable attention of Ronnie, their lives intersect, and soon Beryl is pulled into the compromise. Will Evie allow her reputation to be ruined? Can Sault save Beryl from the callous intentions of both Steppe and Morelle? And whose life will become forfeit when a clash of wills leads to murder?

Jack o' Judgment

◆ ◆ ◆

Captains of Souls

TWO NOVELS BY
EDGAR WALLACE

Stark House Press • Eureka California

JACK O' JUDGMENT / CAPTAINS OF SOULS

Published by Stark House Press
1315 H Street
Eureka, CA 95501, USA
griffinskye3@sbcglobal.net
www.starkhousepress.com

ISBN: 1-933586-74-5
ISBN-13: 978-1-933586-74-8

Book design by Mark Shepard, www.shepgraphics.com
Proofreading by Rick Ollerman

First Stark House Press Edition: October 2014

Edgar Wallace
by Ed Hulse

The recent boom in small-press reprints of works by obscure crime writers and pulp fictioneers has revived interest in a good many storytellers previously forgotten. And yet, strangely, the movement to date has largely ignored Edgar Wallace, an astonishingly prolific British author who was in his time emulated, and imitated, by a host of thriller writers on both sides of the Atlantic. Very little of Wallace's prodigious output remains in print, despite the fact that for many years one of every four books sold in Britain bore his name on its cover. Thankfully, the volume you now hold in your hands begins to redress this lamentable situation.

Richard Horatio Edgar Wallace was born in London on April 1, 1875, the illegitimate son of British stage performers who gave him up for adoption. Taken into the family of "fish porter" George Freeman, the boy shared a cramped home with ten siblings. This modest upbringing led young master Richard to seek employment at an early age, and only upon applying for a job that required the presentation of a birth certificate did he learn the truth about his parentage.

Leaving school at the age of twelve, he toiled in various positions until joining the British army at eighteen. Upon being discharged Wallace—by now using the surname of his birth father—wangled a job as South African correspondent for the Reuters international news agency. The young journalist learned a great deal about Africa and its people while honing his ability as a writer and breaking several important stories. He returned to England an ace reporter for the *London Daily Mail*, mingling effortlessly with members of upper and lower classes alike. Moreover, he developed an uncanny knack for ferreting out news under extraordinary conditions, often relying on shady characters for tips. This experience stood him in good stead when he turned to writing fiction.

In 1905 Wallace self-published his first novel, *The Four Just Men*, under the auspices of Tallis Press. As an inducement to potential buyers unfamiliar with his byline, he offered 500 pounds in prize money to readers who solved the mystery surrounding a supporting character's death at the hands of the Just Men. For this purpose the book included a form that could be filled out, detached, and mailed to the Tallis Press office. The first prize was 250 pounds; the others were lesser amounts. In preparing the promotional copy Wallace failed to restrict the number of contest entrants, and while the novel was a huge best-seller he actually lost money because a larger-than-anticipated number of applicants correctly guessed the murder method. (He actually received financial aid from the *Mail*, which feared his poorly conceived scheme would reflect badly on the paper.) The newly minted author paid dearly for underestimating his readers but established himself as a thriller writer to watch. In the long run his contest payout was money well invested.

Much of Wallace's early fiction drew on his experience in Africa. The exploits of his first series character, Sanders of the River, reflected typical Victorian-era attitudes regarding British colonialism. Commissioner Sanders maintained order among squabbling native tribes using considerable ingenuity and relying on his vast knowledge of human nature. Most readers today find Sanders condescendingly paternalistic at best and arrogantly racist at worst, but in the Twentieth Century's first two decades Wallace's tales in this series were well received and collected in book form on both sides of the Atlantic.

During the First World War, Edgar Wallace wrote about such heroic AEF aviators as Tam o' the Scoots and the Companions of the Ace-High, whose careers were documented in *Everybody's Magazine* and *The Popular Magazine* respectively. After the War he increasingly turned to the production of crime thrillers, especially when the firm of Street & Smith purchased American rights to much of his output for one of its most successful pulps, *Detective Story Magazine*. By this time his yarns were appearing regularly in such British periodicals as *The Strand, The Thriller, The Grand Magazine*, and *The Detective Magazine*. Wallace cleverly rebuffed requests for exclusivity from American pulp-magazine publishers and placed his yarns with multiple houses; during the Twenties his works were just as likely to be seen in Doubleday's *Short Stories* and Munsey's *Flynn's* and *Detective Fiction Weekly* as in *Detective Story*. As his fame grew in the United States, he frequently sold to the prestigious slicks, including *Collier's, Cosmopolitan*, and *The Saturday Evening Post*.

Wallace enjoyed particular success in the pages of *Detective Story*, which serialized more than two dozen of his novels and published multi-entry series of short stories featuring his most popular recurring characters, The Ringer and The Three Just Men. One of his earliest contributions to the venerable Street & Smith pulp was *Jack o' Judgment*, which ran in six weekly installments from March 9 through April 13, 1920. It was published in hard covers the next month by the British house Ward Lock and then again the following year by the Boston-headquartered firm of Small, Maynard & Company.

Jack o' Judgment is a key title in Wallace's *oeuvre*. A pulpy thriller through and through, it marks the first major work in which he employed a "mystery man" protagonist whose motivation remained unknown until the closing chapters. Garbed in slouch hat and cloak, his face masked, Jack mocks his adversaries with a shrill laugh, talks of himself in the third person, and leaves a jack of clubs as his calling card. For reasons known only to himself, this wraith-like figure has sworn vengeance on Colonel Dan Boundary, head of a blackmail ring responsible for the deaths—both suicides and murders—of numerous people whose darkest secrets have been used against them. The Colonel is also sought by Scotland Yard, represented in this story by young inspector Stafford King and distinguished commissioner Stanley Belcom. The inevitable love interest is furnished by Maisie White, stage actress and daughter of Boundary's former partner.

Jack o' Judgment crackles with suspense and melodrama while exhibiting its author's strengths and weaknesses as a storyteller. Wallace often wrote (or dictated) his thrillers at a white heat, and while his speedy composition imparted a breezy quality to these compulsively readable tales, it frequently produced embarrassing lapses in plot and characterization. The early chapters of *Jack*, for example, make a great to-do about incriminating documents collected and hidden by Boundary's clerk, Olaf Hanson, who is working undercover for the police and seems destined to play an important role in the proceedings. Wallace, however, summarily dispatches Hanson in the novel's first *Detective Story* installment and the vitally important papers are never again mentioned, even though the principal characters all know of their existence. Other inconsistencies abound but can't be reported here lest I spoil your enjoyment of the story. Odds are they escaped the notice of *Detective Story* readers who digested the yarn in weekly portions of ten to twelve thousand words.

But therein lays the point: Edgar Wallace thrillers usually move at such a breathless pace, and are crowded with so many exciting incidents and colorful characters, that errors of continuity often go undetected. It doesn't matter that the characters are two dimensional or that certain narrative devices are reused *ad infinitum*. The author is a master at drawing readers into a world of his own creation. Wallace's London is especially magical; its familiar landmarks are carefully and realistically described—the journalist's penchant for conveying shrewd observations in terse sentences is obvious here—but his imagination conjures up a sort of phantom city in which seedy and none-too-bright underworld denizens rub shoulders with grotesquely disguised criminal masterminds and independently wealthy Scotland Yard inspectors.

Jack o' Judgment is relatively straightforward melodrama. One could easily imagine it as a silent-era cliffhanger movie serial with someone like Pearl White in the female lead. The second novel reprinted in this volume, *Captains of Souls*, is ostensibly another thriller cut to a similar pattern. But it is radically different. For all their fanciful aspects, Wallace's crime stories were covered with a patina of realism. It was highly unlikely that a masked and cloaked vigilante would prowl the streets of Limehouse in search of killers on whom to prey. But it *could* have happened. *Captains of Souls*, first published by Small, Maynard & Company in 1922, skirted the boundaries of plausibility by incorporating within its narrative a strong supernatural element.

Most of the characters fall within well-established Wallace parameters.

Ronald Morrelle is an ex-soldier who now works as a reporter for the *Post-Herald*. Evie Colebrook is the poor but pure heroine; her younger sister Christina, an invalid, escapes the confines of her sickbed by projecting herself into the books she reads. Beryl Merville is naïve and sheltered by her ex-physician father, who finds himself implicated in a stock swindle involving a South African diamond mine. The villain of the piece, unscrupulous financier Jan Steppe, has a striking appearance and a magnetic, commanding presence in the accepted Wallace manner.

But *Captains of Souls* is dominated by Ambrose Sault, a stout, shabby, middle-aged man of color with a mane of grey-white hair. He is a mass of contradictions: an apparent illiterate who neither reads nor writes but has committed reams of poetry to memory; an ex-convict and killer capable of great tenderness; a supposed communist whose debt to Moropulos brings him into Steppe's orbit and makes him a trusted henchman.

More to the point, Sault seems to possess the uncanny (and unexplained) ability to transfer his soul into the bodies of other human beings. This questionable gift is put to use several times during the period of time covered by the novel. Describing when and how would be to reveal too much of the plot and possibly ruin your enjoyment of the story. Suffice to say that this storytelling device— employed skillfully by Wallace without making too much of it—lifts *Captains of Souls* above the average and approaches the author's high-water mark. Wallace himself considered it his first attempt at "serious" fiction.

Within a few years of the publication of these novels, Edgar Wallace attained the peak of his popularity. It was reported that in his native England one out of every four books sold bore the Wallace byline. In America, his novels—new and old—anchored the lineup of Doubleday's Crime Club imprint, which issued four books every month for years. His novels and plays were adapted for motion pictures on both sides of the Atlantic; three of the very best (1923's *The Green Archer* and *The Fellowship of the Frog*, and 1926's *The Terrible People*) became top-grossing cliffhanger serials distributed worldwide by Pathé Exchange. His stage thriller *The Terror*, produced in 1928 by Warner Bros. as one of that studio's first all-talking pictures, was a huge success.

Although he ranked among the world's top-earning fictioneers, Wallace squandered his money and was perpetually one jump ahead of creditors. He responded to cash shortfalls by writing even more furiously, in one instance reportedly dictating a fifty-thousand-word novel in a single weekend to meet a financial obligation. His secretary Robert Curtis became an uncredited collaborator, smoothing out the rough edges of Wallace's most hastily crafted yarns.

Edgar Wallace came to Hollywood in late 1931 under contract to RKO Radio Pictures, for which he worked on what became *King Kong*. He died the following February after contracting double pneumonia. The astoundingly prolific author left behind 173 to 181 books (depending upon whose count you believe), as well as hundreds of plays, poems, and uncollected short stories. For several decades his work continued to enjoy worldwide popularity, especially in post-World War II Germany, where film adaptations of his stories were made by the dozens beginning in 1959.

Yet, despite his fecundity and the approbation of readers in countries all over the globe, Edgar Wallace is virtually a forgotten figure in the history of American popular fiction. It's my fervent hope that Stark House, beginning with the publication of these two outstanding novels, will spark a revival of interest in this important and influential author.

—Morris Plains, New Jersey
September 2014

Ed Hulse is a professional writer and editor of *Blood 'n' Thunder* magazine, an amateur journal for aficionados of adventure, mystery, and melodrama in American popular culture of the early 20th century.

Jack o' Judgment

by Edgar Wallace

CHAPTER I
THE KNAVE OF CLUBS

They picked up the young man called "Snow" Gregory from a Lambeth gutter, and he was dead before the policeman on duty in Waterloo Road, who had heard the shots, came upon the scene.

He had been shot in his tracks on a night of snow and storm, and none saw the murder. When they got him to the mortuary and searched his clothes they found nothing except a little tin box of white powder, which proved to be cocaine, and a playing card—the "jack" of clubs.

His associates had called him Snow Gregory because he was a dope fiend, and cocaine is invariably referred to as "snow" by all its votaries. He was a gambler, too, and he had been associated with Colonel Dan Boundary in certain of his business enterprises. That was all. The colonel knew nothing of the young man's antecedents except that he had been an Oxford man who had come down in the world. The colonel added a few particulars designed, as it might seem to the impartial observer, to prove that he, the colonel, had ever been an uplifting quantity.

There were people who said that Snow Gregory in his more exalted moments talked too much for the colonel's comfort, but people were very ready to talk unkindly of the colonel, whose wealth was an offense and a shame.

So they buried Snow Gregory, the unknown, and a jury of his fellow countrymen returned a verdict of "willful murder against some person or persons unknown."

And there was the end of a sordid tragedy, it seemed, until three months later there dawned upon Colonel Boundary's busy life a brand-new and alarming factor.

One morning there arrived at his palatial apartment in Albermarle Place a letter. This he opened because it was marked "Private and Personal." It was not a letter at all—as it proved—but a soiled and stained playing card, the knave of clubs.

He looked at the thing in perplexity, for the fate of his erstwhile assistant had long since passed from his mind. Then he saw writing on the margin of the card and, twisting it sideways, read: "Jack o' Judgment." Nothing more.

"Jack o' Judgment?"

The colonel screwed up his tired eyes as if to shut out a vision.

"Faugh!" he said in disgust and dropped the pasteboard into his waste-paper basket.

For he had seen a vision, a white face, unshaven and haggard, its lips parted in a little grin, the smile of Snow Gregory on the last time they had met.

Later came other cards and unpleasant, not to say disconcerting happenings, and the colonel, taking counsel with himself, determined to kill two birds with one stone.

It was a daring and audacious thing to have done, and none but Colonel Dan Boundary would have taken the risk. He knew better than anybody else that Stafford King had devoted the whole of his time for the past three years to smashing the Boundary gang. He knew that this grave young man with the steady gray eyes, who sat on the other side of the big Louis XV table in the ornate private office of the Spillsbury Syndicate, had won his way to the chief position in the criminal intelligence department by sheer genius, and that he was, of all men, the most to be feared.

No greater contrast could be imagined than that which was presented between the two protagonists—the refined almost esthetic chief of police on the one hand, the big, commanding figure of the redoubtable colonel on the other.

Boundary, with his black hair parted in the center of his sleek head, his big, weary eyes, his long, yellow, walrus mustache, his double chin, his breadth and girth, his enormous hairy hands now laid upon the table, might stand for force, brutal, remorseless, untiring. He stood for cunning, too—the cunning of the stalking tiger.

Stafford was watching him with dispassionate interest. He may have been secretly amused at the man's sheer daring, but if he was, his inscrutable face displayed no such emotion.

"I dare say, Mr. King," said the colonel in his slow, heavy way, "you think it is rather remarkable in all the circumstances that I should ask you to call. I dare say," he went on, "my business associates will think the same, considering all the unpleasantness we have had."

Stafford King made no reply. He sat erect, alert and watchful.

"Give a dog a bad name and hang him," said the colonel sententiously. "For twenty years I've had to fight the unjust suspicions of my enemies. I've been libeled"—he shook his head sorrowfully—"I don't suppose there's anybody been libeled more than me—and my business associates. I've had the police nosing—I mean investigating—into my affairs; and I'll be straight with you, Mr. Stafford King, and tell you that when it came to my ears and the ears of my business associates that you had been put on the job of watching poor old Dan Boundary, I was glad."

"Is that intended as a compliment?" asked Stafford, with the faintest suspicion of a smile.

"Every way," said the colonel emphatically. "In the first place, Mr. King, I know that you are the straightest and most honest police official in England, and possibly in the world. All I want is justice. My life is an open book, which courts the fullest investigation."

He spread out his huge hands as though inviting an even closer inspection than had been afforded him hitherto.

Mr. Stafford King made no reply. He knew, very well he knew, the stories which had been told about the Boundary gang. He knew a little and guessed a lot about its extraordinary ramifications. He was well aware, at any rate, that it was rich, and that this slow-speaking man could command millions. But he was far from desiring to endorse the colonel's inferred claim as to the purity of his business methods.

He leaned a little forward.

"I am sure you didn't send for me to tell me all about your hard lot, colonel," he said a little ironically.

The colonel shook his head.

"I wanted to get to know you," he said with fine frankness; "I've heard a lot about you, Mr. King. I am told you do nothing but specialize on the Boundary enterprises, and I tell you, sir, that you can't know too much about me, nor can I know too much about you." He paused. "But you're quite right when you say that I didn't ask you to come here—and a great honor it is for a big police chief to spare time to come to see me—to discuss the past. It is the present I want to talk to you about."

Stafford King nodded.

"I'm a law-abiding citizen," said the colonel unctuously, "and anything I can do to assist the law, why, I'm going to do it. I wrote you on this matter about a fortnight ago."

He opened a drawer and took out a large envelope embossed with a monogram of the Spillsbury Syndicate. This he opened and extracted a plain playing card. It was a white-backed card of superfine texture, gilt-edged and bore on its face a familiar figure.

"The knave of clubs," said Stafford King, lifting his eyes.

"The jack of clubs," said the colonel gravely; "that is its name, I understand, for I am not a gambling man." He did not bat a lid, nor did Stafford King smile.

"I remember," said the detective chief; "you received one before. You wrote to my department about it."

The colonel nodded.

"Read what's written underneath."

King lifted the card nearer to his eyes, the writing was almost microscopic and read:

"Save crime, save worry, save all unpleasantness. Give back the property you stole from Spillsbury."

It was signed "Jack o' Judgment."

King put the card down and looked across at the colonel.

"What happened after the last card came?" he asked. "There was a burglary or something, wasn't there?"

"The last card," said the colonel, clearing his throat, "contained a diabolical and unfounded charge that I and my business associates had robbed Mr. George Fetter, the Manchester merchant, of sixty thousand pounds by means of card tricks—a low practice, of which I would not be guilty, nor would any of my business associates. My friends and myself knowing nothing of any card game, we, of course, refused to pay Mr. Fetter, and I am sure Mr. Fetter would be the last person who would ask us to do so. As a matter of fact, he did give us bills for sixty thousand pounds, but that was in relation to a sale of property. I cannot imagine that Mr. Fetter would ever take money from us, or that he knew of this business. I hope not, because he seems a very respectable gentleman."

The detective looked at the card again.

"What is this story of the Spillsbury deal?" he asked.

"What is that story of the Spillsbury deal?" said the colonel.

He had a trick of repeating questions; it was a trick which frequently gave him a very necessary breathing space.

"Why, there's nothing to it. I bought the motor works. I admit it was a good bargain. There's no law against making a profit. You know what business is."

The detective knew what business was. Boyd Spillsbury was young and wild, and his wildness assumed an unpleasant character. It was the kind of wildness which people do not talk about—at least, not nice people. He had inherited a considerable fortune, and the control of four factories, the best of which was the one under discussion.

"I know Spillsbury," said the detective, "and I happen to know Spillsbury's works. I also know that he sold you a property worth three hundred thousand pounds in the open market for a sum which was grossly inadequate—thirty thousand pounds, was it not?"

"Thirty-five thousand pounds," corrected the colonel. "There's no law against making a bargain," he repeated.

"You've been very fortunate with your bargains."

Stafford King rose and picked up his hat.

"You bought Transome's Hotel from young Mrs. Rachemeyer for a sum which was less than a twentieth of its worth. You bought Lord Bethon's slate quarries for twelve thousand pounds; their value in the open market was at least one hundred thousand pounds. For the past fifteen years you have been acquiring property at an amazing rate—and at an amazing price."

The colonel smiled.

"You're paying me a great compliment, Mr. Stafford King," he said with a touch of sarcasm, "and I will never forget it. But don't let us get away from the object of your coming. I am reporting to you as a police officer, that I have been threatened by a blackguard, a thief, and very likely a murderer. I will not be responsible for any action I may take. Jack o' Judgment, indeed!" he growled.

"Have you ever seen him?" asked Stafford.

The colonel frowned.

"He's alive, ain't he?" he retorted. "If I'd seen him do you think he'd be writing me letters? It is your job to pinch him. If you people down at Scotland Yard spent less time poking into the affairs of honest business men and more—"

Stafford King was smiling now, frankly and undisguisedly. His gray eyes were creased with silent laughter.

"Colonel, you have some nerve!" he said admiringly, and with no other word he left the room.

CHAPTER II
JACK O' JUDGMENT—HIS CARD

The wrong side of a stage door was the outside on a night such as this was. The rain was bucketing down and a chill northwester howled up the narrow passage leading from the main street to the tiny entry.

But the outside, and the darkest corner of the cul-de-sac from whence the stage door of the Orpheum Music Hall was reached, satisfied Stafford King. He drew farther into the shadow at sight of the figure which picked a way along the passage and paused only at the open doorway to furl his umbrella.

Pinto Silva, immaculately attired with a white rose in the buttonhole of his faultless dress jacket, had no doubt in his mind as to which was the most desirable side of the stage door. He passed in, nodding carelessly to the doorkeeper.

"A rotten night, Joe," he said. "Miss White hasn't gone yet, has she?"

"No, sir," said the man obsequiously; "she's only just left the stage a few minutes. Shall I tell her you're here, sir?"

Pinto shook his head.

He was a good-looking man of thirty-five. There were some who would go further and describe him as handsome, though his peculiar style of good looks might not be to everybody's taste. The olive complexion, the black eyes, the well-curled mustache and the effeminate chin had their attractions, and Pinto Silva admitted modestly in his reminiscent moments that there were women who had raved about him.

"Miss White is in No. 6," said the doorkeeper. "Shall I send somebody along to tell her you're here?"

"You needn't trouble," said the other; "she won't be long now."

The girl, hurrying along the corridor, fastening her coat as she came, stopped dead at the sight of him and a look of annoyance came to her face. She was tall for a girl, perfectly proportioned, and something more than pretty.

Pinto lifted his hat with a smile.

"I've just been in front, Miss White. An excellent performance!"

"Thank you," she said simply. "I did not see you."

He nodded.

There was a complacency in his nod which irritated her. It almost seemed to infer that she was not speaking the truth and that he was humoring her in her deception.

"You're quite comfortable?" he asked.

"Quite," she replied politely.

She was obviously anxious to end the interview, and at a loss as to how she could.

"Dressing room comfortable, everybody respectful and all that sort of thing?" he asked. "Just say the word if they give you trouble, and I'll have them kicked out, whoever they are, from the manager downward."

"Oh, thank you," she said hurriedly; "everybody is most polite and nice." She held out her hand. "I am afraid I must go now. A—a friend is waiting for me."

"One minute, Miss White." He licked his lips, and there was an unaccustomed embarrassment in his manner. "Maybe you'll come one night after the show and have a little supper. You know I'm very keen on you and all that sort of thing."

"I know you're very keen on me and all that sort of thing," said Maisie White, a note of irony in her voice; "but unfortunately I'm not very keen on supper and all that sort of thing." She smiled and again held out her hand. "I'll say good night now."

"Do you know, Maisie—" he began.

"Good night," she said, and brushed past him.

He looked after her as she disappeared into the darkness, a little frown gathering on his forehead; then, with a shrug of his shoulders, he walked slowly back to the doorkeeper's office.

He waited impatiently, chewing his cigar, till the dripping figure of the doorkeeper reappeared with the information that the car was at the end of the passage. He put up his umbrella and walked through the pelting rain to where his limousine stood.

Pinto Silva was angry, and his anger was of the hateful, smouldering type which grows in strength from moment to moment and from hour to hour. How dare she treat him like this? She, who owed her engagement to his influence, and whose fortune and future were in his hands! He would speak to the colonel, and the colonel could speak to her father. He had had enough of this.

He recognized with a start that he was afraid of the girl. It was incredible, but it was true. He had never felt that way about a woman before, but there was something in her eyes, a cold disdain, which cowed even as it maddened him.

The car drew up before a block of buildings in a deserted West End thoroughfare. He flashed on the electric light and saw that the hour was a little after eleven. The last thing in the world he wanted was to take part in a conference that night. But if he wanted anything less, it was to annoy the colonel at this moment of crisis.

He walked through the dark vestibule and entered an automatic elevator, which carried him to the third floor. Here the landing and the corridor were illuminated by one small electric lamp, sufficient to light him to the heavy walnut doors which led to the office of the Spillsbury Syndicate. He opened the door with a latchkey and found himself in a big lobby, furnished in good style.

A man was sitting before a radiator, a paper pad upon his knees, and he was making notes with a pencil. He looked up, startled, as the other entered and nodded. It was Olaf Hanson, the colonel's clerk—and Olaf, with his flat, expressionless face and his stiff, upstanding hair, always reminded Pinto of a *struwwelpeter* which had been cropped.

"Hello, Hanson. Is the colonel inside?"

The man nodded.

"They're waiting for you," he said.

His voice was hard and unsympathetic, and his thin lips snapped out every syllable.

"Aren't you coming in?" asked Pinto in surprise, his hand upon the door.

The man called Hanson shook his head.

"I've got to go to the colonel's flat," he said, "to get some papers. Besides, they don't want me."

He smiled quickly and wanly. It was a grimace rather than an expression of amusement, and Pinto eyed him narrowly. He had, however, the good sense to ask no further questions. Turning the handle of the door, he walked into the large, ornate apartment.

In the center of the room was a big table, and the chairs at its side were, for the most part, filled.

He dropped into a seat on the colonel's right and nodded to the others at the table. Most of the principals were there—"Swell" Crewe, Jackson, Cresswell, and at the farther end of the table Lollie Marsh, with her baby face and her permanent expression of open-mouthed wonder.

"Where's White?" he asked.

The colonel was reading a letter and did not immediately reply. Presently he took off his pince-nez and put them into his pocket.

"Where's White?" he repeated. "White isn't here. No, White isn't here," he repeated significantly.

"What's wrong?" asked Pinto quickly.

The colonel scratched his chin and looked up to the ceiling.

"I'm settling up this Spillsbury business," he said; "White isn't in it."

"Why not?" asked Silva.

"He never was in it," said the colonel evasively; "it was not the kind of business that White would like to be in. I guess he's getting moral or something, or maybe it's that daughter of his."

The eyelids of Pinto Silva narrowed at the reference to Maisie White, and he was on the point of remarking that he had just left her, but changed his mind.

"Does she know anything about—about her father?" he asked.

The colonel smiled.

"Why, no—unless you've told her."

"I'm not on those terms," said Pinto savagely. "I'm getting tired of that girl's airs and graces, colonel, after what we've done for her!"

"You'll get tireder, Pinto," said a voice from the end of the table, and he turned round to meet the laughing eyes of Lollie Marsh.

"What do you mean?" he asked.

"I've been out taking a look at her today," she said, and the colonel scowled at her.

"You were out taking a look at something else, if I remember rightly," he said quietly. "I told you to get after Stafford King."

"And I got after him," she said, "and after the girl, too."

"What do you mean?"

"That's a bit of news for you, isn't it?" She was delighted to drop the bombshell. "You can't shadow Stafford King without crossing the tracks of Maisie White."

The colonel uttered an exclamation.

"What do you mean?" he asked again.

"Didn't you know they were acquainted? Didn't you know that Stafford King goes down to Horsham to see her, and takes her to dinner twice a week?"

They looked at one another in consternation. Maisie White was the daughter of a man who, next to the colonel, had been the most daring member of the gang, who had organized more coups than any other man except its leader. The news that the daughter of Solomon White was meeting the chief of the criminal intelligence department was incredible and stunning.

"So that's it, is it?" said the colonel, licking his dry lips. "That's why Solomon White's fed up with the life and wants to break away."

He turned to Pinto Silva, whose face was set and hard.

"I thought you were keen on that girl, Pinto," he said coarsely. "We left the way open to you. What do you know about it?"

"Nothing," said the man shortly. "I don't believe it."

"Don't believe it?" broke in the girl. "Listen! There was a matinee at the Orpheum today, and King went there. I followed him in and got a seat next to him and tried to be friendly. But he had only eyes for the girl on the stage, and I might as well have been the paper on the wall for all the notice he took of me. After her act he went out and waited for her at the stage door. They went to Roymoyer's for tea. I went back to the theater and saw her dresser. She is the woman I recommended when Pinto put her on the stage."

"What sort of work is Maisie doing?" asked the saturnine Crewe.

"Male impersonations," said the girl. "Say, she looks dandy in men's clothes! She's the best male impersonator I've ever seen. Why, when she talks—"

"Never mind about that," interrupted the colonel. "What did you discover?"

"I discovered that Stafford King comes regularly to the theater, that he takes her to dinner, and that he visits the house at Horsham."

"Solly never told me that—the swine!" exclaimed the colonel. "He's going to double cross us, that fellow."

"I don't believe it."

It was Crewe who spoke, Swell Crewe, whose boast it was that he had a suit for every day in the year.

"I know Solomon and I've known him for years," he said; "I know him as well as you, colonel. As far as we are concerned, Solly is straight. I'm not denying the possibility that he wants to break away, but that's only natural. He's a man with a daughter, and he's made his pile, but I'll stake my life that he'll never double cross us."

"Double cross us?" The colonel had recovered his wonted equanimity. "What has he to double cross?" he demanded almost jovially. "We have a straightforward business! I am not aware that any of us are guilty of dishonest actions. Double cross! Bah!"

He brought his big hand down with a thump on the table, and they knew from experience that this was the gavel of the chairman that ended all discussions.

"Now, gentlemen," said the colonel, "let us get to business. Ask Hanson to come in—he's got the figures. It is the last lot of figures of ours that he'll ever handle," he added.

Somebody went to the door of the anteroom and called the secretary, but there was no reply.

"He's gone out."

"Gone out?" said the colonel, and bent his brows. "Who told him to go out? Never mind; he'll be back in a minute. Shut the door."

He lifted a deed box from the floor at his feet, placed it on the table, opened it with a key attached to his watch chain, and removed a bundle of documents.

"We're going to settle the Spillsbury business tonight," he said. "It looks as though Spillsbury might squeal."

"Where is he?" asked Pinto.

"In an inebriates' home," said the colonel grimly. "It seems there are some trustees to his father's estate who are likely to question the legality of the transfers. But I've had the best legal opinion in London, and there is no doubt that our position is safe. The only thing we've got to do tonight is to make absolutely sure that all those fool letters he wrote to Lollie have been destroyed."

"You've got them," said the girl quickly.

"I had them," said the colonel, "and I burned them, all except one, when the transfer was completed. And the question is, gentlemen," he said, "shall we burn the last?"

He took from the bundle before him an envelope and held it up.

"I kept this in case anything unforeseen should happen, but if he's in a booze home, why, he's not going to be influenced by the threat of publishing a slushy letter to a girl. I guess his trustees are not going to be very much influenced either. On the other hand, if this letter were found among business documents, it would look pretty bad for us."

"Found by whom?" asked Pinto.

"By the police," said the colonel calmly.

"Police?"

The colonel nodded.

"They're getting after us, but you needn't be alarmed," he said. "King is working to get a case, and he is not above applying for a search warrant. But I'm not scared of the police so much." His voice slowed and he spoke with greater emphasis. "I guess there are enough court cards in a Boundary pack to beat that combination. It's the Jack—"

"The Jack—ha! ha! ha!"

It was a shrill bubble of laughter which cut into his speech, and the colonel leaped to his feet, his hand dropping to his hip pocket. The door had opened and closed so silently that none had heard it.

A figure stood confronting them. It was clad from head to foot in a long coat of black silk which shimmered in the half light of the electrolier. The hands were gloved, the head covered with a soft slouch hat, and the face hidden behind a white silk handkerchief.

The colonel's hand was in his hip pocket when he thought better and raised both hands in the air. There was something peculiarly businesslike in the long-barreled revolver which the intruder held, in spite of the silver plating and the gold inlay along the chased barrel.

"Everybody's hands in the air," said the Jack shrilly, "right up to the beautiful sky! Yours too, Lollie. Stand away from the table, everybody, and back to that wall. For the Jack o' Judgment is among you and life is full of amazing possibilities!"

They backed from the table, peering helplessly at the two unwinking eyes which showed through the holes in the handkerchief.

"Back to the wall, my pretties," chuckled the Thing. "I'm going to make you laugh, and you'll want some support. I'm going to make you rock with joy and merriment!"

The figure had moved to the table, and all the time it spoke its nimble fingers were turning over the piles of documents which the colonel had disgorged from the box.

"I'm going to tell you a comical tale about a gang of blackmailers."

"You're a liar," said the colonel hoarsely.

"About a gang of blackmailers," said the Jack with a shrill peal of laughter; "fellows who didn't work like common blackmailers, nor demand money. Oh, no, not naughty blackmailers! They got the fools and the vicious in their power and made them sell things for hundreds of pounds that were worth thousands. And they were such a wonderful crowd! They were such wonderfully amusing fellows. There was Dan Boundary, who started life by robbing his dead mother; there was Crook Crewe, who was once a gentleman and is now a thief."

"Damn you!" said Crewe, lurching forward; but the gun swung round on him and he stopped.

"There was Lollie, who would sell her own—"

He stopped. The envelope that his fingers had been seeking was found. He slipped it beneath the black silk cloak, and in two bounds was at the door.

"Send for the police," he mocked. "Send for the police, Dan! Get Stafford King, the eminent chief; tell him I called! My card!"

With a dextrous flip of his fingers he sent a little pasteboard planing across the room. In an instant the door opened and closed upon the intruder and he was gone.

For a second there was silence, and then, with a little sob, Lollie Marsh collapsed in a heap on the floor. Colonel Dan Boundary looked from one white face to the other.

"There's a hundred thousand pounds for any one of you who gets that fellow," he said, breathing hard.

CHAPTER III

THE DECOY

Colonel Boundary, sitting at his desk the morning after, pushed a bell. It was answered by the thickset Olaf. He was dressed as usual in black from head to foot, and the colonel eyed him thoughtfully.

"Hanson," he said, "has Miss Marsh come?"

"Yes, she has come," said the other resentfully.

"Tell her I want her," said the colonel, and then as the man was leaving the room: "Where did you go last night when I wanted you?"

"I was out," said the man shortly. "I get some time for myself, I suppose?"

The colonel nodded slowly.

"Sure you do, Hanson."

His tone was mild, and that spelled danger to Hanson had he known it. This was the third sign of rebellion which the man had shown in the past week.

"What's happened to your temper this morning, Hanson?" he asked.

"Everything," exploded the man, and in his agitation his foreign origin was betrayed by his accent. "You tell me I shall haf plenty money, thousands of pounds! You say I go to my brother in America. Where is dot money? I go in March, I go in May, I go in July; still I am here!"

"My good friend," said the colonel, "you're too impatient. This is not a moment I can allow you to go away. You're getting nervous; that's what's the matter with you. Perhaps I'll let you have a holiday next week."

"Nervous!" roared the man. "Yes, I am. All the time I feel eyes on me! When I walk in the street every man I meet is a policeman. When I go to bed I hear nothing but footsteps creeping in the passage outside my room."

"Old Jack, eh?" said the colonel, eying him narrowly.

Hanson shivered.

He had seen the Jack o' Judgment once, a figure in gossamer silk who had stood beside the bed in which the Scandinavian lay and had talked wisdom while

Olaf quaked in a muck sweat of fear.

The colonel did not know this. He was under the impression that the appearance of the previous night had constituted the first of this mysterious menace. So he nodded again.

"Send Miss Marsh to me," he said.

Hanson would have got on his nerves if he had nerves. The man at any rate was becoming an intolerable nuisance. The colonel marked him down as one of the problems calling for early solution.

The secretary had not been gone more than a few seconds before the door opened again and the girl came in. She was tall, pretty, in a doll-like way, with an aura of golden hair about her small head. She might have been more than pretty but for her eyes, which were too light a shade of blue to be beautiful. She was expensively gowned, and walked with the easy swing of one whose position is assured.

"Good morning, Lollie," said the colonel. "Did you see him again?"

She nodded.

"I got a pretty good view of him," she said. "Did he see you?"

She smiled.

"I don't think so," she said; "besides, what does it matter if he did?"

"Was the girl with him?"

She shook her head.

"Well," asked the colonel after a pause, "can you do anything with him?"

She pursed her lips.

If she had expected the colonel to refer to their terrifying experience of the night before, she was to be disappointed. The hard eyes of the man compelled her to keep to the matter under discussion.

"He looks pretty hard," said the girl; "he is not the man to fall for that heart-to-heart stuff."

"What do you mean?" asked the colonel.

"Just that," said the girl with a shrug. "I can't imagine his picking me up and taking me to dinner and pouring out the secrets of his young heart at the second bottle."

"Neither can I," said the colonel thoughtfully. "You're a pretty clever girl, Lollie, and I'm going to make it worth your while to get close to that fellow. He's the one man in Scotland Yard that we want to put out of business. Not that we've anything to be afraid of," he added vaguely, "but he's just interfering with—"

He paused for a word.

"With business," said the girl. "Oh, come off, colonel! Just tell me how far you want me to go."

"You've got to put him in as wrong as you can," said the other decidedly. "He must be compromised up to his neck."

"What about my young reputation?" asked the girl with a grimace.

"If you lose it we'll buy you another," said the colonel dryly; "and I reckon it's about time you had another one, Lollie."

The girl fingered her chin thoughtfully.

"It is not going to be easy," she said again. "It isn't going to be like young Spillsbury—Pinto Silva could have done that job without help—or Solomon White even."

"You can shut up about Spillsbury," retorted the colonel. "I've told you to forget everything that has ever happened in our business. And I've told you a hundred times not to mention Pinto or any of the other men in this business. You can do as you're told! And take that look off your face!"

He rose with extraordinary agility and leaned over, glowering down at the girl.

"You've been getting a bit too fresh lately, Lollie, and giving yourself airs! You don't try any of that grand-lady stuff with me; d'ye hear?"

There was nothing suave in the colonel's manner now, nothing slow or ponderous or courtly. He spoke rapidly and harshly, and revealed the brute that many suspected, but few knew.

"I've no more respect for women than I have for men, understand! If you ever get gay with me, I'll take your neck in my hand like that." He clenched his two fists together with a horribly suggestive motion, and the frightened girl watched him, fascinated. "I'll break you as if you were a bit of china! I'll tear you as if you were a rag! You needn't think you'll ever get away from me—I'll follow you to the ends of the earth. You're paid like a queen and treated like a queen, and you play straight. There was a man called Snow Gregory once!"

The trembling girl was on her feet now, her face ashen white.

"I'm sorry, colonel," she faltered; "I didn't intend giving you offense. I—I—"

She was on the verge of tears when the colonel, with a quick gesture, motioned her back to the chair. His rage subsided as suddenly as it had risen.

"Now do as you're told, Lollie," he said calmly. "Get after that young fellow, and don't come back to me until you've got him."

She nodded, not trusting herself to speak, and almost tiptoed from his dread presence.

At the door he stopped her.

"As to Maisie," he said, "why, you can leave Maisie to me."

CHAPTER IV

MISSING

Colonel Dan Boundary descended slowly from the taxicab which had brought him up from Horsham station, and surveyed without emotion the domicile of his partner. It was Colonel Boundary's boast that he was in the act of lathering his face on the tenth floor of a California hotel when the earthquake began, and that he finished his shaving operations, took his bath and dressed himself before the earth had ceased to tremble.

"I shall want you again, so you had better wait," he said to the driver, and passed through the wooden gates toward Rose Lodge.

He stopped halfway up the path, having now a better view of the house. It was a red brick villa, the home of a well-to-do man. The trim lawn with its border of rose trees, the little fountain playing over the rockery, the quality of the garden furniture within view, and the general air of comfort which pervaded the place suggested the home of a prosperous business man, one of those happy creatures who have never troubled to get themselves in line for millions, but have lived happily between the four and five figure mark.

Colonel Boundary grunted and continued his walk. A trim maid opened the door to him, and by her blank look it was evident that he was not a frequent visitor.

"Boundary—just say Boundary," said the colonel in a deep voice, which carried to the remotest part of the house.

He was shown to the drawing-room, and again found much that interested him. He felt no twinge of pity at the thought that Solomon White would very soon exchange this almost luxury for the bleak discomfort of a prison cell, and not even the sight of the girl who came through the door to greet him brought him a qualm.

"You want to see my father, colonel?" she asked.

Her tone was cold but polite. The colonel had never been a great favorite of Maisie White's, and now it required a considerable effort on her part to hide her deep aversion.

"Do I want to see your father?" said Colonel Boundary. "Why, yes, I think I do, and I want to see you, too, and I'd just as soon see you first, before I speak to Solly."

She sat down, a model of patient politeness, her hands folded on her lap. In the light of day she was pretty, straight of back, graceful as to figure, and the clear gray eyes which met his faded blue ones were very understanding.

"Miss White," he said, "we have been very good to you."

"We?" repeated the girl.

"We." The colonel nodded. "I speak for myself and my business associates. If Solomon had ever told you truth you would know that you owe all your education, your beautiful home"—he waved his hand—"to myself and my business associates." His tongue rolled round the last two words. They were favorites of his.

She nodded her head slightly.

"I was under the impression that I owed it to my father," she said with a hint of irony in her voice, "for I suppose that he earned all he has."

"You suppose that he earned all that he has?" repeated the colonel. "Well, very likely you are right. He has earned more than he has got, but pay day is near at hand."

There was no mistaking the menace in his tone, but the girl made no comment. She knew that there had been trouble. She knew that her father had for days been locked in his study and had scarcely spoken a word to anybody.

"I saw you the other night," said the colonel, changing the direction of his attack; "I saw you at the Orpheum. Pinto Silva came with me. We were in the stage box."

"I saw you," said the girl quietly.

"A very good performance, considering you're a kid," said Boundary. "In fact, Pinto says you're the best mimic he has ever seen on the stage." He paused. "Pinto got you your contracts."

She nodded.

"I am very grateful to Mr. Silva," she said.

"You have all the world before you, my girl," said Boundary in his slow ponderous way, "a beautiful and bright future—plenty of money, pearls, diamonds"—he waved his hand with a vague gesture—"and Pinto, who is the most valuable of my business associates, is very fond of you."

The girl sighed helplessly.

"I thought that matter had been finished and done with, colonel," she said. "I don't know how people in your world would regard such an offer, but in my world they would look upon it as an insult."

"And what the devil is your world?" asked the colonel without any sign of irritation.

She rose to her feet.

"The clean, decent world," she said calmly, "the law-abiding world, the world that regards such arrangements as you suggest as infamous. It is not only the fact that Mr. Silva is already married—"

The colonel raised his hand.

"Pinto talks very seriously of getting a divorce," he said solemnly, "and when a gentleman like Pinto Silva gives his word, that ought to be sufficient for any girl. And now you have come to mention law-abiding worlds," he went on slowly, "I would like to speak of one of the law-abiders."

She knew what was coming and was silent.

"There's a young gentleman named Stafford King hanging round you." He saw her face flush but went on: "Mr. Stafford King is a policeman."

"He is an official of the criminal intelligence department," said the girl; "but I don't think you would call him a policeman, would you, colonel?"

"All policemen are policemen to me," said Boundary, "and Mr. Stafford King is one of the worst of the policemen from my point of view, because he's trying to trump up a cock-and-bull story about me and get me into very serious trouble."

"I know Mr. King is connected with a great number of unpleasant cases," said the girl coolly; "it would be a coincidence if he was in a case which interested you."

"It would be a coincidence, would it?" said the colonel, nodding his huge head. "Perhaps it is a coincidence that my clerk, Hanson, has disappeared and has been seen in the company of your friend, eh? It is a coincidence that King is working on the Spillsbury case—the one case that Solly knows nothing about—eh?"

She faced him, puzzled and apprehensive.

"Where does all this lead?" she asked.

"It leads to trouble for Solly, that's all," said the colonel. "He's trying to put me away and put his business associates away, and he has got to go through the mill unless—"

"Unless what?" she asked.

"Pinto's a merciful man; I'm a merciful man. We don't want to make trouble with former business associates, but trouble there is going to be, believe me."

"What kind of trouble?" asked the girl. "If you mean that your so-called business association with my father will cease, I shall be happier. My father can earn his living, and I have my stage work."

"You have your stage work"—the colonel did not smile but his tone betrayed his amusement—"and your father can earn his living, eh? He can earn his living in Portland jail," he said, raising his voice.

"For the matter of that, so can you, colonel."

The colonel turned his head slowly and surveyed the spare figure in the doorway.

"Oh, you heard me, did you, Solly?" he said not unpleasantly.

"I heard you," said Solomon White, his lean face a shade whiter than the girl had seen it, and his breathing was a little labored.

"If you are thinking of sending me to prison," said White, "why, I think we shall make up a pretty jolly party."

"Meaning me?" said the colonel, raising his eyebrows.

"You among others. Pinto Silva, Swell Crewe and Selby, to name a few."

Colonel Boundary permitted himself to chuckle.

"On what charge?" he asked. "Tell me that, Solly. The cleverest men in Scotland Yard have been laying for me for years and they haven't got away with it. May be they have your assistance and that dog Hanson's."

"That's a lie," interrupted White, "so far as I am concerned. I know nothing about Hanson."

"Hanson," said the colonel slowly, "is a thief. He ran off with three hundred pounds of mine, as I've reported to the police."

"I see," said White with a little smile of contempt. "Got your charge in first, eh, colonel? Discredit the witness. And what have you framed for me?"

"Nothing," said the colonel, "except this. I've just had from the bank a check for four thousand pounds drawn in your favor on our joint account and purporting to be signed by Silva and myself."

"As it happens," said White, "it was signed by you fellows in my presence."

The colonel shook his head.

"Obdurate to the last, brazening it out to the end. Why not make a frank confession to an old business associate, Solly? I came here to see you about that check."

"That's the game, is it?" said White. "You are going to charge me with forgery. And suppose I talk?"

"Talk?" asked the colonel innocently. "If by 'talk' you mean make a statement to the police derogatory to myself and my business associates, what can you tell? I can bring a dozen witnesses to prove that both Pinto and I were in Brighton the morning that check was signed."

"You came up by car at night," said White harshly; "we arranged to meet outside Guilford to divide the loot."

"Loot?" said Colonel Boundary, puzzled. "I don't understand you."

"I'll put it plainer," said White, his eyes like smouldering fire. "A year ago you got young Balston, the ship owner, to put fifty thousand pounds into a fake company."

He heard Maisie gasp but went on.

"How you did it I'm not going to tell before the girl, but it was blackmail which you and Pinto engineered. He paid his last installment; the four thousand pounds was my share."

Colonel Boundary rose and looked at his watch.

"I have a taxicab waiting and, with a taxicab, time is money. If you are going to bring in the name of an innocent young man, who will certainly deny that he had any connection with myself and my business associates, that is a matter for your own conscience. I tell you I know nothing about this check. I have made your daughter an offer."

"I can guess what it is," interrupted White; "and I can tell you this, Boundary, that if you are going to 'frame' me, I'll be even with you, if I wait twenty years! If you imagine I am going to let my daughter into that filthy gang"—his voice broke and it was some time before he could recover himself—"do your worst. But I'll get you, Boundary! I don't doubt that you'll convict me. You know the things that I can't talk about, and I'll have to take my medicine, but you are not going to escape."

"Wait, colonel." It was the girl who spoke, in so low a voice that he would not have heard her if he had not been expecting her to speak. "Do you mean that you will—prosecute my father?"

"With law-abiding people," said the colonel profoundly, "the demands of justice come first. I must do my duty to the state, but if you should change your mind—"

"She won't change her mind," retorted White.

With one stride he had passed between the colonel and the door. Only for a second he stood, and then he fell back.

"Do your worst," he said huskily, and Colonel Boundary passed out, pocketing the revolver which had come from nowhere into his hand. Presently they heard the purr of the departing motor.

He went to Horsham station in a thoughtful frame of mind. He was still thinking profoundly when he reached Victoria station.

Then, as he stepped on the platform, a hand was laid on his arm and he turned to meet the smiling face of Stafford King.

"Hello," said the colonel, and something within him went cold.

"Sorry to break in on your reverie, colonel," said Stafford King, "but I've a warrant for your arrest."

"What is the charge?" asked the colonel, his face gray.

"Blackmail and conspiracy," said King, and saw with amazement the look of relief in the other's eyes.

"Boundary," he added between his teeth, "you thought I wanted you for Snow Gregory!"

The colonel said nothing.

CHAPTER V
IN THE MAGISTRATE'S COURT

Never before in history had the dingy little street, in which North Lambeth police court stands, witnessed such scenes as were presented on that memorable fourth of December, when counsel for the crown opened the case against Colonel Dan Boundary.

Long before the building was opened the precincts of the court were besieged by people anxious to secure one of the very few seats which were available for the public. By nine o'clock it became necessary to summon a special force of police to clear a way for the numerous motor cars which came bowling from every point of the compass, and which were afterward parked in the narrow side streets, to the intense amazement and interest of the curious denizens of the unsavory neighborhood in which the court is located.

Admission was by ticket. Even the reporters, those favored servants of democracy, had to produce a printed pass before the scrutinizing policeman at the door allowed them to enter. Every available seat had been allotted. Even the magistrate's sacristy had been invaded, and chairs stood three deep to left and right of him.

There were some who came out of sheer morbid curiosity, in order that they might boast that they were present when this remarkable case was heard. There were others who came, inwardly quaking at the revelations which were promised or hinted at in the daily press, for the influence which the Boundary gang exercised was wide and far-reaching.

A young man stood upon the congested pavement, watching with evident impatience the arrival of belated cars. The magistrate had already come and had disappeared behind the slate-colored gates which led to the courtyard. Stafford saw fashionably dressed women and worried-looking men who were figures in the political and social world, and presently he involuntarily stepped forward into the roadway, as though to meet the electric limousine which came noiselessly to the main entrance.

The solitary occupant of the car was a man of sixty—a gray-haired gentleman of medium height, dressed with scrupulous care, and wearing on his clean-shaven face a perpetual smile, as though life were an amusement which never palled.

Stafford King took the extended hand with a little twinkle in his eye.

"I was afraid we shouldn't be able to keep your place for you, Sir Stanley," he said.

Sir Stanley Belcom, first commissioner of criminal intelligence, accentuated his smile.

"Well, Stafford," he drawled, "I've come to see the culminating triumph of your official career."

Stafford King made a little grimace.

"I hope so," he said dryly.

"I hope so, too," said the baronet; "yet—I'll tell you frankly, Stafford, I have a feeling that the ordinary processes of the law are inadequate to trap this organization. The law has too wide a mesh to deal with the terror which this man exercises. Such men are the only justification of lynch law, the quick, sharp justice which is administered without subtlety and without quibble."

Stafford looked at the other and made no attempt to hide his astonishment.

"You believe in—the Jack o' Judgment?" he asked.

Sir Stanley shot a swift glance at him.

"That is the bugbear of the gang, isn't it?"

"So Hanson says," replied the other. "I verily believe that Hanson is more afraid of that mysterious person than he is of Boundary himself."

The attorney general had begun his opening speech when the two men made their way into the crowded court and found their seats at the end of the lawyer's table.

In the dock sat Colonel Boundary, the least concerned of all that assembly. The colonel was leaning forward, his arms resting on the rails, his chin on the back of his hairy hand, his eyes glued upon the gray-haired lawyer who was dispassionately opening the case.

"The contention of the crown," the attorney general was saying, "is that Colonel Boundary is at the head of a huge blackmailing organization and that in the course of the past twenty years, by such means as I shall suggest, and as the principal witness for the crown will tell you he has built up his criminal practice until he now controls the most complex and the most iniquitous organization that has been known in the long and sordid history of crime.

"Your worship will doubtless hear," he went on, "of a bizarre and fantastic figure which flits through the pages of this story, a mysterious somebody who is called 'The Jack.' But I shall ask your worship, as I shall ask the jury, when this case reaches, as it must reach ultimately, the central criminal court, to disregard this apparition, which displayed no part in bringing Boundary to justice.

"The contention of the crown is, as I say, that Boundary, by means of terrorization and blackmail, through the medium and assistance of his creatures, has from time to time secured a hold over rich and foolish men and women, and from these has acquired the enormous wealth which is now his and his associates'. As to these latter, their prosecution depends very largely upon the fate of Boundary. There are, I believe, some of them in court at this moment, and though they are not arrested, it will be no news to them to learn that they are under police observation."

Swell Crewe, sitting at the back of the court, shifted uneasily, and, turning his head, he met the careless gaze of the tall, military-looking man who had "detective" written all over him.

There had been a pause in the attorney general's speech while he examined short-sightedly the notes before him.

"In the presentation of this case, your worship," he went on, "the crown is in somewhat of a dilemma. We have secured one important and, I think, convincing witness—a man who has been closely associated with the prisoner, a Scandinavian named Hanson, who, considering himself badly treated by this gang, has been for a long time secretly getting together evidence of an incriminating character. As to his object we need not inquire. There is a possibility suggested by my learned friend, the counsel for the defense, that Hanson intended blackmailing the blackmailers and presenting such a weight of evidence against Boundary that he could do no less than pay handsomely for his confederate's silence. That is as may be. The main fact is that Hanson has accumulated this documentary evidence, and that that documentary evidence is in existence in certain secret hiding places in this country, which will be revealed in the course of his examination.

"We are at this disadvantage, that Hanson has not yet made anything but the most scanty of statements. Fearing for his life, since this gang will stop at nothing, he has been closely guarded by the police from the moment he made his preliminary statement. Every effort which has been made to induce him to commit his revelations to writing has been in vain, and we are compelled to take what is practically his affidavit in open court."

"Do I understand," interrupted the magistrate in that weary tone which is the prerogative of magistrates, "that you are not as yet in possession of the evidence on which I am to be asked to commit the prisoner to the Old Bailey?"

"That is so, your worship," said the counsel; "all we could procure from Hanson was the affidavit which was necessary to secure the man's arrest."

"So that if anything happened to your witness, there would be no case for the crown?"

The attorney general nodded.

"Those are exactly the circumstances, your worship," he said, "and that is why we have been careful to keep our witness in security. The man is in a highly nervous condition, and we have been obliged to humor him. But I do not think your worship need have any apprehension as to the evidence which will be produced today, or that there will not be sufficient to justify a committal."

"I see," said the magistrate.

Sir Stanley turned to Stafford and whispered: "Rather a queer proceeding." Stafford nodded.

"It is the only thing we could do," he said. "Hanson refused to speak until he was in court—until, as he said, he saw Boundary under arrest."

"Does Boundary know this?"

"I suppose so," replied Stafford with a little smile; "he knows everything. He has a whole army of spies. Sir Stanley, you don't know how big this organization is. He has roped in everybody. He has members of Parliament, he has the best lawyers in London, and two of the big detective agencies are engaged exclusively on his work."

Sir Stanley pursed his lips thoughtfully and turned his attention to the prosecuting counsel. The address was not a long one, and presently the attorney sat down, to be followed by a leading member of the bar who had been retained for the defense. Presently he, too, had finished, and again the attorney general rose.

"Call Olaf Hanson," he said, and there was a stir of excitement.

The door leading to the cells opened and two tall detectives came through, and two others followed. In the midst of the four walked the short, gray-faced man in whose hands was the fate and, indeed, the life of Colonel Dan Boundary.

He did not so much as glance at the dock, but hurried across the floor of the court and was ushered to the witness stand, his four guardians disposing themselves behind and before him. The man seemed on the point of fainting. His fearful eyes ranged the court, always avoiding the gross figure in the railed dock. The lips of the witness were white and trembling. The hands, which clutched the front of the box for support, twitched spasmodically.

"Your name is Olaf Hanson?" asked the attorney soothingly.

The witness tried to speak, but his lips emitted no sound. He nodded.

"You are a native of Denmark?"

Again Hanson nodded.

"You must speak," said the attorney kindly, "and you need have no fear. How long have you known Colonel Boundary?"

This time Hanson found his voice.

"For ten years," he said huskily.

An usher came forward from the press at the back of the court with a glass of water and handed it to the witness, who drank eagerly. The attorney waited until he had drained the glass before he spoke again.

"You have in your possession certain documentary evidence convicting

Colonel Boundary of illegal acts?''

"Yes," said the witness.

"You have promised the police that you will reveal in court where those documents have been stored?''

"Yes," said Hanson again.

"Will you tell the court now, in order that the police may lose as little time as possible, where you have hidden that evidence?''

Colonel Boundary was showing the first signs of interest he had evinced in the proceedings. He leaned forward, his head craned round as though endeavoring to catch the eye of the witness.

Hanson was speaking, and speaking with difficulty.

"I haf—put those papers—" He stopped and swayed. "I haf put those papers—" he began again, and then, without a second's warning, he fell limply forward.

"I am afraid he has fainted," said the magistrate.

Detectives were crowding round the witness and had lifted him from the witness stand. One said something hurriedly, and Stafford King left his seat. He was bending over the prostrate figure, tearing open the collar from his throat, and presently was joined by the police surgeon, who was in court. There was a little whispered consultation, and then Stafford King straightened himself up and his face was pale and hard.

"I regret to inform your worship," he said, "that the witness is dead."

CHAPTER VI
STAFFORD KING RESIGNS

A week later Stafford King came to the office of the first commissioner of the criminal intelligence department, and Sir Stanley looked up with a kindly but pitying look in his eye.

"Well, Stafford," he said gently. "Sit down, won't you? What has happened?''

Stafford King shrugged his shoulders.

"Boundary is discharged," he said shortly.

Sir Stanley nodded.

"It was inevitable," he said. "I suppose there's no hope of connecting him and his gang with the death of Hanson?''

"Not a ghost of a hope, I am afraid," said Stafford, shaking his head. "Hanson was undoubtedly murdered, and the poison which killed him was in the glass of water which the usher brought. I've been examining the usher again today, and all he can remember is that he saw somebody pushing through the crowd at the back of the court, who handed the glass over the heads of the people. Nobody seems to have seen the man who passed it. That was the method by which the gang got rid of their traitor.''

"Clever," said Sir Stanley, putting his finger tips together. "They knew just the condition of mind in which Hanson would be when he came into court. They had the dope ready, and they knew that the detectives would allow the usher to bring the man water, when they would not allow anybody else to approach him. This is a pretty bad business, Stafford."

"I realize that," said the young chief. "Of course I shall resign. There's nothing else to do. I thought we had him this time, especially with the evidence we had in relation to the Spillsbury case."

"You mean the letter which Spillsbury wrote to the woman Marsh? How did that come, by the way?"

"It reached Scotland Yard by post."

"Do you know who sent it?"

"There was no covering note at all," replied Stafford; "it was in a plain envelope with a typewritten address, and was sent to me personally. The letter, of course, was valueless by itself."

"Have you made any search to discover the documents which Hanson spoke about?"

"We have searched everywhere," said the other a little wearily, "but it is a pretty hopeless business looking through London for a handful of documents. Anyway, Boundary is free."

The other was watching him closely.

"It is a bitter disappointment to you, my young friend," he said; "you've been working on the case for years. I fear you'll never have another chance of putting Boundary in the dock. He's got a lot of public sympathy, too. Your thorough rascal who manages to escape from the hands of the police has always a large following among the public, and I doubt whether the home secretary will sanction any further proceedings unless we have the most convincing proof. What's this?"

Stafford had laid a letter on the table.

"My resignation," said that young man grimly.

The first commissioner took up the envelope and tore it in four pieces.

"It is not accepted," he said cheerfully. "You did your best, and you're no more responsible than I am. If you resign I ought to resign, and so ought every officer who has been on this game. A few years ago I took exactly the same step— offered my resignation over a purely private and personal matter, and it was not accepted. I have been glad since, and so will you be. Go on with your work and give Boundary a rest for a while."

Stafford was looking down at him abstractedly.

"Do you think that we shall ever catch the fellow, sir?"

Sir Stanley smiled.

"Frankly I don't," he admitted. "As I said before, the only danger I see to Boundary is this mysterious individual who apparently crops up now and again in his daily life, and who, I suspect, was the person who sent you the Spillsbury letter—the Jack o' Judgment, doesn't he call himself? Do you know what I think?" he asked quietly. "I think that if you found the Jack, if you ran him to earth, stripped him of his mystic guise you would discover somebody who has a greater grudge against Boundary than the police."

Stafford smiled.

"We can't run about after phantoms, sir," he said, with a touch of asperity in his voice.

The chief looked at him curiously.

"I hear you do quite a lot of running about," he said carelessly as he began to arrange the papers on his table. "By the way, how is Miss White?"

Stafford flushed.

"She was very well when I saw her last night," he said stiffly. "She is leaving the stage."

"And her father?"

Stafford was silent for a second.

"He left his home a week before the case came into court and has not been seen since," he said.

The chief nodded.

"While White is away and until he turns up I should keep a watchful eye on his daughter," he said.

"What do you mean, sir?" asked Stafford.

"I'm just making a suggestion," said the other; "think it over."

Stafford thought it over on his way to meet the girl, who was waiting for him on a sunny seat in Temple Gardens, for the day was fine and even warm, and, two hours before luncheon, the place was comparatively empty of people. She saw the trouble in his face and rose to meet him, and for a moment forgot her own distress of mind, her doubts and fears. Evidently she knew the reason for his attendance at Scotland Yard, and something of the interview which he had had.

"I offered my resignation," he replied in answer to her unspoken question, "and Sir Stanley refused it."

"I think he was just," she said. "Why, it would be simply monstrous if your career were spoiled through no fault of your own."

He laughed.

"Don't let us talk about me," he said. "What have you done?"

"I've canceled all my contracts; I have other work to do."

"How are—" He hesitated, but she knew just what he meant, and patted his arm gratefully.

"Thank you; I have all the money I want," she said; "father left me quite a respectable balance. I am closing the house at Horsham and storing the furniture, and shall keep just sufficient to fill a little flat which I have taken in Bloomsbury."

"But what are you going to do?" he asked curiously.

She shook her head.

"Oh, there are lots of things that a girl can do," she said vaguely, "besides going on the stage."

"But isn't it a sacrifice? Didn't you love your work?"

She hesitated.

"I thought I did at first," she said. "You see, I was always a very good mimic. When I was only a little girl I could imitate the colonel. Listen!"

Suddenly to his amazement he heard the drawling growl of Dan Boundary. She laughed with glee at his amazement, but the smile vanished and she sighed.

"I want you to tell me one thing, Mr. King."

"Stafford—you promised me," he began.

She reddened.

"I hardly like calling you by your Christian name, but it sounds so like a surname that perhaps it won't be so bad."

"What do you want to ask?" he demanded.

She was silent for a moment, then she said:

"How far was my father implicated in this terrible business?"

"In the gang?"

She nodded.

He was in a dilemma. Solomon White was implicated as deeply as any save the colonel. In his younger days he had been the genius who was responsible for the organization, and had been for years the colonel's right-hand man until the more subtle villainy of Pinto Silva, that Portuguese adventurer, had ousted him, and, if the truth be told, until the sight of his girl growing to womanhood had brought qualms to the heart of this man, who, whatever were his faults, loved the girl dearly.

"You don't answer me," she said, "but I think I am answered by your silence. Was my father—a bad man?"

"I would not judge your father," he said. "I can tell you this, that for the past few years he has played a very small part in the affairs of the gang. But what are you going to do?"

"How persistent you are!" She laughed. "Why, there are so many things I am going to do that I haven't time to tell you. For one thing, I am going to work to undo some of the mischief which the gang has wrought. I am going to make such reparation," she said, her lips trembling, "for the evil deeds which I fear my father has committed."

"You have a mission, eh?" he said with a little smile.

"Don't laugh at me," she pleaded; "I feel it here." She put her hand on her heart. "There's something which tells me that, even if my father built up this gang, as you told me once he did—ah! You had forgotten that."

Stafford King had, indeed, forgotten the statement.

"Yes," he said. "You intend to pull it down?"

She nodded.

"I feel, too, that I am at bay. I am the daughter of Solomon White, and Solomon White is regarded by the colonel as a traitor. Do you think they will let me alone? Don't you think they are going to watch me day and night, and get me in their power just as soon as they can? Think of the lever that would be, the lever to force my father back to them."

"Oh, you'll be watched all right," he said easily, and remembered the commissioner's warning; "in fact, you're being watched now. Do you mind?"

"Now?" she asked in surprise.

He nodded toward a lady who sat a dozen yards away and whose face was carefully shaded by a parasol.

"Who is she?" asked the girl curiously.

"A young person called Lollie Marsh." Stafford laughed. "At present she has a mission, too, which is to entangle me into a compromising situation."

The girl looked toward the spy with a new interest and a new resentment.

"She has been trailing me for weeks," he went on, "and it would be embarrassing to tell you the number of times we have been literally thrown into one another's arms. Poor girl," he said with mock concern, "she must be bored with sitting there so long! Let us take a stroll."

If he expected Lollie to follow, he was to be disappointed. She stayed on, watching the disappearing figures, without attempting to rise. Waiting until they were out of sight she walked out on to the embankment and hailed a passing taxi. She seemed quite satisfied in her mind that the plan she had evolved for the trapping of Stafford King could not fail to succeed.

CHAPTER VII
THE COLONEL CONDUCTS HIS BUSINESS

A merry little dinner party was assembled that night in a luxurious apartment in Albermarle House. It was a bachelor party and consisted of three—the colonel, resplendent in evening dress, Swell Crewe and a middle-aged man whose antique dress coat and none too spotless linen certainly did not advertise their owner's prosperity. Yet this man with the stubby mustache and the bald head could write his check for seven figures, being Mr. Thomas Crotin, of the firm of Crotin & Principle, whose woolen mills occupy a respectable acreage in Huddersfield and Dewsbury.

"You're Colonel Boundary, are you?" he said admiringly, and for about the seventh time since the meal started.

The colonel nodded with a good-humored twinkle in his eye.

"Well, fancy that!" said Mr. Crotin. "I'll have something to talk about when I go back to Yorkshire! It is lucky I met your friend, Captain Crewe, at our club in Huddersfield."

There was something more than luck in that meeting, as the colonel knew.

"I read about the trial and all," said the Yorkshire-man. "I must say it looked very black against you, colonel."

The colonel smiled again and lifted a bottle toward the other.

"No, no!" said the spinner. "I'll have no more. I know when I've had enough."

The colonel replaced the bottle by his side.

"So you read of the trial, did you?"

"I did," said the other; "and I said to my missus: 'Yon's a clever fellow. I'd like to meet him.'"

"You have an admiration for the criminal classes, eh?" said the colonel good-humoredly.

"Well, I'm not saying you're a criminal," said the other, taking his host literally, "but I take an interest in these cases. You never know what you can learn."

"And what did your lady wife say?" asked Boundary.

The Yorkshireman smiled broadly.

"Well, she doesn't take any interest in these things. She's a real London lady, my wife. She was in a high position when I married."

"Five years ago," said Boundary, "you married the daughter of Lord West-severn. It cost you a hundred thousand pounds to pay the old man's debts."

The Yorkshireman stared at him.

"How did you know that?" he asked.

"You're nominated for Parliament, too, aren't you? And you're to be mayor of Little Thornhill?"

Mr. Crotin laughed uproariously.

"Well, you've got me properly placed," he said admiringly; and the colonel agreed with a gesture.

"So you're interested in the criminal classes?"

Mr. Crotin waved a hand protestingly.

"I'm not saying you're a member of the criminal classes, colonel," he said. "My friend Crewe here wouldn't think I would be so rude. Of course I know the charge was all wrong."

"That's where you're mistaken," interrupted the colonel calmly; "it was all right."

"Eh?"

The man stared.

"The charge was perfectly sound," said the colonel, playing with his fruit knife. "For twenty years I have been making money by buying businesses at about a twentieth of their value and selling them again."

"But how—" began the other.

"Wait; I'll tell you. I've got men working for me all over the country, agents and sub-agents who are constantly on the lookout for scandal. Housekeepers, servants, valets—you know the sort of people who get hold of information."

Mr. Crotin was speechless.

"Sooner or later I find a very incriminating fact which concerns a gentleman of property. I prefer those scandals which verge on the criminal," the colonel went on.

The outraged Mr. Crotin was rolling his serviette.

"Where are you going? What are you going to do? The night's young," said the colonel innocently.

"I'm going," said Mr. Crotin, very red of face. "A joke's a joke, and when friend Crewe introduced me to you, I hadn't any idea that you were that kind of man. You don't suppose that I'm going to sit in your society—me with my high connections—after what you've said?"

"Why not?" asked the colonel. "After all, business is business, and as I'm making an offer to you for the Riverborne Mill—"

"The Riverborne Mill?" interrupted the spinner. "Ah, that's a joke of yours! You'll buy no Riverborne Mill from me!"

"On the contrary, I shall buy the Riverborne Mill from you. In fact, I have all the papers and transfers ready for you to sign."

"Oh, you have, have you?" said the man grimly. "And what might you be offering me for the Riverborne?"

"I'm offering you thirty thousand pounds cash," said the colonel, and his hearer was stricken speechless.

"Thirty thousand pounds cash!" he said after a while. "Why, man, that property is worth two hundred thousand pounds."

"I thought it was worth a little more," said the colonel carelessly.

"You're a fool or a madman," said the angry Yorkshireman. "It isn't my mill, it is a limited company."

"But you hold the majority of the shares—ninety-five per cent, I think," said the colonel. "Those are the shares which you will transfer to me at the price I suggest."

"I'll see you dead first," declared Crotin, bringing his hand down to smash on the table.

"Sit down again for one moment." The colonel's voice was gentle but insistent. "Do you know Maggie Delman?"

Suddenly Crotin's face went white.

"She was one of your father's mill girls when you were little more than a boy," the colonel proceeded, "and you were rather in love with her, and one Easter you went away together to Blackpool. Do you remember?"

Still Crotin did not speak.

"You married the young lady and the marriage was kept secret because you were afraid of your father, and as the years went on and the girl was content with the little home you had made for her and the allowance you gave her, there seemed to be no need to admit your marriage, especially as there were no children. Then you began to take part in local politics and to accumulate ambitions. You dared not divorce your wife, and you thought there was no necessity for it. You had a chance of improving yourself socially by marrying the daughter of an English lord, and you jumped at it."

The man found his voice.

"You've got to prove that," he said huskily.

"I can prove it all right. Oh, no, your wife hasn't betrayed you—your real wife, I mean. You've betrayed yourself by insisting on paying her by telegraphic money orders. We heard of these mysterious payments, but suspected nothing beyond a vulgar love affair. Then one night, while your placid and complacent wife was in a theater, one of my people searched her rooms and came upon the marriage certificate. Would you like to see it?"

"I've nothing to say," said Crotin thickly. "You've got me, mister. So that is how you do it!"

"That is how I do it," said the colonel. "I believe in being frank with people like you. Here are the transfers. You see the place for your signature marked with a pencil."

Suddenly Crotin leaped at him in a blind fury, but the colonel gripped him by the throat with a hand like a steel vise, and shook him as a dog would shake a rat. And the gentle tone in his voice changed as quickly.

"Sit down and sign!" demanded Boundary. "If you play that game, I'll break your neck! Try any of those tricks with me and I'll smash you. Give him the pen, Crewe."

"I'll see you in jail for this," said the white-faced man shakily.

"That's about the place you will see me, if you don't sign—and it is inside of that jail you'll be to see me."

The man rose up unsteadily, flinging down the pen as he did so.

"You'll suffer for this," he said between his teeth.

"Not unduly," said the colonel.

There was a tap at the door, and the colonel swung round.

"Who's that?" he asked.

"Can I come in?" said a voice.

Crewe was frowning.

"Who is it?" asked the colonel.

The door opened slowly. A gloved hand, and then a white, hooded face, slipped through the narrow entry. "Jack o' Judgment! Poor old Jack o' Judgment come to make a call!" chuckled the hateful voice. "Down, dog down!" He flourished the long-barreled revolver theatrically, then turned with a chuckle of laughter to the gaping Mr. Crotin.

"Poor Jacob!" he crooned. "He has sold his birthright for a mess of pottage! Don't touch that paper, Crewe, or you die!"

His hand leaped out and snatched the transfer, which he thrust into the hand of the wool spinner.

"Get out and go home, my poor sheep," he said, "back to the blankets! Do you think they'd be satisfied with one mill? They'd come for a mill every year and they'd never leave you till you were dead or broke. Go to the police, my poor lamb, and tell them your sad story. Go to the admirable Mr. Stafford King—he'll fall on your neck. You won't! I see you won't!"

The laughter rose again, and then swiftly with one arm he swung back the merchant and stood in silence till the door of the flat slammed.

The colonel found his voice.

"I don't know who you are," he said, breathing heavily, "but I'll make a bargain with you. I've offered a hundred thousand pounds to anybody who gets you. I'll offer you the same amount to let me alone."

"Make it a hundred thousand millions!" said Jack o' Judgment in his curious, squeaky voice; "give me the moon and an apple, and I'm yours!"

He was gone before they could realize he had passed through the door, and he had left the flat before either moved.

"Quick! The window!" said the colonel.

The window commanded a view of the front entrance of Albermarle House, and the entry was well lighted. They reached the window in time to see the Yorkshireman emerge with unsteady steps and stride into the night. They waited for their visitor to follow. A minute, two minutes passed, and then somebody walked down the steps to the light. It was a woman, and as she turned her face the colonel gasped.

"Maisie White!" he said in a wondering voice. "What is she doing here?"

CHAPTER VIII
THE LISTENER AT THE DOOR

Maisie White had taken up her abode in a modest flat in Doughty Street, Bloomsbury. The building had been originally intended for a dwelling house, but its enterprising owner had fitted a kitchenette and a bathroom to every floor and had made each suite self-contained.

She found the one bedroom and a sitting room quite sufficient for her needs. Since the day of her father's departure she had not heard from him, and she had resolutely refused to worry. What Solomon White's association with the Boundary gang had been, she could only guess. She knew it had been an important one, but her fears on his behalf had less to do with the action the police might take against him than with Boundary's sinister threat.

She had other reasons for leaving the stage than she had told Stafford King. On the stage she was a marked woman, and her movements could be followed for at least three hours in the day; she was anxious for more anonymity. She was conscious of two facts as she opened the outer door that night to let herself into the hallway and hurried up to her apartments. The first was that she had been followed home, and that impression was the more important of the two. She did not switch on the light when she entered her room, but, bolting the door behind her, she moved swiftly to the window and raised it noiselessly. Looking out, she saw two men on the opposite side of the street, standing together in consultation. It was too dark to recognize them, but she thought that one figure was that of Pinto Silva.

She was not frightened, but nevertheless she looked thoughtfully at the telephone, and her hand was on the receiver before she changed her mind. After all, they would know where she lived, and an inquiry at her agents or even at the theater, would tell them to where her letters had been readdressed. She hesitated a moment, then pulled down the blinds and switched on the light.

Outside the two men saw the light flash up and watched her shadow cross the blind.

"It is Maisie all right," said Pinto. "Now tell me what happened."

In a few words Crewe described the scene which he had witnessed in the Albermarle flat.

"Impossible!" said Pinto. "Are you suggesting that Maisie is Jack o' Judgment?"

Crewe shrugged his shoulders.

"I know nothing about it," he said. "There are the facts."

Pinto looked up at the light again.

"I'm going across to see her," he said.

Crewe made a grimace.

"Is that wise?" he asked. "She doesn't know we have followed her home. Won't she be suspicious?"

Pinto shrugged his shoulders.

"She's a pretty clever girl," he said, "and if she doesn't know we're outside there's nothing of Solomon White in her composition."

He crossed the road and struck a match to discover which was her bell. He guessed right the first time. Maisie heard the tinkle and knew what it portended. She had not started to disrobe, and after a few moments' hesitation she went down the stairs and opened the door.

"It is rather a late hour to call on you," said Pinto pleasantly, "but we saw you going away from the Albermarle and could not overtake you."

There was a question in his voice, though he did not give it actual words.

"It is rather late for small talk," she said coolly; "is there any reason for your call?"

"Well, Miss White, there were several things I wanted to talk to you about," said Pinto, taken aback by her calm. "Have you heard from your father?"

"Don't you think," she said, "it would be better if you came at a more conventional hour? I don't feel inclined to gossip on the doorstep, and I'm afraid I can't ask you in."

"The colonel is worrying," Pinto hastened to explain. "You see, Solly's one of his best friends."

The girl laughed softly.

"I know," she said. "I heard the colonel talking to my father at Horsham," she added meaningly.

"You've got to make allowances for the colonel," urged Pinto. "He lost his temper, but he's feeling all right now. Couldn't you persuade your father to communicate with us—with him?"

She shook her head.

"I am not in a position to communicate with my father," she responded quietly; "I am just as ignorant of his whereabouts as you are. If anybody is anxious, it is surely myself, Mr. Silva."

"And another point," Silva went on, so that there should be no gap in the conversation, "why did you give up your theatrical engagements, Maisie? I took a lot of trouble to get them for you, and it is stupid to jeopardize your career. I have plenty of influence, but managers will not stand that kind of treatment, and when you go back—"

"I am not going back," she said. "Really, Mr. Silva, you must excuse me tonight. I am very tired after a hard day's work and—" She checked herself.

"What are you doing now, Maisie?" asked Silva curiously.

"I have no wish to prolong this conversation," said the girl, "but there is one thing I should like to say, and that is that I would prefer you to call me 'Miss White.'"

"All right, all right," said Silva genially. "And what were you doing at the flat tonight, Mai—Miss White?"

"Goodnight," said the girl, and closed the door in his face.

He cursed angrily in the dark and raised his hand to rap on the panel of the door, but thought better of it, and, turning, walked back to the interested Crewe, who stood in the shadow of a lamp-post watching the scene.

"Well?" asked Crewe.

"Confound the girl, she won't talk," grumbled Silva. "I'd give something to break that pride of hers, Crewe. By Jove, I'll do it one of these days," he added between his teeth.

Crewe laughed.

"There's no sense in becoming excited because a girl turns you down," he said. "What did she say about the flat? And what did she say about her visit to Albermarle Place?"

"She said nothing," said the other shortly. "Come along; let's go back to the colonel."

On the return journey he declined to be drawn into any kind of conversation, and Crewe, after one or two attempts to procure enlightenment as to the result of the interview, relapsed into silence.

They found the colonel waiting for them, and to all appearances the colonel was undisturbed by the happenings of the evening.

"Well?" he asked.

"She admits she was here," said Pinto.

"What was she doing?"

"You'd better ask her yourself," said the other with some asperity; "I tell you, colonel, I can't handle that woman."

"Nobody ever thought you could," said the colonel. "Did she give you any idea as to what her business was?"

Pinto shook his head, and the colonel paced the room thoughtfully, his big hands in his pockets.

"Here's the situation," he said. "There's some outsider who's following every movement we make, who knew that boob from Huddersfield was coming, and who knew what our business was. That somebody was this infernal Jack o' Judgment, but who is Jack o' Judgment, hey?" He looked round fiercely. "I'll tell you who he is," he went on, speaking slowly; "he's somebody who knows our gang as well as we know it ourselves, somebody who has been on the inside, somebody who has access, or who has had access, to our working methods; in fact," using his pet phrase, "a business associate."

"Rubbish!" said Pinto.

This polished man of Portugal, who had come into the gang very late in the day, was one of the few people who were privileged to offer blunt opposition to the leader of the Boundary gang.

"You might as well say it is I, or that it is Crewe, or Dempsey, or—"

"Or White," said the colonel slowly. "Don't forget White."

They stared at him.

"What do you mean?" asked Crewe with a frown. White had been a favorite of his. "How could it be White?"

"Why shouldn't it be White?" said the colonel. "When did Jack o' Judgment make his first appearance? I'll tell you. About the time we started getting busy framing up something against White. Did we ever see him when White was with us? No! Isn't it obviously somebody who has been a business associate and knows our little ways? Why, of course it is. Tell me somebody else. You don't suggest it is Snow Gregory, anyway," he added sarcastically.

Crewe shivered and half closed his eyes.

"For Heaven's sake don't mention Snow Gregory," he said irritably.

"Why shouldn't I?" retorted the colonel. "He's worth money and life and liberty to us, Crewe. He's an awful example that keeps some of our business associates on the straight path. Not," he added with elaborate care, "not that we were in any way responsible for his untimely end. But he died—providentially. A dope fiend's bad enough, but a dope fiend who talks and boasts and tells me, as he told me in this very room, just where he'd put me, is a mighty dangerous man, Crewe."

"Did he do that?" asked Crewe with interest.

The colonel nodded.

"In this very room where you're standing," he said impressively. "At the end of that table he stood, all lit up with coke, and he told me things about our organization that I thought nobody knew but myself. That's the worst of drugs," he said, shaking his head reprovingly, "you never know how clever they'll make a man, and they made Snow a bit too clever. I'm not saying that I regretted his death—far from it. I don't know how he got mixed up in the affair, but—"

"Oh, shut up!" interrupted Pinto. "Why go on acting before us? We were all in it."

"Hush!" said the colonel with a glance at the door. There was a silence. All eyes were fixed on the door.

"Did you hear anything?" asked the colonel under his breath.

His face was a shade paler than they had ever remembered seeing it.

"It is nothing," said Pinto. "That fellow's got on your nerves."

The colonel walked to the sideboard and poured out a generous portion of whisky and drank it at a gulp.

"Lots of things are getting on my nerves," he said, "but nothing gets on my nerves so much as losing money. Crewe, we've got to go after that Yorkshireman again—at least somebody has got to go after him."

"And that somebody is not going to be me," said Crewe quietly; "I did my part of the business. Let Pinto have a turn."

Pinto Silva shook his head.

"We'll drop him," he said decisively; and for the first time Crewe realized how dominating a factor Pinto had become in the government of the band. "We'll drop him—"

Suddenly he stopped and craned his head round.

It was he who had heard something near the door, and now, with noiseless steps, he tiptoed across the room, went to the door, and, gripping the handle, opened it suddenly. A gun had appeared in his hand, but he did not use it. Instead, he darted through the open doorway, and they heard the sound of a struggle. Presently he came back, dragging by the collar a man.

"Got him!" he said triumphantly, and hurled his captive into the nearest chair.

CHAPTER IX

THE COLONEL EMPLOYS A DETECTIVE

Their prisoner was a stranger. He was a lean, furtive-looking man of thirty-five, below middle height, respectably dressed, and, at first glance, the colonel, whose hobby was distinguishing at a look the social standing of humanity, was unable to place him.

Crewe locked the door.

"Now then," said the colonel, "what were you doing, listening at my door? Was that his game, Mr. Silva?"

"That was his game," said the other, brushing his hands.

"What have you got to say before I send for the police?" asked the colonel virtuously. "What have you got to say for yourself? Sneaking about a gentleman's flat, listening at keyholes!"

The man, who had been roughly handled, had risen and was putting his collar straight. If he had been taken aback by the sudden onslaught, he was completely self-possessed now.

"If you want to send for the police you'd better start right away," he said. "You've got a telephone, haven't you? Perhaps I'll have a job for the policeman, too. You've no right to assault me, my friend," he said, addressing Pinto resentfully.

"What were you doing?" asked the colonel.

"Find out," said the man sharply.

The colonel stroked his long mustache, and his manner underwent a change.

"Now look here, old man," he said almost jovially, "we're all friends here, and we don't want any trouble. I dare say you've made a mistake, and my friend has made a mistake. Have a whisky-and-soda?"

The man grinned crookedly.

"Not me, thank you," he said emphatically. "If I remember rightly, there was a young gentleman who took a glass of water in North Lambeth Police Court the other day, and—"

The colonel's eyes narrowed.

"Well, sit down and be sociable. If you're suggesting that I'm going to poison you, you're also suggesting that you know something which I don't want you to tell, or that you have discovered one of those terrible secrets that the newspapers are all writing about. Now be a sensible man; have a drink."

The man hesitated.

"You have a drink of whisky out of the same bottle, and I'll join you."

"Help yourself," said the colonel good-naturedly; "give me any glass you like."

The man went to the sideboard, poured out two portions and sent the soda water sizzling into the long glasses.

"Here's yours and here's mine," he said. "Good luck!"

He drank the whisky off, after he had seen the colonel drink his, and wiped his mouth with a gaudy handkerchief.

"I'm taking it for granted," said the colonel, "that we've made no mistake and that you were listening at our door. Now we want no unpleasantness, and we'll talk about this matter as sensible human beings, and man to man."

"That's the way to talk," said the other, smacking his lips.

"You've been sent here to watch me."

"I may have and I may not have," said the other.

Pinto shifted impatiently, but the colonel stopped him with a look.

"Now let me see what you are," mused the colonel, still wearing that benevolent smile of his. "You're not an ordinary tradesman. You've got a look of the book canvasser about you. I have it—you're a private detective!"

The man smirked.

"Perhaps I am," said he; "and," he added, "perhaps I'm not."

The colonel slapped him on the shoulder.

"Of course you are," he said confidently. "We don't see shrewd-looking fellows like you every day. You're a detective!"

"Not official," said the man quickly.

He had all the English private detective's fear of posing as the genuine article.

"Now look here," said the colonel, "I'm going to be perfectly straight with you, and you've got to be straight with me. That's fair, isn't it?"

"Quite fair," said the man. "If I've been misconducting myself in any manner—"

"Don't mention it," said the colonel politely. "My friends here will apologize for handling you roughly, I'm sure; won't you, Mr. Silva?"

"Sure!" said the other without any great heartiness. He was tired of this conversation and was anxious to know where it was leading.

"You're not in the private detective business for your health," said the colonel, and the man shook his head. "I bet you're working for a firm that's paying you about three pounds a week and your miserable expenses—a dog's life."

"You're quite right there," said the man—and he spoke with the earnestness of the ill-used wage earner. "It is a dog's life; out in all kinds of weather, all hours of the day and night, and never so much as 'thank you' for any work you do. Why, we get no credit at all, sir. If we go into the witness box the lawyers treat us like dirt."

"I absolutely agree with you," said the colonel, shaking his head. "I think the private detective business in this country isn't appreciated as it ought to be. And it is very curious we should have met you," he went on. "Only this evening I was saying to my friends here that we ought to get a good man to look after our interests. You've heard about me, I'm sure, Mr.—"

"Snakit," said the other. "Here's my card."

He produced a card from his waistcoat pocket, and the colonel read it.

"Mr. Horace Snakit," he said, "of Dooby & Somes. Now what do you say to coming into our service?"

The man blinked.

"I've got a good job—" he began inconsistently.

"I'll give you a better—six pounds a week, regular expenses and an allowance for dressing."

"It's a go!" said Mr. Snakit promptly.

"Well you can consider yourself engaged right away. Now, Mr. Snakit, as frankness is the basis of our intercourse, you will tell me at once whether you were engaged in watching me?"

"I'll admit that, sir," said the man readily. "I had a job to watch you and to discover if you knew the whereabouts of a certain person."

"Who engaged you?"

"Well," the man hesitated, "I don't know whether it isn't betraying the confidence of a client." He waited for some encouragement to pursue the path of rectitude and honor, but received none. "Well, I'll tell you candidly, our firm has been engaged by a young lady. She brought me here tonight."

"Miss White, eh?" said the colonel quickly.

"Miss White it was, sir," said Snakit.

"So that was why she was here? She wanted to show you—"

"Just where your rooms were, sir," said the man. "She also wanted to show me the back stairs, by which I could get out of the building if I wanted to."

"What were your general instructions?"

"Just to watch you, sir, and if I had an opportunity, when you were out, to sneak in and look around."

"I see," said the colonel. "Crewe, just take Mr. Snakit downstairs and tell him where to report. Fix up his pay—you know." He gave a significant sideways jerk of his head, and Crewe escorted the gratified little detective from the apartment.

When the door had closed the colonel turned on Silva.

"Pinto," he said—and there was a rumble in his voice which betrayed his anger—"that girl is dangerous. She may or may not know where her father is; this detective business may be a blind. Probably Snakit was sent here knowing that he would be captured and would talk."

"That struck me, too," said Pinto.

"She's dangerous," repeated the colonel. He resumed his promenade up and down the room. "She's an active worker, and she's working against us. Now I'm going to settle with Miss White," he said gratingly; "I'm going to settle with her for good and all. I don't care what she knows, but she probably knows too much. She's hand in glove with the police and maybe she's working with her father. You'll get Phillopolis here tomorrow in the morning—"

The other's eyes opened.

"Phillopolis?" He almost gasped. "You're not going to—"

The colonel faced him squarely.

"You've had your chance with the girl and you've missed it," he said; "you've tried your fancy method of courting and you've fallen down."

"But I'm not going to stand for Phillopolis," said the other, with tense face. "I tell you I like the girl. There's going to be none of that smuggling—"

"Oh, there isn't, isn't there?" said the colonel in his silkiest tone.

Then suddenly he leaned forward across the table, and his face was the face of a devil.

"There's only one Boundary gang, Pinto, and this is it," he said between his clenched white teeth; "and there's only one Dan Boundary, and that's me! Do you get me, Pinto? You can go a long way with me if I happen to be going that way. But you stand in the road and you're going to get what's coming to you! I've been good to you, Pinto. I've stood your interference because it amused me.

But you oppose me, really oppose me, and you'll know it. Did you get that?"

"I got it," said Pinto sullenly.

CHAPTER X
THE GREEK

The upbuilding of the Boundary gang had neither been an accident, nor was it exactly designed on the lines which it ultimately followed.

The main structure was Boundary himself, with his extraordinary financial genius, his plausibility, his lightning exploitation of every advantage which offered. Outwardly he was the head of three trading corporations which complied with the laws, paid small but respectable dividends, and cloaked other operations which never appeared in the official records of the companies.

The side lines of the gang came through force of circumstances. Men, good, bad, and indifferent, were drawn into the orbit of its activities, as extraordinary circumstances arose or dire necessities dictated. Throughout the length and breadth of Britain, through France, Italy, and, in the days before the war, in Germany, in Russia, and in the United States, were men, who, if they could not be described as agents, were at least ready tools.

He had a finger in every unsavory pie. The bank robber discharged from jail did not ask Colonel Boundary to finance him in the purchase of a new kit of tools—an up-to-date burglar's kit costs a considerable amount—but there were people who would lend the money, which eventually came out of the colonel's pocket. Some of the businesses he financed were on the border line of respectability. Some into which his money was sunk were frankly infamous. But it was a popular fiction that he knew nothing of these, or, if he did know that he was financing a scoundrel, it was insisted that that scoundrel was engaged in—so far as the colonel knew—legitimate enterprise.

Paul Phillopolis was a small Greek merchant, who had an office in Mincing Court—a tiny room at the top of four flights of stairs. On the glass panel of its door was the announcement: "General Exporter."

Mr. Phillopolis spent three or four hours at his office daily, and for the rest of the time, particularly toward the evening, was to be found in a café in Soho. He was a dark little man, with fierce mustache and a set of perfect white teeth which he displayed readily, for he was easily amused. His most intimate acquaintances knew him to be an exporter of Greek produce to South America, and he was, in the large sense of the word, eminently respectable.

Occasionally he would be seen away from his customary haunt, discussing with a compatriot some very urgent business, which few knew about. For there were ships which cleared from the Greek ports, carrying cargoes to the order of Mr. Phillopolis, which did not appear in any bill of lading. Armenian girls, girls from South Russia, from Greece, from Smyrna, en route to a promised land, looked forward to the realization of those wonderful visions which the Greek agent had so carefully sketched.

In half a dozen South American towns the proprietors of as many dance halls would look over the new importations approvingly and remit their bank drafts to the merchant of Mincing Court.

The colonel departed from his usual practice and met the Greek himself, the place of meeting being a small hotel in Aldgate. Whatever other pretenses the colonel made, he did not attempt to continue the fiction that he was ignorant of the Greek's trade.

"Paul," he said, after the first greetings were over, "I've been a good friend to you."

"You have, indeed, colonel," said the man gratefully. He spoke English with a very slight accent, for he had been born and educated in London. "If ever I can render you a service—"

"You can," said the colonel, "but it is not going to be easy."

The Greek eyed him curiously.

"Easy or hard," he said, "I'll go through with it."

The colonel nodded.

"How is the business in South America?" he asked suddenly.

The Greek spread out his hands in deprecation.

"Very poor," he said tragically. "All those beautiful girls waiting for music-hall engagements and impossible to send them because of the unsettled condition of their countries. I must have lost thousands of pounds."

"The demand hasn't slackened off, eh?" asked the colonel, and the Greek smiled.

"South America is full of money. They have millions—billions. Almost every other man is a millionaire. The music halls have patrons but no talent."

The colonel smiled grimly.

"Cut that stuff out, Paul," he said brutally, "and let us get down to facts. There's a girl in London of exceptional ability. She has appeared in a music hall here, and she's as beautiful as a dream."

"English?" asked the Greek.

"Irish," said the other. "As pretty as a picture, I tell you. She will make a great hit."

The Greek look puzzled.

"Does she want to go?" he asked, and the colonel snarled round at him.

"Do you think I should come and ask you to book her passage if she wanted to go?" he demanded. "Of course she doesn't want to go, and she doesn't know she's going. But I want her out of the way. You understand?"

Mr. Phillopolis pulled a long face.

"To take her from England?"

"From London," said the colonel.

The Greek shook his head.

"It is impossible," he said. "Passports are required, and unless she was willing to go it would be impossible to take her. You can't kidnap a girl and rush her out of the country, colonel."

Boundary interrupted him impatiently.

"Don't you think I know that?" he asked. "Your job is, when she's in a fit state of mind, to take her across and put her somewhere where she's not coming back for a long time, and not caring much whether she ever comes back. Do you understand?"

"I understand that part of it very well," said the Greek. "You get her to Rio and I'll do the rest."

"You'll get her to Rio," said Boundary. "I'm not to be mixed up in it. The only thing I can promise you is that she'll go quietly. I'll have her passports fixed. She'll be traveling for her health—you understand? And I promise you that her health will be so bad that she'll give you no trouble. When you get to South America I want you to take her into the interior of the country. You're not to leave her in one of these coast towns where English and American tourists are likely to meet her."

"What do I get out of it?" asked the Greek frankly.

"You'll get out of it what she's worth to the music halls," said the colonel shortly; "you know your own beastly business better than I do. I tell you she's worth a gold mine."

"But how are you going to—"

"That's my business," said the colonel. "You understand what you have to do. I'll send you the date you leave, and I'll pay her passage and yours. For any extra expenses you can send the bill to me; you understand?"

Obviously it was not a job to the liking of Phillopolis, but he had good reason to fear the colonel and acquiesced with a nod. Boundary went back to where he had left Pinto and found the Portuguese biting his finger nails—a favorite spare-time occupation of his.

"Did you fix it?" he asked in a low voice,

"Of course I fixed it," said the colonel sharply.

"I'm not going to have anything to do with it," said the other, and the colonel smiled.

"Maybe you'll change your mind," he said significantly.

There was a knock at the door and the colonel himself answered it. He took the card from the servant's hand and read: "Mr. Stafford King, Criminal Intelligence Department." He looked from the card to Pinto, then said: "Show him in."

CHAPTER XI
THE COLONEL AT SCOTLAND YARD

The two men had not met since they had parted at the door of the North Lambeth Police Court, and there was in Colonel Boundary's smile something of forgiveness and gentle reproach.

"Well, Mr. King," he said, "come in, come in, won't you?"

He offered his hand to the other, but Stafford apparently did not see it.

"No malice, I trust, Mr. King?" said the colonel genially. "You know my friend Mr. Silva? A business associate of mine, a director of several of my companies."

"I know him all right," said Stafford, and added, "I hope to know him better."

Pinto recognized the underlying sense of the words, but not a muscle of his face moved. For Stafford King the hatred with which he regarded the law took on a personal character. This man was something more than a thief taker and a tracker of criminals. Pinto chose to regard him as the close friend of Maisie White, and, as such, his rival.

"And to what are we indebted for this visit?" asked the bland colonel.

"The chief wants to see you."

"The chief?"

"Sir Stanley Belcom. Being the chief of our department, I should have thought you had heard of him."

"Sir Stanley Belcom," repeated the other. "Why, of course, I know Sir Stanley by repute. May I ask what he wants to see me about? And how is my young friend—er—Miss White?"

"When I saw her last," replied Stafford steadily, "she was looking pretty well, so far as I could tell."

"Indeed!" said the colonel politely. "I have a considerable interest in the welfare of Miss White. May I ask when you saw her?"

"Last night," replied Stafford. "She was standing at the door of her apartments in Doughty Street, having a little talk with your friend"—he nodded to Pinto and Pinto started. "Also," added the cheerful Stafford, "another mutual friend of ours, Mr. Crewe, was within hailing distance, unless I am greatly mistaken."

"So you were watching, eh?" burst out Pinto. "I thought after the lesson you had a couple of weeks ago you'd have—"

"Let me carry on this conversation if you don't mind," said the colonel, and the fury in his eyes silenced the Portuguese.

"We have agreed to let bygones be bygones, Mr. King, and I am sure it is only his excessive zeal on my behalf that induced our friend to be so indiscreet as to refer to the unpleasant happenings—which we will allow to pass from our memories."

So the girl was being watched. That made things rather more difficult than he had imagined. Nevertheless, he anticipated no supreme obstacle to the actual abduction. His plans had been made that morning, when he saw in the columns of the daily newspaper a four-line advertisement which, to a large extent, had cleared away the greatest of his difficulties.

"And if Mr. King is looking after our young friend, Maisie White, the daughter of one of our dearest business associates—why, I'm glad," he went on heartily. "London, Mr. King, is a place full of danger for young girls, particularly those who are deprived of the loving care of a parent, and one of the chief attractions, if I may be allowed to say so, which the police have for me, is the knowledge that they are the protectors of the unprotected, the guardians of the unguarded."

He made a little bow, and for all his amusement Stafford gravely acknowledged the handsome compliment which the most notorious scoundrel in London had paid the metropolitan police force.

"When am I to see your chief?"

"You can come along with me now if you like, or you can go tomorrow morning at ten o'clock," said Stafford.

The colonel scratched his chin.

"Of course, I understand that this summons is in the nature of a friendly—" He stopped questioningly.

"Oh, certainly," said Stafford, his eyes twinkling; "it isn't the customary 'come-along-o'-me' demand. I think the chief wants to meet you, to discover just the kind of person you are. You will like him, I think, colonel. He is the sort of man who takes a tremendous interest in—er—"

"In crime?" said the colonel gently.

"I was trying to think of a nice word to put in its place," admitted Stafford; "at any rate, he is interested in you."

"There is no time like the present," said the colonel. "Pinto, will you find my hat?"

On the way to Scotland Yard they chatted on general subjects till Stafford asked:

"Have you had another visitation from your friend?"

"The Jack o' Judgment?" asked the colonel. "Yes, we met him the other night. He's rather amusing. By the way, have you had complaints from anywhere else?"

Stafford shook his head.

"No, he seems to have specialized on you, colonel. You have certainly the monopoly of his attentions."

"What is going to happen, supposing he makes an appearance when I happen to have a lethal weapon ready?" asked the colonel. "I have never killed a person in my life, and I hope the sad experience will not be mine. But from the police point of view, how do I stand, supposing—there is an accident?"

Stafford shrugged his shoulders.

"That is his lookout," he said. "If you are threatened I dare say a jury of your fellow countrymen will decide that you acted in self-defense."

"He came the other night," the colonel said reminiscently, "when we were fixing up a particularly difficult—er—business negotiation."

"Bad luck!" said Stafford. "I suppose the mug was scared?"

"The what?" asked the puzzled colonel.

"The mug," said Stafford. "You may not have heard the expression. It means 'cad'—'fool'—'dupe.'"

The colonel drew a long breath.

"You still bear malice, I see, Mr. King," he said sadly. He entered the portals of Scotland Yard without so much as a tremor, passed up the broad stairs and along the unlovely corridors, till he came to the double doors which marked the first commissioner's private office. Stafford disappeared for a moment and presently returned with the news that the first commissioner would not be able to see his visitor for half an hour. Stafford apologized, but the colonel was affability itself and kept up a running conversation until a beckoning secretary notified him that the great man was disengaged.

It was King who ushered the colonel into the commissioner's presence. Sir Stanley was writing at a big desk and looked up as the colonel entered.

"Sit down, colonel," he said, nodding his head to a chair on the opposite side of the desk. "You needn't wait, King. There are one or two things I want to speak to the colonel about."

When the door had closed behind the detective, Sir Stanley leaned back in his chair. Their eyes met, the gray and the faded blue, and for the space of a few seconds they stared. Sir Stanley Belcom was the first to drop his eyes.

"I've sent for you, colonel," he said, "because I think you might give me a great deal of information if you're willing."

"Command me," said the colonel grandly.

"It is on the matter of a murder which was committed in London a few years ago," said the commissioner quietly, and for a moment Colonel Boundary did not speak.

"I presume you are referring to the Snow Gregory murder," he said at last.

"Exactly." The commissioner nodded. "We have had an inquiry from America as to the identity of this young man. Now you knew him better than anybody else in London, colonel. Can you tell me, was he an American?"

"Emphatically not," said the colonel with a little sigh, as though he were relieved at the turn the conversation was taking. "I came to know him through—er—circumstances, and exactly what they were I cannot for the moment remember. I had a lot to do with him. He did odd jobs for me."

"Was he well educated?" asked the commissioner.

"Yes, I should say he was," said the colonel slowly. "There was a story that he had been at Oxford, and that's very likely true. He spoke like a college man."

"Do you know if he had any relations in England?"

The commissioner eyed the other straightly, and the colonel hesitated. "How much does this man know?" he wondered, and decided that he could do no harm if he told all the truth.

"He had no relations in England," he said, "but he had a father who was abroad."

"Ah! Now we're getting at some facts," said the commissioner, and drew a slip of paper toward him. "What was the father's name?"

The colonel shook his head.

"That I can't tell you, sir," he said. "I should like to oblige you, but I have no more idea of what his name was than the man in the moon. I believe he was in India because letters from India used to come to Gregory."

"Was Gregory his name?"

"His Christian name, I think," said the colonel after a moment's thought. "He got into some scrape at college and was not graduated. Then he went to Paris and started to study art, and he got in bad there, too. That's as much as he ever told me."

"He had no brothers?" asked the commissioner.

"None," said the colonel emphatically. "I am certain of that, because he once declared he was thankful that he was the only child."

"I see," nodded the commissioner again. "You have formed no theory as to why he met his death or how?"

"No theory at all," said the colonel, but corrected himself. "Of course, I've had ideas and opinions, but none of them has ever worked out. So far as I know, he had no enemies, although he was a quick-tempered chap, especially when he was recovering from a dose of cocaine, and would quarrel with his own grandmother."

"You've no idea why he was in London? Apparently he did not live there."

The colonel shrugged his massive shoulders.

"No; I couldn't tell you anything about that, sir," he said.

"He was not an American?" asked the commissioner again.

"I could swear to that," answered the colonel.

There was a pause, and he waited.

"There's another matter." The commissioner spoke slowly. "I understand that you are being bothered by a mysterious individual who calls himself the Knave of Judgment."

"Jack o' Judgment," corrected the colonel with a contemptuous smile. "That sort of monkey tricks don't bother me, I can assure you."

"I have my theories about the Jack o' Judgment," said the commissioner. "I have been looking up the circumstances of the murder, and I seem to remember that on the body was found a playing card."

"That's right," said the colonel, who had remembered the fact himself many times. "The jack of clubs."

"Do you know what that jack of clubs signified?" asked the commissioner, but the colonel could honestly say that he did not. Its presence on the body had frequently puzzled him and he had never found a solution. "There is a certain type of ruffian to be found, particularly in Paris, who affects this sort of theatrical trademark. Did you know that?"

The colonel was suddenly stricken to silence. He did not know this fact, in spite of his extraordinary knowledge of the criminal world.

"These men have their totems and their sign manuals," said the commissioner; "for example, the apache who was executed at Nantes the other day invariably left a domino—the double-six—near his victim."

This was news to the colonel, too.

"I've been giving a great deal of thought and time to this old case," said the commissioner, "and I was hoping that perhaps you could help me. The most workable theory that I can suggest is that this unfortunate man was destroyed by a French criminal of the class which I have indicated, the bullying apache type, which is so common in France. Why the murder was committed"—the commissioner fingered his paper knife carelessly—"what led to it and who committed it, and more especially who instigated the crime, are matters which seem to me to defy detection. Do you agree?"

"I quite agree," said the colonel, licking his dry lips.

"Now I suggest to you," said the commissioner, "that your Jack o' Judgment, whoever he is, is some relation to the dead man."

He spoke slowly and emphatically, and the colonel did not raise his eyes from the desk.

"It is not my business to make life any easier for you," the commissioner was saying, "or to assist you in any way. But as the Jack o' Judgment seems to me to be engaged in a wholly illegal practice and as I, in my capacity, must suppress illegal practices, I make you a present of this suggestion."

"That the Jack o' Judgment is related to Snow Gregory?" asked the colonel huskily.

"That is my suggestion," said the commissioner.

"And you think—"

The commissioner raised his shoulders.

"I think he is your greatest danger, colonel," he said; "far greater than the police, far greater than the clever minds which are planning to bring you to prison and possibly," he added, "to the gallows."

Ordinarily the colonel would have protested at the suggestion in the speech, protested laughingly or with dignity, but now he was stricken dumb, both by the seriousness of the commissioner's voice and by the consciousness of a new and a more terrible danger than any that had confronted him. He rose, realizing that the interview was ended.

"I am greatly obliged to you, Sir Stanley," he said, clearing his throat; "it is good of you to warn me, but I'd like you to think that I am not engaged in any dishonest—"

"We'll let that matter stand over for discussion until another time," said the commissioner dryly. As Stafford King came into the room he turned to him. "You might show the colonel the way to the street. Otherwise he will be getting himself entangled in some of our detention rooms. Good morning, Colonel Boundary. Don't forget."

"I'm not likely to," said the colonel.

He recovered his poise quickly enough, and by the time he was in the street he was back in his old mood. But he had had a shock. That sunny afternoon was filled with shadows. The booming bells of Big Ben tolled "Jack o' Judgment"; the very wheels of the taxi droned the words. And Colonel Boundary went back to Albermarle Place for the first time in his life with his confidence in Colonel Boundary shaken.

There was nobody in save the one man servant he kept by the day, and he passed into the dining room overlooking the street. He had work to do, and it had to be done quickly. In one of the walls was set a stout safe, and this he opened, taking from it a steel box, which he carried to the table. There was a fire laid on the hearth, and to this he put a match, though the day was warm enough. Then he proceeded to unlock the box. Apparently it was empty, but, taking out his scarfpin, he inserted the point in a tiny hole which would have escaped casual observation, and pressed.

Half the steel bottom of the box leaped up, disclosing a shallow cavity beneath. The colonel stared. There had been two letters put in there, letters which he had secreted until such time as it might be necessary to bring a recalcitrant agent to heel. They were gone. He slid his fingers beneath the half of the bottom which had not opened, and felt a card. He drew this out and looked at it, licking his lips the while.

For the space of a minute he stared and stared at the knave of clubs he held in his hand, a knave of clubs signed with a flourish across its face: "Jack o' Judgment." Then he flung the card into the fire, and, walking to the sideboard, splashed whisky into a tumbler with a hand that shook.

CHAPTER XII

BUYING A NURSING HOME

The building in which Colonel Boundary had this beautiful home was of a type not uncommonly met with in the West End of London. The street floor was taken up entirely with shops, the first floor with offices, and the remainder of the building was practically given over to the colonel. One by one, he had ousted every tenant from the building, and practically the whole of the fourteen sets of apartments which constituted the residential portion of the building was held by him in one name or another. Some he had obtained by the payment of heavy premiums, some he had secured when the lease of the former tenant had lapsed, some he had gathered in by subletting. He had tried to buy the building, since it served his purpose well, but came against a deed of trust and the Court of Chancery, and had wisely refrained from going any further into a matter which must bring him *vis-à-vis* with a master in Chancery, with all the publicity which such a transaction entailed.

Nor had he been successful in acquiring any of the premises on the first floor. They were held by three very old-established businesses—an estate agent, a firm of land surveyors, and the offices of a valuer. He missed his opportunity, at any rate, of securing the business of Lee & Hol, the surveyors, and did not know it was in the market until after it had been transferred to a new owner. But they were quiet, sober tenants, who closed their offices between five and six every night and did not open them until between nine and ten on the following morning, and their very respectability gave him a certain privacy.

The new proprietor of Lee & Hol was a short-sighted, elderly man of no great conversational power, and apparently of no fixed purpose in life except to say "no" to the very handsome offers which the colonel's agents made when they discovered there was a chance of repurchasing the business. Boundary had personally inspected all the offices. He had found an excuse to visit them several times, duly noted the arrangements of the furniture, the sizes of the staffs and the general character of the business which was being carried on. This was a necessary precaution because these offices were immediately under his own flat. But just now they had a special value because it was a practice during the daytime for the three firms to employ a receiving clerk, who occupied a little glass-partitioned office on the landing and attended impartially to the needs of all three tenants to the best of his ability.

Boundary descended the stairs and found the elderly man in his office, leisurely and laboriously affixing stamps to a pile of letters. The colonel called him from his task.

"Judson," he said, "have you seen anybody go up to my room this afternoon?"

The man thought.

"No, sir; I haven't," he replied.

"Have you been here all the time?"

"Yes; since one o'clock I have been in my office," said the commissioner. "None of our tenants wanted anything."

"You didn't go out to go to the mail box?"

"No, sir," said the man. "I've practically not stirred from this office except for one minute when I went into Mr. Lee's office to get these letters."

"And you've seen nobody go upstairs?"

"Not since Mr. Silva came down, sir. He came down after you, if you remember."

"Nobody's been up?" insisted the other.

"Not a soul. Your servant came down before you, sir."

"That's true," said the colonel, remembering that he had sent the man on a special journey to Huddersfield with a letter to the bigamous Mr. Crotin. "You haven't seen a lady go up at all?" he asked suddenly.

"Nobody has gone up them stairs," said the doorman emphatically. "I hope you haven't lost anything, sir?"

The colonel shook his head.

"No, I haven't lost anything. If anything, I've found something," he said grimly.

He slipped half a crown into the man's hand.

"You needn't mention the fact that I've been making inquiries," he said, and went slowly up the stairs again.

The card had been put there that day. He would swear to it. The ink on the card had not had time to darken, and when he made a further search of his room, this view was confirmed by the appearance of his blotting pad. The card had been dried there, and the pen, which had been left on the table, was still damp.

The colonel passed into his bedroom and took off his coat and vest. He searched his drawer and found what looked to be like a pair of suspenders made of light fabric. These he slipped over his shoulder, adjusting them so that beneath his left arm hung a canvas holster. From another drawer he took an automatic pistol, pulled the magazine from the butt and examined it before he returned it and forced a cartridge into the breach by drawing back the cover of the pistol. This he carefully oiled, and then, pressing up the safety catch, he slipped the pistol into the holster and resumed his coat and vest.

It was a long time since the colonel had carried a gun under his arm, but his old efficiency was unimpaired. He practiced before a mirror and was satisfied with his celerity. He loaded a spare magazine, and dropped it into the capacious pocket of his waistcoat. Then, putting the remainder of the cartridges away neatly, he closed the box, shut the drawer and went back to his room. If all the commissioner had hinted were true, if this mysterious visitor was laying for him because of the Snow Gregory affair, he should have what was coming to him.

The colonel was no coward, and if this eerie experience had got a little on his nerves, it was not to be wondered at. He drew up a chair to the table, sitting in such a position that he could see the door, took a pencil and a sheet of paper, and began to write rapidly.

The man's knowledge was encyclopedic. Not once did he pause or refer to a catalogue, and he was still writing when Crewe came in. The colonel looked up.

"You're the man I want," he said.

He handed the other three sheets of paper, closely covered with writing.

"What's this?" asked Crewe, and read: "Twenty-three iron bedsteads, twenty-three mattresses, twenty-three—why, what's all this, colonel?"

"You can go down to Tottenham Court Road and you can order all that furniture to be taken into No. 3 Washburn Avenue.''

"Are you furnishing a children's orphanage or something?'' asked the other in surprise.

"I am furnishing a nursing home, to be exact,'' said the colonel slowly. "I bought it this morning, and I'm going to furnish it tomorrow. Send Lollie Marsh to me. Tell her I want her to get three women of the right sort to take charge of a mental case which is coming to my nursing home. By the way, you had better telegraph to old Boyton, or, better still, go in a cab and get him. He'll probably be drunk, but he's still on the medical register, and he's the man I want. Take him at once to Washburn Avenue, and don't forget that it's his nursing home and not mine. My name doesn't occur in this matter. You'd better get a dummy to do the buying for you from the furniture people.''

"Who is the mental case?'' asked the other.

"Maisie White,'' snapped the colonel, and Crewe stared.

"Mad?'' he said incredulously. "Is Maisie mad?''

"She may not be at present,'' said Boundary, "but by the time I'm through with her—''

He did not finish his sentence. Crewe, who was once a gentleman and was now a thief, swallowed something—but he had swallowed too much to choke at the threat to a girl in whom he had not the slightest interest.

CHAPTER XIII
THE LOVE OF STAFFORD KING

Maisie White had no illusions. When the report came to her that the detective she had employed had passed his services over to the man he was engaged to watch, she knew that the full force of the Boundary gang would be employed to her extinction. Strangely enough, she did not appear to be disturbed, as she confessed to Stafford King. They were lunching together at the Hotel Palatine, and the detective was unusually thoughtful.

"Why don't you go out of London?'' he asked.

"I must go on with my work,'' she said.

"What is your work?'' he asked.

"I have told you once,'' she replied; "I am trying to disentangle my father from disgrace. I am working to put him apart when the day of reckoning comes.''

"You've not heard from him?'' he asked.

She shook her head, and her eyes filled with tears.

"He has been a good father to me,'' she said, "the kindest and best of daddies. It is dreadful to think—'' Her lips quivered and she could go no further.

Nor could Stafford King make matters any easier for her. He knew better than she the depth of Solomon White's commitments. If the gang was ever smashed, and if by good fortune the law ever took its course, there was no hope for

Solomon White's escape from his share of the responsibility.

"Why do you think your father went away?" he asked, to turn the subject to a new aspect.

She did not reply instantly.

"I think he was scared," she said after a while. "I was shocked when I discovered how much in awe of the colonel he stood. He was just terrified at the threat, and yet I know he would have given his life to protect me from harm. I think it was just my being about that spurred him on to make the plans he did."

Stafford King agreed with a gesture.

"Now what are we going to do about you?" he asked, half humorously, half seriously. "I cannot let you go wandering alone about London—I'm scared to death as it is."

She smiled at him.

"You had better lock me up," she said flippantly, and he nodded in the same spirit.

"I know a little house in St. Johns Wood that would serve us beautifully as a prison," he said. "It has ten rooms and two admirable bathrooms. There is central heating and a large shady garden, and if you will only let me take you before a clergyman or a justice of the peace—"

She shook her head.

"That isn't prison," she said quietly, and put out her hand over the table.

He caught it in his and held it tight.

"Maisie," he said, "you know I love you. I love you more dearly than anything in the world."

She did not speak.

"As my wife," he went on, "you would be safe, and I should be happy. I just want you all the time."

Gently she disengaged her hand, shaking her head with a little smile.

"What would that mean, Stafford?" she said. "You know you are deceiving me when you agree that my father—" Again her voice shook. "No, no!" she said. "It would ruin your career to have the daughter of a convict for your wife. I realize very well what it will mean, for I know—I know—I know!"

"What do you know?" he asked in a low voice.

"I know that all my work will be in vain. But I must go on with it. I must, or I shall go mad. I know nothing on earth can clear my father, but I'm not going to tell you that again. I just want to think there is a possibility that some miracle will happen, that all the evidence which even I have against him will be explained away."

He took her unresisting hand in his, and under the cover of the tablecloth held it tight.

"That is why I wanted to leave the service," he said.

She looked at him quickly.

"Because you thought that it would mean ruin?"

He smiled.

"No, not that. It would hurt you; that is all. Of course, if such a thing happened I would be obliged to resign."

"And you'd never forgive yourself."

"I wanted to anticipate such a happening, and, darling, you've got to face the future without any other illusions."

She winced at the word "other" but he went on, unnoticing:

"Boundary is a tiger. If he thinks there is reason to fear you he will never let up on you till he has you in his grip. I tell you this," he said earnestly, "for all the power of the police, for all their organization and the backing which the law gives them, they may be helpless against this man if he has marked you down for punishment."

"I'm not afraid," she said quietly.

"But I am," said he. "I'm so afraid that I'm sick with apprehension sometimes."

"Poor Stafford!" she said softly, and there was a look in her eyes which compensated him for much. "But you mustn't worry, dear. Truly, truly, you mustn't worry. I'm quite capable of looking after myself."

"And that's the greatest of all your illusions," he said half laughingly and half irritably. "You're the meekest little mouse that ever came under the paw of a cat."

She shook her head smilingly.

"But I tell you I'm speaking seriously," he went on. "I'll do my best to look after you. I'll have a man watching you day and night."

"But you mustn't," she protested. "There's no immediate cause for worry."

He saw her to the door of the restaurant and showed her into the taxi-cab which came at his whistle, and she leaned out of the window and waved her hand in farewell as she drove off.

Two men stood on the opposite side of the road and watched her depart. Crewe was one, and a dark-faced man with a fierce mustache was the other.

"That's the girl," said Crewe.

The Greek smiled broadly, unpleasantly.

CHAPTER XIV
THE ABDUCTION OF MAISIE WHITE

A week passed without anything exceptional happening, and Maisie White had ceased even to harbor doubts as to her own safety—doubts which had been present in spite of the courageous showing she had made before Stafford King. Undeterred by her previous experience, she had made arrangements with another and a more responsible detective agency and had chosen a new watcher, though she had small hopes of obtaining results. She knew his task was one of almost insuperable difficulty, and she was frank in exposing to him what those difficulties were. Still there was a faint chance that he might discover something, and moreover, she had another purpose to serve.

She had seen Pinto Silva once. He had called, and she had noticed with surprise that the debonair, sell-confident man she had known, whose air of conscious superiority had been so annoying to her, had undergone a considerable change. He was ill at ease, almost incoherent at moments, and it was a long time before she could discover his business.

This time she received him in her tiny sitting room, for Pinto was somehow less alarming to her than he had been. Perhaps she was conscious that at the corner of the street stood a quietly dressed man doing nothing in particular, who was relieved at the eighth hour by an even less obtrusive-looking gentleman from Scotland Yard.

She waited for Pinto to disclose his business, but the Portuguese was apparently in no hurry to do so. Presently he blurted it out.

"Look here, Maisie," he said. "You've got things all wrong. Things are going to be very rotten for you unless—unless—" He floundered.

"Unless what?" she asked.

"Unless you make up with me," he said in a low voice. "I'm not so bad, Maisie, and I'll treat you fair. I've always been in love with you."

"Stop," she said quietly. "I dare say it is a great honor for a girl that any man should be in love with her, but it takes away a little of the compliment when the man is already married."

"That's nothing," he said eagerly. "I can divorce her by the laws of my country. Maisie, she hates me, and I hate her."

"No, Mr. Silva," she replied, "if you were single or divorced, or if you were ever so eligible, I would not marry you."

"Why not?" he demanded truculently. "I've got money."

"So have I," she said, "of a sort."

"My money's as clean as yours, if it is Solomon White's money."

She nodded.

"I'm well aware of that, too," she said. "It is gang money, isn't it? Stolen money. I don't see what good I shall get out of exchanging mine for yours, anyway. It is just as dirty. The money doesn't come into it at all, Mr. Silva—it is just liking people well enough—for marriage. And I don't like you that way."

"You don't like me at all," he muttered.

"You're very nearly right." She smiled.

"You're a fool, you're a fool!" he exclaimed. "You don't know what's coming to you. You don't know."

"Perhaps I do," she said; "perhaps I can guess. But whatever is coming to me, as you put it, I prefer that to marrying you."

He started back as though she had struck him across the face, and his face was livid.

"You won't say that when—"

He checked himself and without another word left the room, and she heard his heavy feet blundering down the stairs.

And then she met him again. It was two nights after. She met him in a horrible dream. She dreamed he was flying after her, that they were both birds, she a pigeon and he a hawk; and as she made her last desperate struggle to escape, she heard his hateful voice in her ear:

"Maisie, it is your last chance!"

She had gone to bed at ten o'clock that night, and it seemed that she had hardly fallen asleep before the vision came. She struggled to sit up in bed, she tried to speak, but a big hand was over her mouth and another was gripping her by her shoulder.

"Maisie, Maisie, it is your last chance!"

Then it was true, it was no dream. He was in the room, his hand upon her mouth, his voice in her ear. She struggled again, but he held her in a grip of iron. The room was in darkness. There was no sound save the sound of his heavy breathing and his voice.

"They'll be up here in five minutes," he whispered. "I can save you, I can save you, Maisie! Will you marry me?"

She summoned all the strength at her command to shake her head.

"You won't, eh?"

There was a note of savagery in his voice which made her feel sick.

"Keep quiet!"

For a second the hand was withdrawn, and she filled her lungs to scream, but at that instant a mass of cotton wool was thrust over her face, and she began to breathe in a sickly sweet vapor. Somebody else was in the room now. They were holding her feet. The voice in her ear said:

"Breathe. Take a deep breath!"

She sobbed and writhed in an agony of mind, but all the time she was breathing, all the time she was drawing into her lungs the chloroform with which the wool was saturated.

At two o'clock in the morning a uniformed constable, patrolling his beat, saw an ambulance drawn up outside a house in Doughty Street. He crossed the road to make inquiries.

"A case of scarlet fever," said the driver.

"You don't say," said the sympathetic constable.

The door opened and two men walked out, carrying a figure in a blanket. The policeman stood by and saw the "patient" laid upon a stretcher and the back of the ambulance closed. Then he continued his walk to the corner of the street, where he found, huddled up in a doorway, the unconscious figure of a Scotland Yard detective, whose observation had been interrupted by a well-directed blow from a blackjack.

CHAPTER XV
THE COMMISSIONER HAS A THEORY

From station to station throughout the night, the following communication was flashed:

To all stations. Stop Ambulance Motor No. LKO.9943 Arrest and detain driver and any person found therein. Warn all garages and report. COMMISSIONER.

Before the dawn, nine thousand policemen were on the lookout for the motor ambulance.

"There's a chance, of course," said Stafford, "but it is a poor chance."

He was looking white and heavy-eyed.

"I don't know, sir," said Southwick, his subordinate. "There's always a chance that a crook will do the obviously wrong thing. I suppose you've no theory as to where they have gone?"

"Not out of town—of that I'm certain," said King; "that is why the quest is so hopeless. Why, they'll have reached their destination hours before the message went out!"

They were standing in the girl's bedroom, which still reeked with chloroform, and all the clews were piled together on the table. There were not many. There was a pad of cotton wool, a half empty bottle of chloroform, bearing the label of a well-known wholesaler, and one of a pair of old wash-leather gloves, which had evidently been worn by somebody in his desire to avoid leaving finger prints.

"We've not much to go on there," said Stafford disconsolately. "The chloroform may have been sold a long time ago. Any chemist would have supplied the cotton wool, and as for the glove—" He picked it up and looked at it, then he carried it to the light.

Old as it was, it was of good shape and quality and when new had probably been supplied to order by a first-class glovemaker.

"There's nothing here," said Stafford again, and threw the glove back on the table.

A policeman came into the room and saluted.

"I've cycled over from the Yard, sir. We have had a message asking you to go at once to Sir Stanley Belcom's private house."

"How did Sir Stanley know about this affair?" asked Stafford listlessly.

"He telephoned, sir, about five o'clock this morning. He often makes an early inquiry."

Stafford looked round. There was nothing more that he could do. He passed down the stairs into the street and jumped on to the motor cycle which had brought him to the scene.

Sir Stanley Belcom lived in Cavendish Place, and Stafford had been a frequent visitor to the house. Sir Stanley was a widower, who was wont to complain that he kept up his huge establishment in order to justify the employment of his huge staff of servants. Stafford suspected him of being something of a sybarite. His dinners were famous, his cellar was the best in London, and because of his acquaintances and friendships in the artistic sets, he was something of a dabbler in the arts he patronized.

The door was opened, and an uncomfortable-looking butler was waiting on the step to receive Stafford.

"You'll find Sir Stanley in the library, sir," he said.

Despite his sorrow, Stafford could not help smiling at this attempt on the part of an English servant to offer the conventional greeting in spite of the hour.

"I'm afraid we've got you up early, Perkins," he said.

"Not at all, sir."

The man's stout face creased in a smile.

"Sir Stanley often gets up in the middle of the night and orders a meal."

Stafford found his gray-haired chief, arrayed in a flowered silk dressing gown, balancing bread on an electric toaster.

"Bad news, eh, Stafford?" he said. "Sit down and have some coffee. The girl is gone?"

Stafford nodded.

"And our unfortunate detective-constable who was sent to watch is half-way to the mortuary, I presume?"

"Not so bad as that, sir," said Stafford, "but he got a pretty bad knock. He's recovered consciousness but remembers nothing that happened."

Sir Stanley nodded.

"Very scientifically done," he said admiringly. "This, of course, is the work of the Boundary gang."

"I wish—" began Stafford between his teeth.

"Save your breath, my friend"—Sir Stanley smiled—"wishing will do nothing. You could arrest every known member of the gang, and they'd have twenty alibis ready, and very good alibis, too. It is years since the colonel staged an outrage of this kind, but his right hand has not lost its cunning.

"Look at the organization of it! The men get into the house without attracting the attention of your watcher. Then, at the exact second that the ambulance is due, along comes their thug and knocks down the policeman on duty. I don't suppose the thing took more than ten minutes. Everything was timed. They must have known the hour the policeman on the beat passed along the street."

Sir Stanley poured out the coffee with his own hands, and relapsed back into his armchair.

"Why do you think they did it?"

"They were afraid of her, sir," said Stafford.

Sir Stanley laughed softly.

"I can't imagine Boundary being afraid of a girl."

"She was Solly White's daughter," said Stafford.

"Even then I can't understand it," replied the chief, "unless—by Jove. Of course."

He hit his knee a smack, and Stafford waited.

"Probably they've got some other game on; but I'll tell you one of the ideas of taking that girl—it is to bring back Solomon White. He disappeared, didn't he?"

Stafford nodded.

"That's the game—to bring back Solomon White. And whatever is the danger to himself, he'll be in London tomorrow, as soon as this news is known." Sir Stanley sat with his chin in his hand, thinking, his forehead wrinkled in thought. "There's some other reason, too. Now, what is it?"

Stafford guessed, but did not say.

"That girl will take some recovering before harm comes to her," said Sir Stanley softly. "Your only hope is that friend Jack comes to your rescue."

"Jack o' Judgment?"

Sir Stanley nodded, and the other smiled sadly.

"That's unlikely," he said; "indeed, it is impossible. I think I might as well tell you my own theory as to why she was abducted and why Boundary took so much trouble to capture her."

"What is your theory?" asked Sir Stanley curiously.

"My theory, sir, is, that she is Jack o' Judgment," said Stafford King.

"She—Jack o' Judgment?" Sir Stanley was on his feet, staring at him. "Impossible! It is a man."

"You seem to forget sir," said Stafford, "that Miss White is a wonderful mimic."

"But why?"

"She wants to clear her father. She told me that only a week ago. And then I've been making inquiries on my own account. I found that she was seen coming out of the Albermarle mansions the night that 'Jack' made his last visit to Boundary's flat."

Sir Stanley rose.

"Wait," he said, and left the room.

Presently he came back.

"If Miss White is Jack o' Judgment, and if she was captured tonight, how do you account for this? It was under my pillow when I woke up."

He laid on the table the familiar jack of clubs.

CHAPTER XVI
IN THE TURKISH BATHS

Colonel Boundary had a breakfast party of three. Though he had been up the whole of the night, he showed no signs of weariness. Not so Pinto or Crewe, who seemed tired out, and were all the more weary looking because they were both conspicuously unshaven.

"Half the game's won," said the colonel. "We'll get rid of this girl and Solly White by the same stroke. I'm afraid of Solly—he knows too much. By the way, Raoul is coming over."

"Raoul!" said Crewe, sitting up suddenly. "Why, colonel, you're crazy! Didn't the Scotland Yard man say—"

"That he suspected a French hand in the case of Snow Gregory? All the more reason why Raoul should come," said the colonel calmly. "He ought to report this morning."

"You're taking a risk," muttered Pinto.

"Nothing unusual," replied the colonel, shelling a plover's egg; "it is the last thing in the world they would suspect at Scotland Yard after their warning, that I should bring Raoul over again. Besides, they don't know him anyway. He's just a harmless young French cabinet maker. He doesn't talk, and I will get him out of the silly habit of leaving his visiting card."

There was a silence, which Crewe broke.

"You want him for—"

He did not finish the sentence.

"For work," replied the colonel. "It is a thousand pities, but it would be a thousand times a thousand pities if you and I were arrested and waiting in the condemned cell for the arrival of the eminent hangman. Raoul's a workman. We can trust him. He doesn't try any funny business. He lives out of this country, and I can cover his tracks. Besides," the colonel went on, "I shall give him enough to live in comfort for the next two years. Raoul is a grateful little beast, and, thank goodness he can neither read nor write."

"I don't like it," said Crewe; "I hate that kind of thing. Why not give Solly a chance? Why not get up a fight—a duel, anything but murder?"

The colonel turned his cold eyes upon the other, and his lips parted in a mirthless smile.

"You're speaking up to your character now, aren't you, Crewe?" he said unpleasantly. "You're 'Gentleman Crewe' once again, eh? Want to do everything in the correct fashion? Well, you cut out all that stuff. I'm Dan Boundary, looking forward to a pleasant old age. There's nothing of the Knights of the Round Table about me."

Crewe flushed.

"All right," he said; "have it your own way."

"You bet your life I'm going to have it my own way," said the colonel. "Have you seen the girl this morning, Pinto?"

Pinto shook his head.

"You'll keep away from there for a couple of days. I've got Boyton on the spot, and he'll be feeding her with bromide till she won't care where she is. Besides, we'll all be shadowed for the next day or two. Make no mistake about that. Stafford King won't let the grass grow under his feet. And now go home and try to look as though you've had a night's rest."

After their departure the colonel made his own preparations. There were Turkish baths in Westminster, and it was to the Turkish baths he went. Clad in a towel, he passed from hot room to hot room, and finally came to the big, vaulted saloon, tiled from floor to roof, where in canvas-backed chairs the bathers dozed and read. The colonel lay back in his chair, his eyes closed, apparently oblivious to his surroundings. Nor was it to be observed that he saw the thin little man who came and sat beside him. The newcomer was sallow-skinned and lantern-jawed, and his long arms were tattooed from shoulder to wrist.

"Here!" said a soft voice in French.

The colonel did not open his eyes. He merely dropped the palm fan which he was waving idly to and fro, so that it hid his mouth.

"Do you remember a Mr. White?" he said in the same tone.

"Perfectly," replied the other. "He was the man who would not have your little 'snow' friend—disposed of."

"That is the man," said the other. "You have a good memory, Raoul."

"Monsieur, my memory is wonderful, but, alas! One cannot live on memory," he added sententiously.

"Then remember this: There is a place near London called Putney Heath."

"Putney Heath," repeated the other.

"There is a house called Bishopsholme."

"Bishopsholme," repeated the other.

"It is empty—to let, you understand? It is in a sad state of desolation. The garden, the house—you know the kind of place?"

"Perfectly, monsieur."

"At nine o'clock to-night and at nine o'clock tomorrow night you will be near the door. There is a large clump of bushes, behind which you will stand. You will stay there until ten. Between those hours Mr. White will approach and go into the house. You understand?"

"Perfectly, monsieur," said the voice again.

"You will shoot him so that he dies immediately."

"He is a dead man," said the other.

There was a long pause.

"I will pay you sixty thousand francs, and I will have a motor car to take you directly to Dover. You will catch the night boat for Ostend. Your passports will be in order, and you can make your way to Paris at your leisure. The payment you will receive in Paris. Is that satisfactory?"

"Eminently so, monsieur," said the other. "I need a little for expenses for the moment. Also I wish information as to where the motor car will meet me."

"It will be waiting for you at the corner of the first road past the house, on the way from London. You will, in fact, pass it on your way to the house. You will not speak to the chauffeur and he will not speak to you. In the car you will find sufficient money for your immediate needs. Is there any necessity to explain further?"

"None whatever, monsieur," said the soft voice, and Raoul dropped his head on one side as though he were sleeping.

As for the colonel, he did not simulate slumber, but passed into dreamland, sleeping quietly and calmly, with a look of benevolence upon his big face.

The only other occupant of the cooling room, a big-framed man who was reading a newspaper, closed his eyes, too—but he did not sleep.

CHAPTER XVII
SOLOMON COMES BACK

At nine o'clock that night the colonel, in immaculate evening dress, sat playing double-dummy bridge with his two companions. In the light of the big shaded lamp overhead there was something particularly peaceful and innocent in their occupation. No word was spoken save of the game.

It was a quarter to nine, noted the colonel, looking at the little French clock on the mantelpiece. He rose, walked to the window and looked out. It was a stormy night and the wind was howling down the street, sending the rain in noisy splashes against the windowpanes. He grumbled his satisfaction and returned to the table.

"Did you see the paper?" asked Pinto presently.

"I saw the paper," said the colonel, not looking up from his hand. "I make a point of reading the newspapers."

"You see they've made a feature of—"

"Mention no names," said the colonel. "I know they've made a feature about it. So much the better. Everything depends—"

It was as he spoke that Solomon White came into the room. Boundary knew it was he before the door handle turned, before the hum of voices in the hall outside had ceased, but it was with a great pretense of surprise that he looked up.

"Why, if it isn't Solomon White!" he said.

The man was haggard and sick looking. He had evidently dressed in a hurry, for his cravat was ill tied and the collar gaped. He strode slowly up to the table, and Boundary's manservant, with a little grin, closed the door.

"Where have you been all this time, Solomon?" asked Boundary genially. "Sit down and play a hand."

"You know why I've come," breathed Solomon White.

"Surely I know why you've come. You've come to explain where you've been, old boy. Sit down," said Boundary.

"Where is my daughter?" asked White.

"Where is your daughter?" repeated the colonel. "Well, that's a queer question to ask us. We've been saying, 'Where is Solomon White?' all this time."

"I've been to Brighton," said the man, "but that's nothing to do with it...."

"Been at Brighton? A very pleasant place, too," said Boundary. "And what were you doing at Brighton?"

"Keeping out of your way," said White fiercely, "trying to cure the fear of you which has made a rank coward of me! If you wanted to find a method for curing me, colonel, you've found it. I've come back for my daughter. Where is she?"

The colonel pushed his chair back from the table and looked up with a quizzical smile.

"Now you're not going to take it hard, Solomon," he said. "We had to have you back and that was the only scheme we could think of. You see, there are lots of little bits of business that have to be cleared up, business in which you had a hand the same as my other business associates."

"Where is the girl?" asked the man steadily.

"Well, I'm going to admit to you," said the colonel with a fine show of frankness, "that I've put her away. No harm has come to her, you understand. She's at a little place at Putney Heath, a house I took specially for her, surrounded by loving guardians."

"Like Pinto?" asked the man, looking down at the silent Silva.

"Like Lollie. Now you can't deny that Lollie's a very nice girl," said the colonel. "Sit down, Solomon, and talk things over."

"When I've got my girl I'll talk things over with you. Where is this place?"

"It is on Putney Heath," said the colonel. "Now am I not being straightforward with you? If I had any bad designs against the girl should I tell you where she is? If you go there, Solomon, take some of your police friends."

"I have no police friends," said the man angrily; "you know it well enough. What am I that I should go to the police? Can I go to them with clean hands?"

"Well, that's a question I've often asked myself," said the colonel. "I've often said—"

"What is the name of the house?" interrupted White. "I want to see whether you're playing square with me, Boundary, and if you're not, by—"

"Don't threaten me, don't threaten me, Solomon," said the colonel with a good-humored gesture; "I'm a nervous man and I suffer from heart disease. You ought to know better than that. Bishopsholme is the place. It is the fourth big house after passing Tredennis Road—a fine villa standing in its own grounds.

It looks a bit deserted because it was empty until a few days ago, when I put a scrap or two of furniture into it. Why not wait—"

"First I'll find whether you're speaking the truth, and if you're not—"

"Stay a while," said Boundary, "it is only just nine—"

But White was gone.

He pushed past the servant, one of the readiest and most dangerous of the colonel's instruments, and into the half-dark corridor. There was a light on the landing below, and as he ran down the stairs he thought he saw somebody standing there. It looked like a woman, till the figure turned, and then Solomon White stood stock-still. It was the first time he had seen Jack o' Judgment. The shimmer of the black silk coat, the curious suggestion of pallor which the white mask conveyed, the slouch hat, throwing a black bar of shadow diagonally across the face, lent the figure a peculiarly sinister aspect.

"Stand!"

The voice was commanding, the glittering revolver in the figure's hand more so.

"Who are you?" gasped Solomon White.

"Jack o' Judgment! Have you ever heard of little Jack?"

The figure chuckled. "Oh, here's a new one—Solomon White, too, and never heard of Jack o' Judgment! Didn't you see me when they took me out of Snow Gregory's pocket? Little Jack o' Judgment!"

Solomon White stepped back, his face twitching.

"I had nothing to do with that," he said hoarsely; "nothing to do with that, do you hear?"

"Where are you going? Won't you tell Jack something, give him a bit of news? Poor old Jack hears nothing these days." The figure sighed, laughter bubbling between the words.

"I'm going on private business. Get out of my way," said the other, remembering the urgency of his mission.

"But you'll tell Jack o' Judgment?" wheedled the figure. "You'll tell poor old Jack where you are going to find your beautiful daughter?"

"You know!" said the man.

He took a step forward, but the revolver waved him back.

"You'll speak or you don't pass," said Jack o' Judgment. "You don't pass until you speak. Do you hear, Solomon White?"

The man thought.

"It is a place called Bishopsholme," he said gruffly; "on Putney Heath. Now, let me pass."

"Wait, wait!" said the figure eagerly. "Wait for me—only five minutes. I won't keep you! But don't go! There's death there, Solomon White! It is waiting for you. Don't you feel it in your bones?"

The voice sank to a whisper, and in spite of himself a cold shiver passed down White's spine. He half turned to go back.

"Wait!" said the figure again eagerly, fiercely. "I shall keep you but a minute—a second!"

Solomon White stood irresolutely, and the mask seemed to melt into the darkness. White strained his ears to hear the soft patter of its shoes as it mounted the stairs, but no sound came. Then with a start he seemed to awake as if from a bad dream, and without a word strode down the remaining stairs into the night.

On the landing above, the strange being who called himself "Jack o' Judgment" stood outside the door of Boundary's flat. He had taken a key from his pocket and had it poised, when he heard the clatter of the other's feet. He stood undecidedly, but only for a second; then the key slipped into the lock and the door opened. The butler from his little pantry saw the figure and slammed his own door, bolting it with trembling fingers.

In a second Jack o' Judgment was in the room, facing the paralyzed trio.

He spoke no word, but suddenly his right arm was raised, some shining object flew from his hand and there was a crash of glass and instantly a vile odor. On the opposite wall, where the bottle had broken, appeared a dark and irregular stain.

Then, without so much as a laugh, he stepped back through the door and raced down the stairs in pursuit of White. It was too late; the man had disappeared. Jack o' Judgment stood for a moment listening, then he slipped off the black coat and ripped off the mask. The coat was of the finest silk, for he rolled it into the space of a pocket handkerchief and slipped it into his pocket. The handkerchief went the same way. If there had been observers they would have caught a glimpse of a man in evening dress as he went swiftly down the half lighted stairway.

He turned and walked in the shadow of the building and passed down a side street, where a big closed limousine was awaiting him. He gave a murmured direction to the driver, and the car sped on its way.

CHAPTER XVIII
THE JUDGMENT OF DEATH

Solomon White had a taxi waiting and gave his directions. He was sufficiently loyal to the band to avoid calling especial attention to the house where the girl was imprisoned, and he told his cab to wait at the end of Putney Heath. The night was wild and boisterous and very dark, but he carried an electric torch, and presently he came to weather-stained gates bearing in letters, which had half faded, the name he sought. He pushed open the gate with some trouble. There was a curving carriage drive which led to the front door, which stood at the head of a flight of steps under a square and ugly portico.

He looked up at the building, but it was in darkness. Apparently it was empty, but he knew enough of the colonel's methods to be sure that Boundary would not advertise the presence of the girl to the outside world.

He stood hesitating, wondering. The whole thing might be a trap, but Solomon White was not easily scared. He took a revolver from his pocket, drew back the hammer and walked forward cautiously. There was no sign of life. The rustling of shrubs and trees was the only mournful sound which varied the roar of the storm.

He was opposite the door, and one foot was raised to surmount the first step, when there came a sound like the sharp tap of a drum.

"Rap, rap!"

Solomon White stood for fully a second before he crumpled and fell, and he was dead before he reached the ground.

Still there was no sign or sound of life. A church clock boomed out the quarter to ten. A motor car went past, and then the laurel bushes by the side of the steps moved, and a man in a black mackintosh stepped out. He bent over the dead man, picked up the fallen torch and flashed the light on the dead man's face; then, with a grunt of satisfaction, Raoul Pontarlier unscrewed his silencer and slipped his automatic into the wet pocket of his mackintosh.

Feeling in an inside pocket for a cigarette, he found one and lit it from the smouldering end of a tinder lighter. Then, carefully concealing the lighted cigarette in the palm of his hand, he walked softly and noiselessly down the drive, keeping to the shadow of the bushes and watching to left and right for signs of approaching pedestrians. At two points he could see the heath road, and nobody was in sight. There was plenty of time, and men had been ruined by haste. He reached the gate and carefully looked over. The road was deserted. His hand was on the gate when something cold and hard was pushed against his ear and he turned round.

"Put up your hands!" said a mocking voice. "Put them up!"

The Frenchman's hands slowly rose.

"Now turn round and face the house. Quick!" said the voice, "*marcher! Halt!*"

Raoul stopped. If he could only get his hands down and duck, one lightning dive—

His captor evidently read his thoughts, for he felt a hand slip into his mackintosh pocket and he was relieved of the weight of his automatic.

"Go forward, up the steps. Stop!"

The stranger had seen the huddled figure of White, and stooped over him. He made no comment. He knew the man was dead before his hands had touched him.

"Mount the steps, *canaille!*" said the voice; and Raoul walked slowly up the steps of the house and halted with his face against the door.

A hand came up under his uplifted arm and sought the keyhole. A few minutes' fumbling until the prongs of the skeleton key had found its corresponding wards, and then the door swung open, emitting a scent of mustiness and decay.

"Marchez!" said the stranger, and Raoul walked forward and heard the door slam behind him.

The house was not empty, in the sense that it was unfurnished. The unknown was using an electric torch of extraordinary brilliancy, and revealed a dilapidated hallstand and a musty chair. He took a brief survey and then said: "Down those stairs!" and the murderer obeyed.

They were in the kitchen now, and again the bright light gleamed about. The windows were heavily shuttered, the grate was rusty, and a few old pieces of china on the sideboard were dirty. There was a gas bracket in the center, over a large deal table, and this the stranger turned on. He heard the hiss of escaping gas, struck a match and lit it, and then for the first time Raoul gazed in fear and astonishment upon the man who held him.

"Monsieur," he stammered, "who are you?"

The masked figure slipped his hand into his pocket and flicked a card upon the table, and Raoul, looking down, saw the jack of clubs and knew that his end was near.

For three hours the Frenchman had lain on the floor, tied hand and foot, a gag in his mouth, and the clocks were striking two when Jack o' Judgment came back. This time he wore neither mask nor coat, but over his arm he carried a coil of fine rope. Raoul watched him, fascinated, as he walked about the kitchen, whistling softly to himself, and now and again breaking into song.

"Monsieur, monsieur," blubbered the terrified man, "I would make a confession. I will make a statement before the judge."

Jack o' Judgment smiled.

"You shall make a statement before your judge, for I am he," he said, "and I think this is the place."

He glanced up at the high roof of the kitchen, for there was a stout hook, where in old times heavy sides of bacon hung. He drew the table under the place and put a chair on top. Then he mounted, and with a skillful cast of his rope caught the hook and drew the rope slowly through. He did not move the table or take any notice of the man on the floor but stood as a workman might stand who was calculating distances, and all the time he whistled softly.

"Monsieur, monsieur, spare me! I will make reparation!"

"You speak truly," said the other, without taking his eyes from the rope, "for it is reparation you make this night for two dead men, and Heaven knows how many besides."

"Two?"

The murderer twisted his head.

"For a man called Gregory particularly," said Jack o' Judgment, "shot down like a mad dog."

"I was paid to do it. I knew nothing against him. I had no malice in my heart," said the man eagerly.

"Nor have I," said Jack o' Judgment, "for behold! I shall kill you without passion, as a warning to all villains of all nationalities."

"This is against the law," whined the man, beads of sweat standing on his forehead; "give me a knife and let me fight you, you coward!"

"Give Solomon White a pistol and let him fight you," said the other. "It is against the law—well I know it. But it is much more speedy than the law, my little cabbage!"

He was busy making a slipknot at one end of the rope, and presently he had finished it to his satisfaction.

"Raoul Pontarlier," he said, "this is a moment for which I have waited many years."

The man screamed and twisted his head, but the noose was about his neck and tightening. Then with a wrench Jack o' Judgment jerked him to his feet.

"On to the table," he said sternly; "mount! It is quicker so!"

"I will not, I will not!" yelled the Frenchman. His voice rose to a shrill scream. "Help!"

Half an hour later Jack o' Judgment came down the dark path, stopping only for a second to look down upon the figure of Solomon White.

"God have mercy on you all!" he said soberly, and passed into the night.

CHAPTER XIX
THE COLONEL IS SHOCKED

"The Putney mystery," said the *Daily Megaphone*, "surpasses any of recent years in its sensational character. There is a touch of the bizarre in this grim spectacle of the dead man at the door of the empty house and the swaying figure of his murderer hanging in the kitchen, with no other mark of identification than a playing card pinned to his breast.

"The tragedy can be reconstructed up to a point. Mr. White was evidently killed in the garden by the Frenchman who was found hanging. The automatic pistol in his pocket, which had recently been discharged might support this theory, even if the police had not found tracks of his feet in the laurels. But who hanged the man Raoul with a hangman's rope? That is the supreme mystery of all. The Putney police can offer no information on the subject, and Scotland Yard is as reticent. The circumstances of the discovery are as follows: At three o'clock on the morning of the fourth, Police Constable Robinson, who was patrolling his beat, entered the garden, as is customary when houses are empty, to see if any doors had been forced. There has been an epidemic of burglaries in the region of Putney Heath during the past two or three months, and the police are exercising unusual vigilance in relation to these houses. The constable might not have made his inspection that night but for the fact that the garden gate had been left wide open."

Here followed an account of how the body was found, and how further investigation led the constable to the kitchen to make his second gruesome discovery.

Colonel Boundary folded up the paper slowly and put it down. He had bought a copy of an early edition of the evening newspaper as he was stepping into his car, and now he was driving slowly through the park. He lit a cigar and gazed stolidly from the window. But his face showed no sign of mental perturbation.

The car had made the circuit of the park twice when, turning again by Marble Arch, he saw Crewe standing on the sidewalk. A word to his chauffeur, and the machine drew up.

"Come in," he said curtly, and the other obeyed.

The hand that he lifted to take his cigarette from his lips trembled, and the colonel eyed him with quiet amusement.

"They've got you rattled, too, have they?" he said.

"It is awful!" said Crewe. "Awful!"

"What's awful about it?" asked the colonel. "White's dead, ain't he? And Raoul's dead, ain't he? Two men who might talk and give a lot of trouble."

"What did he say before he died? That's what I've been thinking. What did he say?"

"Who—Raoul?" demanded the colonel. He had asked himself the same question before. "What could he say? Anyway, if he had a statement to make, and his statement was worth taking, why, he'd be alive today! Raoul was the one witness that they wanted, if they only knew it. They've bungled pretty badly, whoever they are."

"This Jack o' Judgment," quavered Crewe, his mouth working, "who is he? What is he?"

"How do I know?" retorted the colonel. "You ask me these fool questions—do you expect a reply? They're dead and that's done with. I'd sooner he killed Raoul than made a mess of my room. The smell—phew!"

"Why did he do it?" asked Crewe.

The colonel growled something about fools and their questions, but offered no explanation.

"It may have been a monkey trick to make us change our quarters—the stuff was sulphurated hydrogen and asafetida. It may have been just bravado, but if he thinks he can scare me—"

He sucked viciously at his cigar butt.

"I've got workmen in to strip the walls and repaper the part that's soiled," he said. "I'll be back there tonight."

The colonel threw the end of his cigar from the window and relapsed into moody reverie. When he spoke it was in a more cheerful tone.

"Crewe," he said, "that guy at Scotland Yard has given me an idea."

"Which guy?" asked Crewe, steadying his voice.

"The first commissioner," said the colonel, lighting another cigar. "He particularly wanted to know if Snow had any relations. Curse Snow!" he said between his teeth and dropping his mask of urbanity. "I wish he'd—Well, it doesn't matter; he's dead anyway—he's dead."

"Relations?" said Crewe. "Did you tell him anything?"

"I told him all I knew and that was very little," said the colonel, "but it struck me that Sir Stanley knows much more about this fellow Snow than we do. At any rate, somebody's been making inquiries, and I guess that somebody is the fellow who settled Raoul."

"Jack o' Judgment?"

"Jack o' Judgment," repeated the colonel grimly "You brought Snow Gregory into the gang. What do you know about him?"

Crewe shook his head.

"Very little," he said. "I met him in Monte Carlo. He was down and out. He seemed a likely fellow—educated, a gentleman and all that sort of thing—and when I found that he'd hit the dope, I thought he'd be the kind of man you might want."

The colonel nodded.

"He never talked about his relations. The only thing I know was that he had a father or an uncle who was in India, and I gathered that he had forged his name to a bill. When I arrived in Monte Carlo he was spending the money as fast as he could. I guess that was why he called himself Gregory, for I'm sure it wasn't his name."

"You're sure he never spoke of a brother?"

"Never," said Crewe; "he never talked about himself at all. He was generally under the influence of dope or was recovering from it."

The colonel pushed back his hat and rubbed his forehead.

"There must be some way of identifying him," he said. "He came from Oxford, you say?"

"Yes, I know that," said Crewe; "he spoke of it once."

"What house in Oxford? There are several colleges, aren't there?"

"From Balliol," said Swell Crewe; "I distinctly remember him talking about Balliol."

"What year would that be?"

Crewe reflected.

"He left college two years before I met him at Monte Carlo," he said, "that would be—." He gave the year.

"Well, it is pretty simple," said the colonel. "Send a man to Oxford and get the names of all the men who left Balliol in that year. Find out how many you can trace, and I dare say that will narrow the search down to two or three men. Now get after this at once, Crewe. Spare no expense. If it costs half a million, I'm going to discover who Mr. Jack o' Judgment is, when he's at home."

He dismissed Crewe and gave fresh instructions to his driver, and ten minutes later he was stepping out of his limousine at the entrance to Scotland Yard.

Stafford King was not in, or at any rate was not available. Greatly daring, the colonel sent his card to the first commissioner. Sir Stanley Belcom read the name and raised his eyebrows.

"Show him in," he said; and for the second time the colonel was ushered into the presence of the chief.

"Well, colonel," said Sir Stanley, "this is rather a dreadful business."

"Terrible, terrible!" said the colonel, shaking his head. "Solomon White was one of my best friends. I've been searching for him for weeks."

"So I've heard," said Sir Stanley dryly. "Have you any theory?"

"None whatever."

"What about this man called Raoul? Is he unknown to you?" asked Sir Stanley.

"That's what I've come to see you about, sir," said the colonel in a confidential tone. "You remember the last time I was here you suggested that possibly the murderer of poor Gregory might be a Frenchman. You remember how you told me that these French assassins have a trick of leaving some fantastic card or sign of their handiwork?"

Sir Stanley nodded.

"Well, here you have the same thing repeated," said the colonel triumphantly, "and the identical card. Do you think, sir, that the murderer of my poor friend Gregory and my poor friend, White, was the same man?"

"In fact, Raoul?" asked Sir Stanley.

The colonel nodded, and for a few moments Sir Stanley communed with his well-kept finger nails.

"I don't think it will do any harm if I tell you that is my theory also, Colonel Boundary," he said, "and, giving confidence for confidence, would you have any objection to telling me whether Raoul is one of your—er—business associates?"

There was just the slightest shade of irony in the last two words, but the colonel preferred to ignore it.

"I'm very glad you asked me that question, sir," he said with a sigh, so palpably a sigh of relief that the recording angel might be excused if he were deceived. "I have never seen Raoul before. In fact, my knowledge of Frenchmen is a very small one. I do very little business in France, and I certainly do no business at all with men of that class."

"What class?" asked the other quickly.

The colonel shrugged his big shoulders.

"I am only going on what the newspapers say," he said; "they suggest that this man is an apache."

"You do not know him?" asked Sir Stanley after a pause.

"I have never seen him in my life," said the colonel.

Again Sir Stanley examined his finger nails as though searching for some flaw.

"Then you will be surprised to learn," he drawled at last, "that you sat next to him in the cooling room of the Yildiz Turkish Baths."

The colonel's heart missed a beat, but he did not flinch.

"You surprise me," he said. "I have only been to the Turkish Baths once during the past three months, and that was yesterday."

Sir Stanley nodded.

"According to my information, which was supplied to me by my very able assistant, Mr. Stafford King, that was also the morning when Raoul was seen to enter that building."

"And he sat next to me?" said the colonel incredulously.

"He sat next to you," said Sir Stanley, with evidence of enjoyment.

"Well, that is the most amazing coincidence," exclaimed the colonel, "I have ever met with in my life! To imagine that that scoundrel sat shoulder to shoulder with me—good heavens! It makes me hot to think about it."

"I was afraid it would," said the first commissioner.

He pressed the bell, and his secretary came in.

"See if Mr. Stafford King is in the building and tell him to come to me, please," he said. "You see, colonel, we were hoping that you would supply us with a great deal of very useful information. We naturally thought it was something more than a coincidence that this man and you should foregather at a Turkish bath— a most admirable rendezvous, by the way."

"You may accept my word of honor," said Colonel Boundary impressively, "that I had no more idea of that man's presence, or of his identity, or of his very existence than you had."

Stafford King came in at that moment, and the colonel, noting the haggard face and the look of care in the dark-lined eyes, felt a certain amount of satisfaction.

"I've just been telling the colonel about his meeting in the Turkish baths," said Sir Stanley. "I suppose there is no doubt at all as to that happening?"

"None whatever, sir," said Stafford shortly. "Both the colonel and this man were seen by Sergeant Livingstone."

"The colonel suggests that it was a coincidence, and that he had never spoken to the man," said Sir Stanley. "What do you say to that, King?"

Stafford King's lips curled.

"If the colonel says so, of course it must be true."

"Sarcasm never worries me," said the colonel. "I'm always getting into trouble and I'm always getting out again. Give a dog a bad name and—"

He stopped. There arose in his mind a mental picture of a man swinging in an underground kitchen, and in spite of his self-control he shuddered.

"And hang him, eh?" said Sir Stanley. "Now, I'm going to put matters to you very plainly, colonel. There have been three or four very unpleasant happenings. There has been the death of the chief witness for the crown against you;

there has been the death of this unhappy man White, who was closely associated with you in your business deals, and who has recently broken away from you, unless our information is inaccurate; there is the death of Raoul, who was seen seated next to you and apparently carrying on a conversation behind a fan.''

"He never spoke a word to me," protested the colonel.

"And we have the disappearance of Miss White, which is one of the most important of the happenings, because we have reason to believe that Miss White, at any rate, is still alive," said Sir Stanley, taking no notice of the interruption. "Now, colonel, you may or may not have the key to all these mysteries. You may or may not know who your mysterious friend, the Jack o' Judgment—"

"He's no friend of mine, by Heaven!" said the colonel, and neither man doubted that he spoke the truth.

"As I say, you may know all these things. But principally at this moment we are anxious to secure authentic news concerning Miss White. Both I and Mr. Stafford King have particular reasons for desiring information on that subject. Can you help me?"

The colonel shook his head.

"If by spending a hundred thousand pounds I could help you, I would do it," he said fervently, "but as to Miss White and where she is, I am as much at sea as you. Do you believe that, sir?"

"No," said Sir Stanley truthfully; "I don't."

CHAPTER XX
SWELL CREWE BACKS OUT

The colonel left Scotland Yard with a sense that he had spent the morning not unprofitably. It was his way to beard the lion in his den, and, after all, the police department was no more formidable than any other public department. He spent the morning quietly in Pinto's flat, making certain preparations.

The workmen were doing a thorough job with his damaged wall, as he found when he looked in, and the horrible odor had almost disappeared. It was to be a much longer job than he thought. It had been necessary to cut away and replace the plaster under the paper, for the infernal mixture had soaked deep.

Still the colonel had plenty to occupy his mind. What he called his legitimate business had been sadly neglected of late. Reports had come in from all sorts of agencies, reports which might by careful study be turned to the greatest advantage. There was the affair of Lady Glenmerrin. He had been months accumulating evidence of that lady's marital delinquencies, and now the iron was ready to strike—and he simply had no interest in a deal which might very easily transfer the famous Glenmerrin farms to his charge at a nominal figure.

And there were other prospects as alluring. But for the moment the colonel was mainly interested in the stock value of Colonel Dan Boundary and the possibility of violent fluctuations. He was losing grip. The story of Jack o' Judgment had circulated with amazing rapidity by all manner of underground channels, to people vitally concerned. Crewe, who had been a standby in almost every big coup he had pulled off, was as stable as pulp. White, his right-hand man, was dead. Pinto—well, Pinto would go his own way just when it suited him. He had no doubt whatever as to Pinto's loyalty. Silva had big estates in Portugal, to which he would retire just when things were getting warm and interesting. Moreover, the British government could not extradite Pinto from his native land.

The colonel found himself regretting that he had missed the opportunity of taking up American citizenship during the seven years he had spent in San Francisco. And what of Crewe? Crewe was to reveal himself most unmistakably. He came in in the late afternoon and found the colonel working through the litter on his desk.

"Have you started your search at Oxford?" asked the colonel.

"I've sent two men down there—the best men in London," replied Crewe. He drew up a chair to the desk and flung his hat on a near-by couch.

"I want to have a little talk with you, colonel."

Boundary looked up sharply.

"That sounds bad," he said. "What do you want to talk about—the weather?"

"Hardly," said Crewe. A little pause, and then he announced: "Colonel, I'm going to quit."

The colonel made no reply. He went on writing his letter, and not until he had reached the end of the page and carefully blotted the epistle did he meet Crewe's eyes, "So you're going to quit, are you?" said Boundary. "Cold feet?"

"Something like that," said Crewe. "Of course, I'm not going to leave you in the lurch."

"Oh, no," said the colonel with elaborate politeness, "nobody's going to leave me in the lurch. You're just going to quit, that's all, and I've got to face the music."

"Why don't you quit, too, colonel?"

"Quit what?" asked Boundary, "and how? You might as well ask a tree to quit the earth, to uproot itself and go on living. What happens when I walk out of this office and take a first-class stateroom to New York? You think the Boundary gang collapses, fades away, just dies off, eh? The moment I leave there's a squeal, and that squeal will be loud enough to reach me in whatever part of the world I may be. There are a dozen handy little combinations which will think that I am double crossing them, and they'll be falling over one another to get in with the first tale."

Crewe licked his dry lips.

"Well, that certainly may be in your case, colonel, but it doesn't happen to be in mine. I've covered all my tracks so that there's no evidence against me."

"That's true," said the colonel, "you've just managed to keep out of taking an important part. I congratulate you."

"There's no sense in getting riled about it," said Crewe; "it has just been my luck, that's all. Well, I want to take advantage of this luck."

"In what way?"

"I'm out of any bad trouble. The police, if they search for a million years, couldn't get a scrap of evidence to convict me," he said. "Even if they'd had you when Hanson betrayed you, they couldn't have convicted me also."

"That's true," said the colonel again. He shook his head impatiently. "Well, what does all this lead to, Crewe? Do you want to be demobilized?" he asked humorously.

"That's about the size of it," said Crewe. "I don't want to be in anything new, and I certainly don't want to be in this—"

"What?"

"In this Maisie White business," said Crewe doggedly. "Let Pinto do his own dirty work."

"My dirty work, too," said the colonel. "But I reckon you've overlooked one important fact."

"What's that?" demanded Crewe suspiciously.

"You've overlooked a young gentleman called Jack o' Judgment," said the colonel, and enjoyed the look of consternation which came to the other's face. "There's a fellow that doesn't want any evidence. He hanged Raoul all right."

"Do you think he did it?" said Crewe in a hushed voice.

"Do I think he did it?" The colonel smiled. "Why who else? And when he comes to judge you, I guess he's not going to worry very much about affidavits and sworn statements, and he's not going to take you before a magistrate before he hands you over to the coroner."

Crewe jumped to his feet.

"What have I done?" he asked harshly.

"What have you done? Well, you know best," said the colonel with a wave of his hand. "You say the police haven't got you and haven't a case against you. Maybe you're right. That Greek was saying the same sort of thing to me. He was here this afternoon squealing about taking the girl to the Argentine; wanted us to send the doctor while he would wait to meet us when we land. There's no evidence against him either. Maybe there's more evidence than you imagine. I wouldn't bank too much upon the police passing you by, if I were you, Crewe. There's something about Mr. Stafford King that I don't like. He's got more brains in his little finger than that dude commissioner has in the whole of his body. He doesn't say much, but I guess he thinks a lot, and I'd give something to know what he's thinking about me just now."

CHAPTER XXI
THE BRIDE OF DEATH

Time had long ceased to have any significance for Maisie White. There was daylight and night light. She seemed to remember that she had made a great fight on the day she arrived at this strange house when the hard-faced nurses had strapped her to the bed, and an old man, with trembling fingers, had pushed a needle into her arm. She remembered it hurt, and then she remembered very little else. She viewed life with a dull apathy and without much understanding. She ceased to resent the presence of the women who came and went, and even the uncleanly old doctor no longer filled her with a sense of revulsion.

She just wanted to be left alone to sleep, to dream the strangest dreams that any girl had ever had. She did not know that this was the action of a drug, consistently administered in every drink she took, in every morsel of food she ate. Bromide in bread, in coffee, in mashed potatoes, in rice, in all the vehicles by which the drug could be administered.

Sometimes by reason of her sheer vitality she flung off the effects of the dope, and was keenly conscious of her surroundings. There was one girl, who came and went, a pretty girl with fluffy golden hair, who looked at her dispassionately and made no reply to the questions with which Maisie plied her. And once she had seen Pinto and would have screamed, but they stopped her in time. And then a dark man had come, a little man with long curling mustaches, who had looked down and showed his even white teeth in a smile.

One night the old doctor had come into the room very drunk. He was crying and moaning in a maudlin fashion about some mysterious position which he had lost, and he had sat on the bed and cursed his passion for strong drink with such vehemence that she, in her half-dazed state of mind, had found herself interested against her will.

In one of her lucid intervals she had realized a vital fact, that she was under the influence of a drug, and instinctively knew that she was becoming more and more immune to its action. She formed a vague plan, which she had almost forgotten the next morning. She must always be sleepy, almost dazed; she must never show signs of returning consciousness. She had been a week in the "nursing home" before she made this plan. She could lie now with her eyes shut, picking up the threads. She heard somebody talk of a ship and of a passport, and learned that she was to be removed in another week. She could not find where, but it was somewhere on a ship. She tried once, when the nurses were out of the room, to get out of bed and walk to the window. Her legs gave way beneath her, and it was with the greatest difficulty that she managed to crawl back to bed.

There was no escape that way. There was no help either from the nurses who were not nurses at all, nor from the maudlin little doctor, nor from the pretty girl who came sometimes and looked down on her with undisguised contempt—or was it pity? Then one night she woke in a fright.

Two people were talking. She half turned her head and saw that Pinto Silva was in the room and his face was flaming fury. She had seen that look before, but now his rage was directed at somebody else, and with a start she recognized the pretty girl that the nurses called Lollie.

"You're not in this, Lollie," said the man, and she laughed.

"That's just where you're wrong, Silva," she replied; "I'm very much in it. What happens to this girl when she leaves here, I don't know—I guess it's up to the colonel. But while she's here, I'm looking after her."

"You are, are you?" he said between his teeth. "Well, now you can go and take a walk."

"I can also take a seat, too," she said. He walked over to her and glowered down at the girl, and she puffed a cloud of cigarette smoke in his face.

"I'm a crook because it pays me to be a crook," said the girl calmly. "If it's jollying along one of the colonel's blue-eyed innocents, or keeping a watchful eye upon Mr. King—why, I'm ready and willing, because that's my job. But this is a different matter altogether. If the colonel says she's got to go abroad, why, I suppose she's got to go. But she's not going to be subjected to your persecution while she's under my charge," said Lollie.

"Oh, that's all, is it?" repeated Pinto. "Now, just come outside; I've a few words to say to you."

They passed through the door into a smaller room where the night watchers sat. Lollie made as though to sit at the table, when he gripped her arm and swung her round. She put up her hands to defend herself, but she was thrown against the wall and his grip was on her throat.

"Do you know what I'll do to you?" he threatened.

"I don't care what you do," she said. She was on the verge of tears. "You're not going into that room!"

She sprang at him, but with a snarl like a wild beast, he turned and struck at her, and she fell against the wall.

"Now get out"—he pointed to the door—"get out and don't show your face here again or I'll mark it for you."

She slunk from the room, sick at heart, and he locked the door behind her.

All that was worst in him was alive and active this night. Here was a girl who had rejected him, who had poured contempt upon offers which he honestly believed were generous. Pinto Silva was nine-tenths brute. He had neither conscience nor pity, and he went back to the room where the girl lay, determined to mar her beauty with the acid he carried in his pocket, if she still refused to marry him as soon as he should obtain a divorce.

He knelt down beside the bed.

"Covered your head with a blanket, my pretty, eh?" he said with a sneer.

"Pinto must see that pretty face, and now."

He laid hold of the blanket's edge and pulled it down. He wanted to see the eyes panic-stricken, and the drawn mouth that he had glimpsed in that second before Lollie Marsh had intruded upon his plan of revenge.

But the blankets would not come away. They were being clutched tightly. The resistance inflamed him.

With a jerk he wrenched them down, then stumbled backward to the floor, a grotesque and ludicrous figure, for the white silk mask of Jack o' Judgment confronted him and the hateful voice of his enemy shrilled:

"I'm Death! Who wants me as a bride? Jack o' Judgment! Poor old Jack! Jack Ketch, the hangman. You'll meet him one day, Pinto—meet him now!"

Pinto collapsed—he had fainted.

CHAPTER XXII
MAISIE TELLS HER STORY

"There is one fact which I would impress upon you," said Sir Stanley Belcom, addressing the heads of his departments at the early morning conference at Scotland Yard, "and it is this: that the criminal has nine chances against the one which the law possesses. He has the initiative in the first place, and if he fails to evade detection, the law gives him certain opportunities of defense and imposes certain restrictions which prevent one taking a line which would bring the truth of his assertions or denials to light. It protects him; it will not admit evidence against him; it will not allow the jury to be influenced by the record of his previous crimes until they have delivered their verdict upon the one on which he stands charged; in fact, gentlemen, the criminal, if he were intelligent, would score all the time."

"That's true enough, sir," said Cole, of the record office, "I've never yet met a criminal who wasn't a fool."

"And you never will till you meet Colonel Boundary," said Sir Stanley with a good-natured smile; "and the reason you do not meet him is because he is not a fool. But, gentlemen, every criminal has one weak spot, and sooner or later he exposes the chink in his armor to the sword of justice—if you do not mind so theatrical an illustration. Here again, I do not think that Boundary will make any such exposure. One of you gentlemen has again brought up the question as to the prosecution of the Boundary gang, and particularly the colonel himself. Well, I am all in favor of it, though I doubt whether the home secretary or the public prosecutor would agree with my point of view. We have a great deal of evidence, but not sufficient evidence to convict. We know this man is a blackmailer and that he engages in terrorizing his unfortunate victims, but the mere fact that we know is not sufficient. We need the evidence, and that evidence we have not got. And that is where our mysterious Jack o' Judgment is going to score. He knows, and it is sufficient for him that he does know. He calls for no corroborative evidence, but convicts and executes his judgment without recourse to the law books. I do not think that the official police will ever capture Boundary, and if it is left to them, he will die sanctified by old age and ten years of comfortable repentance. He will probably end his life in a cathedral town, and may indeed become a member of the town council. Hello, King, what is the matter?"

Stafford King had rushed in. He was dusty and hot of face, and there was a light of excitement in his eye. "She's found, sir; she's found!"

"She's found?" Sir Stanley frowned. "To whom are you referring—Miss White?"

Stafford could only nod.

With a gesture the commissioner dismissed the conference, then he asked: "Where was she found?"

"In her own flat, sir. That is the amazing thing about it."

"What? Did she come back herself?"

Stafford shook his head.

"It is an astonishing story, sir. She was, of course, detained and held prisoner somewhere, and last night—she will not give me any details—she was carried from the house where she had been kept prisoner. She had an awful experience, at which she only hints, poor girl! Apparently she fainted, and when she came to she was in a motor car, being carried along rapidly. And that is about all she'll tell me."

"But who brought her away?" asked the commissioner.

Again Stafford shook his head.

"For some reason or other she is reticent, and will give me no information at all. It is evident she has been drugged, for she looked wretchedly ill—of course, I haven't pressed her for further particulars."

"It is a strange story," said the commissioner.

"I have a feeling," Stafford went on, "that she has given a promise to her unknown rescuer that she will not tell more than is necessary."

"But it is necessary to tell the police," said the commissioner, "and even more important for the young lady to tell her—fiance, I hope, King?"

The young man reddened and smiled.

"I agree with you that this is not the moment when you can cross-examine the girl, but I want you to see her as soon as you possibly can and try to induce her to tell you all she knows."

Maisie White lay on the sofa in her own room. She was still weak, but, oh! The relief of being back again and of ending that terrible nightmare which had oppressed her for—how long? Even the depressing effect of the drug could not quench the exaltation of finding herself free. She went over the details of the night one by one. She must do it, she thought. She must never lose grip of what happened or forget her promise.

First she recalled seeing the weird figure of Jack o' Judgment. He had lifted her from the bed and had laid her on the floor. She remembered seeing him slip beneath the blankets, and then Pinto had come. She recalled the cracked voice of her rescuer, his fantastic language.

She had awakened to consciousness to find herself in a big car which was passing quickly through the dark and deserted streets. She had no recollection of being carried from the room or of being handed to the thickset man who stood on a ladder outside the open window. All she recalled was her waking to consciousness and seeing in the half light the gleam of a white silk handkerchief.

She was too dazed to be terrified, and the soft voice which spoke into her ear quelled any inclinations she might have had to struggle. For the man was holding her in his arms as tenderly as a brother might hold a sister, or a father a child.

"You're safe, Miss White," said the voice. "Do you understand? Are you awake?"

"Yes," she whispered.

"You know what I have saved you from?"

She nodded.

"I want you to do something for me now. Will you?" She nodded again. "Are you sure you understand?" said the voice anxiously.

"I quite understand," she replied.

She could have almost smiled at his consideration.

"I am taking you to your home, and tomorrow your friends will know that you have returned. But you're not to tell them about the house where they have kept you. You must not tell them about Silva or anybody that was in that house. Do you understand?"

"But why?" she began, and he laughed softly.

"I am not trying to shield them," he said, answering her unspoken thought, "but if you give information you can only tell a little, and the police can only discover a little, and the men can only be punished a little. And there's so much that they deserve, so many lives they have ruined, so much sorrow they have caused, that it would be a hideous injustice if they were only punished—a little. Will you leave them to me?"

She struggled to an erect position and stared at him.

"I know you," she whispered fearfully, "you are Jack o' Judgment!"

"Jack o' Judgment!" He laughed a little bitterly. "Yes, I am Jack o' Judgment."

"Who are you?" she asked.

"A living lie," he replied bitterly, "a masquerader, a nobody."

She did not know what impelled her to do the thing, but she put out her hand and laid it on his. She felt the silky smoothness of the glove, and then his other hand covered hers.

"Thank you," he said simply. "Do you think you can walk? We are just turning into Doughty Street. We've passed the policeman on his beat; he is going the other way. Can you walk upstairs by yourself?"

"I—I'll try," she said; but when he assisted her from the cab she nearly fell, and he half carried, half supported her into her room.

He stood hesitating near the door.

"I shall be all right." She smiled. "How quickly you understand my thoughts!"

"Wouldn't it be well if I sent somebody to you—a nurse? Have you the key I gave you?"

"How did you get it?" she asked suddenly; and he laughed again.

"Jack o' Judgment," he said mockingly. "Wise old Jack o' Judgment! He has everything and nothing! Suppose I send a nurse to you, a nice nurse. I could send the key to her by messenger. Would you like that?"

She looked doubtful.

"I think I would," she said with a weak smile; "I am not quite sure of myself."

He did not take off the soft felt hat which was drawn tightly over his ears, nor did he remove his mask or cloak. She was making up her mind to take closer stock of when unexpectedly he backed towards the door and with a little nod was gone. He had left her on the couch, and there she was, half dozing and half drugged, when the matronly nurse from St. George's Institute arrived half an hour later.

Stafford called in the afternoon and was surprised and delighted to learn that he could speak to the girl. He found her looking better and more cheerful. He bent over and kissed her cheek and her hand sought his.

"Now, I'm going to be awfully official." He laughed. "I want you to tell me all sorts of things. The chief is very anxious that we should lose no time in getting your story."

She shook her head.

"There's no story to tell, Stafford," she said.

"No story to tell?" he said incredulously. "But weren't you abducted?"

She nodded.

"There's so much you know," she said; "I was abducted and taken away. I have been detained and, I think, drugged."

"No harm has come to you?" he asked anxiously.

Again she shook her head.

"But where did they take you? Who was it? Who were the people?"

"I can't tell you," she said.

"You don't know?"

She hesitated.

"Yes, I think I know, but I can't tell you."

"But why?" he asked in astonishment.

"Because the man who rescued me begged me not to tell, and, Stafford, you don't know what he saved me from."

"He—he—who was it?" asked Stafford.

"The man called Jack o' Judgment," said the girl slowly, and Stafford jumped up with a cry.

"Jack o' Judgment!" he said. "I ought to have guessed! Did you see his face?" he demanded eagerly.

She shook her head again.

"Did he give you any clew to his identity?"

"None whatever," she replied with a little gleam of amusement in her eyes. "What a detective you are, Stafford! And I thought you were coming down here to tell me"—the color went to her cheeks—"well, to tell me the news," she added hastily. "Is there any news?"

"None, except—"

Then he remembered that she knew nothing whatever of her father's death and its tragic sequel, and this was not the moment to tell her. Later, when she was stronger, perhaps.

She was watching him with trouble in her eyes. She had noted how quickly he had stopped, and guessed that there was something to be told which he was withholding for fear of hurting her. Her father was uppermost in her mind, and it was natural that she should think of him.

"Is there any news of my father?" she asked quietly.

"None," he lied.

"You're not speaking the truth, Stafford." She put her hand on his arm. "Stafford, is there any news of my father?"

He looked at her, and she saw the pain in his face.

"Why don't you wait a little while, and I'll tell you all the news," he said with an assumption of gaiety. "There have been several fashionable weddings and—"

"Please tell me," she said. "Stafford, I've been for weeks under the influence of a drug, and somehow it has numbed pain, even mental pain, and perhaps you will never find me in a better condition to hear—the worst."

"The worst has happened, Maisie," he said gently.

"He has been arrested?" she asked.

He shook his head.

"No, dear; worse than that."

"Not—not suicide?" she said between her set teeth.

Again he shook his head.

"He is dead," he said softly.

"Dead!"

There was a long silence, which he did not break.

"Dead!" she said again. "How?"

"He was shot by—we think it was by a member of the Boundary gang, a man named Raoul."

She looked up at him.

"I have never heard my father speak of him."

"He was a man imported from France, according to our theory."

"And was he captured?"

"He was killed, too," said Stafford; "he was caught in the act and instantly executed."

"By whom?" she asked.

"By Jack o' Judgment," replied Stafford.

"Jack o' Judgment!" She breathed the words. "And I—I never thanked him! I never knew!"

He told her the story, step by step, of the discovery which the police had made and the theories they had formed.

"He was lured there," said the girl.

She did not cry; she seemed incapable of tears.

"He was lured there and murdered, and Jack o' Judgment slew his murderer? Poor father! Poor, dear daddy!"

And then the tears came.

Half an hour later he left her in charge of the nurse and went back to Scotland Yard to report.

CHAPTER XXIII

THE GANG FUND

The news of the girl's escape had been received in another quarter. Colonel Boundary had sat in his favorite chair and listened without comment to Pinto's halting explanation.

"Oh, they went out of the window and down a ladder, did they?" said the colonel sarcastically when the Portuguese had finished. "And you had a fit on the mat, I suppose! Well, that's a fine story! And what did you do—you who were plastered all over with guns? Couldn't you shoot?"

"Did you shoot when you saw Jack o' Judgment?" said the other sullenly. "It is no good your telling me what I ought to do."

"Maybe it isn't," said the colonel. "Well, there's nothing to do now, anyway. The girl's gone and all our plans are undone."

The colonel bit off the end of his cigar and lit it, sitting back in the chair and contemplating the ceiling reflectively.

"We can only wait and see what will happen," he said; "the odds are all in favor of our being raided."

Pinto went pale.

"Yes," said the colonel talking to himself, "I guess this is our last day of freedom. Well, Pinto, I hope you can pick oakum."

"Oh, shut up about oakum," retorted the other. "It isn't a joke."

"It is not a joke," said the colonel; "and if it is, it is one of those jokes that make people laugh the most. And do you know the kind of joke that makes people laugh the most, Pinto? It is when somebody gets hurts and we are the people who are going to get hurt."

"Do you think she'll tell the police?"

"It is extremely likely," said the colonel; "in fact, it is extremely unlikely that she won't tell the police. I am rather glad I'm out of it."

Pinto leaped up.

"You're out of it!" he shouted. "You're in it up to the neck!"

The colonel shook his head.

"I'm absolutely out of it, Pinto," he said, flicking the ash of his cigar into the fireplace; "I cannot be identified with this unhappy affair by so much as a finger print."

The Portuguese scowled down at him.

"So that's the game, is it? You're going to double cross us? You're going to be out of it and we're going to be in it!"

"Sit down, you fool! Double cross you! You are easily scared. I'm merely pointing out that it is not a matter in which I am greatly interested. It is a good thing for you I'm not. Whom are the police after? You and Crewe and the rest of the gang? Not on your life! They're after me. They get the trunk and all the branches come down with it. Do you see? There's no sense in lopping off a few branches, even of dead wood. It won't be good enough if they connect you with the case, unless they connect me, too. They're after the big horns; they're not shooting the little bucks. If she tells the police, they're going to snoop around for two or three days seeing how far they can connect me with it. Why, they'll arrest you without a doubt, but they'll arrest me, too."

The colonel blew a blue ring of smoke into the air and watched it float to the ceiling.

"The advantage of having a business associate like me is that I'm a sort of insurance to you little crooks. I am the big fish they're trying to hook, and their bait isn't the kind of bait that you'd swallow."

"I've burned all the papers I had," explained Pinto, "and covered my trail."

"When you burned your boats and came in with me," said the colonel, "you burned everything that was worth burning. I tell you it isn't you they're trailing. It is me or nothing. Maybe they'll scare you," he said reflectively, "hoping you'll turn king's evidence. I've got a feeling that you won't—if I had a feeling the other way about, Pinto, you wouldn't see the curtain rise at the Orpheum tonight. And now," said the colonel, "we'll go out."

He rose abruptly, walked into his bedroom, and came out wearing his broad felt hat. He found Pinto biting his finger nails nervously and looking out of the window.

"I don't want to go out," said Pinto.

"Come out," said the colonel. "What's the good of staying here, anyway? Besides, if they are going to arrest you, I don't want them to arrest you in my rooms. It would look bad."

They walked downstairs into the street, and a few minutes later they were strolling across Green Park, the colonel a picture of a contented bourgeois, with his half-smoked cigar, and his hands clasped together under the tails of his alpaca coat.

"I don't see how you can say they've no evidence against you. Suppose Crotin squeals?"

"He ain't stopped squealing yet," said the colonel philosophically, "but I don't see what difference it makes. Pinto, you haven't got the hang of my methods, and I doubt if you ever will. You're a clever, useful fellow, but if you were allowed to run the gang you'd have it in jail in a month. Take the manufacturer, Crotin," he said. "I dare say he's feeling sore, and maybe this cursed Jack o' Judgment is standing behind him telling him—" He stopped. "No, he wouldn't either," he said after a moment's thought; "Jack o' Judgment knows as much about it as I do."

"What are you talking about?" asked the other impatiently.

"Crotin," said the colonel; "he hasn't any evidence against me. You see, I do not do any business by letters. You fellows have often wanted me to write to this person and that, but writing is evidence. Do you get me? And what evidence has Crotin? Absolutely none. I have never written a line to him in my life. Crewe brought him down to the flat. We gave him a dinner and put the proposal to him in plain language. There's nothing he could take before a judge and jury—absolutely nothing."

He took the cigar from his mouth and blew a cloud of smoke.

"That's the way I've built the business up—no letters, no documents, nothing that a lawyer can make head or tail of."

"What about the documents that Hanson talked about?"

The colonel frowned and then laughed.

"They're nothing but records of our transactions, and they're not evidence. Why, even the police have given up the search for them. By the way, I haven't done with Crotin," he said after a while.

"He's done with you, I should think," said Pinto grimly.

The colonel nodded.

"I guess so, but he hasn't done with the gang. You can take him on next."

"I?" said Pinto in affright. "Now look here, colonel, don't you think it's time we lay low?"

"Lay low!" said the colonel scornfully. "We're either going to get into trouble or we're not. If we're not going to get into trouble we might as well go on. Besides, we want the money. The business has slackened off, and we haven't had a deal since the Spillsbury affair, and that won't last very long. We've got to split our loot six ways, Pinto, and that leaves very little for anybody."

"Where are you going now?" asked the other, as the colonel changed his direction.

"It just struck me that we might as well go over to the bank and see how our balance stands. Also, with the exchange going against us, I want to tell Ferguson to buy dollars."

The handsome premises of the Victoria & City Bank, in Victoria Street, were only a stone's throw from the park; and, whatever might be the views of Ferguson, the manager, as to the colonel's moral character, he had a Considerable respect for him as a financier, and Dan Boundary was shown immediately into the manager's office.

He was gone some time, while Pinto waited impatiently outside. The colonel never invited other members, even of the inmost council, to share his knowledge of finances. They all knew roughly the condition of the exchequer, but really the balance at the Victoria & City was the colonel's own. It was the practice of the Boundary gang to share after each coup, every man taking that to which he was entitled. The money was split among five, the sixth share going to what was known as the "Gang Account," a common fund upon which all could draw in moments of necessity.

The gang fund was not so described in the books of the bank. It was known as "Account B." The expenses of operations were usually paid out of the colonel's private account, and credited to him when the next division took place. He was absolute master of his own balance, but it required three signatures to extract a check from account B. One of the objects of the colonel's visit was to reduce this number to two, the death of Solomon White having removed one of the signatories.

He returned to Pinto, apparently not too well satisfied.

"There's quite a lot of money in the gang account," he said. "I've struck off Solly's name; and your signature and mine, or mine and Crewe's are sufficient now."

"Or mine and Crewe's, I suppose?" suggested Pinto, and the colonel smiled.

"Oh, no," said he. "I'm not a great believer in the indispensability of any man, but I'm making the signature of Dan Boundary indispensable before that account is touched."

They walked back through the park, and the colonel expounded his philosophy of wrong living.

"The man who runs an honest business and mixes it with a little crooked work is bound to be caught," he said, "because his mind is concentrated on the unpaying side of the game. You've got to run a crook business in an honest way if you want to escape the law, and pay big dividends. They call our system blackmail, but it ain't. A blackmailer asks for something for nothing, and he's bound to get caught sooner or later. We offer spot cash for all the things we steal, and that baffles the law. And we're not the only people in London, or in England, or in the world, who are pulling bargains by scaring the fellow we buy from. It is done every day in London; it is done every day by the trusts that control the little shops in the suburbs; it is done even by the big proprietary companies that tell a miserable little tradesman that, if he doesn't stop selling one article, they won't supply him with theirs. Living, Pinto, is preying. The only mistake a crook ever makes is when he goes outside of his legitimate business and lets some other consideration than the piling up of money influence him."

"How do you mean?" asked Pinto wearily. He hated the colonel when he was in this communicative mood of his.

"Well," said the colonel slowly, "I shouldn't have been so keen to go after Maisie White if it hadn't been that you were fond of her and wanted her. That's what I call letting love interfere with business."

"But you said you were afraid of her blabbing. You don't put the blame onto me," said the indignant Pinto.

"I was, and I wasn't," said the colonel. "I think I almost persuaded myself that the girl was a danger. Of course, she isn't. Even Solomon White wasn't a danger."

He stopped dead, and, speaking slowly and pointing his words with a huge forefinger on the other's chest, he said:

"Bear this fact in mind, Pinto, that I have no malice against Miss White, and I don't think that she can harm me. As far as I'm concerned, I will never hurt a hair of her head or do her the slightest harm. I believe that she has nothing against me, and I give orders to anybody who's connected with me—in fact, to any of my business associates—that that girl is not to be interfered with."

Slowly, emphatically, every word emphasized, the colonel spoke; but Pinto did not smile. He had seen the colonel in this gentle mood before, and he knew that Maisie White was doomed.

CHAPTER XXIV
PINTO GOES NORTH

Had Pinto been a psychologist, which he was not, he might have been struck by the unusual reference on the part of the colonel to the funds of the gang. It was a subject to which the colonel very seldom referred, and it was certainly one which he did not emphasize. The truth was that the colonel's investigations into his own private affairs had not been as satisfactory as he had hoped would be the case.

He was in the habit of advancing money, and the gang owed him a considerable sum, money which had been advanced for the pursuit of various enterprises. To draw from that money would leave the gang funds sadly depleted. Yet he could not afford to draw upon it at a moment when they were all on edge. Not only were the two principal subordinates in the condition of mind which led them to jump at every knock and start at every shadow, but he had been receiving urgent messages from all parts of the country from the other men, and he had determined upon a step which he had not taken for three years—a meeting of the full "Board" of his lawless organization.

That night summonses went forth calling his "business associates" to an "Extraordinary General Meeting of the North European Smelter Syndicate." This was one of the companies which he operated, and the existence of which was justified by a small smelting works in the north of England, and owed its international character to the fact that it had a branch works in Sweden. Its turnover was small, its list of stockholders was select. A summons to a general meeting of the North European Smelter Syndicate meant that the affairs of the gang were critical, and in this spirit the call was obeyed.

The meeting was held in the banquet hall of a West End restaurant, and the twenty men who assembled differed very little in appearance from twenty other provincial business men who might have been gathered to discuss the affairs of any company.

Their coming excited no comment and apparently did not even arouse the attention of a vigilant Scotland Yard. Nor, had the colonel's speech been taken down by a shorthand writer and submitted to the police, could any suggestion be found of the significance of the meeting. He spoke of the difficulties of trading, of the "competition" with which the company was faced, and called upon all the shareholders to assist loyally the executive in a very critical and trying time. But those who listened knew very well that the "competition" was the competition of the police, and they had their own ideas as to what constituted the trying time to which the colonel made reference.

It was a very commonplace, ordinary company meeting, which ended in a conventional way by a vote of confidence in the directors. It was when that had been passed, and the meeting had broken up, and members and officials were talking together, that the real business started.

Then it was that Selby, the stout little man, whose special job was to act as intermediary between the company and its more criminal enterprises, received his instructions to speed up. Selby was the receiver of letters. A burglar or a pickpocket who acquired in the course of his activities documents and letters which had hitherto been worthless found a ready market through Selby. Eighty letters out of every hundred were absolutely valueless, but occasionally they would find a rich gem, a love letter indiscreetly cherished, on which a new operation would be based. Then would begin the subtle torturing of a human soul, the opening of new vistas of despair, the stage cleared for a new tragedy.

The colonel was to find that the chief anxiety of his "shareholders" was not as to the future of the company or as to the success of its trading. Again and again he was asked a question couched in identical words, and again and again he replied with a shrug of his big shoulders:

"What's the good of worrying about a thing like that? Jack o' Judgment is a crook! That's all he is, boys, a crook. He's not the sort of man who'll go to the police; he wouldn't dare put his face inside a police station. You leave him to us; we'll fix him sooner or later."

"But," somebody asked uneasily, "what about Raoul, that fellow who was killed at Putney?"

The colonel lifted his eyebrows.

"Raoul?" he said. "He had nothing to do with us. I never heard the fellow's name until I read it in the paper. As to White"—he shrugged his shoulders again—"we can't prevent people having private quarrels, and may be this Frenchman and White had one. My theory is," he said, elaborating an idea which had only at that moment occurred to him, "that Raoul, White, and this Jack o' Judgment, were working together. May be it isn't a bad thing that White was killed under the circumstances." He dropped his hand on the other man's shoulder and oozed geniality. "Now, back you go, my lads, and don't worry. Leave it to old Dan to fix Jack o' Judgment, or Bill o' Judgment, or Tom o' Judgment, whoever he may be; and that we'll fix him, you can be certain."

Coming away from the meeting, he expressed himself as being perfectly satisfied with its results. He brought Pinto and Crewe back with him in his car, and dropped the latter at Piccadilly Circus. Pinto would have been glad to have joined the Swell, but the colonel detained him.

"I want to talk to you, Pinto," he said.

"I've had enough business for today," said the Portuguese.

"So have I," said the colonel, "but that doesn't prevent my attending to pressing affairs. I was talking to you today—or was it yesterday—about Crotin."

"The Yorkshire woolen merchant?" said Pinto.

"That's the fellow," replied the colonel. "I suggested you should go and see him."

"And I suggested that I shouldn't," said Pinto. "Let him alone. You'll never get another chance like you had before."

"Alone, nothing," said the colonel testily. "You're scared because you imagine Crotin is warned? What do you think?"

Pinto was silent.

"I suppose you think that, because Jack o' Judgment intervened at the right moment, he went back to Yorkshire feeling fine? Well, you're wrong! You don't understand one side of the psychology of this business. That little fellow is quaking in his shoes and wondering what his grand wife would say if the fact that he was a bigamist was revealed. And there's more reason for his fear today than there was before. Look here!"

He took a newspaper out of his pocket, and Pinto remembered that even during the meeting the colonel had twice made reference to its columns, and he had wondered why. He had suspected that there had been some reference to the Boundary gang, but this was not the case. The paragraph which the colonel pointed out with his thick forefinger was short.

"By the death of Sir George Tressillian Morgan an ancient baronetcy has become extinct. His estate, which has been estimated at over a million, passes to his niece, Lady Sybil Crotin, the daughter of Lord Westsevern, Sir George's son and heir having died previously. Lady Sybil is the wife of a well-known Yorkshire mill owner."

"I didn't know that," said Pinto, interested in spite of himself.

"Nor did I, till today," said the colonel. "The fact is, this cursed Jack o' Judgment has put everything else out of our minds. And you can see for yourself, Pinto, that this business is important."

Pinto nodded.

"We are not only after the factory, but here's a chance of making a real big coup. Now I can't send anybody else to Yorkshire—Crewe is impossible. Crotin knows him, and the moment he put in an appearance, as likely as not, Crotin would lose his head and give the whole show away. It is you or nobody." He rubbed his chin thoughtfully. "You know there are times when I'm sorry about Solomon White," he said; "he was the boy for this kind of business—that is to say, in the old days—he got a bit scrupulous toward the end."

Pinto was to find that the colonel had made all arrangements, and that for the previous two days he had been planning a predatory raid on the Yorkshireman.

There was to be a bazaar in Huddersfield on behalf of a local hospital, in which Lady Sybil Crotin took a great interest. She was organizing the fete and had invited subscriptions.

"They're not coming in very fast, according to their local paper," said the colonel, "and that has given me an idea. You're a presentable sort of fellow, Pinto, and it is likely you'll be all the more successful because you're a foreigner. You'll go up to Yorkshire and you'll take a thousand pounds, and, if necessary, you'll subscribe pretty liberally to the fund, but it must be done through Lady Sybil. You can make yourself known to her, and invite yourself to the house, where you can meet Crotin himself."

He made other suggestions, for he had worked out the whole scheme in detail for the other to carry into effect. Pinto's objections slowly dissipated. He was a vain man and had all the vices of his vanity. A desire to be thought well of, to be regarded as a rich man when he was in fact on the verge of ruin, had brought him into crooked practices and eventually into the circle of the colonel's acquaintances.

To appear among the fair as a giver of largesse on a magnificent scale suited him down to the ground. It was a part for which he was eminently fitted, as the colonel, a shrewd judge of humanity, knew quite well.

"I'll do it," said Pinto. "But do you think he'll squeal?"

Boundary shook his head.

"I never knew a man who was caught on the rebound to squeal," he said. "No, no, you needn't worry about that. All you have to do is to use your discretion, choose the right moment, preparing him by a few hints for what is coming, and you'll find he'll sit down, like the hardheaded business man he is, and talk money."

Pinto looked discontented.

"I know what you're thinking," said the colonel; "you hate the idea of the generous donor being unmasked and appearing to anybody as a blackmailer. Well, you needn't worry about that. Lady Sybil will not know, nor will anybody else that counts. And, believe me, Crotin doesn't count. Anyway, you can pretend that you're a perfectly innocent agent in the matter, that you know me slightly, and that I've dropped hints which made you curious and which you are anxious to verify."

Pinto went off to make preparations for the journey. He had one of the top flats in the Albermarle Buildings, a suite of rooms which, if they were not as expensively furnished as the colonel's, were more artistic. He had recently acquired the services of a new "daily valet"—a step he could take without fear that his secrets would be betrayed, since he had no secrets in his own rooms, kept no documents of any kind, and received no visitors.

The man opened the door to his ring.

"No, sir; nobody has been," said the servant in answer to his query, and Pinto was relieved.

For the past two days he had been living in a condition bordering on panic. It seemed unlikely that the colonel's confidence would be justified and that the police would take no action. And yet the incredible had happened. There had not been so much as an inquiry, and not once, though he had been on his guard, had he detected one shadow trailing him. His spirits rose and he whistled cheerfully as he directed the packing of his trunk, for he was traveling north, fully equipped for any social events which might await him.

"I am going to Yorkshire," he explained. "I'll give you my address before I leave, and you can let me know if there are any inquiries and who the inquirers were."

"Certainly, sir," said the man respectfully, and Pinto eyed him approvingly.

"I think you'll suit me, Cobalt," he said. "My last valet was rather a fool and inclined to stick his nose into business which did not concern him."

The man smiled.

"I shan't trouble you that way, sir," he said.

"Of course, there's nothing to hide," said Pinto with a shrug, "but you know what people are. They think that because you're associated in business with Colonel Boundary you're up to all sorts of tricks."

"That's what Mr. Snakit said, sir," remarked the man.

"Snakit?" said the puzzled Pinto. "Who is Snakit?"

Then he remembered the little detective whom Maisie had employed and who had been bought over by the colonel.

"Oh, you see him, do you?" he asked carelessly.

"He comes up, sir, now and again. He's the colonel's valet, isn't he, sir?"

Pinto grinned.

"Not exactly," he said. "I shouldn't discuss things with Snakit. That man is quite reliable and—"

"Anyway, sir, I should not discuss your business," said the valet with dignity.

He finished packing and, after assisting his master to dress, was dismissed for the night.

"A useful fellow that," thought Pinto, as the door closed behind the man. The "useful fellow" reached the street and, after walking a few hundred yards, found a disengaged taxi and gave an address.

Maisie White was writing when her bell rang. It rang three times—two long and one short peals—and she went downstairs to admit her visitor. She did not speak until she was back in her room, and then she faced the polite little man whom Pinto had called Cobalt.

"Well, Mr. Gray," she said.

"I wish you'd call me Cobalt, miss," said the man, with a smile. "I like to keep up the name; otherwise I'm inclined to give myself away."

"Have you found anything?"

"Very little, miss," said the detective. "There's nothing to find in the apartment itself."

"You secured the situation as valet?"

He nodded.

"Thanks to the recommendations you got me, miss, there was no difficulty at all. Silva wanted a servant, and accepted the testimonials without any question."

"And you've discovered nothing?" she said in a disappointed tone.

"Not in Mr. Silva's room. The only thing I found was that he is going to Yorkshire tomorrow."

"For long?" she asked.

"For some considerable time," said the detective; "at least, I guess so, because he has packed half a dozen suits, top hats, and all sorts of things which I should imagine he wouldn't take away unless he intended making a long stay."

"Have you any idea of the place he's going to?"

"I shall discover that tomorrow, miss," said Cobalt. "I thought I'd tell you now as much as I know."

"And you have not been into the colonel's flat?"

The man shook his head.

"It is guarded inside and out, miss, now. He has not only his butler, who is a tough customer, to look after him, but he has Snakit, the man you employed, I understand."

"That's the fellow," said the girl, with a grim little smile. "Very good, Cobalt. You'll phone me if you make any other discoveries."

She was sitting at her solitary breakfast the next morning when the telephone bell rang. It was from a call office, and presently she heard Cobalt's voice.

"Just a word, miss. He leaves by the ten-twenty-five train for Huddersfield," said the voice; "and the person he is going to see is Lady Sybil somebody, and there's money in it."

"How do you know?" she asked quickly.

"I heard him speaking to the colonel on the landing, and I heard the words: 'He'll pay.'"

She thought a moment.

"Ten-twenty-five," she repeated. "Thank you very much, Mr. Cobalt."

She hung up the receiver and sat a moment in thought, then passed quickly to her bedroom and began to dress.

CHAPTER XXV
A PATRON OF CHARITY

Lady Sybil Crotin was not a popular woman. She was conscious that she had married beneath her, more conscious lately that there had been no necessity to make the marriage, and she had grown a little soured. She could never mix with the homely wives of local millionaires; she professed a horror of the vulgarities with which she was surrounded; hated and loathed her lord and master's flamboyant home, which she described as something between a feudal castle and a moving-picture palace; and openly despised her husband's friends and their feminine relatives.

She made a point of spending at least six months of the year away from Yorkshire, and came back with protest at her lot written visibly upon her face.

A thin, angular woman, with pale-green eyes and straight, tight lips, she had never been beautiful, but five or six years in an uncongenial environment had hardened and wasted her. That her husband adored her and never spoke of her save in a tone of awe was common property and a favorite subject for local humor. That she regarded him with contempt and irritation was as well known.

In view of Lady Sybil Crotin's unpopularity, it was perhaps a great mistake that she should make herself responsible for the raising of funds for the local women's hospital. But she was under the impression that there was a magic in her name and station, which would overcome what she described as shyness, but which was in point of fact the frank dislike of her neighbors. A subscription list that she had opened had a weak and unpromising appearance. She had with the greatest difficulty secured help from the bazaar, and knew, even though it had been opened by a duchess, that it was a failure even from the very first day.

Had she herself made a generous contribution to the bazaar fund, there might have been a hope; but she was mean, and the big bleak hall she had chosen because of its cheapness was quite unsuitable for the entertainment she sponsored.

On the afternoon of the second day, Lady Sybil was pulling on her gloves, eying her husband with an unfriendly gaze as he sat at lunch.

"It was no more than I expected," she said bitterly. "I was a fool ever to start the thing. This is the last time I ever attempt to help local charities."

Mr. Crotin rubbed his bald head in perplexity.

"They'll come," he said hopefully, referring to the patrons whose absence was the cause of Lady Sybil's annoyance; "they'll come when they hear what a fine show it is. And if they don't, Syb, I'll come along and spend a couple of hundred pounds myself."

"You'll do no such thing," she snapped. "And please get out of that ridiculous habit of reducing my name to one syllable. If the people of the town can't help to support their own hospital, then they don't deserve to have one, and I'm certainly not going to allow you to waste our money on that sort of nonsense."

"Have your own way, love," said Mr. Crotin meekly.

"Besides," she said, "it would be all over the town that it was your money which was coming in and these horrible people would be laughing at me."

She finished buttoning her gloves and was looking at him curiously.

"What is the matter with you, John?" she asked suddenly, and he almost jumped.

"With me, love?" he said with a brave attempt at a smile. "Why, there's nothing the matter with me. What should there be?"

"You've been very strange lately," she said; "ever since you came back from London."

"I think I ate something that disagreed with my digestion," he said uneasily. "I didn't know that I'd been different."

"Are things well at your—factory?" she asked.

"At the mills? Oh, aye, they're all right," he said. "I wish everything was as right as them."

"As they," she corrected.

"As they," said the humble Mr. Crotin.

"There's something wrong," she said, and shook her head, and Mr. Crotin found himself going white. "I'll have a talk with you when I've got this wretched bazaar business out of my head," she added, and with a little nod she left him.

He walked to the window of the long dining hall and watched her car disappearing down the drive, and then with a sigh went back to his thoughts.

When Colonel Dan Boundary surmised that this unfortunate victim of his blackmail would be worried, he was not far from the mark. Crotin had spent many sleepless nights since he came back from London, nights full of terror, that left him a wreck to meet the fears of the days which followed. He lived all the time in the shadow of vengeful justice and exaggerated his danger to an incredible degree. Perhaps it was in anticipating what his wife would say that he experienced the most poignant misery.

He had taken to secret drinking, too; little nips at odd intervals, both in his room and in his private office. Life had lost its savor, and now a new agony was added to the knowledge that his wife had detected the change. He went to his office and spent a gloomy afternoon wandering about the mills, and came back an hour before his usual time. He had not the heart to make a call at the bazaar, and speculated unhappily upon the proceeds of the afternoon session.

It was therefore with something like pleasure that he heard his wife on the telephone speaking more cheerfully than he had heard her for months.

"Is that you, John?" She was almost civil. "I'm bringing somebody home to dinner. Will you tell Phillips?"

"That's right, love," said Mr. Crotin eagerly.

He would be glad to see some new face, and that it was a new face he could guess by the interest in Lady Sybil's tone.

"It is a Mr. de Silva. Have you ever met him?"

"No, love; I've not. Is he a foreigner?"

"He's a Portuguese gentleman," said his wife's voice, "and he has been most helpful and most generous."

"Bring him along," said Crotin heartily; "I'll be glad to meet him. How has the sale been, love?"

"Very good, indeed," she replied, "splendid, in fact—thanks to Mr. de Silva."

John Crotin was dressing when his wife returned, and it was not until half an hour later that he met Pinto Silva for the first time. Pinto was a man who dressed well and looked well. John Crotin thought he was the most impressive personality he had met when he stalked into the drawing-room and took the proffered hand of the little millionaire.

"This is Mr. de Silva," said his wife, who had been waiting for her guest. "As I told you, John, Mr. de Silva has been awfully kind. I don't know what you're going to do with all those perfectly useless things you've bought," she added to the polished Portuguese, and Pinto shrugged his shoulders.

"Give them away," he said. "There must, for example be a lot of poor women in the country who would be glad of the linen I have bought."

At this point dinner was announced and he took Lady Sybil in. The meal was approaching its end when she revived the question of the disposal of his purchases.

"Are you greatly interested in charities, Mr. de Silva?"

Pinto inclined his head.

"Both here and in Portugal I take a very deep interest in the welfare of the poor," he said solemnly.

"That's fine," said Mr. Crotin, nodding approvingly. "I know what these poor people have to suffer. I've been among them."

His wife silenced him with a look.

"It frequently happens that cases are brought to my notice," Pinto went on. "I have one or two cases of women in my mind where these purchases of mine would be most welcome. For example, I heard the other day, quite by accident, of a poor woman in Wales, whose husband deserted her."

Mr. Crotin had his fork halfway to his mouth, but put it down again.

"I don't know much about the case personally," said Pinto carelessly, "but the circumstances were brought to my notice by a friend. I think these people suffer more than we imagine, and I'll let you into a secret, Lady Sybil," he said, speaking impressively. He did not look at Crotin but went on. "A few of my friends are thinking of buying a mill."

"A woolen mill?" she said, raising her eyebrows.

"A woolen mill," he repeated.

"But why?" she asked.

"We wish to make garments and blankets for the benefit of the poor. We feel that, if we could run this sort of thing on a co-operative basis, we could manufacture the stuff cheaply, always providing, of course, that we could purchase a mill at a reasonable figure."

For the first time he looked at Crotin, and the man's face was ghastly white.

"What a queer idea!" said Lady Sybil. "A good mill will cost you a lot of money."

"We don't think so," said Pinto; "in fact, we expect to purchase a very excellent mill at a reasonable sum. That was my object in coming to Yorkshire, I may tell you, and it was only by accident that I saw the advertisement of your bazaar and called in."

"A fortunate accident for us," said Lady Sybil.

Crotin's eyes were on his plate and he did not raise them.

"I think it is a great mistake to be too generous with the poor," said Lady Sybil, shaking her head; "these women are very seldom grateful."

"I realize that," said Pinto gravely, "but I am not seeking their gratitude. We find that many of these women are in terrible circumstances owing to no fault of their own. For example, this woman in Wales, whose husband is supposed to have deserted her—now there is a bad case."

Lady Sybil was interested.

"We found on investigation," said Pinto, speaking slowly and impressively, "that the man who deserted her, has since married, and occupies a very important position in a town in the north of England."

Mr. Crotin dropped his knife with a crash, and with a mumbled apology, picked it up.

"But how terrible!" said Lady Sybil. "What a shocking thing! The man should be exposed! He is not fit to associate with human beings. Can't you do something to punish him?"

"That could be done," said Silva; "it could be done, but it would bring a great deal of unhappiness to his present wife, who is ignorant of her husband's treachery."

"Better she knew now than knew later," said the militant Lady Sybil. "I think you do very wrong to keep it from her."

Mr. Crotin rose, and his wife looked at him with suspicion.

"Aren't you feeling well, John?" she asked with asperity.

It was not the first time she had seen her husband's hand shaking and had diagnosed the cause more justly than she was doing at present, for John Crotin had scarcely taken a drink that evening.

"I'm going into the library if you'll excuse me, love," he said. "Maybe Mr.—Mr. de Silva will join me. I'd—I'd like to talk over the question of that mill with him."

Pinto nodded.

"Then run along now," said Lady Sybil. "And when you've finished talking, come back to me, Mr. de Silva. I want to know something about your charitable organizations in Portugal."

Pinto followed the other at a distance, saw him enter the big room and switch on the lights, and followed, closing the door behind him.

Mr. Crotin's library was the most comfortable room in the house. It was lighted by French windows which opened to a small terrace. Long, red velvet curtains were drawn, and a little fire crackled on the hearth.

When the door closed Crotin turned upon his guest. "Now," he said harshly, "what's your proposition? Make it a reasonable sum and I'll pay you."

CHAPTER XXVI
THE SOLDIER WHO FOLLOWED

In the train which had carried Pinto Silva to Huddersfield were one or two remarkable passengers, and it was not a coincidence that they did not meet. In a third-class carriage at the far end of the train was a soldier who carried a kit bag and who whiled away the journey by reading a seemingly endless collection of magazines.

He got out at Huddersfield, too, and Pinto might, and probably did, see him as he passed through the barrier. The soldier left his kit bag at the cloak room and eventually became one of the two dozen people who patronized Lady Sybil's bazaar on that afternoon. He passed Pinto twice, and once made a small purchase at the same stall where the Portuguese was buying lavishly. If Pinto saw him he did not remember the fact. One soldier looks very much like another, anyway.

Lady Sybil had reason to notice the representative of his majesty's forces, and herself informed him severely that smoking was not allowed, and the man had put his cigarette under his heel with an apology and had walked out of the building. When Lady Sybil and her guest had entered her car and were driven away to Mill Hall, the soldier had been loitering near the entrance, and a few minutes later he was following the party in a taxicab which had been waiting at his order for the past two hours.

The taxi did not turn in at the stone-pillared gates of the Hall, but continued some distance beyond, when the soldier alighted, and, turning back, walked boldly through the main entrance and passed up the drive. It was dusk by now, and nobody challenged him.

He made a reconnaissance of the house, and found the dining room without any difficulty. The blinds were up and the servants were setting the table. Then he passed around to the wing of the building and discovered the library. He actually went into that room, because it was one of Lady Sybil's standing orders that the library should be "aired" and that the scent of Mr. Crotin's atrocious tobacco should be cleared out.

He sniffed the stale fragrance and was satisfied that this was a room which was lived in.

If there was any real confidential talk between the two men, it would be here, he thought, and looked round for a likely place of concealment. The room was innocent of cupboards. Only a big settee drawn diagonally across a corner of the room promised cover and that looked too dangerous. If anybody sat there and by chance dropped something—a pipe, an ash tray—

He walked back to the terrace to take his bearings in case he had to make a rapid exit. He looked around and then dropped suddenly to the cover of the balustrade, for he had seen a dark figure moving across the lawn, and it was coming straight for the terrace. He slipped back into the room, and as he did so he heard a step in the passage without. He stepped lightly over the settee and crouched down.

It was evidently a servant, for he heard the French windows closed and the clang of the shutters. They were evidently very ordinary folding shutters, fastened with an old-fashioned steel bar—he made a mental note of this. Then he heard the swish of the curtain rings upon the brass pole as the curtains were drawn. A dim light was switched on, somebody poked the fire and then the light was put out and the door closed softly.

The intruder did some rapid thinking. He crossed to the nearest of the windows, noiselessly opened the shutters and pushed them back to the position in which they stood when not in use. Then he unlatched the French window and left it, hoping that it would not blow open and betray him. This done, he again pulled the heavy curtains across and returned to his place of concealment. That was to be the way out for him if the necessity for a rapid retreat should arise.

There was no sound save the ticking of the clock and the noise of falling cinders for ten minutes, and then he heard something which brought him to the alert, all his senses awakened and concentrated. It was the sound of a light and stealthy footstep on the terrace outside. He wondered whether it was a servant and whether he would see that one of the windows was unshuttered. He had half a mind to investigate, when there came another sound—a lumbering foot in the passage. Suddenly the door was opened, the lights were flashed on and the man behind the settee hugged the floor and held his breath.

"How much do I want?"

Pinto laughed and lit a cigarette.

"My dear Mr. Crotin, I really don't know what you mean."

"Let's have no more foolery," said the Yorkshireman roughly. "I know that you've come up from Colonel Boundary, and I know what you've come for. You want to buy my mill, eh? Well, I'll make it worth your while not to buy my mill. You can take the money instead."

"I really am honest when I tell you that I don't understand what you are talking about. I have certainly come up to buy a mill that is true. It is also true that I want to buy your mill."

"And what might you be thinking of paying for it?" asked Crotin between his teeth.

"Twenty thousand pounds," said Pinto nonchalantly.

"Twenty thousand, eh? It was thirty thousand the last time. You'll want me to give it to you soon. Nay, nay, my friend, I'll pay, but not in mills."

"Think of the poor," murmured Pinto.

"I'm thinking of them," said the other. "I'm thinking of the poor woman in Wales too, and the poor woman in there." He jerked his head. Then, in a calmer tone: "I guessed at dinner where you came from. Colonel Boundary sent you."

Pinto shrugged his shoulders.

"Let us mention no names," he said politely. "And who is Colonel Boundary anyway?"

Crotin was at his desk now. He had taken out his check book and slapped it down upon the writing pad.

"You've got me," he said, and his voice quavered. "I'll make an offer to you. I'll give you fifty thousand pounds if you write an agreement that you will not molest or bother me again."

There was a silence, and the soldier crouched behind the settee, listening intently. He heard Pinto laugh softly as one who is greatly amused.

"That, my good friend," said Pinto, "would be blackmail. You don't imagine that I would be guilty of such an iniquity? I know nothing about your past; I merely suggest that you should sell me one of your mills at a reasonable price."

"Twenty thousand pounds is reasonable for you, I suppose," said Crotin sarcastically.

"It is a lot of money," replied Pinto.

The Yorkshireman pulled open the drawer of his desk and slammed in the check book, closing it with a bang. "Well, I'll give you nothing," he said, "neither mill nor money. You can clear out of here."

He crossed the room to the telephone.

"What are you going to do?" asked Pinto, secretly alarmed.

"I'm going to send for the police," said the other grimly. "I'm going to give myself up and I'm going to have you arrested, too!"

If Crotin had turned the handle of the old-fashioned telephone, if he had continued in his resolution, if he had shown no sign of doubt, a different story might have been told. But with his hand raised, he hesitated, and Pinto clinched his argument.

"Why have all that trouble?" he said. "Your liberty and reputation are much more to you than a mill. You're a rich man. Your wife is wealthy in her own right. You have enough to live on for the rest of your life. Why make trouble?"

The little man dropped his head with a groan and walked wearily back to the desk.

"Suppose I sell this," he said in a low voice, "how do I know you won't come again?"

"When a gentleman gives his word of honor," began Pinto with dignity, but was interrupted by a shrill laugh that made his blood run cold.

He swung round with an oath. Framed in an opening of the curtains which covered one of the windows was The Figure.

The black silk gown, the white masked face, the soft felt hat, pulled down over the eyes. His teeth chattered at the sight of it, and he fell back against the wall.

"Who wouldn't trust Pinto?" squeaked the voice. "Who wouldn't take Pinto's word of honor! Jack o' Judgment wouldn't, poor old Jack o' Judgment!"

Jack o' Judgment! The soldier behind the settee heard the words and gasped. Without any thought of consequence he raised his head and looked. The Jack o' Judgment was standing where he expected him to be. He had come through the window which the soldier had left unbarred. This time he carried no weapon in his hand, and Pinto was quick to see the possibilities. The electric switch was within reach, and his hand shot out. There was a click and the room went dark.

But the figure of Jack o' Judgment was silhouetted against the night, and Pinto whipped out the long knife which never left him and sent it hurtling at his enemy. He saw the figure duck, heard the crash of broken glass, and then Jack o' Judgment vanished. In a rage which was three parts terror, he sprang through the open door onto the terrace in time to see a dark figure drop over the balustrade and fly across the park.

CHAPTER XXVII
THE CAPTURE OF "JACK"

Pinto leaped the parapet and was following swiftly in its wake. He guessed rather than knew that for once Jack o' Judgment had come unarmed, and a wild exultation filled him at the thought that it was left to him to unveil the mystery which was weighing even upon the iron nerve of the colonel.

The figure gained the shrubbery, and the pursuer heard the rustle of leaves as it plunged into the depths. In a second he was blundering after. He lost sight of his quarry and stopped to listen. There was no sound.

"Hiding," Pinto grunted. And then aloud: "Come out of it. I see you and I'll shoot you like a dog if you don't come to me!"

There was no reply. He dashed in the direction he thought Jack o' Judgment must have taken, and again missed. With a curse he turned off in another direction and then suddenly glimpsed a shape before him and leaped at it. He was flung back with little or no effort and stood bewildered, for the coat his hand had touched was rough, and he had felt metal buttons.

"A soldier!" he gasped. "Who are you?"

"Steady," said the other; "don't get rattled, Pinto."

"Who are you?" asked Pinto again.

"My name is Stafford King," said the soldier, "and I think I shall want you."

Pinto half turned to go, but was gripped.

"You can go back to Huddersfield and pack your boxes," said Stafford King; "you won't leave the town except by my permission."

"What do you mean?" demanded Pinto, breathing heavily.

"I mean," said Stafford King, "that the unfortunate man you blackmailed must prosecute you, whatever be the consequence to himself. Now, Pinto, you've a grand chance of turning king's evidence."

Pinto made no reply. He was collecting his thoughts. Then, after a while, he said:

"I'll talk about that later, King. I'm staying at the Huddersfield Arms. I'll meet you there in an hour."

Stafford King did not move until the sound of Pinto's footsteps had died away. Then he began a systematic search, for he, too, was anxious to end the mystery of Jack o' Judgment. He had followed Pinto when he had dashed from the room, and had heard the Portuguese calling upon Jack o' Judgment to surrender. That mysterious individual, who was obviously lying low, could not be very far away.

He was in a shrubbery which proved later to be a clump of rhododendrons, in the center of which was a summer-house. To the heart of this shrubbery led three paths, one of which Stafford discovered quite close at hand. The sound of gravel under his feet gave him an idea, and he began walking backwards till he came to the shadow of a tree, and then, simulating the sound of retreating footsteps, he waited. Presently he heard a rustle but did not move.

Somebody was coming cautiously through the bushes, and that somebody appeared as a shadowy, indistinct figure not twenty yards away. Only the keenest eyesight could have detected it, and still Stafford waited. Presently he heard the soft crunch of gravel under his feet and at that moment leaped toward it. The figure stood as though paralyzed for a second, and then, turning quickly, fled back to the heart of the bushes. Before it had gone a dozen paces Stafford had reached it, and his arm was about its neck.

"My friend," he breathed. "I don't know what I'm to do with you now I've got you, but I certainly am going to register your face for future reference."

"No, no," said a muffled voice from behind the mask, "no, no, don't, I beg of you!"

But the mask was plucked away, and, fumbling in his pocket, Stafford produced his electric lamp and flashed it on the face of his prisoner. Then, with a cry of amazement, he stepped back—for he had looked upon the face of Maisie White!

For a moment there was silence, neither speaking. Then Stafford found his voice.

"Maisie!" he said in bewilderment. "Maisie! You are Jack o' Judgment?"

She did not answer.

"Phew!" whistled Stafford.

Then, sitting on a trunk, he laughed.

"It is Maisie, of all people in the world. And I suspected it, too!"

The girl had covered her face with her hands and was crying softly, and he moved toward her and put his arm about her shoulder.

"Darling, it is nothing very terrible. Please don't go on like that."

"Oh, you don't understand, you don't understand!" she wailed. "I wanted to catch Silva. I guessed that he was coming north on one of his blackmailing trips, and I followed him."

"Did you come up by the same train?"

He felt her nod.

"So did I," said Stafford with a little grin.

"I followed him to the bazaar," she said, "and then I watched him from a little eating house on the opposite side of the road. Do you know, I wondered whether you were here, too, and I looked everywhere for you, but apparently there was nobody in sight when Pinto came out with Lady Sybil, only a soldier."

"I was that soldier," said Stafford.

"I discovered where Mr. Crotin lived and came up later," she went on. "Of course, I had no very clear idea of what I was going to do, and it was only by the greatest luck that I found the window of the library open. It was the only window open," she said with a laugh.

"It wasn't so much your luck as my forethought." Stafford smiled.

"Now I want to tell you about Jack o' Judgment," she began, but he stopped her.

"Let that explanation wait," he said. "The point is, that with your evidence and mine, we have Pinto by the throat. What was that?"

There was the sound of a shot.

"Probably a poacher," said Stafford after a moment; "I can't imagine Pinto using a gun. Besides, I don't think he carries one. What did he throw at you?"

"A knife," she said, and he felt her shiver; "it just missed me. But tell me, how have we got Pinto?"

They had left the shrubbery and were walking toward the house. She stopped a little while to take off her long black cloak, and he saw that she was wearing a shirt-skirted dress beneath.

"We must compel Crotin to prosecute," said Stafford. "With our evidence nothing can save Pinto, and probably he will drag in the colonel, too. Even your evidence isn't necessary," he said, after a moment's thought, "and if it is possible, I will keep you out of it."

A woman's scream interrupted him.

"There's trouble there," he said, and raced for the house. Somebody was standing on the terrace as he approached, and hailed him excitedly.

"Is that you, Terence?"

It was a servant's voice.

"No," replied Stafford; "I am a police officer."

"Will you come up, sir?" said the man on the terrace. "I thought it was the gamekeeper I was speaking to."

"What is the matter?" asked Stafford, as he vaulted over the parapet.

"Mr. Crotin has shot himself, sir," said the butler in quavering tones.

Twelve hours later Stafford King reported to his chief, giving the details of the overnight tragedy.

"Poor fellow!" said Sir Stanley. "I was afraid of it ending that way."

"Did you know he was being blackmailed?" asked Stafford.

Sir Stanley nodded.

"We had a report which apparently emanated from Jack o' Judgment, who of late has started sending his communications to me direct," said Sir Stanley. "You can, of course, do nothing to Pinto. Your evidence isn't sufficient. What a pity you hadn't a second witness!" He thought for a moment. "Even then it wouldn't have been sufficient unless we had Crotin to support you."

Stafford cleared his throat.

"I have a second witness, sir," he said.

"You have?" Sir Stanley raised his eyebrows. "Who was your second witness?"

"Jack o' Judgment," said Stafford, and Sir Stanley jumped to his feet.

"Jack o' Judgment?" he repeated. "What do you mean?"

"Jack o' Judgment was there," said Stafford, and told the story of the remarkable appearance of that mysterious figure.

He told everything, reserving the identification of "Jack" till the last.

"And then you flashed the lamp on his face," said Sir Stanley. "Well, who was it?"

"Maisie White," said Stafford.

"Good Lord!"

Sir Stanley walked to the window and stood looking out, his hands thrust into his pockets. Presently he turned.

"There's a bigger mystery here than I suspected," he said. "Have you asked Miss White for an explanation?"

Stafford shook his head.

"I thought it best to report the matter to you, sir, before I asked her to—"

"To incriminate herself, eh? Well, perhaps you did wisely, perhaps you did not. I should imagine that her explanation is a very simple one."

"What do you mean, sir?"

"I mean," said Sir Stanley, "that unless Jack o' Judgment has the gift of appearing in two places at once, she is not Jack."

"But I don't understand, sir."

"I mean," said Sir Stanley, "that Jack o' Judgment was in the colonel's room last night, was in fact sitting by the colonel's bedside when that gentleman awoke; and according to the statement which Colonel Boundary made to me about two hours ago in this room, warned him of his approaching end."

It was Stafford's turn to be astonished.

"Are you sure, sir?" he asked incredulously.

"Absolutely!" said Sir Stanley. "You don't imagine that the colonel would invent that sort of thing? For some reason or other, possibly to keep close to the trouble that's coming, the colonel insists upon bringing all his little chitchat to me. He asked for an interview about ten o'clock this morning and reported to me that he had had this visitation. Moreover, the experience has had the effect of upsetting the colonel, and for the first time he seems to be thoroughly rattled. Where is Miss White?"

"She's here, sir."

"Here, eh?" said the commissioner. "So much the better. Can you bring her in?"

A few minutes later the girl sat facing the first commissioner.

"Now, Miss White, we're going to ask you for a few facts about your masquerade," said Sir Stanley kindly. "I understand that you appeared wearing the costume, and giving a fairly good imitation of the voice of Jack o' Judgment. Now I'm telling you before we go any further that I do not believe for one moment that you are Jack o' Judgment. Am I right?"

She nodded.

"Perfectly true, Sir Stanley," she said. "I don't know why I did such a mad thing, except that I knew Pinto was scared of him. I got the cloak from my dress basket and made the mask myself. You see, I didn't know whether I might want it, but I thought that in a tight pinch, if I wished to terrify this man, that was the role to assume."

Sir Stanley nodded.

"And the voice, of course, was easy."

"But how could you imitate the voice if you have never seen Jack o' Judgment?"

"I saw him once." She shivered a little. "You seem to forget, Sir Stanley, that he rescued me from that dreadful house."

"Of course," said Sir Stanley. "And you imitated him, did you?" He turned to his subordinate. "I'm accepting Miss White's explanation, Stafford, and I advise you to do the same. She went up to watch Silva, as I understand, and took the costume with her as a sort of protection. Well, Miss White, are you satisfied with your detective work?''

She smiled ruefully.

"I'm afraid I'm a failure as a detective," she said.

"I'm afraid you are." Sir Stanley laughed as he rose and offered his hand. "There is only one real detective in the world—and that is Jack o' Judgment!"

CHAPTER XXVIII
THE PASSING OF PHILLOPOLIS

If Pinto Silva had a hobby, it was the Orpheum Theater. The Orpheum had been in low water and had come into the market at a moment when theatrical managers and proprietors were singularly unenterprising and money was short. Pinto had bought the property for a song, and had converted his purchase into a moderate success. The theater served a double purpose; it provided Pinto with a hobby, and offered an excuse for his wealth. Since it was a one-man show, and he produced no balance sheet, his contemporaries could only make a guess as to the amount of money he made. If the truth be told, it was not very large, but small as it was, its dividends more or less justified his own leisure.

There had been one or two scandals about the Orpheum which had reached the public press—scandals of a not particularly edifying character. But Pinto had managed to escape public opprobrium.

The Orpheum, at any rate, helped to baffle the police, who saw Silva living at the rate of twenty thousand a year, and were unable to trace the source of his income. That he had estates in Portugal was known; but they had been acquired, apparently, on the profits of the music hall. He was not a speculator, though he was a shareholder in a number of companies which were controlled by the colonel; and he was certainly not a gambler, in the generally accepted sense of the term.

While he was suspected of being intimately connected with several shady transactions, he could boast truly that there was not a scrap of evidence to associate him with any breach of the law. He was less inclined to boast that evening, when he turned into the stage box at the Orpheum, and, pulling his chair into the shadow of the draperies, sat back and considered his position. He had returned from Yorkshire in a panic, and had met the fury of the colonel's reproaches. It was the worst quarter of an hour that Pinto had ever spent with his superior, and the memory made him shiver.

The stage box at the Orpheum was never sold to any member of the public. It was Pinto's private possession, his sitting room and his office. He sat, watching with gloomy interest the progress of the little revue which was a feature of the Orpheum programme, and his mind was occupied by a very pressing problem. He was shaken, too, by the interview he had had with the Huddersfield police.

He had had to fake a story to explain why he left the library, and why, in his absence, Mr. Crotin had committed suicide. Fortunately he had returned to the house by the front hall, and was in the hall inventing a story of burglars to the agitated Lady Sybil, when they had heard the shot which ended the wretched life of the bigamist. That had saved him from being suspected of actual complicity in the crime. Suppose they had—he grew cold at the thought.

There was a knock on the door of the box, and an attendant put in his head.

"There's a gentleman to see you, sir," he said. "He says he has an appointment."

"What is his name?"

"Mr. Cartwright."

Pinto nodded.

"Show him in, please," he said and dismissed all unpleasant thoughts.

The newcomer proved to be a dapper little man with a weather-beaten face. He was in evening dress, and spoke like a gentleman.

"I had your letter, Mr. Silva," he said. "You received my telephone message?"

"Yes," said Silva. "I wanted to see you particularly. You understand that what I say is wholly confidential?"

"That I understand," said the man called Cartwright.

He took Pinto's proffered cigarette and lit it.

"I have been reading about you in the papers," said Pinto. "You're the man who did the non-stop flight for the Western Aeroplane Company?"

"That's right." Cartwright smiled. "I have done many long flights. I suppose you are referring to my San Sebastian trip?"

Pinto nodded.

"Now I want to ask you a few questions, and if they seem to be prying or personal you must believe that I have no other wish than to secure information which is vital to myself. What position do you occupy with the Western Company?"

Cartwright shrugged his shoulders.

"I am a pilot," he said. "If you mean, am I a director of the firm or am I interested in the company, financially; I regret that I must answer no. I wish I were," he added, "but I am merely an employee."

Pinto nodded.

"That is what I wanted to know," he said. "Now here is another question. What does a first-class aeroplane cost?"

"It depends," said the other. "A long-distance machine, such as I have been flying, would cost anything up to five thousand pounds."

"Could you buy one? Are they on the market?" asked Pinto quickly.

"I could buy a dozen tomorrow," said the other promptly, "and I know just where I could get one machine of the best in Britain."

Pinto was looking at the stage, biting his lips thoughtfully.

"I'll tell you what I want," he said. "I am not very keenly interested in aviation, but it may be necessary that I should return to Portugal in a great hurry. It is no news to you that we Portuguese are generally in the throes of some revolution or other."

"So I understand," the pilot said, with a twinkle in his eye.

"In those circumstances," Pinto went on, "it may be necessary for me to leave this country without going through the formality of securing a passport. I want a machine which will carry me from London to, say, Cintra, without a stop, and I want a pilot who can take me across the sea by the direct route."

"Across the Bay of Biscay?" asked the aviator in surprise, and Pinto nodded.

"I should not want to touch any other country en route, for reasons which, I tell you frankly, are political."

Cartwright thought a moment.

"Yes, I think I can get you the machine, and I'm certain I can find you the pilot," he said.

"To put it bluntly," said Pinto, "would you take on an engagement for twelve months, secure the machine, house it and have it ready for me? I will pay you liberally." He mentioned a sum which satisfied the airman. "It must not be known that the machine is mine. You must buy it and keep it in your own name."

"There's no difficulty about that," said Cartwright. "Am I to understand that I must go ahead with the purchase of the aeroplane?"

"You can start right away," said Pinto; "the sooner you have the machine ready for a flight, the better. I am here almost every night, and I will give orders to the ticket collectors that you are to come to me whenever you want. If you will meet me here tomorrow morning, say at eleven o'clock, I can give you cash for the purchase of the machine, and I shall be happy to pay you half a year's salary in advance."

"It will take some time to finish up my old job," said Cartwright thoughtfully, "but I think I can do it for you. At any rate, I can get time off to buy the machine. You say that you do not want anybody to know that it is yours?"

Pinto nodded.

"Well, that's easy," said the other. "I've been thinking about buying a machine of my own for some time, and have made inquiries in several quarters."

He rose to leave and shook hands.

"Remember," said Pinto as a final warning, "not a word about this to any human soul."

"You can trust me," said the man.

Pinto watched the rest of the play with a lighter heart. After all, there could be nothing very much to fear. What had thrown him off his balance for the moment was the presence of Stafford King in Yorkshire, and when that detective did not make his appearance either at the police inquiry nor seek him in his hotel, it looked as though the colonel's words were true and that Scotland Yard were after Boundary himself and none other.

He sat the performance through and then went to his club—an institution off Pall Mall, which had been quite satisfied to accept Pinto to membership, without making any too close inquiries as to his antecedents.

He spent some time before the stock ticker, watching the news tick forth, then strolled into the smoking-room and read the evening papers for the second time. Only one item of news really interested him. It had interested the colonel, too. The diamond smith's premises in Regent Street had been burgled the night before and the contents of the safe taken. The colonel had arrested his flow of vituperation to speculate as to the "artist" who had carried out this neat job.

Pinto read for a little while, then threw the papers down. He wondered what made him so restive, and why he was so anxious to find something to occupy his attention, and then he realized with a start that he did not want to go back to face Colonel Boundary. It was the first time he had ever experienced this sensation, and he did not like it. He had held his place in the gang, by the assurance, which was also an assumption, that he was at least the colonel's equal. This irritated him. He put on his overcoat and turned into the street.

It was a chilly night, and a thin drizzle of rain was falling. He pulled up his coat collar and looked about for a taxicab. Neither outside the club nor in Pall Mall was one visible.

He started to walk home, but still felt that disinclination to face the colonel. Then a thought struck him; he would go and see Phillopolis, the little Greek.

Phillopolis patronized a night club in Soho, where he was usually to be found between midnight and two in the morning. Having an objective, Pinto felt in a happier frame of mind and walked briskly the intervening distance. He found his man sitting at a little marble-topped table by himself, contemplating a half bottle of sweet champagne and a half-filled glass. He was evidently deep in thought, and started violently when Pinto addressed him.

"Sit down," he said with evident relief. "I thought it was—"

"What did you think it was? You thought it was the police, I suppose?" said Pinto with heavy jocularity, and to his amazement he saw the little man wince.

"What has happened to Colonel Boundary?" asked the Greek irritably. "There used to be a time when anybody he spoke for was safe. I'm getting out of this country, and I'm getting out quick," he added.

"Why?" asked Pinto, who was vitally interested.

The Greek threw out his hands with a little grimace.

"Nerves," he said. "I haven't got over that bungled job of the White girl."

"Pooh!" said the other. "If the police were moving in that matter they'd have moved long ago. You're worrying yourself unnecessarily, Phillopolis."

De Silva's words slipped glibly from his tongue, but Phillopolis was unimpressed.

"I know when I've had enough," he said. "I've got my passports and I'm clearing out at the end of this week."

"Does the colonel know this?"

The Greek raised his shoulders indifferently.

"I don't know whether he does or whether he doesn't," he said; "anyway, Boundary and I are only remotely connected in business, and my movements are no affairs of his."

He looked curiously at the other.

"I wonder that a man like you, who is in the heart of things, stays on when the net is drawing round the old man."

"Loyalty is a vice with me," said Pinto virtuously; "besides, there's no reason to run away—as yet."

"I'm going while I'm safe," said Phillopolis, sipping his champagne. "At present the police have nothing against me, and I'm going to take good care they have nothing. That's where I've the advantage of people like you."

Pinto smiled.

"You've nothing on me," he said easily; "I have an absolutely clean record."

It disturbed him, however, to discover that even so minor a member of the gang as Phillopolis was preparing to desert what he evidently regarded as a sinking ship. More than this, it confirmed him in the wisdom of his own precautions, and he was rather glad that he had taken it into his head to visit Phillopolis on that night.

"When do you leave?" he asked.

"The day after tomorrow," said Phillopolis. "I think I'll go down into Italy for a year. I've made enough money now to live without worrying about work, and I mean to enjoy myself."

Pinto looked at the man with interest. Here, at any rate, was one without a conscience. The knowledge that he had accumulated his fortune through the miseries of innocent girls shipped to foreign dance halls did not weigh greatly upon his mind. Though every penny he had stood for the sob of heart-broken womanhood, though his big bank balance had been built up on broken lives and broken hearts, he thought no more of the source of his income than did the butcher think of the sufferings of the lambs he had slaughtered and offered for sale.

"Lucky you!" said Pinto, as they walked out of the club together. "Where do you live, by the way?"

"In Somers Street, Soho. It is just around the corner," said Phillopolis. "Will you walk there with me?"

Pinto hesitated.

"Yes, I will," he said.

He wanted to see the sort of establishment which Phillopolis maintained. They chatted together till they same to the street, and then Phillopolis stopped.

"Do you mind if I go ahead?" he said. "I have a—friend there who might be worried by your coming."

Pinto smiled to himself.

"Certainly," he said. "I'll wait on the opposite side of the road until you are ready."

The man lived above a big furniture shop, and admission was gained by a side door. Pinto watched him pass through the portals and heard the door close. He was a long time gone, and evidently his friend was unprepared to receive visitors at that hour, or else Phillopolis himself had some reason for postponing the invitation.

The reason for the delay was explained in a sensational manner. Suddenly the door opened and a man came out. He was followed by two others, and between them was Phillopolis, and the street lamp shone upon the steel handcuffs on his wrists. Pinto drew back into a doorway and watched. Phillopolis was talking—it would perhaps be more accurate to say that he was raving—at the top of his voice, cursing and sobbing in a frenzy.

"You planted them—it is a plant!" he yelled. "You devils!"

"Are you coming quietly," said a voice, "or are you going to make trouble? Take him, Dempsey!"

Phillopolis seemed to have forgotten Pinto's presence, for he went out of the street without once calling upon him to testify to his character and innocence. Pinto waited till he was gone, and then strolled across the road to the detective who stood before the door lighting his pipe.

"Good evening," he said. "Has there been some trouble?"

The officer looked at him suspiciously. But Pinto was in evening dress and talked like a gentleman, and the policeman thawed.

"Nothing very serious, sir," he said, "except for the man. He's a 'fence.'"

"A what?" said Pinto with well-feigned innocence.

"A receiver of stolen property. We found his lodgings full of stuff."

"Good heavens!" gasped Pinto.

"Yes, sir," said the man, delighted that he had created a sensation; "I never saw so much valuable property in one room in my life. There was a big burglary in Regent Street last night. A jeweler's shop was cleaned out of about twenty thousand pounds' worth of necklaces, and we found every bit of it here tonight. We've always suspected this man," he went on confidentially; "nobody knew how he got his living, but from information we received today we were able to catch him red-handed."

"Thank you," said Pinto faintly and walked slowly home, for now he no longer feared to meet the colonel. He had something to tell him, something that would inspire even Boundary with apprehension.

CHAPTER XXIX
THE VOICE IN THE ROOM

As Silva anticipated, the colonel was up and waiting for him. He was playing patience on his desk and looked up with a scowl as the Portuguese entered.

"So you've been sulking, have you, Pinto?" he began, but the other interrupted him.

"You can keep all that talk for another time," he said. "They've taken Phillopolis!"

The colonel swept his cards aside with a quick, nervous gesture.

"Taken Phillopolis?" he repeated slowly. "On what charge?"

"For being the receiver of stolen property," said the other. "They found the proceeds of the Regent Street burglary in his apartments."

The colonel opened his mouth to speak, then shut it again, and there was silence for two or three minutes. "I see. They've planted the stuff on him, have they?"

"What do you mean?" asked Pinto.

"You don't suppose that Phillopolis is a fence, do you?" said the colonel scornfully. "Why, it is a business that a man must spend the whole of his life at before he can be successful. No, Phillopolis knows no more about that burglary or the jewels than you or I. The stuff has been planted in his rooms."

"But the police don't do that sort of thing."

"Who said the police did it?" snarled the colonel. "Of course they didn't; they haven't the sense. That's Mr. Jack o' Judgment once more, and this time, Pinto, he's real dangerous."

"Jack o' Judgment!" gasped Pinto. "But would he commit a burglary?"

The colonel laughed scornfully.

"Would he commit murder? Would he hang Raoul? Would he shoot you? Don't ask such fool questions, Silva! Of course it was Jack o' Judgment. I tell you, the night you were in Yorkshire making a mess of that Crotin business, Jack o' Judgment came here, to this very room, and told me that he would ruin us one by one and that he would leave me to the last. He mentioned us all—you, Crewe, Selby—" He stopped suddenly and scratched his chin. "But not Lollie Marsh," he said. "That's queer; he never mentioned Lollie Marsh!"

He was deep in thought for a few moments, then he went on:

"So he's done for Phillopolis, has he? Well, Phillopolis has got to take his medicine. I can do nothing for him."

"But surely he can prove—" began Pinto.

"What can he prove?" asked the other. "Can he prove how he earns his money? He's been taken with the goods; he hasn't that chance." He snapped his fingers. "I'll make a prophecy," he said; "Phillopolis will get five years penal servitude, and nothing in the world can save him from that."

"An innocent man!" said Pinto in amazement. "Impossible!"

"But is he innocent?" asked the colonel sourly. "That's the point you've got to keep in your mind. He may be innocent of one kind of crookedness and be so mixed up in another that he cannot prove he is innocent of either. That's where they've got this fellow. He dare not appeal to the people who know him best, because they'd give him away."

He squatted back in his chair, pulling at his mustache.

"Phillopolis, Crewe, Pinto, Selby and then me," he said speaking to himself, "and he never mentioned Lollie Marsh. And Lollie has been the decoy duck that has been in every hunt we've had. This wants looking into, Pinto."

As he finished speaking, there was a little buzz from the corner of the room, and Pinto looked up, startled. The colonel looked up too, and a slow smile dawned on his face.

"A visitor," he said softly. "Not our old friend, Jack o' Judgment, surely!"

"What is it?" asked Pinto.

"A little alarm I've had fixed under one of the treads of the stairs," said the other. "I don't like to be taken unawares."

"Perhaps it is Crewe," suggested the other.

"Crewe went home an hour ago," said the colonel. "No, this is a genuine visitor."

They waited for some time and then there was a knock at the outer door.

"Open it, Pinto." As the other did not instantly move, he commanded: "Open it, do you hear! What are you afraid of?"

"I'm not afraid of anything," retorted the Portuguese, and flung out of the room.

Yet he hesitated again before he turned the handle of the outer door. He flung it open and stepped back. He would have gone farther but the wall was at his back and he could only stand with open mouth, staring at the visitor. It was Maisie White.

She returned his gaze steadily.

"I want to see Colonel Boundary," she said.

"Certainly, certainly," said Pinto huskily.

He shut the door and ushered her into the colonel's presence. Boundary's eyes narrowed as he saw the girl. He suspected a trap and looked past her as though expecting to see an escort behind her.

"This is an unexpected honor, Miss White," he said suavely, and he looked meaningly at the clock on the mantelpiece. "We do not usually receive visitors so late, and especially charming lady visitors."

She was carrying a thick package, and this she laid on the table.

"I'm sorry it is so late," she said calmly, "but I have been all the evening checking my father's accounts. This is yours."

She handed the package to the colonel.

"That parcel contains bank notes to the value of twenty-seven thousand, three hundred pounds," said the girl quietly. "It represents what remains of the money which my father drew from your gang."

"Tainted money, eh?" said the colonel humorously. "I think you're very foolish, Miss White. Your father earned this money by legitimate business enterprises."

"I know all about them," she said. "I won't ask you to count the notes, because it is only a question of getting the money off my own conscience, and the amount really doesn't matter."

"So you came here alone to make this act of reparation?" asked the colonel.

"I came here to make this act of reparation," she replied steadily.

"Not alone, eh? Surrounded entirely by police. Mr. Stafford King is in the offing, waiting outside in a taxi, or probably waiting on the mat," said the colonel in the same tone. "Well, well, you're quite safe with us, Miss White."

He took up the package and tore off the wrapping, revealing two wads of bank notes, and ran his finger along the edges.

"And how are you going to live?" he asked.

"By working," said the girl. "That's a strange way of earning a living, don't you think, colonel?"

"You'll never work harder than I have worked," said Colonel Dan Boundary good-humoredly. And, looking down at the money, he added: "So that's Solly White's share, is it? And I suppose it doesn't include the house he bought, or the car?"

"I've sold everything," said the girl quietly. "Every piece of property he owned has been realized, and that is the proceeds."

With a little nod she was withdrawing, but Pinto barred her way.

"One moment, Miss White," he said, and there was a dangerous glint in his eyes. "If you chose to come here alone in the middle of the night—"

The colonel stepped between them and swept the Portuguese backward. Without a word he opened the door.

"Good night, Miss White," he said. "My kind regards to Mr. Stafford King, who, I suppose, is somewhere on the premises, and to all the bright lads of the criminal intelligence department who are at this moment watching the house."

She smiled, but did not take his proffered hand.

"Good-by," she said.

The colonel accompanied her to the outer door and switched on all the stair lights, as he could from the master switch near the entrance to his flat, and waited until the echo of her footsteps had passed away before he came back to the man.

"You're a clever fellow, you are, Pinto," he said quietly; "you have one of the brightest minds in the gang."

"If she comes here alone—" began Pinto.

"Alone!" snarled the colonel. "I hinted a dozen times, if I hinted once, that she'd come with a young army of police. The first shout she made would have been the signal for your arrest and mine. Haven't you had your lesson tonight? How long do you think it would take Stafford King to trump up a charge against you and put you where the dogs wouldn't bite you, eh?"

He walked to the window and watched the girl. There was a taxicab waiting at the entrance, and, as he had suspected, a man was standing by the door and followed the girl into the cab before it drove away.

"She timed her visit. I suppose she gave herself five minutes. If she'd been here any longer they would have been up for her, make no mistake about that, Pinto."

The colonel drew down the blinds with a crash and began pacing the room. He stopped at the farther end and looked at the wall.

"Do you know, I've often wondered why Jack o' Judgment damaged that wall?" he said. "He got me guessing and I've been guessing ever since."

"You thought it was a foolish stunt?" said Pinto, glad to keep his master off the subject of his Huddersfield blunder.

The colonel shook his head.

"I shouldn't think it was that," he said. "It was not like Jack o' Judgment to do foolish things. He has an object in everything he does."

"Perhaps it was to get you out of the room for the morning and make a search of your papers," suggested Pinto. Again the colonel shook his head.

"He knows me better than that. He knew very well that I would shift every document from the room, and that there was nothing for his bloodhounds to discover." He thought a moment, pulling at his long, yellow mustache. "May be," he said to himself, "may be—"

"May be what?" asked Pinto.

"The workmen may have been up to some kind of deviltry. They might have been policemen, for all I know." He shrugged his shoulders. "Anyway, that's long ago, and if he's made a discovery, why, I think we should have heard about it. Now, Pinto"—his tone changed—"I'm not going to talk to you any more about Crotin. You've made a mess of it, and I ought never to have sent you. We have two matters to settle. Crewe wants to quit, and I think you're getting ready to run away."

"Me?" said Pinto with virtuous indignation. "Do you imagine I should leave you, colonel, if you were in for a bad time?"

"Do I imagine it?" The colonel laughed. "Don't be a fool. Sit down. When did you see Lollie Marsh last?"

Pinto considered.

"I haven't seen her for weeks."

"Neither have I," said the colonel. "Of course she has an excuse for staying away. She never comes unless she's sent for. If we've got a 'prospect' we want to lead down the easy path, why, there's nobody in London who can do it like Lollie. And I understand you had some disagreement with the young lady over

Maisie White?"

"She interfered—" began Pinto.

"And probably saved your life," remarked the colonel meaningly. "No, you have no kick against Lollie for that."

He pulled open the drawer of his desk, took out a card and wrote rapidly.

"I'll put Snakit on her trail," he said.

"Snakit!" said the other contemptuously.

"He's all right for this kind of work," said the colonel. "Snakit can trail her. He does nothing for his keep—and Lollie doesn't know him, does she?"

"I don't think so," said Pinto absently. "If you believe that Lollie is double-crossing you why don't you—"

"I'll write to you when I want any suggestions as to how to run my business," said the colonel unpleasantly. "Where does Lollie live?"

"Tavistock Avenue," said Pinto. "I wish you'd be a little more decent to me, colonel. I'm trying to do the right thing by you."

"And you'll soon get tired of trying," said the colonel. "Don't worry, Pinto. I know just how much I can depend upon you and just what your loyalty is worth. You'll sell me at the first opportunity, and you'll be dead about the same day. I only hope for your sake that the opportunity never arises. That's that," he said as he finished the card and put it on one side. "Now what is the next thing?" He looked up at the ceiling for inspiration. "Crewe," he said; "Crewe is getting out of hand, too. I put him on a job to trace Snow Gregory's past. I haven't seen or heard of him for two days, either."

Somebody laughed. It was a queer little far-away laugh, but Pinto recognized it, and his hair almost stood on end. He looked across at the colonel with ashen face and then swung round apprehensively toward the door.

"Did you hear that?" he whispered.

"I heard it—thank the Lord!" said the colonel, and fetched a long sigh.

Pinto gazed at him in amazement.

"Why," he said in a low voice, "that was Jack o' Judgment!"

"I know," said the colonel, nodding, "but I still thank the Lord!"

He got up slowly and walked round the room, opened the door that led to his bedroom and put on the light. The room was empty and the only cupboard which might have concealed an intruder was wide open. He came back, walked into the entrance hall and opened the door softly. The landing was empty, too. He returned after fastening the door and slipping the bolts—bolts which he had fixed during the previous week.

"You wonder why I held a thanksgiving service?" said the colonel slowly. "Well, I've heard that laugh before, and I thought my brain was going—that's all. I'd rather it were Jack o' Judgment in the flesh than Jack o' Judgment wandering loose around my nut."

"You heard it before?" said Pinto. "Here?"

"Here in this room," said the colonel. "I thought I was going daft. You're the first person who has heard it beside myself." He looked at Pinto. "A fierce prospect isn't it?" he said gloomily. "Let's talk about the weather!"

CHAPTER XXX
DIAMONDS FOR THE BANK

There was no hope for Phillopolis from the first. The case against him was so clear and so damning that the magistrate before whom the preliminary inquiry was heard had no hesitation in committing him to trial at the Old Bailey on a charge of receiving stolen goods. Every article which had been stolen from the diamond smith's company had been recovered in his flat. The police experts gave evidence to the effect that he had been a suspected man for years, and that his method of earning a living had on several occasions been the subject of police inquiry. He was known to be, so the evidence ran, the associate of criminal characters.

The woman who passed as his wife had nothing good to say of him. It was not she who had admitted the police. Indeed, they found her in an upper room, locked in. Phillopolis was something of a tyrant, and on the day of his arrest he had had a quarrel with the woman, who had threatened to expose him to the police for some other breach of the law. He had beaten her and locked her into an upper bedroom, and this act of tyranny had proved his downfall, if it were true, as he swore so vehemently, that the articles which were found in his room had been planted there.

The colonel was not present, nor were any other members of the gang, save Selby, who had been summoned to the colonel's presence and had arrived in the early morning.

"He hasn't a ghost of a chance," reported Selby, who had a lifelong acquaintance with criminals of the meaner sort, and had spent no small amount of his time in police courts, securing evidence as to the virtue of his protégés. "If he doesn't get ten years I'll be surprised."

"What does Phillopolis say?"

"He swears that the goods were not in his flat when he went out that night," he said; "but if they were planted the work was done thoroughly. The detectives found jewel cases under cushions, hidden in cupboards, on the tops of shelves, and one of the best bits of swag—a wonderful diamond necklace—was discovered in his boot, at the bottom of his trunk."

The conversation took place in Green Park, which was a favorite haunt of the colonel's. He loved to sit on a chair by the side of the lake, watching the children sailing their boats and the ducks mothering their broods. He was silent. His eyes were bent upon the efforts of a small boy to bring a little waterlogged boat to a level keel, and apparently he had no other interest.

"Have a cigar, Selby," he said at last. "What is the news in your part of the world?"

Selby was carefully biting off the end of his gift.

"Nothing much," he said. "We got some letters the other day from Mrs. Crombie-Brail. Her son has got into trouble at the Cape. Lew Litchfield got them. He was doing a job in Manchester."

Lew Litchfield was a bright young burglar of whom the colonel had heard, and he knew the kind of "job" on which Lew was engaged.

"You bought 'em?" he asked.

"I gave him a tenner for them," said Selby. "I don't think they're much use."

The colonel shook his head.

"That's not the kind of letter that brings in money," he said. "You can't bleed a mother because her son got into trouble—at least, not for more than a hundred."

"Letters have been scarce lately," said his agent disconsolately; "I think people have either given up keeping or writing them."

"Maybe," said the colonel. "Anyway, I didn't bring you down to talk about letters. I've work for you."

Selby looked uneasy, and that in itself was a discouraging sign. Usually the little crook from the north hailed any job of any kind with enthusiasm.

It was an unmistakable proof to the colonel that he was losing grip, that the magic of his name and all that he implied in the way of protection from punishment was less than it had been

"You don't seem very pleased," he said.

Selby forced a smile.

"Well, colonel," he said, "I've a feeling they're after us, and I don't want to take any risks."

"You'll take this one," said the colonel. "There's somebody to be put away."

The man licked his lips.

"Well, I'm not in it," he said. "I had enough with that Hanson business."

"By 'put away' I don't mean murdered or ill-treated in any sense," said the colonel, "and, besides, it is one of our own people."

But even this assurance did not satisfy the man.

"I don't like it," he said. "They tell me that this Jack o' Judgment—"

"Just forget Jack o' Judgment for a minute and think of yourself," retorted the colonel. "You've made your pile, and you find that England's getting a bit too hot for you, don't you?"

"I do indeed," said the man fervently. "You know, colonel, I was thinking that a trip to America wouldn't be a bad idea."

"There are plenty of places to go to without going to America," said the colonel. "I tell you that I mean Lollie no harm."

"Lollie?" Selby was surprised and showed it. "She hasn't—"

"I don't know what she's done yet, but I think it is time she went away," said the colonel; "and so far as I can judge, it is time you went, too, Selby. I don't know whether Lollie is betraying us, and maybe I'm doing her an injustice," he went on, "but if I put up to her a suggestion that she should leave the country maybe she'd turn me down. You know how suspicious these women are. The only idea I can think of is to scare her and make her run quick and sudden, and I want you to provide the means."

Selby was waiting.

"I bought a motor boat, a swift one. I have it ready at Twickenham, and you can get all your goods on board and go to—"

"Where?"

"Anywhere you like," said the colonel; "Holland, Denmark—one place is as good as another, and it'll be a good sea-going boat. You see, my idea is this: If I think Lollie is negotiating to put us away I can give her a fright which will make her jump at the means of getting out of England by the quickest and shortest route. You can go with her and keep her under your eye until the trouble blows over."

He saw a look in the man's face and correctly interpreted it.

"I'm not worried about you double-crossing me," he said, "even if you are abroad. I've enough evidence against you to bring you back under an extradition warrant." He laughed as Selby's face fell. "You see, Selby, there's nothing in it that you can take exception to. I don't even know that Lollie will refuse to go in the ordinary way, but I must make preparations."

"It is a reasonable suggestion," said Selby after considering the matter for a few minutes. "I'll do it, colonel."

"You'd better bring a couple of men to London who can handle Lollie if she gives any trouble. No, no," said the colonel, raising his hand in dignified protest, "there's going to be nothing rough. How can there be? You'll be in charge of it all, and it is up to you as to how Lollie is treated."

It did not occur to Selby until an hour later to ask the colonel how he knew that his hobby was motor boating, but by that time the colonel had gone.

It was true, as Boundary said, that the gang was badly scared. It was equally true that they needed only one jar before it became a case of every man for himself. Already even the minor members were making their preparations to break away. The red light was burning clear before all eyes. But none knew how readily the colonel had recognized the signs, and how, in spite of his apparent philosophy and his contempt of danger, he, more than any of the others, was preparing for the inevitable crash.

Jack o' Judgment, he told himself, was playing his game better than he could play it himself. The arrest of Phillopolis had removed one of the men who might have been an inconvenient witness against him. White was gone, Raoul was gone. He had planned the disappearance of Selby, a most dangerous man, and Lollie Marsh, an even more dangerous woman, and there remained only Pinto and Crewe.

When he had taken leave of his agent the colonel walked to Westminster and boarded a car which carried him along the Embankment to Blackfriars. He might have been followed, and probably was, but this possibility did not worry him. He walked across Ludgate Circus, up St. Bride Street to Hatton Garden, and turned into the office of Myglebergs.

Mr. Mygleberg, a very suave and polite gentleman, received him and ushered him into a private room. This shrewd Dutchman had no illusions as to the colonel's probity, but he had no doubt either that the big man could pay handsomely for everything he bought.

"I'm glad you've come, colonel," he said. "I have been expecting you for a couple of days. We have just had a wonderful parcel of stones from Amsterdam, and I think some of them would suit you."

He disappeared and came back with a tray covered with the most beautiful diamonds that had ever left the cutter's hands. The colonel went over them slowly, examining them and putting a select number aside.

"I'll take those," he said; and Mr. Mygleberg laughed.

"They're the best," he conceded. "Trust you to know a good thing when you see it, Colonel!"

"What have I to pay for these?"

Mygleberg made a rapid calculation and put the figures before Colonel Boundary.

"It is a big price," said the colonel, "but I don't think you have overcharged. Besides, I could always sell them again for as much as that."

Mr. Mygleberg nodded.

"I think you are wise to put your money into stones, colonel," he said; "they always go up and never go down in value. You can lose other things. They're easy, and they're always convertible. I always tell my partner that if I ever become a millionaire I shall invest every penny in stones. "

The colonel paid for the gems from a thick wad of notes he took from his hip pocket. They were, in point of fact, the identical notes which Maisie White had handed to him the night previous. He waited while the jewels were made up into a little oblong package, heavily sealed and inscribed with the colonel's name and address, and then, shaking hands with Mygleberg and fixing a further appointment, he went out into Hatton Garden, whistling a little song and apparently the picture of contentment.

He was getting ready for flight, too. This, the first of the many packages which he intended depositing in the private safe of his bank, would go with the ever-increasing pile of American gold bonds of high denomination which filled that steel repository. For months the colonel had been converting his property into paper dollars. They were more easily negotiated and less traceable than English bank notes, and they were more get-at-able. A big balance in the books of the bank might be creditable but took time to convert into cash. Now nobody knew but himself the amount standing to his credit. He was not at the mercy of prying bank clerks or a manager who might be reached by the police. At a minute's notice, and without anybody's being the wiser, he could demand the contents of his safe-deposit box and walk from the bank premises without a soul being aware that he was carrying the bulk of his fortune away.

He took a cab and drove now to the bank premises. Ferguson, the manager, received him.

"Good morning, colonel," he said. "I was just writing you a note. You know your account is getting very low."

"Is that so?" said the colonel in surprise.

"I thought you wouldn't realize the fact," said Ferguson, "but you've been drawing very heavily of late."

"I'll put it right," said the colonel. "It is not overdrawn?" he asked jocularly, and Ferguson smiled.

"You've eighty thousand pounds in account B," he said. "I suppose you don't want to touch that?"

"Unless you're anxious that I should get penal servitude for fraudulently converting the company's funds," said the colonel in the same strain. "No, I'll fix my account some time today. In the meantime"—he produced a package from his hip pocket—"I want this to go into my safe-deposit box."

"Certainly," said Ferguson, and struck a bell. A clerk answered the call. "Take Colonel Boundary to the vaults. He wants to deposit something in his box," he said. "Or would you like me to do it, colonel?"

"I'll do it myself," said the colonel.

He followed the clerk down the spiral staircase to the well-lit vault, and with the key which the man handed him opened box twenty. It was divided into two compartments, that on the left consisting of a deep drawer, which he pulled out. It was half filled with American paper currency, as he knew—currency neatly parceled and carefully packed by his own hands.

"I often wonder, Colonel Boundary," said the interested clerk, "why you don't use the bank safe. When a customer has his own, you know, we are not responsible for any of his losses."

"I know that," said the colonel genially. "Still, one must take a risk."

He placed the package on the top of the money, pushed back the drawer, locked the safe and handed the key to the young man.

"I think the bank takes enough risks without asking them to accept any more," he said, "and, besides, I like to take a little risk myself sometimes."

"So I've heard," said the clerk innocently, and the colonel shot a questioning look at the young man.

CHAPTER XXXI
THE VOICE AGAIN

He left the bank with the sense of having done his duty by himself. He had not planned the route by which he was leaving the country, or the hour. Much was to happen before he shook the dust of England from his feet, and as he had arranged matters he would have plenty of time to think things over before his departure. A great deal happened in the next few days to make him believe that the necessity for getting away was not very urgent. He met Stafford King in the park one morning, and Stafford had been unusually communicative and friendly. Then the whispering voices in the flat had temporarily ceased and Jack o' Judgment had given him no sign of his existence. It was five days after he had made his deposit in the bank that the first shock came to him. He found Snakit waiting on returning from a matinee, and the little detective was so important and mysterious that the colonel knew something had been discovered.

"Well," he asked, closing the door, "what have you found?"

"She is in communication with the police," said Snakit; "that's what I've found."

"Lollie?"

"Miss Marsh is the lady. In communication with the police," said the other impressively.

"Now just tell me what you mean," said the colonel. "Do you mean she's on speaking terms with the policeman on point duty at Piccadilly Circus?"

"I mean, sir," said Snakit with dignity, "that she's in the habit of meeting Mr. Stafford King, who is a well-known man at Scotland Yard."

"He is well known here, too," interrupted the colonel; "where does she meet him?"

"In all sorts of queer places—that's the suspicious part of it," said Snakit, who had joyously entered thoroughly into the work which had been given to him, without realizing its unlawful character.

He had accepted the colonel's story that he was the victim of police persecution without question, and as this was the first news of any importance he had been able to bring to his employer, he was naturally inclined to make the most of it.

"He has met her twice at eleven o'clock at night, at the bottom of St. James' Street, and walked up with her, very deeply engaged in conversation," said Snakit, consulting his note book. "He met her once at the foot of the steps leading down from Waterloo Place, and they were together for an hour. This morning," he went on speaking slowly, and evidently this was his titbit, "this morning Mr. Stafford King went to the Cunard office in Cockspur Street and booked cabin seventeen on the shelter deck of the *Lapland* for New York."

"In what name?"

"In the name of Miss Isabel Trenton."

The colonel nodded. It was a name that Lollie had used before and the story rang true.

"When does the *Lapland* sail?" he asked, and again the detective consulted his book.

"Next Saturday," he said, "from Liverpool."

"Very good," said the colonel. "Thank you, Snakit; you've done very well. See if you can pick them up tonight, or"—he thought a moment—"no, don't shadow her tonight. I'll have a talk with her."

The news disturbed him. Lollie was getting ready to run away—that was unimportant. But she was running away with the assistance of the police, who had booked her passage. That meant that they had got as much out of her as she had to tell, and were helping her out of the country before the blow fell. That was not only important, but it was grave. Either the police were going to strike at once or—

An idea struck him and he telephoned to Pinto. Another call got him into touch with Crewe, and these three were in consultation when Selby came that afternoon.

He arrived at an unpropitious time, for the colonel was in a cold fury, and the object of his wrath was Crewe, who sat with folded arms and tense face, looking down at the table.

"That gentleman business is played out, Crewe," stormed the colonel, "and I'm just about tired of hearing what you won't do and what you will do! If Lollie's given us away she has got to go through it."

"What use will it be, supposing she has?" said the other doggedly. "I don't for a moment believe she has done anything of the sort. But suppose she has given you away, what are you going to do? Add to the indictment? She's sick of the game and wants to get away somewhere where she can live a decent life."

"Oh, you've been discussing it with her, have you?" said the colonel with dangerous calm. "And maybe you also are sick of the game and want to get away and live a decent life? I remember hearing you say something of that sort a few weeks ago."

"We're all sick of it," said Crewe. "Look at Pinto. Do you think he's pleased?"

Pinto started.

"Why do you bring me into it?" he complained. "I'm standing by the colonel to the last. And I agree with him that we ought to know what Lollie told the police."

"She's told them nothing," said Crewe; "she isn't that kind of girl. Besides, what does she know?"

"She knows a lot," said the colonel. "I'll put a supposition to you. Suppose she's Jack o' Judgment."

Crewe looked at him in astonishment.

"That's an absurd suggestion," he said. "How could she be?"

"I'll tell you how she could be," said the colonel. "She has never been with us when Jack made his appearance. You'll grant that?"

Crewe thought for a moment.

"There you're wrong," he said; "she was with us the night Jack first came."

The colonel was taken aback. A theory which he had formed was destroyed by that recollection.

"So she was. That's right, she was there! I remember he insulted her. But I'm certain she's seen him since; I am certain she's been working hand in glove with him since. Who was the Jack who went to Yorkshire?"

It was Crewe's turn to be nonplussed.

"Jack o' Judgment must be working with a pal," the colonel went on triumphantly, "and I suggest that that pal is Lollie Marsh."

"That's a lie!"

The colonel looked up quickly.

"Who said that?" he demanded harshly.

Crewe shook his head.

"It was not me," he said.

"Was it you, Selby?"

"Me?" said the astonished Selby. "No. I thought it was you who said it. It came from your end of the table, colonel."

The colonel got up.

"There's something wrong here," he said.

"I've got it!" It was Pinto who spoke. "Did you notice anything peculiar about the voice, colonel?" he asked eagerly. "I did, the first time I heard it, and I've been wondering how I'd heard it before, and just now it has struck me. It was a gramophone voice!"

"A gramophone voice?"

"It sounded like a voice on a speaking machine."

The colonel nodded slowly.

"Now you come to mention it, I think you're right," he said. "It sounded familiar to me. Of course it was a gramophone voice."

They made a careful search of the apartment, taking down every book from the big shelf in one of the alcoves, and turning the leaves to discover the hidden machine. With this idea to guide them the search was more complete than it had been before. Every drawer in the desk was taken out, every scrap of furniture was minutely examined, even the massive legs of the colonel's writing table were tapped.

Crewe took no part in the search, but watched it with a slight smile of amusement, and the colonel, turning, detected this.

"What the devil are you grinning about?" he said. "Why aren't you helping, Crewe? You've got an interest in this business."

"Not such an interest that I'm going to fool around looking for a gramophone voice that goes off at appropriate intervals," said Crewe. "Doesn't it strike you that it would have to be a pretty smart gramophone to chip in at the right moment?"

The colonel pondered this a minute and then went back to his place at the table, mopping his forehead.

"Pinto's right," he said. "The fellow has smuggled some fool machine into the flat, and we shall discover it sooner or later. I don't know how he controls it, or who controls it"—he looked suspiciously at Crewe—"or who controls it," he repeated.

"You said that before," said Crewe coolly.

The colonel had something on his lips to say, but swallowed it.

"We'll meet here tonight at eleven. I told Lollie to come. Now, Crewe," he said in a more gentle tone, "you're in this up to the neck, and you've got to go through with it. After all, your life and liberty are at stake as much as ours. If Lollie's played us false we've got to be—"

"Lollie has not played you false, colonel," said Crewe. His face was very pale, the colonel noticed. "I like that girl, and—"

"So that's it?" said the colonel. "A little love romance introduced into our sordid commercial lives? Maybe you know what she's been talking to Stafford King about?"

Crewe did not immediately reply.

"Do you?" asked the colonel.

"I know she has been trying to get out of the country, to break with the gang, but that she has given you or any of us away is a lie. Lollie's had a rotten life, and she's just sick of it, that's all. Do you blame her?"

"There's no question of blaming her or praising her," said the colonel patiently; "the question is whether we condemn her, or whether she still has our confidence; and that we shall know tonight. You will be present, Crewe?"

"I shall be present, you may be sure," said Crewe, and there was a look in his face which Pinto, for one, did not like.

CHAPTER XXXII
LOLLIE GOES AWAY

It seemed to Swell Crewe that the scene was curiously reminiscent of a trial in which he had once participated. The colonel, at the end of the long table, sat aloof and apparently noncommittal, a veritable judge and a merciless judge at that. Pinto sat at his right, Selby on the left, and Crewe himself sat halfway between the girl at the further end of the table, and Pinto.

Lollie Marsh had no doubt as to why she had been summoned. Her pretty face was drawn, the hands which were clasped on the table before her were restless, but what Crewe noticed more particularly was a certain untidiness both in her costume and in her usually well-coiffured hair. As though wearying of the part she had been playing, she was already discarding her make-up.

"I hate to bring you here, Lollie, and ask you these questions," the colonel was saying, "but we are all in some danger and we want to know just where we stand with you."

She made no reply.

"The charge against you is that you've been in communication with the police. Is that true?"

"If you mean that I've been in communication with Mr. Stafford King, that's true," she said. "You told me to get after him. Haven't I been for weeks—"

"That's a pretty good excuse," interrupted the colonel, "but it won't work, Lollie. You don't get after a man like Stafford King and meet him secretly in St. James' Street. And you don't get after him by seeing him for half an hour at a time, and I haven't heard of you ever getting after a fellow to the extent of his paying for your passage to America."

She started.

"You know the way it is done. You did it before, Lollie," the colonel went on. "Now, you've got to be a good girl and tell us how far you've gone."

She did not reply.

"Come, Lollie," said Pinto in his most engaging voice; "we don't mean you any harm, but we've got to look after ourselves. What have you told Stafford King?"

"I've told him nothing," said the girl; "at least, nothing about you people. And what do you think I could tell him that he doesn't already know?" she asked scornfully. "Why, Pinto, he's got you sized right down to the ground! He's got you in half sizes! Tell him indeed! Why, he told me things about you that I had never heard before in my life."

Pinto went a dusky red.

"That won't go," he said roughly; "he didn't meet you to give you information."

"Didn't he, though?" said the girl, nodding. "He told me all about the Orpheum, and the man who horsewhipped you, and—"

With an oath the other started to his feet, touched in the tenderest spot.

"Dry up, Pinto," said the colonel; "we all know that story's true. But why did he tell you this, Lollie?"

She hesitated.

"I'll tell you the truth," she said. "I'm sick of this life, colonel. I want to get away out of it all, and—and—he's going to help me."

"A social reformer, eh?" said the colonel. "I didn't know the police went in for that sort of stunt. And when did he take this sudden liking for you, Lollie?"

"It wasn't a sudden liking at all," she said, "but I think it was because—well, because I stopped Pinto in the nursing home—and Miss White told him. I think that's all."

The colonel looked down on his pad.

"There's something in that," he said; "it sounds feasible. Didn't he question you?" raising his eyes.

"About you?" she said.

"About us!" corrected the colonel.

"He asked me nothing about you, nothing about your habits or your methods or about any of our funny business. I'll swear it," she said.

"You're not going to believe that, are you, colonel?" demanded Pinto. "You can see that she is lying and that she's double-crossing you?"

"She's neither lying nor double-crossing us." It was Crewe who spoke. "I don't know what you think about it, colonel, but I am convinced that Lollie is speaking the truth."

"You!" Pinto laughed loudly. "I think you're in a state of mind when you'd believe anything Lollie said. And anyway you're probably in league with her."

"You're a liar," said Crewe, so quietly that no one suspected the surprising thing that would follow, for of a sudden his fist shot out and caught Pinto under the jaw, sending him sprawling to the floor.

The colonel was instantly on his feet, his hand outspread.

"That's enough, Crewe," he said harshly. "I'll have none of that!"

Pinto picked himself up, his face livid.

"You'll pay for that," he said breathlessly; but Swell Crewe had walked to the girl and had laid his hand on her shoulder.

"Lollie," he said, "I'm believing you, and I think the colonel is, too. If you're going out of the country, why I'll say good luck to you. You've made a very wise decision, and one which we shall all make—some of us perhaps too late."

"Wait a moment," said the colonel. He exchanged a glance with Selby, and the man slipped quietly from the room. "Before we do any of that fare-thee-well stuff I've got a few words to say to you, Lollie. I'm with Crewe. I think it is time you went out of the country, but you're going out my way."

"What do you mean?" she asked.

Her hand clutched Swell Crewe's sleeve.

"You're going out my way," said the colonel, "and I swear no harm will come to you. You're leaving tonight."

"But how?" she asked, affrighted.

"Selby will tell you. You'll meet him downstairs. Now be a sensible girl and do as I tell you. Selby will go with you and see you safe. We made all preparations for your departure tonight."

"What's this, colonel?" asked Crewe.

"You're out of it," said the colonel savagely; "I'm running this show myself. If you want to join Lollie later, why, you can. For the present she's going just where I want her to go and in the way I have planned."

He held out his hand to the girl and she took it.

"Good-by and good luck, Lollie!" he said.

"But can't I go back to my rooms?" she asked.

He shook his head.

"Do as I tell you," he said shortly.

She stood at the door, and for a moment her eyes met Crewe's and he moved toward her.

"Wait." The colonel gripped his arm. "Good-by, Lollie," and the door shut on the girl.

"Let me go," said Crewe between his teeth. "If she trusts you I don't. This is some trick of that dirty half-breed!"

With a snarl of rage Pinto whipped his ever-ready knife from his hip pocket and flung it. It was the colonel who drew Crewe aside, or that moment would have been his last. The knife whizzed past and was buried almost to the hilt in the wall. The colonel broke the tense silence which followed.

"Pinto," he said in his silkiest voice, "if you ever want to know what it feels like to be a dead man just repeat that performance, will you?" Then his rage burst forth. "I'll shoot either of you if you play the fool in front of me again. You dirty little pickpockets that I've taken from the gutter! You miserable little sneak thieves!"

He let loose a flood of abuse that made even Crewe wince.

"Now sit down, both of you," he finished up, out of breath.

He went to the window and looked out. The car which he had hired for the occasion was still standing at the door, and he distinguished Selby talking to the chauffeur.

"Listen you," he said, "and especially you, Crewe. You're too trusting with these females. Maybe Lollie's speaking the truth, but it is just as likely she's lying. I'm not going to take your corroboration, you know, Crewe," he said. "We've got to depend on her word. There's nobody else can speak for her, is there?"

Before Crewe could speak the colonel was answered.

"Jack o' Judgment! Poor old Jack o' Judgment! He'll speak for Lollie!"

The colonel looked up with a curse. There was nobody in the room, but the voice had been louder than ever he had heard it before. It seemed as though it emanated from a disembodied spirit that was floating through the air. There was a knock at the outer door.

CHAPTER XXXIII
WHERE THE VOICE LIVED

"Open it," said the colonel in a low voice; "open it, Crewe." He pulled open the drawer and took out something. "And if it is Jack o' Judgment—"

Crewe opened the door, his heart beating at a furious rate, but it was Selby who came into the room and faced the half leveled gun of the colonel.

"What do you want?" asked Boundary quickly. "You fool, I told you not to lose sight of her!"

"But when is she coming down?" asked Selby. "I've been waiting there all this time, and there's a policeman at the corner of the street. I wondered whether you had seen him, too."

"Not come down?" said the colonel. "She left here five minutes ago!"

Selby shook his head.

"She hasn't come down," he said, "and I've certainly not passed her on the stairs. Is there any other way out?"

"No way that she could use," said the colonel, shaking his head. "I've had new locks put on all the doors."

He thought a moment. "If she hasn't come down she went up."

They went up the stairs together and searched, first Pinto's flat, and then the storerooms and empty apartments on the floor higher up.

"Go down to the door and wait, in case she tries to get out," said the colonel.

He returned to the room with the two men, and they looked at one another in frank astonishment.

"Have you any idea what's happened, Crewe?" asked the colonel suspiciously.

"No idea in the world," said Crewe.

"But she went downstairs," said the colonel; "I heard the alarm click."

"The alarm?" questioned Crewe.

"I've got a buzzer under one of the treads of the stairs," said the colonel; "it is useful to know when people are coming up. It went off about twenty seconds after she left."

Ten minutes passed, and Selby returned to say that the policeman had been making inquiries as to whom the car belonged.

"You'd better get it away," said the colonel, "and send away your men."

"They've gone," said the other. "I wasn't taking any risks."

He disappeared to carry out the colonel's instructions, and they heard the whine of the moving car.

Boundary unlocked a cabinet and took out a full decanter of whisky. Without a word he poured three stiff doses into as many glasses and filled them with soda. Each man was thinking, and thinking after his own interests.

Boundary looked up and saw the dagger which Pinto had thrown. It was still embedded in the wall.

"It isn't enough that I should have Jack o' Judgment messing my room about," he said, "but you must do something to the same wall! Pull it out and don't let me see it again, Pinto."

The Portuguese smiled sheepishly, walked to the wall and gripped the handle. Evidently the point had embedded in a lath, for the knife did not move. He pulled again, exerting all his strength, and this time succeeded in extracting not only the knife but a large portion of the plaster and a strip of the wall paper.

"You fool!" said the colonel angrily. "See what you have done! Jumping Moses!"

He walked to the wall and stared, for the dislodgment of plaster and paper had revealed three round, black disks, set flush with the plaster and only separated from the room by the wall-paper, which had been stripped.

"Jumping Moses!" said the colonel softly. "Detectaphones!"

He took Pinto's knife from his hand and pried one of the disks loose. It was attached to a wire which was embedded in the plaster, and this the colonel severed with a stroke of the knife.

"This is the business end of a microphone," he said.

"The voice!" gasped Pinto; and the colonel nodded.

"Of course. I was mad not to guess that," he said; "that's how he heard and that's how he spoke. Now, we're going to get to the bottom of this."

With a knife he slashed the plaster and exposed three wires that led straight downward and apparently through the floor. The colonel rested and eyed the debris thoughtfully.

"What is under this flat? Lee's office, isn't it? Of course—Lee's!" he said. "I'm the fool!"

He handed the knife back to Pinto, took an electric torch from his pocket and led the way from the flat. They passed down the half darkened stairs to the floor beneath, on which was situated the three sets of offices. The colonel took a bunch of keys and tried them on the door of the surveyor's office. Presently he found one that fitted, and the door opened. He fumbled about for the electric switch, found it and flooded the room with light. It was a very ordinary clerk's office, with a small counter, the flap of which was raised. Inside the flap he saw something white on the floor, and, stooping, picked it up. It was a lady's handkerchief.

"L," he read. "That sounds like Lollie. Do you know this, Crewe?"

Crewe took the handkerchief and nodded.

"That is Lollie's," he said shortly.

"I thought so. This is where she was when we were looking for her. Here with Jack o' Judgment, eh? Let's try the inner office."

The inner office was locked, but he had no difficulty in gaining admission. Inside this was a private office which was simply furnished and had in one corner what appeared to be a telephone box. He opened the glass door and flashed his lamp inside. There was a little desk, a pair of receivers fastened to a headpiece, and a small vulcanite transmitter.

"This is where he sat," said the colonel meditatively, pointing to a stool, "and this"—he lifted up the earpieces—"is how he heard all our very interesting conversations. Go upstairs, Pinto. I want to try this transmitter."

He fixed the receiver to his ears and waited, and presently he heard distinctly the sound of Pinto closing the door of the room upstairs. Then he spoke through the receiver.

"Do you hear me, Pinto?"

"I hear you distinctly," said Pinto's voice.

"Speak a little lower. Carry on a conversation with yourself and let me try to hear you."

Pinto obeyed. He recited something from the Orpheum revue, a line or two of a song, and the colonel heard distinctly every syllable. He replaced the earpieces where he had found them, closed the door of the box and that of the outer office, and led the way upstairs. The whisky still stood upon the table and he lifted a glass and drained it at a draught.

"If you're a linguist, Crewe, you'll have heard of the phrase: *'Sauve qui peut.'* It means 'Git!' And that's the advice I'm giving and taking. Tomorrow we'll meet to liquidate the Boundary gang and split the gang fund."

He turned his companions out to get what sleep they could. For him there was little sleep that night. Before the dawn came he was at Twickenham, examining a big motor launch that lay in a boat house. It was the launch which should have carried Lollie Marsh and Selby on their river and sea journey. It was provisioned and ready for the trip, but first the colonel had to take from a locker in the stern of the boat a small black box and disconnect the wires from certain terminals before he stopped a little clock which ticked noisily. He had timed his bomb to go off at four in the morning, by which time, he calculated, Lollie Marsh and her escort would be well out to sea. For the colonel regarded no evidence that might be brought against him as unimportant.

CHAPTER XXXIV
CONSCIENCE MONEY

The colonel was sleeping peacefully when Pinto rushed into his bedroom with the news. He was awake in a second and sat up in bed.

"What!" he said incredulously.

"Selby's arrested," said Pinto, his voice shaking. "It's awful! It's dreadful! Colonel, we've got to get away today. I tell you they'll have us——"

"Just shut up for a minute, will you?" replied the colonel swinging out of bed and searching for his slippers with the detached interest of one who was hearing a little gossip from the morning papers. "What is the charge against him?"

"Loitering with intent to commit a felony," said Pinto. "They took him to the station and searched his bag. He had brought a bag with him in preparation for the journey. And what do you think they found?"

"I know what they found," said the colonel; "a complete kit of burglar's tools. The fool must have left his bag in the hall, and of course Jack o' Judgment planted the stuff. It is simple!"

"What can we do?" Pinto asked pleadingly. "What can we do?"

"Engage the best lawyer you can. Do it through one of your pals," said the colonel. "It will go hard with Selby. He's had a previous conviction."

"Do you think he'll talk?" asked Pinto.

He looked yellow and haggard and he had much to do to keep his teeth from chattering.

"Not for a day or two," said the colonel, "and we shall be away by then. Does Crewe know?"

Pinto shook his head.

"I haven't any time to run about after that swine," he said impatiently.

"Well, you'd better do a little running now, then," said the colonel; "we may want his signature for the bank."

"What are you going to do?"

"I'm going to draw every penny we've got, and I advise you to do the same. I suppose you haven't made any preparations to get away, have you?"

"No," lied Pinto, remembering with thankfulness that he had received a letter that morning from the aviator Cartwright, telling him that the machine was in good order and ready to start at any moment; "no, I have never thought of getting away, colonel. I've always said I'll stick to the colonel—"

"H'm!" said the colonel, and there was no very great faith in Pinto revealed in his grunt.

Crewe came along an hour later and seemed the least perturbed of the lot.

"Here's the check book," said the colonel, taking it from a drawer. "Now the balance we have"—he consulted a little waistcoat pocket notebook, "is eighty-one thousand, three hundred and seventeen pounds. I suggest we draw eighty thousand pounds, split it three parts and separate tonight."

"What about your own private account?" asked Pinto.

"That's my business," said the colonel sharply. He filled in the check, signed his name with a flourish and handed the pen to Crewe.

Crewe put his name beneath, saw that the check was made payable to bearer, and handed the book to the colonel.

"Here, Pinto." The colonel detached the form and blotted it. "Take a taxicab, see Ferguson, and bring the money straight back here. Or, better still, go on to the New York Guaranty and change it into American money."

"Do you trust Pinto?" asked Crewe bluntly after the other had gone.

"No," said the colonel; "I don't trust Pinto or you. And if Pinto had plenty of time I shouldn't expect to see that money again. But he's got to be back here in a couple of hours and I don't think he can get away before. Besides, at the present juncture," he reflected, "he wouldn't run away because he doesn't know how serious the position is."

"Where are you going, colonel?" asked Crewe curiously. "I mean, when you get away from here."

Boundary's broad face creased with smiles.

"What a foolish question to ask!" he said. "Timbuctoo, Tangier, South America, Buenos Aires, Madrid, China—"

"Which means you're not going to tell, and I don't blame you," said Crewe.

"Where are you going?" asked the colonel. "If you're a fool you'll tell me." Crewe shrugged his shoulders.

"To jail, I guess," he said bitterly; and the colonel chuckled.

"Maybe you've answered the question you put to me," he said, "but I'm going to make a fight first. Dan Boundary is too old in the bones and hates exercise too much to survive the keen air and the bracing employment of Dartmoor—if we ever get there," he said ominously.

"What do you mean?" demanded Crewe.

"I mean that, when they've photographed Selby and circulated his picture, somebody is certain to recognize him as the man who handed the glass of water over the heads of the crowd when Hanson was killed."

"Was it Selby?" gasped Crewe. "I wasn't in on it. I knew nothing about it." The colonel laughed again.

"Of course you're not in on anything," he bantered. "Yes, it was Selby; and it is ten chances to one that the usher would recognize him again if he saw him. That would mean—well, they don't hang folks at Dartmoor." He looked at his watch again. "I expect Pinto will be about an hour and a half," he said. "You will excuse me," he added with elaborate politeness; "I have a lot of work to do."

He cleared the drawers of his writing table by the simple process of pulling them out and emptying their contents upon the top. He went through these with remarkable rapidity, throwing the papers one by one into the fire; and he was engaged in this occupation when Pinto returned.

"Back already?" said the colonel in surprise; and then, after a glance at the other's face, he demanded: "What's wrong?"

Pinto was incapable of speech. He just put the check down upon the table.

"Haven't they cashed it?" asked the colonel with a frown.

"They can't cash it," said Pinto in a hollow voice; "there's no money there." The colonel picked up the check.

"So there's no money there to meet it?" he said softly. "And why is there no money there to meet it?"

"Because it was drawn out three days ago. I thought—" said Pinto incoherently. "I saw Ferguson and he told me that a check for the full amount came through from the Bank of England."

"In whose favor was it drawn?"

Pinto cleared his throat.

"In favor of the chancellor of the exchequer," he said. "That's why Ferguson passed it without question. He said that otherwise he would have sent a note to you."

"The chancellor of the exchequer?" asked the colonel. "What does it mean?"

"Look here! Ferguson showed it to me himself." He took a copy of the *Times* from his pocket and laid it on the table, pointing out the paragraph with trembling fingers.

It was in the advertisement column and it was brief:

"The chancellor of the exchequer desires to acknowledge the receipt of eighty-one thousand pounds conscience money from Colonel D. B."

"Conscience money!"

The colonel sat back in his chair and laughed softly. He was genuinely amused.

"Of course we can get this back," he said at last. "We can explain to the chancellor of the exchequer the trick that has been played upon us, but that means delay, and at the moment delay is really dangerous. I suppose both you fellows have money of your own. I know Pinto has. How do you stand, Crewe?"

"I have a little," said Crewe, "but honestly I was depending upon my share of the gang fund."

"What about you, colonel?" asked Pinto meaningly. "If I may suggest it we should pool our money and divide."

The colonel smiled.

"Don't be silly," he said tersely. "I doubt whether my balance at the bank is more than a couple of thousand pounds."

"But what about your private safe-deposit box?" persisted Pinto. "Aha! You didn't know I knew that, did you? As a matter of fact, Ferguson told me that—"

"What the devil does Ferguson mean by discussing my business?" said the colonel wrathfully. "What did he tell you?"

"He told me that the package was received and that he had put it with the other in your safe."

"Package?" The colonel's voice was quiet, almost inaudible. "The package was received? When was the package received?"

"Yesterday," said Pinto. "He said it came and he put it with the other. Now what have you got in—"

But the colonel was walking toward his bedroom with rapid strides. Presently he reappeared with his hat and his coat on.

"Come with me, Crewe, we'll go down to the bank," he said. "You stay here, Pinto, and report anything that happens."

When they were on their way he confided to the other:

"I have a little money put aside and I'm willing to finance you. You haven't been a bad fellow, Crewe. The only rotten turn you ever did us was introducing that fellow, Snow Gregory, and you didn't even do that, for I had met him before you brought him from Monte—Which reminds me. Have you found anything about him?"

"I have a letter here from Oxford," said Crewe, putting his hand in his pocket.

"I hadn't opened my letters when Pinto came. You'll find all the news there, if there is any news."

He handed the envelope to the other, and the colonel transferred it to his pocket.

"That'll keep," he said. "What was I talking about? Oh, yes—Gregory. The whole of this business has come about through Gregory. Gregory made Jack o' Judgment and Jack o' Judgment has ruined us."

He sprang from the taxi at the door of the bank with an agile step and went straight to the manager's office. Without any preliminary he began.

"What is this package that came for me yesterday, Ferguson?"

The manager looked surprised.

"It was an ordinary package, similar to that which you put in the safe the other day. It was sealed and wrapped, and had your name on it. I rather wondered you hadn't brought it yourself, but it was put into your safe in the presence of two clerks."

"I'd like to see it," said the colonel.

Ferguson led the way down the stairs to the vault and snapped back the lock of box twenty. As he did so Crewe was conscious of a faint musty odor.

"I smell something," said the colonel suspiciously.

He reached his hand into the box and pulled open the long drawer, and as he did so a cloud of sickly smelling vapor rose from its interior. For the first time Crewe heard Boundary groan. He pulled the drawer out under the light and looked in. There was nothing but a black mass of pulp, out of which glinted and gleamed a dozen pin points of light.

With a howl of rage the colonel turned the contents upon the stone floor of the vault and raked it over with the end of his walking stick. The diamonds were intact, and they at least were something; but the greater part of eight hundred thousand dollars was indistinguishable from any other kind of paper that had been treated with one of the most destructive acids known to chemical science.

CHAPTER XXXV
THE AVIATOR

The colonel wiped his burned and discolored hands after he had dropped the last diamond into a medicine bottle which the bank manager happened to have in the room.

"That's something saved from the wreck, at any rate," he said.

He had gone suddenly old and his mouth trembled, as many a younger mouth had trembled in despair so that Colonel Boundary might become a rich man.

"Something saved from the wreck," he repeated slowly.

The manager's grave eyes were fixed on his.

"I'm not blaming you, Ferguson," said the colonel. "It was a plot to ruin me, and it succeeded."

"What do you think happened?" asked the troubled Ferguson.

"The second package was a box filled with a very strong acid," said the colonel. "Probably the box was made of soft metal, through which the acid would eat in a few hours. It was placed in the safe, and in time the corrosive worked through."

He shrugged his shoulders and left the room without another word.

"Thirty-five years' work that represents, Crewe," he said as they were driving back to the flat; "thirty-five years of risk and thought and organization, and ended in pulp that burns your fingers when you touch it.

"Jack o' Judgment!" he went on wonderingly. "Jack o' Judgment! Well, he's had his judgment, all right, and I'm going to have mine. You needn't tell Pinto what happened this morning. Leave him guessing. He's got a pretty thick bank roll, and I'll agree to that grand scheme of his for sharing."

The thought seemed to cheer him, and by the time they reached the flat he was almost jovial.

"Well, what's the news?" asked Pinto eagerly.

"Fine," said the colonel. "Everything is as it should be."

"Stop fooling," replied the other. "What is the news?"

"The news," said the colonel, "is that I've decided to agree to your unselfish suggestion."

"What's that?" said the unsuspicious Pinto.

"That we should pool and divide."

"Jack o' Judgment's got your money, too!" said Pinto, who cherished no illusions about the colonel's generosity.

"How well he knows me!" said Boundary. "Now come, Pinto; we're all in this, sink or swim. I told Crewe going down that I intended dividing; didn't I, Crewe?"

"You said something like that," said Crewe cautiously.

"Now we'll pool our money," said the colonel, "and divide it three ways. I'll make a fair proposition. We'll divide it into four, and the man who puts in the most shall take two shares. Is it a bet?"

"I suppose so," said Pinto reluctantly. "What is the truth about your money? Did Jack o' Judgment get it?"

"I hadn't any money," said the colonel blandly. "I've about a thousand pounds hidden away in this room; that is all—if Jack hasn't been in."

He unlocked the safe and made an inspection.

"Yes, a little over a thousand, if anything. How much have you, Crewe?"

"Three thousand," said Crewe.

"That makes four thousand. Now what have you got, Pinto?"

"I've about five thousand," said Pinto, trying to appear unconcerned.

The colonel made a little whistling noise through his teeth.

"Bring fifty," he said. "I'm dead serious, Pinto. Bring fifty!"

"But how can I get it?" demanded the other frantically.

"Get it," said the colonel. "It is highly probable that it will be no use to any of us. Let us at least have the illusion of being well off."

In greater leisure than either of her three companions in crime were exhibiting, Lollie Marsh was preparing to take her departure to New York. She was packing at leisure in her cozy flat on Tavistock Avenue, stopping now and again to consider the problem of the superfluous article of clothing—a problem which presents itself to all packers.

Between whiles she arrested her labors to think of something else. Kneeling down by the side of her trunk, she would give herself up to long reveries which ended in a sigh and the resumption of her packing.

By the commonly accepted standards of civilization she was a wicked woman, but there are degrees of wickedness. She had searched her mind to recall all the qualms she had felt in her long association with the Boundary gang, and took an unusual pleasure in her strange collection. She remembered when she had refused to be drawn into the Crotin fraud; she recalled her stormy interview with the colonel, when she declined to take a part in the ruining of young Debenham.

But mostly she was glad that she had never gone any further to carry out the colonel's instructions in regard to Stafford King. Not that she would have succeeded, she told herself, with a little smile, but she was glad she had never seriously tried.

Her mind switched to Crewe and switched back again. Crewe was the one face she did not wish to see, the one member of the gang that she put aside from the others and willfully veiled. Crewe had always been kind to her, always courteous, her champion in all bad times. She wondered what had brought him down to his present level, and why a man possessed of education, and who at one time, as she knew, had been an officer in a crack regiment, should have fallen so readily under Boundary's influence.

She made a little face and went on with her packing. She did not want to think about Crewe for obvious reasons. Yet, as he had said—but he hadn't said, she told herself.

She took a delight in torturing herself with pictures of her own humiliation, though she may have counted it to the good that she was capable of feeling humiliated at all. She finished her trunk, squeezed in the last article; and locked down the lid. She looked at her wrist watch, it was half past nine. Stafford King had not asked to see her, and she had the evening free.

She had only spoken the truth when she had told Boundary that the police chief had made no inquiries as to the gang. Stafford King knew human nature rather well, and he would not make the mistake of questioning her. Or perhaps it was because he did not wish to spoil the value of his gifts by fixing a price—the price of treachery.

She wondered what the colonel was doing, and Pinto—and Crewe. She stamped her foot impatiently. She was indulging in the kind of insanity of which hitherto she had shown no symptoms. She looked at her watch again and then remembered the Orpheum. It was a favorite house of hers. She could always get a free box, if there was one vacant, and she had spent many of her lonely evenings in that way. She had always declined Pinto's offer to share his own, and of late he had not been inviting her.

She dressed and took a taxi to the Orpheum. The booking-office clerk knew her and, without asking her desires, drew a slip from the ticket rack.

"I can give you box C tonight, Miss Marsh," he said. "That is the one above the 'governor's'."

The governor was Pinto.

"Have you a good house?"

The youth shook his head.

"We are not having the houses we had when Miss White was here," he said. "What's become of her, miss?"

"I don't know," said Lollie shortly.

She had to pass to the back of Pinto's box to reach the little staircase which led to the box above. She thought she heard voices, and, stopping in the door, listened. Perhaps Crewe had come down or the colonel. But it was not Crewe's voice she heard. The door was slightly ajar, and the man who was talking was evidently on the point of departure, because she glimpsed his hand upon the handle and his voice was so distinct that he must have been quite near her.

"—three o'clock in the morning. You can't miss the aerodrome. It is a mile out of Bromley on the main road and on the right. You will see three red lamps burning in a triangle."

The aerodrome! She put her hand to her mouth to suppress an exclamation. Pinto was talking, but his voice was a mumble.

"Very good," said the strange voice. "I can carry three or four passengers if you like. There's plenty of room. Of course, if you're by yourself, so much the better. I shall expect you at three o'clock. The weather's fine."

The door opened, and she crouched against the wall so that the opening door hid her, and heard Pinto call the man back by name.

"Cartwright," she repeated; "Cartwright. A mile out of Bromley on the main road. Three lamps in a red triangle!"

She was going to slip up the stairs, but the door had closed on Cartwright, and making a swift decision, she passed his box and came again into the vestibule of the theater. Presently she saw the man appear. She guessed it was he by the smile on his face, and when he said "Good night" to the attendant at the barrier she recogsized his voice. She followed him, but let him get outside the theater before she spoke to him. Then suddenly she laid her hand on his arm.

"Isn't it Mr. Cartwright?" she asked.

He looked round into her smiling face in surprise, taking off his hat.

"That is my name," he said with a smile. "I don't remember—"

"Oh, I'm a friend of Mr. Silva," she said. "I've heard a lot about you."

"Oh, indeed?" said he.

He was a little puzzled because he thought that the projected flight was a dead secret, and she guessed his thoughts.

"You won't tell Mr. Silva I told you? He begged me not to repeat it to anybody, even to you. But I know he's leaving tomorrow morning; isn't he?"

He nodded.

"I know an awful lot," she said; and then: "Won't you come and have supper with me? I'm starving!"

Cartwright hesitated. He had not expected so charming a diversion and really there was no reason why he should not accept the invitation. He was not due at Bromley until early in the morning, and the girl was young and pretty and evidently a friend of his employer. It was she who hailed the taxi, and they drove to a select little restaurant at the back of Shaftesbury Avenue.

"You're not seeing Pinto—I mean, Mr. Silva—again tonight, are you?" she asked.

"No; I'm not seeing him until—well, until I see him." He smiled again.

"Well, I want to tell you something."

He thought she was charmingly embarrassed, and in truth she was to invent the story she had to tell.

"You know why Mr. Silva is leaving England in such a hurry?"

He nodded. She wished she knew, too, or had the slightest inkling of the yarn which Pinto had spun. And then the man enlightened her.

"Political," he said.

"Exactly; political," she said easily. "But you will realize that it is not necessarily he who is making this flight."

"I did understand that he was making the flight himself," said the aviator in surprise.

"But"—she was desperate now—"has he never told you of the other gentleman who was coming, the other political person who really must go to Portugal at once?"

"No, he certainly did not," said Cartwright; "he told me distinctly that he was going himself."

The girl leaned back in her chair, baffled but thoughtful.

"Oh, of course he told you that," she said with a knowing smile. "You see, there are some things he is not allowed to tell you. But do not be surprised if you have two passengers instead of one."

"I shan't be surprised; I shall be pleased. The machine will carry half a dozen," said Cartwright readily, "but I certainly thought—"

"Wait till you see him," said the girl, waving a finger with mock solemnity.

He found her a cheerful companion through the meal, but there were certain intervals of abstraction in her cheerfulness, intervals when she was thinking very rapidly and reconstructing the plan which Pinto had made. So he was one of the rats who were deserting the sinking ship and leaving the colonel and Crewe to face the music. And Crewe—that was the thought uppermost in her mind.

When she parted from the pilot she had only one thought—to warn the colonel of Pinto's treachery—and to warn Crewe. And somehow Crewe seemed to bulk most importantly at that moment.

CHAPTER XXXVI
LOLLIE PROPOSES

What should she do? It was her sense of loyalty which brought the colonel first to her mind. She must warn him. She went into a tube-station telephone box and rang his apartment, but received no answer. Her quest for Crewe had as little result. She drove off to the flat, thinking that possibly the telephone might be out of order, or that they would have returned by the time she reached there, but there was no answer to her ring. She went out again into the street in despair and walked slowly toward Regent Street. Then she saw two people ahead of her and recognized the swing of the colonel's shoulders. She broke into a run and overtook them. The colonel swung round as she uttered his name and peered at her.

"Lollie!" he said in surprise, and he looked past her as though seeking some police shadow.

"I have something important to tell you," she said. "Let us go up here."

They turned into a deserted side street, and rapidly she told her story.

"So Pinto's getting out, is he?" said the colonel thoughtfully. "Well, it is no more than I expected. An aeroplane, too! Well, that's enterprising. I thought of something of the sort, but there's nowhere I could go, except to America." He dropped his head onto his chest and was considering something. "Thank you, Lollie," he said simply. "I'm glad that you didn't go with Selby; you would never have got to the Continent alive."

He said this in an ordinary conversational tone, and the girl gasped. She did not ask him for an explanation and he offered none. Crewe, standing in the background, looked at the man with something like bewilderment.

"And now I think you'd better make a real get-away and not trust to the police," said the colonel. "Maybe with the best intentions in the world Stafford King can't save you if I happen to be arrested. And you, too, Crewe." He turned to the other.

"So Pinto is going, eh?" He bit his nether lip. "And that is why he promised to bring the fifty thousand tomorrow morning. Well, somehow I don't think Pinto will go." He spoke deliberately. "I don't think Pinto will go."

"It is too dangerous for you to stop him," said Crewe.

"I shall not try to stop him," said the other. "There's somebody besides myself on Pinto's track, and that somebody is going to pull him down."

"But why don't you escape, colonel?" she urged. "There is the aeroplane waiting at Bromley. We could easily persuade the man that Pinto sent us."

He shook his head.

"You take your own advice," he said, "and clear out tonight. Get her away,

Crewe. Don't worry about the police. You've got twenty-four hours. This is Pinto's night," he said between his teeth. "Pinto's night—the dirty hound!"

Slowly they paced the street together in silence. When they came to the end the colonel turned.

"I want to shake hands with you, Lollie. I shook hands with you once before, intending to send you to a very quick decease. You're carrying your money with you, aren't you, Crewe?"

"Yes," said the other.

"Good!" responded the colonel. "Now get away."

He took no other farewell, but turned abruptly and left them. Crewe was following him, but the girl caught his arm.

"Don't go," she said in a low voice; "don't you know the colonel better?"

"I hate leaving him like this," he said.

"So do I," said the girl quietly; "I've still got some decent feeling left. We're all in this together. We're all crooks as bad as we can possibly be, and if he's used us we've been willing tools. What is your Christian name?" she asked.

He looked at her in surprise.

"Jack," he said. "What a weird question to ask!"

"Isn't it?" she said with a laugh but a little catch in her throat. "Only we're to be comrades and stick to one another, and I hate calling you by your surname, so I'm going to call you Jack."

It was his turn to be amused. They walked in the opposite direction to that which the colonel had taken. "You're very quiet," she said after a while.

"Aren't I?" He laughed.

"Have I offended you?" she asked quickly. "Was it wrong to call you Jack? Oh, yes, somebody else must have called you Jack."

"No, no, it isn't that," he said, "but I haven't been called by my Christian name for years and years, and somehow it seems to span all the bad times and take me back to the—the—"

"The 'Jack' days?" she suggested, and he nodded.

Then after another period of silence he said:

"This is a queer ending to it all, isn't it?" Her heart skipped a beat.

"Ending?" she whispered. "No, no, not ending! It may be the beginning of a new life and a new way of living that life. I'm not getting sentimental," she added quickly. "Only I've faith that there's something better in life than I've ever found."

"I should think there is," said Crewe. "It couldn't be much worse, could it?"

"I haven't been bad," she said, "not bad like you probably think I have."

"I never thought you were bad," he said; "you were just a victim like the rest of them. You were only a kid when you started working for the colonel, weren't you?"

She nodded.

"Well, there's a chance for you, Lollie. Your passage is booked and all that sort of thing. Have you sufficient money?"

"I've plenty of money," she said.

"Fine!" He dropped his hand lightly on her shoulder. "There's a big chance for you, my girl."

"And for you?" she asked.

He laughed.

"There is no chance for me at all," he said simply; "they'll take me and they'll take Pinto, and last of all they'll take the colonel. It is written," he added philosophically. "Why, what is the matter?"

She stood stock-still and was holding onto his arm with both hands.

"You mustn't say that, you mustn't say that!" she said brokenly. "It isn't finished for you, Jack. There's a chance to get out, and the colonel has told you there's a chance. He meant it. He knows much more than we do. If you've got murder on your soul, or something worse, if you feel that you're altogether so bad that there isn't a chance for you, that there's no goodness in your life which can be expanded, why, just wait and take what's coming. But if you feel that in another land, with—with some one who loves you by your side—"

Her voice broke.

"Why, Lollie," he said gently, "you don't mean—"

"I'm just as shameless as I've ever been," she said, "and I'm proposing to—to—" She stopped, blushing. Then she took a fresh start. "I'm going away to a new land and a new life. Do you want—will you—"

"Will I go?" he asked.

She nodded.

"I'll go anywhere with that prospect in sight." He slipped his arm round her shoulders, and, bending, kissed her on the cheek.

CHAPTER XXXVII
THE FALL OF PINTO

While Pinto was putting the finishing touches to his scheme of flight, the colonel paced his room, whistling jerkily. He was restless and nervous, and rendered all the more irritable by the disappearance of his servant, a minor member of the gang, who had been a participant in every act of villainy, and who had been in charge of the arrangements for the abduction of Maisie White. Twice in the course of the evening he wandered through the hall, opened the outer door, and looked out onto the landing.

On the first occasion there was nothing to see, but on the second it was only by the narrowest margin of time that he failed to detect a dark figure moving noiselessly up the stairs and disappearing onto the second landing. The man above heard the door open and close again, and stood waiting. Then, when no sound reached him, he moved to the door of Pinto's flat, opened it, deposited the suit case which he was carrying in the hall, and closed the door softly behind him.

He was within for about a quarter of an hour; then he reappeared, and, still carrying his suit case, passed swiftly down the stairs and out into the street. The clock struck half past nine as he disappeared, and a quarter of an hour later Stafford King received by special messenger a communication which gave him something to think about. He read it through twice, then called up the first commissioner and gave him the gist of it.

"That's the third time we've had this sort of message," he said.

"The others have proved right," said the commissioner's voice; "why shouldn't this?"

"But it seems incredible," said Stafford in perplexity. "We've been watching these people for years and we've never found them with the goods."

"I should certainly act on it, King, if I were you," said the commissioner. "Let me know what happens. Of course you may make a mistake, but you must take a chance on that."

Pinto had a lot of business to do at the theater that night. For a week he had not banked the theater's earnings, but had converted them into paper money, and now he took from his safe the last penny he could carry. It was half past eleven when he arrived at his club, where supper had been prepared for him. He paid the bill from notes he had taken from the bank that day. Presently the waiter came back.

"I beg your pardon, sir, but the cashier says that this note is a bad one."

"A bad one?" said Pinto in surprise, and took it in his hand.

There was no doubt whatever that the man was right. It was the most obvious forgery he had ever handled.

"Then I've been stung." He smiled. "Here's another."

He took the second note and examined it. That also was bad, as he could tell at a glance. In the tail pocket of his dress coat he had the money he had taken from the theater, and was able to settle the bill.

He was worried on the journey back to the flat. He had drawn a hundred pounds from the bank that morning in five-pound notes. He remembered putting them into his pocketbook and had had no occasion to disturb them since. It was unlikely that the bank would have given him such obvious forgeries. He was stepping from the taxi when the awful truth dawned on him. The notes had been planted, the forgeries substituted for the good paper! He was putting his hand in his pocket, intending to take out the money and push it down the nearest drain, when he was gripped.

"Sorry and all that," said a voice.

He turned round, shaking like an aspen.

"Stafford King!" he said dully.

"Stafford King it is. I have a warrant for your arrest, Silva, on a charge of counterfeiting and passing forged notes. Bring him up to his rooms."

The colonel heard the noise on the stairs and came to the door. He stood, a silent spectator, watching with unmoved face the procession as it passed up to the floor above.

"I want your key," said Stafford; and humbly the Portuguese handed it to him.

Stafford opened the door and snapped on the light. "Bring him in," he said to the detective who held Pinto. "What room is this?"

"My dining room," said Pinto faintly.

Stafford entered the room, turning on the light as he did so.

"Hello, Pinto!" he said.

Pinto could only look.

The table was littered with copper plates and ink rollers. There was a thick pad of counterfeit money on one corner of the table, held down by a paper weight; little bottles of acids were scattered about, and near the table was a small lever press, so small that a man might carry it in a corner of his hand bag.

"I think I have got you, Pinto," said Stafford King; and Pinto Silva nodded before he fell limply into the arms of his captor.

Maisie White had gone to bed early. The bell rang three times before she awoke. She slipped into a dressing gown and, going to the window, leaned out. She looked down upon the upturned face of a girl, and in spite of the distance and the darkness of the night, recognized her. The man who stood in the background, however, she could not for the moment place. Nevertheless, she did not hesitate to go downstairs.

"Is that Miss White?" asked the girl.

"Yes. It is Lollie Marsh, isn't it? Won't you come in?"

Lollie was hesitant.

"Yes," she said after a while, and they went upstairs together. "I'm very sorry I disturbed you, Miss White, but it is a matter which can't very well wait. You know that Mr. Stafford King has been kind to me?"

Maisie nodded. She was looking at the girl with interest, and was surprised to note how pretty she was. She could not forget what Lollie Marsh had done for her that dreadful night at the nursing home, and if the truth be told, she had inspired the assistance which Stafford had been giving the girl.

"Mr. King has booked my passage to America, as you probably know," Lollie went on, "but at the last moment I have been obliged to change my plans."

"I'm sorry to hear that," said the girl; "I was hoping that you'd get away before—"

"I am hoping to get away before"—Lollie smiled faintly—"but, you see, one has to be very quick, because things are moving at such a rapid rate. They arrested Pinto tonight—we only just heard of it."

"Arrested Silva?" said the girl in surprise. "That is news to me. What is the charge?"

"I didn't quite understand what the charge was. I know he's arrested," said

Lollie. "And the colonel has advised me to get out as quickly as I can. And there's a big chance for me, Miss White. I'm going to be married!"

She blurted the words out, and Maisie stared at her. Somehow she had never thought of Lollie Marsh as a person who would get married, and it was amazing to see the confusion and shyness into which her confession had thrown her.

"I congratulate you with all my heart," said Maisie. "Who is the fortunate man?"

"I can't tell you. Yes, I will," said the girl; "I'll trust you—I'm marrying Jack Crewe."

"Crewe? I remember. Mr. King spoke about him. But isn't he one of the—isn't he a friend of the colonel's?"

Lollie nodded.

"Yes, but we're going away tonight. That is why I came to see you."

Maisie White clasped the girl's hands in hers.

"You yourself are facing a great happiness and a beautiful new life," pleaded Lollie, her eyes filling with tears; "can't you feel some sympathy with me? For I want love and happiness and security more even than you, because you have never known anything of the dreadful apprehensions and uncertainties such as I have passed through. And I want you to help me in this. I'm not going to ask you to influence Mr. King to do anything but his duty. But I want just a chance for Jack."

Maisie shook her head.

"I don't know that I can promise that," she said. "Mr. King has always spoken of your friend as one of the least dangerous of the gang. When are you leaving?"

"Tonight."

"Tonight? But how?"

"That's a secret."

"But it is a secret I won't reveal." Maisie smiled.

"By aeroplane," said Lollie after a moment's hesitation, and told the story of Pinto's preparation.

"You'd better not tell me where you're going," warned Maisie, but she didn't stop Lollie in time. "Well, I wish you luck and I'll do my best for you."

She stooped and kissed the girl.

"There's one warning I want to give you, Miss White," said Lollie as she stood in the doorway. "The colonel is a desperate man, and I don't think, somehow, that he's coming through this with his life. He's been a good friend of mine up to a point and according to his lights, but you've been good and Mr. King has been more than good. Beware of the colonel now that you have him at bay! That is all!"

Then she was gone.

CHAPTER XXXVIII
OLD FILMS

They brought Pinto Silva into the magistrate's court at Bow Street the following morning in a condition of collapse. The man was dazed by his misfortune, incapable of answering the questions which were put to him, or even of instructing the exasperated solicitor who had been with him for an hour.

By the solicitor's side was a gray-faced, shrunken man, whose clothes did not seem to fit him and who at the end of the proceedings whispered something into the lawyer's ear. But the application which was made for bail was rejected. The evidence was too damning, and the knowledge that the prisoner was not English and that it would be impossible to extradite him if he managed to make his escape to another country, all helped to influence the magistrate in his refusal.

Colonel Boundary did not speak to the man under arrest or as much as look at him. He got out of court after the proceedings had terminated, the cynosure of every policeman's eye, and drove back to his apartments. He had not heard from Crewe or Lollie that morning, and he guessed that the two had left by aeroplane. So he was alone, he thought, and the very knowledge had the effect of stiffening him.

He could go through the remainder of his papers at his leisure, without fear of interruption. The lesser members of the gang had been controlled by Selby or Crewe, and they would not approach him directly, but he did not doubt that there were a score of little men waiting to jump into the witness box the moment he was caught, but he had by no means given up hope of escaping.

For days he had carried in his pocket the means of disguise—a safety razor, scissors, and a small bottle of a solution to darken his face.

Despite his sixty-one years, he was a healthy and virile man, capable of undergoing hardships if the necessity arose, but, above all, he had a plan and an alternative plan.

He finished the destruction of his correspondence, and then began to search his pocket for any stray letters which he might have put away absent-mindedly. In making this search he came upon a long white envelope addressed to Crewe, and wondered how it had come into his possession. Then he remembered that Crewe had handed him a letter.

He looked at the postmark from the college town where Snow Gregory had once been a resident.

This was the report of the agents whom Crewe had sent down to discover the names of the men who had left the university in a certain year. Snow Gregory, who had been found shot in the streets of London, had left the college in that year. It was certain that it was a relative of Snow Gregory who was called Jack o' Judgment and who had taken upon himself the task of avenging the man's death.

What was Snow Gregory's real name? If he could find that, he might find Jack o' Judgment.

Slowly, as though with a sense that the great discovery was imminent, he tore open the letter and pulled out the three foolscap pages which, with a covering note, constituted the contents. There were two lists of names of graduates who had passed out in the year which, if Snow Gregory spoke the truth in a moment of unusual confidence, was the year of his leaving.

The colonel's finger traced the lines one by one, and he finished the first list without discovering a name which was familiar. He was halfway through the second list when he stopped and his finger jumped. For fully three minutes he sat glaring at the paper open-mouthed. Then:

"Merciful Heaven!" he whispered.

He sat there for the greater part of an hour, his chin on his hand, his eyes glued to the name. And all the time his active mind was running back through the years, piecing together the evidence which enabled him to identify Jack o' Judgment without any shadow of doubt.

He rose and went to his bookcase and took down volume after volume. They were mostly reference books, and for some time he searched in vain. Then he found a year book which gave him the data he wanted and he brought it back to the table and scribbled a few notes. These he read through and carefully burned.

He finished his labors with a bright look in his eye and strutted into his bedroom ten years younger in appearance than he had been that afternoon. He put out all the lights and sat for a little while in the shadow of the curtain, watching the street from the open window. At the corner of the block a street band was playing, and he was surprised that he had not noticed the fact.

Very keenly he scrutinized the street for some sign of a lurking figure, and once he saw a man walk past under the light of a street lamp and melt into the shadow of a doorway on the opposite side of the road. He went into his bedroom and brought back a pair of night glasses, and focused them upon the figure.

He chuckled and went out of the flat into the street, turning southward. He did not go far, however, before he stopped and looked back, and his patience was rewarded by the sight of a figure crossing the road and entering the building he had just left.

The colonel gave him time, and then retracted his steps. He took off his boots in the vestibule and went upstairs quietly. He was halfway up when he heard the soft thud of his own door closing and grinned again. He gave the intruder time to get inside before he, too, inserted his key, and, turning it without a sound, came into the darkened hall. There was a light in his room, and he heard the sound of a drawer being pulled open. Then he gripped the handle, and, flinging the door open, stepped in. The man who was looking through the desk sprang up in affright.

As Boundary had suspected, it was his former butler, the man who had deserted him the day before without a word. He was a big, heavy-jowled man of powerful build, and the momentary look of fright melted to a leer at the sight of the colonel's face.

"Well, Tom," said Boundary pleasantly, "come back for the pickings?"

"Something like that, guv'nor," said the other. "You don't blame me?"

"I've been pretty good to you, Tom," said the colonel.

"Ugh! I don't know that I've anything to thank you for."

Here was a man who a month before would have cringed at the colonel's up-raised finger.

"Oh, don't you, Tom?" said Boundary softly. "Come, come, that's not very grateful."

"What have I got to be grateful to you for?" demanded the man.

"Grateful that you're alive, Tom," said the colonel and the servant's face went hard.

"None of that, colonel," he retorted, "you can't afford to talk fresh with me. I know a great deal more about you than you suppose. You think I've got no brains."

"I know you have brains, Tom," said the colonel, "but you can't use 'em."

"Can't! Eh? I haven't been looking after you for four or five years and doing your dirty work, colonel, without picking up a little intelligence—and a little information! You'd look funny if they put me in the witness box!"

He was gaining courage at the very mildness of the man of whom he once stood in terror.

"So you've come for the pickings?" said the colonel ignoring the threat. "Well, help yourself."

He went to the sideboard, poured himself out a little whisky, and sat down by the window to watch the man search. Tom pulled open another drawer and closed it again.

"Now look here, colonel," he said; "I haven't made so much money out of this business as you have. Things are pretty bad with me, and I think the least you can do is to give me something to remember you by."

The colonel did not answer. Apparently his thoughts were wandering.

"Tom," he said after a while, "do you remember three months ago I bought a lot of old moving-picture films?"

"Yes, I remember," said the man, surprised at the change of subject. "What's that to do with it?"

"There were about ten boxes, weren't there?"

"A dozen, more likely," said the man impatiently. "Now look here, colonel, I—"

"Wait a moment, Tom. I'll discuss your share when you've given me a little help. Meeting you here—by the way, I saw you out of the window, skulking on the other side of the street has given me an idea. Where did you put those films?"

The man grinned.

"Are you starting a moving-picture company, colonel?"

"Something like that," replied Boundary; "it was the band that gave me the idea really. Do you hear what an infernal noise that drum makes?"

The man made a gesture of impatience.

"What is it you want?" he asked. "If you want the film, I put it in my pantry, underneath the silver cupboard. I suppose now that the partnership's broken up you don't object to me taking the silver? I might be starting a little house of my own."

"Certainly, certainly, you can take the silver," said the colonel genially. "Bring me the film."

The man was halfway out of the room when he turned round.

"No tricks, mind you," he said, "no doing funny business when my back's turned."

"I shall not move from the chair, Tom. You don't seem to trust me."

The ex-valet made two journeys before he deposited a dozen shallow tin boxes on the desk.

"There they are," he said. "Now tell me what's the game."

"First of all," said the colonel, "were you serious when you suggested that you knew something about me that would be worth a lot to the police? There goes that drum again, Tom. Do you know what use that drum is to me?"

"I don't know," replied the man. "Of course I meant what I said. And what's this stuff about the drum?"

"Why, the people in the street can hear nothing when that's going," said the colonel softly.

He put his hand in the inside of his coat, as though searching for a pocket-book, and so quick was he that the man, leaning over the table, did not see the weapon that killed him. Three times the colonel fired. The man slid in an inert heap to the ground.

"Might as well be hung for a sheep as a lamb, Tom," said the colonel, replacing the weapon, and turning the body over; he took the scarfpin from his own tie and fastened it in that of the dead man. Then he took his watch and chain from his pocket and slipped them in the waistcoat pocket of the other. He had a signet ring on his little finger, and this he transferred to the finger of the limp figure.

Then he began opening the boxes of old films and twisted their contents about the floor, pinning them to the curtains, twining them about the legs of the chairs, all the time whistling. He found a candle in the butler's pantry and planted it with a steady hand in the heap of celluloid coils. This he lighted with great care and went out, closing the door softly behind him. Half an hour later Albermarle Place was blocked with fire engines and a dozen horses were playing in vain upon the roaring furnace behind the gutted walls of Colonel Dan Boundary's residence.

Stafford King was an early caller at Doughty Street, and Maisie knew, both by the unusual hour of the visit and by the gravity of the visitor, that something extraordinary had happened.

"Well, Maisie," he said, "there's the end of the Boundary gang—the colonel is dead."

"Dead?" she said, open-eyed.

"We don't know what happened, but the theory is that he shot himself and set fire to the house. The body was found in the ruins, and I was able to identify some of the jewelry—you remember the police had it when he was arrested, and we kept a special note of it for future reference."

She heaved a long sigh.

"That's over at last. It is the end of a nightmare," she said, "a horrible, horrible nightmare. I wonder—"

"What do you wonder?"

"I wonder if this is also the end of Jack o' Judgment," she replied, "or whether he will continue working to bring to justice those people whom the law cannot touch."

"Heaven only knows," said Stafford, "but I'll admit that Jack o' Judgment has been a most useful person so far as we are concerned. We should never have collected Pinto or Selby, or even the colonel, but for Jack. By the way, there is no news of Crewe and the girl."

"I suppose they've reached their destination by now?" she asked.

"Oh, yes," said Stafford, "hours and days ago. Where were they going, by the way?"

She shook her head.

"I'm not going to tell you that."

"You needn't." Stafford smiled. "They've gone to Portugal. It was Pinto's machine and I don't suppose he had any other idea in the world than to get back to his own beloved land. By the way, it looks as though Pinto would get ten years. To satisfy myself in regard to Crewe, I telegraphed to an Englishman at Finisterre, who is a good friend of mine, and who lives in a wild and isolated spot somewhere near the lighthouse, and he sent me back a message to the effect that an aeroplane passed over Finisterre yesterday afternoon soon after lunch time. That must be friend Loilie."

She nodded.

"Do you know, I hope they get away. Is that rather dreadful of me?" she said.

He shook his head.

"No, I don't think so. I believe the chief shares your hope. He has queer views on things, and they irritate me sometimes. For example, he doesn't think that the colonel is dead."

"But I thought you had found the body?"

"He gets over that by saying that it isn't the body," said Stafford with a little laugh of annoyance. "It rather worries you after you have decided that you've rounded up the gang. I still believe that it is the colonel."

She thought a moment.

"I am inclined to agree with Sir Stanley," said she. "It isn't the sort of thing that the colonel would do. Men like Colonel Boundary are never without hope."

Stafford scratched his head.

"Well, if it isn't the colonel, he's gone, and we'll probably never see him again! There is only the question of rounding up the little people of the gang, and that won't be much trouble."

She put both her hands on his shoulders and looked at him smilingly.

"You're an optimist, dear," she said.

"Who wouldn't be?" he replied cheerfully. "You said that when the gang was wound up we would drop our sad and lonely lives apart and form a little gang of our own."

She laughed and kissed him, and he went back to his office to find that his chief had already arrived and had asked for him. Sir Stanley was reading the morning paper when Stafford came into his room, and his first words brought consternation to the younger man.

"Stafford," he said, "this is not the body of the colonel. I've just been to see it and I'm certain. Now you've got to send a call out to all stations throughout the country, particularly the south of England, to look for a man, possibly clean shaven, certainly without mustaches, who will be disguised as a tramp."

"Why a tramp, sir?" asked Stafford, with a heroic attempt to preserve an open mind on a subject concerning which he had reached a definite decision.

"Fifteen years ago," replied Sir Stanley, "when the colonel did most of his own dirty work, it was his favorite disguise. Search the casual wards, the common lodging houses, and the jails. It is just likely that the colonel will commit a small offense, with the object of getting himself three months in jail—there's no hiding place like jail, you know, Stafford. The real danger is that he may not actually tramp or assume the guise of the real lowdown loafer. He may have the sense to become a poor but honest workman, traveling third-class from town to town in search of work. Then he will present the greatest difficulty." He saw the look of doubt on the young man's face and laughed. "You think he's dead, don't you?" he said.

"I'm perfectly sure he is, sir," replied Stafford frankly.

"An optimist to the last." Sir Stanley smiled and dismissed him with a nod.

Later he was to come to Stafford's little bureau and tell him things which he did not know before. Then for the first time Stafford King discovered how closely his lackadaisical chief had followed the developments of the past few months. He learned for the first time of the big part which Jack o' Judgment had played in the detection of the gang.

"He had an office under the colonel's flat," said Sir Stanley. "Apparently it was bought with no other object than to provide our friend with an opportunity of spying on the colonel. He discolored the wall, brought in his own workmen, and in the colonel's absence—he was driven from the occupation of the room by the smell—he installed microphones. With the aid of these he was able to listen to all the conversation downstairs and sometimes to chime in. It was Jack o' Judgment who—well, perhaps I'd better not tell you that, because officially I am not supposed to know it. At any rate, Stafford," he said more seriously, "we have seen the smashing of one of the most iniquitous, villainous gangs that ever existed. Heaven knows how many broken hearts there are in England today, how many poor souls who have been brought to a suicide's grave through the machinations of Colonel Boundary and his tools. I do not think there has been a more immoral force in existence in our time, and I hope we shall never see its like again. You sent out the message?" he asked at parting.

"Yes, sir. I warned all stations and all chief constables."

"Good!" said Sir Stanley; and his last words were: "Don't forget—Boundary is not dead!"

CHAPTER XXXIX
JACK O' JUDGMENT REVEALED

A stoutish, gray-haired man descended from a third-class carriage at Chatham Station and inquired of the porter the way to the dockyard. He carried a kit of carpenter's tools in a straw bag and smoked a short clay pipe. The porter looked at the man with the white, stubby beard critically.

"Trying to get a job, mate?" he asked.

"Why, yes," said the man.

"How old might you be?" demanded the porter.

"Sixty-four," said the other, and the porter shook his head.

"You won't get work easy. They're not very keen on us old fellows," he said. "Why don't you try at Markham's, the builders, in the High Street? They're short of men. I saw a notice outside their yard only this morning."

The workman thanked the porter, shouldered his basket, and tramped down the High Street. He was respectably dressed, and policemen on the lookout for suspicious tramps did not give him a second glance. He spent the greater part of the day walking from yard to yard, everywhere receiving the same answer. Late in the afternoon he had better luck. A small firm of ship repairers was in want of a jobbing carpenter and put him to work at once.

It was many years since Colonel Boundary had wielded a saw—this colonelcy was an honorary title which he held by custom rather than law—but he made a good showing. After two hours' work, however, his back was aching and his hands were sore. He was glad when the yard bell announced the hour for knocking off.

He had yet to find a lodging, but this did not worry him. He was careful to avoid the cheaper kind of lodging house and went to one which catered to the artisan, where he could get a room of his own and a clean bed. He paid a deposit, washed himself and left his tools, then went out in search of some refreshment.

At seven o'clock the next morning he was back at the yard. He thought several times during the day that he would have to throw the work up. His back ached, his arms were like lead. But he persevered, and again another day drew to a close. By the third day he had got his muscles into play and found the work easy. He was asked by the foreman if he would care to go into the country to work at a house that the head of the firm was building, but he declined. He wanted to remain in the town, where there were crowds.

At the end of the week came his great chance. He had been sent down to the docks to do some repairs on a small steamer and had pleased the skipper, who was himself an elderly man, by the ability he had shown.

"You're worth twice some of these young men," grumbled the old man. "Are you married?"

"No," said the other.

"Why don't you sign on with me?" asked the skipper. "I want a carpenter bad."

"Where are you going?" asked Boundary, breathing more quickly.

"We're going to Valparaiso first, then we're going to work down the coast, round the Horn to San Francisco, and maybe we'll get a cargo across to China."

"I'll think it over," said the colonel.

That night he called on the captain and told him that he had made up his mind to go.

"Good!" said the skipper. "But you'll have to sign on tonight. I'm leaving tomorrow by the first tide."

The colonel nodded, not daring to speak. Here was luck, the greatest in the world. Nobody would suspect a carpenter, taken from a local firm and shipped with the captain's good will.

At seven o'clock the next morning he was standing on the deck of the *Arabelle Sands,* watching the low coast line slipping past. The ship was to make one call at Falmouth, and two days later she reached that port. Boundary went ashore to buy some wood and a few tools that he found he needed, and pulled back to the ship in the afternoon. In the evening he accompanied the captain ashore.

"We shan't leave till tomorrow at twelve," said the captain. "You might as well spend a night on solid earth while you can. It will be a long time before you smell dirt again."

The colonel secured lodgings in the town and retired to his room early. He had purchased all the newspapers he could find, and he wanted to study them quietly. It was with unusual relish that he read the account of an inquest on himself. There was no breath of suspicion that he was not dead.

"Old Dan Boundary has tricked them all."

He chuckled at the thought. He had deceived all those clever men at Scotland Yard—Sir Stanley Belcom, Stafford King, Jack o' Judgment! Yes, he had deceived Jack o' Judgment, and that seemed the least believable part of the affair. All the rest of the gang were captured or fugitives. He wondered whether Lollie Marsh and Crewe had reached Portugal, and what they were doing there, and how long their money would last, and how they would earn more. He had his own money well secured. He had managed to get together quite a large sum, for there were other banks than the Victoria and City—odd accounts in assumed names which he had drawn upon on the very day of his supposed death.

There was a tap at the door.

"Come in," said Boundary, thinking it the landlady.

He was in the middle of the room as he spoke, and he went back step by step as the visitor entered. His tongue clove to the roof of his mouth, his eyes were starting out of his head.

"You! You!" he gasped.

"Little Jack o' Judgment," said the mask mockingly; "poor old Jack! Come to take farewell of the colonel before he goes to foreign parts!"

"Stop!" cried Boundary hoarsely. "I know you, damn you! I know you!"

He pulled back the curtains and glared out of the window. There was no need to ask any further questions. The house was surrounded. He swung round again at his tormentor and faced the white mask in a blind fury of rage.

"You're clever, aren't you," he said, "cleverer than all the police! But you weren't clever enough to save your son from death!"

The masked figure reeled back.

"Ah, that got you, little Jack o' Judgment!" mocked the colonel. "That's hit you where it hurts you most, hasn't it? Your only son, too! And he went to the devil all the faster because of me—me—me!" He struck his breast with his clenched fist. "You can't bring him back to life, can you? That's one I've scored against you."

"No," said Jack o' Judgment in a low voice, "I cannot bring him back to life, but I can destroy the man who destroyed him, who blighted his young life, who taught him vicious practices, who sapped his vitality with drugs."

"That's a lie!" said the colonel. "Crewe picked him up at Monte Carlo, when he was on his beam ends."

"Who sent him to Monte Carlo?" asked the other. "Who was the gambler who brought him down and received the wreck he had made with the pretense that he had never met him before? It was you, Boundary!"

The colonel nodded.

"It was I," he said with satisfaction. "I was a fool to deny it. I pretended to Crewe that I hadn't met him before. Yes, it was I, and I glory in it. You think you're going to arrest me now, and put me where I belong—on the scaffold, maybe. But, you can never wipe that memory out of your mind—that you had a son who died in the gutter, that you're a childless old man who has no son to follow you!"

"I can't wipe that out!" said Jack o' Judgment. "I can't wipe that out!" He raised his hand to his masked face as though to hide the picture which Boundary conjured. "But I can wipe you out," he said fiercely, "and I've given my life, my career, my reputation, all that I hold dear to get you! I've smashed your schemes, I've ruined you, even if I've ruined myself. They're waiting for you downstairs, Boundary. I told them to be here at this very minute. Stafford King—"

"You'll never see me taken," said Boundary.

Two shots rang out together, and the colonel sprawled back over the bed, dead. Propped against the wall was Jack o' Judgment, and the hand that gripped his breast dripped red.

They heard the shots outside. Stafford King was the first to enter the room. One glance at the colonel was sufficient, and then he turned to the man who had slipped to the floor and was sitting with his back propped against the wall.

"Jack o' Judgment," said Stafford wonderingly.

"Poor old Jack!" said the mocking voice.

Stafford's arm was about his shoulder, and he laid the head gently back upon his bent knee. He lifted the mask gently, and the light of the oil lamp which swung from the ceiling fell upon the white face.

"Sir Stanley Belcom! Sir Stanley!" he whispered.

Sir Stanley turned his head and opened his eyes. The old look of good humor shone.

"Poor old Jack o' Judgment!" he mimicked. "This is going to be a first-class scandal, Stafford. For the sake of the service you ought to hush it up."

"But nobody need know, sir," said Stafford. "You can explain to the home secretary—"

Sir Stanley shook his head.

"I'm going to see a greater Home Secretary than ever lived in Whitehall," he said slowly. "I'm finished, Stafford. Strip this mummery from me if you can."

With shaking hands Stafford King tore off the black cloak and flung it under the bed.

"Now," said Sir Stanley weakly, "you can introduce me to the provincial police as the head of our department and you can keep my secret, Stafford—if you will."

Stafford laid his hand upon Sir Stanley's.

"I told my solicitor"—Sir Stanley spoke with difficulty—"to give you a letter in case—in case anything happened. I know I haven't played the game as I should. I ought to have resigned years ago when I found what had happened to my poor boy. I was chief of police in one of the provinces of India at the time, but they wouldn't let me go. I came to Scotland Yard and was promoted. No, I haven't played the game as I should with the department. And yet perhaps I have."

He did not speak for some time.

His breathing was growing fainter and fainter, and when Stafford asked him, he said he was in no pain.

"I had to deceive you," he said after a while; "I had to pretend that Jack o' Judgment called on me, too. That was to take suspicion from your—Miss White." He smiled. "No; I haven't played the game. I stood for the law, and yet—I broke that gang, which the law could not touch. I broke them! I broke them!" he whispered. "If Boundary hadn't known me I should have been gone before you came, and resigned tomorrow," he said; "but he must have discovered the boy's name. I wonder he hadn't tried before. I smashed them; didn't I, Stafford? It cost me thousands. I have committed almost every kind of crime. I robbed the diamond smiths'—but you must give me your word you will never tell. Phillopolis must suffer. They must all be punished."

Stafford had sent the police from the room, but the police surgeon would not be denied. He had the sense to see that nothing could be done for the dying man, however, and that a change of position would probably hasten the end. He, too, left him alone with King.

"Stafford, I have quite a lot of money," said the first commissioner; "it is yours. There's a will—yours."

Then he ceased to speak, and Stafford thought that the end had come, but did not dare move in case he were mistaken. After five minutes the man in his arms stirred slightly, and his voice sounded strangely clear and strong.

"Gregory, my boy! Good old Gregory! Father's here, old man!"

His voice died away to a rumble and then to a murmur.

The tears were running down Stafford's face. He sensed all the tragedy, all the loneliness of this man who had offered so cheerful a face to the world. Then Sir Stanley struggled to draw himself to his feet and Stafford held him.

"Gently, sir, gently," he said; "you're only hurting yourself."

The dying man laughed. It was a little shrill chuckle of merriment, and Stafford's blood ran cold.

"Here I am, poor old Jack o' Judgment! Little old Jack o' Judgment! Give me the lives you took and the hopes you've blasted. Give them to Jack o' Judgment—Jack o' Judgment!"

They were his last words.

A year later First Commissioner Sir Stafford King received a letter from South America. It contained nothing but a photograph—of a very good-looking man and a singularly pretty woman, who held in her lap a very tiny baby.

"Here is the last of the Boundary gang," said Sir Stafford to Maisie. "It is the one happy ending that has emerged from so much misery and evil."

"Why, it is Lollie Marsh!"

"Lollie Crewe, I think her name is now," said Stafford. "It was queer how Sir Stanley recognized the only human members of the gang."

"Then they got away after all?" said the girl. "I've often wondered what happened at that aerodrome."

Stafford laughed.

"Oh, yes," he said dryly, "they got away. They left at twenty minutes past three, after a long argument with the aviator, a man named Cartwright."

"How do you know?" she asked.

"Sir Stanley and I watched them go off," said Stafford.

He looked at the photograph again and shook his head.

"There were times when the judgment of Jack was very merciful," he said soberly.

THE END

Captains of Souls

by Edgar Wallace

Dedicated to "Tookie"

BOOK THE FIRST

I

Beryl Merville wrote:

"Dear Ronnie: We are back from Italy, arriving this afternoon. Daddy thought you would be there to meet us, and I was so disappointed to find nobody but Mr. Steppe. Oh, yes! I know that he is a most important person, and his importance was supported by his new car; such an impressive treasure, with a collapsible writing-table and cigar-lighter and library—actually a library in a cunning little locker under one of the seats. I just glanced at them.

I am a little afraid of Mr. Steppe, yet he was kindness itself, and that bull voice of his, bellowing orders to porters and chauffeur and railway policemen was comforting in a way. Daddy is a little plaintive on such occasions.

I thought he was looking unusually striking—Steppe I mean. People certainly do look at him, with his black, pointed beard and his bristling, black eyebrows. You like him, don't you? Perhaps I should too, only—he is very magnetic; a commanding person, he frightens me, I repeat. And I have met another man, I don't think you know him, he said he had never met you. Daddy knows him rather well, and so does Mr. Steppe. Such a queer man, Ronnie!

He arrived after Daddy had gone to his club, to collect some correspondence. The maid came and told me there was a strange man in the hall who said Dr. Merville had sent for him; so I went down to see him.

He made the queerest impression on me. You will be amused, but not flattered, when I confess that the moment I saw him, I thought of you! I had a sort of warm impulse toward him. I felt as though I were meeting you, as I wanted you to be. That sounds feeble, and lame, but employing my limited vocabulary to the best of my poor ability, I am striving to reduce my mad impression to words. How mad it was, you'll understand. For, Ronnie, he was a stoutish man of middle age—no more like you than I am like Mr. Steppe! Yet when I saw this shabbily dressed person (the knees of his trousers shone and the laces of his untidy boots were dragging) I just gasped. He sat squarely on one of the hall chairs, a big, rough hand on each knee, and he was staring in an absent-minded way at the wall. He didn't even see me when I stood almost opposite to him. But his head, Ronnie! It was the head of a conqueror; one of those heroes of antiquity. You see their busts in the museums and wonder who they are. A broad, eagle face, strangely dark, and on top a shock of gray-white hair brushed back into a mane. He had the most beautiful eyes I have ever seen in a man, and when they turned in my direction, and he got up from his chair, not awkwardly as I expected, but with the ease of an Augustus, there was within them so much loving-kindness that I felt I could have cried.

And please, Ronnie, do not tell me that I am neurotic and over-tired. I was just mad—nothing worse than that. I'm mad still, for I cannot get him out of my mind. His name is Ambrose Sault, and he is associated with daddy and Mr. Steppe, though I think that he is really attached to that horrid Greek person to whom daddy introduced me—Moropulos. What sort of work he does for Moropulos I have not discovered. There is always a great deal of mystery about Mr. Moropulos and Mr. Steppe's business schemes. Sometimes I am very uncomfortable—which is a very mild way of describing my feelings—about daddy and things.

Ronnie, you have some kind of business dealings with father, what is it all about? I should so like to discover. It is to do with companies and corporations, isn't it? I know Mr. Steppe is a great financier, but I don't quite know how financiers work. I suppose I ought not to be curious, but it worries me—no, bothers is a better word—sometimes.

Come and see me soon, Ronnie. I promise you I won't—you know. I've never forgiven myself for hurting you so. It was such a horrid story—I blame myself for listening, and hate myself for telling you. But the girl's brother was so earnest, and so terribly upset, and the girl herself was so wickedly circumstantial. You have forgiven me? It was my first experience of blackmailers and I ought to have known you better and liked you better than to believe that you would be such a brute—and she was such a common girl, too—"

She stopped writing and looked round. "Come in."

The maid was straightening her face as she entered. "That gentleman, miss, Mr. Sault, has called."

Beryl tapped her lips with the feathered penholder. "Did you tell him that the doctor was out?"

"Yes, miss. He asked if you were in. I told him I'd go and see." Something about the visitor had amused the girl, for the corners of her lips twitched.

"Why are you laughing, Dean?" Beryl's manner was unusually cold and her grave eyes reproving. For no reason that she could assign, she felt called upon to defend this man, against the ridicule which she perceived in the maid's attitude.

"Oh, miss, he was so strange! He said: 'Perhaps she will see me.' 'Do you mean Miss Merville?' says I. 'Merville!' he says in a queer way. 'Of course, Beryl Merville,' and then he said something to himself. It sounded like 'how pitiful.' I don't think he is quite all there, miss."

"Show him up, please," said Beryl quietly. She recognized the futility of argument. Dean and her type found in the contemplation of harmless lunacy a subject for merriment—and Dean was the best maid she had had for years. She sat waiting for the man, uncertain. Why did she want to see him? She was not really curious by nature and the crude manners of the class to which he belonged usually rubbed her raw. The foulness of their speech, the ugliness of their ideals and their lives; the gibberish, almost an unknown language to her, of the cockney man and woman, all these things grated. Perhaps she was a neurotic after all; Ronnie was quite sure of his judgment in most matters affecting her.

Ambrose Sault, standing in the doorway, hat in hand, saw her bite her lower lip reflectively. She looked around with a start of surprise and, seeing him, got up. He was a colored man! She had not realized this before, and she was unaccountably hurt; just colored and yet his eyes were gray!

"I hope I haven't disturbed you, mademoiselle," he said. His voice was very soft and very sweet. Mademoiselle? A creole—a Madagascan—an octoroon? From one of the French foreign territories, perhaps. He spoke English without an accent, but the "mademoiselle" had come so naturally to his lips.

"You are French, Mr. Sault—your name of course?" She smiled at him questioningly and wondered why she troubled to ask questions at all.

"No, mademoiselle," he shook his great head and the mask of a face did not relax. "I am from Barbadoes, but I have lived in Port de France, that is, in Martinique, for many years. I was also in Noumea, in New Caledonia, that is also French."

There was an awkward silence here. Yet he was not embarrassed and displayed no incertitude of his position. Her dilemma came from the fact that she judged men by her experience and acquaintance with them, and the empirical method fails before the unusual—Ambrose Sault was that.

"My father will be home very soon, Mr. Sault. Won't you please sit down?" As he chose a chair with some deliberation it occurred to her that she would find a difficulty in explaining to the fastidious Dr. Merville, why she had invited this man to await him in the drawing-room. Strangely enough, she herself felt the capacity of entertaining and being entertained by the visitor and she had no such spasm of dismay as had come to her, when other, and more presentable, visitors, had settled themselves for a lengthy call. This fact puzzled her. Ambrose Sault was—an artisan perhaps, a messenger, more likely. The shabbiness of his raiment and the carelessness of his attire suggested some menial position. One waistcoat button had been fastened into the wrong buttonhole; the result was a little grotesque.

"Have you been working very long, with my father?" she asked.

"No—not a very long time," he said. "Moropulos and Steppe know him better than I."

He checked himself. She knew that he would not talk any more about his associates and the enigma which their companionship presented would remain unsolved, so far as he could give a solution. "Moropulos"—"Steppe"? He spoke as an equal. Even Ronnie was deferential to Mr. Steppe and was in awe of him. Her father made no attempt to hide his nervousness in the presence of that formidable person. Yet this man could dispense with the title. It was not bravado on his part, the conscious impertinence of an underling, desirous of asserting his equality. Obviously, he thought of Mr. Steppe as "Steppe." What would he call her father? No occasion arose, but she was certain he would have been "Merville" and no more.

Sault's eyes were settled on her, absorbing her; yet his gaze lacked offence, being without hostility, or notable admiration. She had a ridiculous sensibility of praise. So he might have looked upon Naples from the sea, or upon the fields of narcissi above Les Avants, or the breath-taking loveliness of the hills of Monticattini in the blue afterlight of sunset. She could not meet his eyes—yet was without discomfort. The praise of his conspection was not human.

She laughed, artificially, she thought, and reached out for a book that lay on the table.

"We have just returned from Italy," she said. "Do you know Italy at all, Mr. Sault?"

"I do not know Italy," he said, and took the book she held to him.

"This is rather a wonderful account of Lombardy and its history," she said. "Perhaps you would like to read it?"

He turned the leaves idly and smiled at her. She had never seen a man smile so sweetly.

"I cannot read," he said simply.

She did not understand his meaning for a while thinking that his eyesight was failing.

"Perhaps you would care to take it home."

He shook his head and the book came back to her.

"I cannot read," he said, without shame, "or write—at least I cannot write words. Figures, yes, figures are easy; somebody told me—he was a professor of English I think, at one of the universities—that it was astonishing that I could work out mathematical problems and employ all the signs and symbols of trigonometry and algebra without being able to write. I wish I could read. When I pass a bookshop I feel like an armless man who is starving within hands' reach of salvation. I know a great deal and I pay a man to read to me—Livy and Prescott and Green, and, of course, Bacon—I know them all. Writing does not worry me—I have no friends."

If he had spoken apologetically, if he had displayed the least aggression, she might have classified, and held him in a place. But he spoke of his shortcomings as he might have spoken of his gray hair, as a phenomenon beyond his ordering.

She was thunderstruck; possibly he was so used to shocking people from this cause that he did not appear to observe the effect he had produced.

He was so completely content with this, the first contact with his dream woman, that he was almost incapable of receiving any other impression. Her hair was fairer than he had thought, the nose thinner, the molding of her delicate face more spiritual. The lips redder and fuller, the rounded chin less firm. And the eyes—he wished she would turn her head so that he could be sure of their color. They were big, set wide apart, there was depth in them and a something upon which he yearned. The figure of her he knew by heart. Straight and tall and most gracious. A patrician; he thought of her as that. And oriental. He had pictured her as a great lady at Constantine's court; he set her upon the marble terrace of a decent villa on the hills above the Chrysopolis; a woman of an illustrious order.

She could never suspect that he thought of her at all as a distinct personality. She could not guess that he knew her as well as his own right hand; that, day after day, he had waited in the Row, a shabby and inconspicuous figure amongst the smart loungers: waited for the benison of her presence. She had not seen him in Devon in the spring—he had been there. Lying on the rain-soaked grass of Tapper Downs to watch her walking with her father; sitting amidst gorse on the steep slope of the cliff, she unconscious of his guardianship, reading in her chair on the smooth beach.

"How curious, I nearly said 'sad.' But you do not feel very sad about it, Mr. Sault, do you?" Amused, he shook his head.

"It would be irritating," he said, "if I were sorry for myself. But I am never that. Half the unhappiness of life comes from the vanity of self-pity. It is the mother of all bitterness. Do you realize that? You cannot feel bitter without feeling sorry for yourself." She nodded.

"You miss a great deal—but you know that—poetry, I suppose you have that read to you?"

Ambrose Sault laughed softly. "Yes—poetry.

> "'Out of the dark which covers me,
>   Black as a pit from pole to pole,
> I thank whatever gods there be,
>   For my unconquerable soul—'

"That poem and Theocrite, and only two lines of Theocrite, are the beginning and the end of my poetical leanings. I attend lectures of course. Lectures on English, on architecture, music, history—especially history—oh, a hundred subjects. And mathematics. You can get those in the extension classes only, unfortunately, I cannot qualify for admission to the classes themselves."

"Have you never tried to— to—"

"Read and write? Yes. My room is packed with little books and big books. A-b, ab; c-a-t, cat; and copy books. But I just can't. I can write the letters of the alphabet, a few of them that are necessary for mathematical calculations, very well; but I cannot go any further. I seem to slip into a fog, a sort of impenetrable wall of thick mist that confuses and baffles me. I know that c-a-t is 'cat' but when I see 'cat' written it is a meaningless combination of straight and curved lines. It is sheerly physical—the doctors have a word for it—I cannot remember what it is for the moment, I just can't read—"

Dr. Merville came in at that moment, a thin colorless man, myopic, irritable, chronically worried. He entered the drawing-room hurriedly. Beryl thought he must have run upstairs. His frowning, dissatisfied glance was toward Sault; the girl he ignored.

"Hello, Sault—had no idea you were here. Will you come into my study?" He was breathless and Beryl knew by the signs that he was angry about something. It occurred to her instantly, that he was annoyed with her for entertaining the untidy visitor. The study was next door to the drawing-room and he walked out with a beckoning jerk of his chin.

"I am glad to have met you, mademoiselle." Ambrose Sault was not to be hurried. Returning to the open doorway, Dr. Merville, clucking his impatience, witnessed the leisurely leave-taking.

The study door had scarcely closed on the visitor before it opened again and her father returned. "Why the deuce did you ask that fellow up, Beryl? He could have very well waited in the servants' hall—or in the breakfast room or anywhere. Suppose—somebody had called!"

"I thought he was a friend of Mr. Steppe's," she said calmly. "You know such extraordinary people. What is he?"

"Who, Sault? Well, he is—"

Dr. Merville was not immediately prepared to define the position of his visitor.

"In a sense he is an employee of Moropulos—picked him up in his travels. He is an anarchist."

She stared. "A what?"

"Well, not exactly an anarchist—communist—anyway, he has quaint views on—things. Believes in the equality of the human race. An extraordinary fellow, a dreamer, got a crazy idea of raising a million to found a college, that's what he calls it, The Mother College—can't stop now, darling, but please don't make a fuss of him. He is just a little difficult as it is. I will tell you about him some day." He bustled out of the room and the study door closed with a thud.

Beryl Merville considered Ambrose Sault for a very long time before she turned to her writing-table, where the unfinished letter to Ronald Morelle invited a conclusion.

II

"Well, Sault, why have you come? Anything wrong?" Beryl would have thought Dr. Merville's manner strangely mild and conciliatory after his show of antagonism toward the visitor.

Sault had seated himself on the edge of a low chesterfield under the curtained window. "Moropulos is worried about some people who called at his bureau to-day. They came to ask him about a letter that had been sent to him from South Africa by the assistant manager of the Brakfontein Diamond Mine."

Merville was standing by the library table, in the center of the room. The hand that played with the leaves of a magazine was trembling ever so slightly. "What has happened—how did they know—who were they?" he demanded shakily.

"I think it was the managing director, the American gentleman. He was very angry. They discovered that the manager had been receiving money from London soon after he made his report. Moropulos told me that the shares had dropped thirty points since yesterday morning. Mr. Divverly said that Moropulos and his gang, those were the words I think, had bribed the manager to keep back the report that the mine was played out. I suppose he did. I know very little about stocks and shares."

Dr. Merville was biting his knuckles, a weak and vacillating man; Sault had no doubts as to this, and it hurt him every time he realized that this invertebrate creature was Beryl Merville's father. How and why had he come into the strange confederation?

"I can do nothing," the doctor was fretful, his voice jerky; he fixed and removed his pince-nez and fixed them again. "Nothing! I do not know why these people make inquiries. There was nothing dishonest in selling stock which you know will fall—it is a part of the process of speculation, isn't it, Sault? All the big houses work on secret information received or bought. If—if Moropulos or Steppe care to buy information, that is nobody's affair—"

"There may be an inquiry on the Stock Exchange," said Sault calmly. "Moropulos asked me to tell you that. The Johannesburg committee have taken up the matter and have called for information. You see, the manager has confessed."

"Confessed!" gasped the doctor and went white.

"So Mr. Divverly says. He has told the directors that Moropulos had the information a month before the directors."

The doctor sat down heavily on the nearest chair. "I don't see—that it affects us," he protested feebly. "There is no offense in getting a tip about a failing property, is there, Sault?"

"I don't know. Moropulos says it is conspiracy. They can prove it if—"

"If—?"

"If they find the letters which the manager wrote. Moropulos has them in his desk."

Merville sprang up. "Then they must be destroyed!" he cried violently. "It is madness to keep them—I had no idea—of course he must burn them. Go back and tell him to do this, Sault."

Ambrose Sault put his hand into the fold of his shabby jacket and brought out a bundle of documents. "They are here," he said in a matter of fact tone. "Moropulos says that you must keep them. They may get a warrant to search his house."

"Keep them—I?" Merville almost screamed. "Moropulos is a fool—burn them!"

Sault shook his head. "Steppe says 'no.' They may be useful later. You must keep them, doctor. It is Steppe's wish. Tomorrow I will start working on the safe."

Dr. Merville took the papers from the outstretched hand and looked around helplessly. There was a steel box on his desk. He took out his key, looked again and more dubiously at the packet of letters and dropped them into the box. "What is this safe, Sault? I know that you are a devilish clever fellow with your hands and Moropulos mentioned something about a safe. You are not making it?"

Sault nodded and there was a gleam in his fine eyes.

"But why? Moropulos has a safe and Steppe must possess dozens. Why not buy another, if he must have a special place for these wretched things?"

"You cannot buy the safe that I shall make," said the dark man quietly. "It has taken me a year to invent the dial—eh? Yes, combination. They are easy, but not this one. A word will open it, any other word, any other combination of letters, and there will be nothing to find."

The doctor frowned.

"You mean if any other person—the police for example, try to open the safe the contents are destroyed?"

Sault nodded.

"How?"

The visitor, his business at an end, rose.

"That is simple, a twist of the hand, unless the combination is true, releases a quart of acid, any of the corrosive acids will serve."

Merville bent his head in thought. Presently he saw a flaw in the invention. "Suppose they don't touch the lock?" he asked. "Suppose they burn out the side of the safe—it can be done, I believe—what then?"

Ambrose Sault gave that soft laugh of his. "The sides will be hollow, and filled from the inside of the safe, with water pumped in at a pressure. Cut through the safe, and the water escapes and releases a plunger that brings about the same result—the contents of the safe are destroyed."

"You are a strange creature—the strangest I have met. I don't understand you," Merville shook his head. "I hope you will hurry with that safe." As Sault was at the door he asked: "Where did Moropulos find you, Sault?"

The man turned. "He found me in the sea," he said. "Moropulos was trading in those days. He had a sloop pearl smuggling, I think. I thought he had told you. I never make any secret about it."

"In the sea—for heavens sake what do you mean? Where?"

"Ten miles off the Isle of Pines. I got away from Noumea in a boat. Noumea is the capital of New Caledonia. I and three *Canaques*—they were under sen-

tence for cannibalism. We ran into a cyclone and swamped, just as we were trying to make the sloop which was standing in to the lee of the island. Moropulos took me on board and the natives; when he found that I was a convict—"

"A convict—a French convict!"

Sault was leaning easily, his cheek against the hand that gripped the edge of
the open door. He nodded. "I thought he had told you. Of course, he would
have taken me back to Noumea for the reward, only he had a cargo on board
which he did not want the French to see. I found afterwards that when we called
at the Loyalty Island, he tried to sell me back, but couldn't get a price."

He smiled broadly as at a very pleasant recollection. "Moropulos would sell
me now," he said, "only I am useful."

"But why—why were you imprisoned?" asked Merville, awe-stricken at the
tremendous revelation.

"I killed a man," said Sault. "Good night, doctor."

III

It was a Monday morning and a bank holiday. A few regular habituées of the
park to whom the word "holiday" had no especial significance, had overlooked the fact and took their cantering exercise a little selfconsciously under
admiring eyes of the people who seldom saw people riding on horseback for the
pleasure of it. The day was fine and warm, the hawthorn trees were thickly
frosted with their cerise and white blossoms; stiff crocuses flamed in every bed
and the banners of the daffodils fluttered in the light breeze that blew half-
heartedly across the wide green spaces. On every path the holiday-makers strag-
gled, small mothers laden with large babies; shopboys in garments secretly
modelled on the supermen they served; girls from the stores in their bargain-
price finery; young men with and without hats, the waitresses of closed
teashops, and here and there a pompous member of the bourgeoisie conscious
of his superiority to the crowd with which, in his condescension, he mingled.

There is one shady place which faces Park Lane—a stretch of wooded lawn
where garden chairs are set six deep. Behind this phalanx there is an irregular
fringe of seats, usually in couples, and greatly in request during the darker hours.
In the early morning, before the energies of the promenaders are exhausted, the
spot is deserted. But two young people occupied chairs this morning. There was
nothing in the appearance of the girl that would have made the companionship
seem incongruous. In her tailored costume, the unobtrusive hat and the sim-
plicity of her toilette, she might as well have been the youngest daughter of a
duke or a workgirl with a judgment in dress. Her clothes would not be "priced"
by the most expert of women critics and even stockings and shoes, the last hope
of the appraiser, would have baffled. No two glances would have been required
to put the man in his class. If he was a thought dandified, it was the dandifica-

tion of a gentleman. He looked what he was, a man of leisure; the type which is to be found in the Guards or the smartest regiment of cavalry. Yet Ronald Morelle was no soldier. He had served during the war, but had seen none of its devastations. He hated the violence of battle and despised the vulgarity of noisy patriotism. His knowledge of Italian had secured him a quasi-diplomatic appointment, nominally at the Italian headquarters, actually in Rome. He had used every influence that could be employed, pulled every string that could be pulled, to keep him from the disorder of the front line, and fortune had favored him to an extraordinary extent. On the very day he received instructions to report to the regiment with which he had trained, the armistice was signed—he saw the last line of trenches which the British had prepared but never occupied, south of Amiens, saw them from the train that carried him home, and thought that they looked beastly uncomfortable.

The girl by his side would not be alone in thinking him good-looking. He was that rarity, a perfectly featured man. His skin was faultless; his straight nose, his deep-set brown eyes, his irreproachable mouth, were excellent. The hyper-critical might cavil at the almost feminine chin. A small brown moustache was probably responsible for the illusion that he favored the profession of arms.

Evie Colebrook thought he was the most beautiful man in the world, and when he smiled, as he was smiling now, she dared not look at him. He was talking about looks, and she was deliciously flattered. "How ridiculous you are, Mr. Morelle," she protested. "I suppose you have said that to thousands and thousands of girls?"

"Not quite so many, Evie," he answered. "To be exact, I can't remember having been so shamelessly complimentary to any girl before. You need not call me 'Mr. Morelle' unless you wish to—my friends call me 'Ronnie'."

She played with the handkerchief on her lap. "It seems so familiar. Honestly, Ronnie, aren't you rather—what is the word? The book you lent me—a play?"

"A philanderer?" suggested the other. "My dear child, how silly you are. Of course I'm not. Very few people have impressed me as you have. It must have been fate that took me into Burts—I never go into shops, but François—that's my man—"

"I know him," she nodded, "he often comes in. I used to wonder who he was."

"He was out and I wanted—I forget what it was I wanted, even forget whether I bought it. I must have done, otherwise I should not have found myself staring over a paydesk at the most lovely girl in all the world."

She laughed, a gurgling laugh of sheer happiness, and looked at him swiftly before she dropped her eyes again.

"I like to hear that," she said softly. "It is so wonderful—that you like me, I mean. Because I'm nothing, really. And you, you're a—well, gentleman. I know you hate the word, but you are. Miles and miles above me. Why, I live in a miserable little house in a horrible neighborhood—full of thieves and terrible creatures who drink. And my mother does odd jobs for people. And I'm not very well educated—really. I can read and write, but I'm not half so clever as Christina, that is my sister. She's an invalid and reads all day and all night too, if I'd let her."

He was watching her as she spoke. The play of color in her pretty face, the rise and fall of her narrow chest, the curve of chin and the velvet smoothness of her throat—he marked them all with the eye of the gourmet who watches lambs frisking in the pasture and sees, not the poetry and beauty of young life, but a likeable dish that will one day mature. "If you were a beggar-maid and I were a prince—" he began.

"I'm not much better, am I?" she asked ruefully, "and you are a prince, to me, Ronnie—" she was thinking.

"Yes?"

"How can anything come right for us? I don't want to think about it and I try ever so hard to keep it out of my thoughts. I'm so happy meeting you—and loving you—and tomorrow never comes, but—"

"You mean how will this dear friendship end?" She nodded.

"How would you like it to end?"

Evie Colebrook poked the furrel of her sunshade into the grass and turned up a tuft of clover. "There is only one way it can ever end—happily," she said in a low voice, "and that is—well, you know, Ronnie."

He laughed. "With you in a beautiful white dress and a beautiful white veil and a wreath of orange blossoms round your glorious hair, and a fat and nasty old man in a surplice reading a few passages from a book; and people leering at you as you go down the aisle and saying—well, you know what they say. I think a wedding is the most indelicate function which society affects."

She said nothing, but continued prodding at the turf. "It can be done quietly," she said at last.

Leaning toward her, he slipped his hand under her arm. "Evie, is love nothing?" he asked earnestly, "isn't it the biggest thing? What is the most decent, a wedding between two people who half hate one another, but are marrying because one wants money and the other a swagger wife, or an everlasting love union between a man and a woman whom God has bound with bonds that a parson cannot strengthen or a snuffy judge cannot break?"

She sighed, the quick, double sigh of one half convinced.

"You make me feel that I'm common and—and brainless, and anyway, I don't want to talk about it. Ronnie, I suppose you're awfully busy this morning?" She looked wistfully at the big Rolls that was drawn up by the side of the road.

"I am rather," he said, "I wish I weren't. I'd love to drive you somewhere—anywhere so long as you were by my side, little fairy. When shall I see you again?"

"On Sunday?" she asked as they strolled toward the car.

"Why not come up to the flat to tea on Saturday afternoon?" he suggested, but she shook her head.

"I'd rather not, Ronnie—do you mind? I—well, I don't want to somehow. Am I an awful pig?"

He smiled down on her. "Of course not—oh, damn!"

A girl on a horse had just cantered past. She saw him and lifted her whip to acknowledge his raised hat.

"Who is that?" Evie was more than curious.

"A girl I know," he said suavely. "The daughter of my doctor, and rather a gossip."

"You're ashamed of being seen with me."

"Rubbish!" he laughed. "I am so proud of you that I wish she had stopped, confound her!" He took her hand and smiled into her eyes. "Goodbye, beloved," he breathed.

Evie Colebrook watched the car until it had turned out of sight. It was following the gossiping girl, but she did not care. She went home walking on air.

At the corner of the Row, the big car drew abreast of the rider. "Why on earth are you riding on Bank Holiday, Beryl—the park is full of louts, and there aren't half-a-dozen people in the Row!"

Beryl Merville looked at him quizzically. "And why on earth are *you* in the park, Ronnie; and who was your beautiful little friend?"

He frowned. "Friend? Oh, you mean the girl I was speaking to? Would you call her beautiful—yes, I suppose she is pretty, but quite a kid. Her father is an old friend of mine—colonel—I forget his name, he's something at the War Office. I have an idea they live near the park. I saw her walking and stopped the car to talk to her. Frankly I was so bored that I almost fell on her neck. I wasn't with her for five minutes."

Beryl nodded and dismissed the matter from her mind. She was more interested in another subject.

"Yes, dear, I had your letter. I'm an awful brute not to have come over and seen you. But the fact is, I have been working hard. Don't sneer, Beryl. I really have. Sturgeon, the editor of the *Post-Herald*, has discovered in me a latent genius for writing. It is rather fun—apparently I have a flair for that kind of work."

"But, Ronnie, this is great news! Stop your car by the corner and find a man to hold my horse—there is an awful lot I want to talk to you about."

He parked his car and, helping her dismount, handed the reins to an idle groom. A watchful attendant drew near.

"You will have to pay for the seats, Ronnie, I have no money."

"Happily I have two tickets," he said and realized his mistake before he drew them from his pocket.

"I thought you hadn't been with your colonel's daughter more than five minutes?" she challenged and laughed. "I sometimes think that you'd rather lie than eat!"

"My dear Beryl," Mr. Morelle's tone revealed both shock and injury. "Did I say that I didn't sit with her? I couldn't be so uncivil as to expect her to stand.

The fact is, that she hinted that she would like me to drive her round the park and I had no wish to."

"Never mind your guilty secret," she said gaily, "tell me all about your new job. Poor Ronnie, so they have made you work at last! I feared this."

Ronnie smiled good-naturedly. "It is amusing," he said. "I was always rather keen on that kind of work, even when I was at Oxford. Sturgeon saw some verses of mine in one of the quarterlies and asked me if I would care to describe a motor-car race—the Gordon Bennett cup. I took it on and he seemed immensely pleased with the account I wrote. I feel that I am doing some poor devil out of a job, but—"

"But it doesn't keep you awake at nights," she finished. "But how lovely, Ronald. You will be able to describe Mr. Steppe's trial—everybody says that one of these days he *will* be tried—"

Ronald Morelle was not amused. She saw a frown gather on his forehead and remembered that he and Mr. Steppe had some association.

"Of course I'm joking, Ronnie. How awfully touchy you are! Mr. Steppe is quite nice, and people invariably say unpleasant things about a successful man."

"Steppe—" he paused. There was a nervousness in his manner and in his tone which he could not disguise. "Steppe is quite a good fellow. A little rough, but he was trained in a rough school. He is very nearly the cleverest financier in this country or any other." He would have changed the conversation had she not interpolated a question.

"I do not know him—Sault you said? No, I've never met him. He does odd jobs for Moropulos. A half-caste, isn't he? What nerve the fellow had to come to the house! Why didn't you kick him out?"

"It is obvious that you haven't seen him or you wouldn't ask such a question," she replied, her eyes twinkling.

"I don't know what he does," Ronnie went on. "Steppe has a good opinion of him. That is all I know. He has three decorations for something he did in the war. He was in the Field Ambulance and brought in a lot of people from No Man's Land. He is quite old, isn't he?"

She nodded. "Moropulos isn't anything to boast about. Steppe likes him, though." Apparently the cachet of Mr. Steppe satisfied Ronnie in all things. "He's a Greek—you've met him? A sleek devil. They say that he's afraid except when he is drunk."

"Ronnie!"

"A fact. Moropulos drinks like a fish. Absinthe and all sorts of stuff. Steppe told me. That is why this nigger fellow Sault is useful. Sault is the only man who can handle him. He's as strong as an ox. There isn't a smarter devil than Moropulos. He has the brain of a cabinet minister, and is as close as an oyster. But when the fit is on him he'd stand up in the street and talk himself into gaol. And others—not Steppe, of course," he added hastily, "Steppe has nothing to be afraid of, only—well, Moropulos might say things that would look bad."

"And is that all?" she asked with an odd sense of disappointment. "Doesn't Mr. Sault do anything else but act as a sort of keeper?"

Ronnie, already weary of the subject, yawned behind his hand. "Awfully sorry, but I was up late last night. Sault? Oh, yes, I believe he does odd jobs. He is rather an ugly brute, isn't he?"

She did not answer this. Her interest in the man puzzled her. He appealed in a strange fashion to something within her that was very wholesome. She was glad, very glad, about his war decorations. That he should have done fine things—she liked to forget Ronnie's war services.

"I wish I had decided to ride this morning," complained Ronnie. "I never dreamed you would be out on a day like this. Why I came into the park at all I really do not know. I didn't realize it was a bank holiday and that all these dreadful people would be unchained for the day. How is the doctor—well?"

She nodded.

"He looked a little peaked when I saw him last. Look, Beryl—Steppe!" A car, headed for Marble Arch, had swerved across the road in response to the signal of its occupant. It pulled up behind Ronald's machine and Mr. Steppe, with his queer sideways smile, alighted, waving a white-gloved hand.

"Oh, dear," said. Beryl plaintively, "why did I get off that horse? I could have pretended that I had not recognized him."

"My dear girl!"

Ronald was genuinely distressed and it came to Beryl in the nature of an unpleasant discovery that he was so completely in awe of the financier, that his manner, his attitude, the very tone of his voice, changed at the sight of him. And Steppe seemed to expect this homage, took it as his right, dismissed and obliterated Ronnie from participation with a jerk of his head intended as an acknowledgment of his greeting and as an excusal of his presence.

Beryl could not help realizing his unimportance in the millionaire's scheme of life.

The photographs of Jan Steppe which have from time to time appeared in the public press, at once flatter and disparage him. The lens has depicted faithfully the short black beard, the thick black eyebrows, the broad nose and the thick bull neck of him. They missed his immense vitality, the aura of power which enveloped him, his dominant and forceful ego. His voice was thick and deep, sometimes in a moment of excitement guttural, for his grandfather had been a Transvaal Boer, a *bywoner* who had become, successively farmer and mine owner. Jan Cornelius Steppe, the first, had spoken no English; his son Commandant Steppe, an enlightened and scholarly man, spoke it well. He had been killed at Tugela Drift in the war, whilst Jan the third was in England at a preparation school.

"Huh! Beryl! Very good luck, huh? I shall miss my train but it is worth while. Riding? God! I wish I wasn't so fat and lazy. Motor cars are the ruin of us. My grandfather rode twenty miles a day and my father was never off a horse. Huh!"

Beryl often asked her father why Mr. Steppe grunted at the end of his every question. But it was not a grunt. It was a throaty growl cut short, a terrifying mannerism of his, meaningless but menacing. She used to wonder whether the impression of ruthless ferocity which he gave, was not more than half due to this peculiarity. He towered above her, a mountain of a man, broad of shoulder and long of arm. There was something simian about him, something that was almost obscene. He was fond of describing himself as fat, but this was an exaggeration. He had bulk, he was in the truest sense gross, but she would not have described him as fat.

"Sit down," he commanded, "I haven't seen you since Friday. The doctor came in yesterday morning. Nerves, huh? What's the matter with him?"

Beryl laughed. "Father receives a great deal of misplaced sympathy. He is really very well. He has been jumpy ever since I can remember."

Steppe nodded. He was sitting by her side in the chair vacated by Ronnie, and Ronnie was standing.

"Sit down, Ronnie," she pointed to a chair at the other side of her.

"No—no thank you, Beryl," he said hastily, for all the world like a schoolboy asked to sit in the presence of his master.

"Sit down," growled Steppe, and to the girl's amazement, Ronnie sat. It was the only notice Jan Steppe took of his presence throughout the interview, and Ronnie neither showed resentment nor made the slightest attempt to intrude into the conversation that followed.

Presently Steppe looked at his watch. "I can catch that train," he said, and got up. "You're coming to dinner with me next week—I'll fix the date with the doctor." She said she would be delighted. Something of the mastership extended to her.

"You saw Sault?" He turned back after he had taken her hand. "Queer fellow, huh? Big man, huh?"

"I thought he was—interesting," she admitted.

"Yes—interesting. A man." He glowered at Ronald Morelle. "Interesting," he repeated, and went away with that. Her fascinated gaze followed him as he strode toward the car. "Paddington—get me there, damn you," she heard him say, and when the car had gone—

"Dynamic," she said with a sigh. "He is like a power house. When I shake hands with him, I feel as though I'm going to get a bad burn! You were very silent, Ronnie."

"Yes—" absently. "Old Steppe is rather a shocker, isn't he? How did he know you had seen Sault?"

"Father told him, I suppose. Ronnie, are you afraid of Mr. Steppe?"

He colored. "Afraid? How stupid you are, Beryl! Why should I be afraid of him? He's—well, I do business with him. I am a director of a company or two, he put me into them. One has to—how shall I put it? One has to be polite to these people. I'll go along now, Beryl—lot of work to do."

He was uncomfortable, and she did not pursue the subject. The knowledge brought a little ache to her heart—that Ronnie was afraid of Jan Steppe! She would have given her soul to respect Ronald Morelle as she respected the swarthy gray-haired man whom even Steppe respected.

IV

"Children," said Mrs. Colebrook peering into the saucepan that bubbled and splashed and steamed on the kitchen fire, "are a great responsibility—especially in this neighborhood where, as you might say, there is nothing but raffle."

Sometime in her youth, it is probable that Mrs. Colebrook had to choose between "rabble" and "riff-raff" and had found a compromise.

"That man Starker who lives up the street, Number 39, I think it is—no maybe it's 37—it is the house before the sweep's. Well, I did think he was all right, geraniums in his window too, and canaries. A very homely man, wouldn't say boo to a goose. He got nine months this morning."

Ambrose Sault, sitting in a wooden chair which was wedged tightly between the kitchen table and the dresser, drummed his fingers absently upon the polished cloth table-cover and nodded. His dark sallow face wore an expression of strained interest.

"Evie—well I'm worried about Evie. She sits and broods—there's no other word for it—by the hour and she used it to be such a bright, cheerful girl. I wonder sometimes if it is through her working at the drug stores. Being attached to medicines in a manner of speaking, you're bound to hear awful stories—people's insides and all that sort of thing. It is depressing for a young girl. Christina says she talks in her sleep and moans and tosses about. It can't be over a young man, or she'd bring him home. I asked her the other day—I think a girl's best friend is her mother—and all I got was, 'Oh shut up, mother'. In my young days I wouldn't have dared speak to my mother like that, but girls have changed. They want to go to business, cashiering and typewriting, and such nonsense. I went out to service when I was sixteen and was first parlormaid before I was twenty. But talk to these girls about going into domestic service and they laugh at you." A silence followed which Sault felt it was his duty to break.

"I suppose they do. Life is very hard on women, even the most favored of women. I hardly blame them for getting whatever happiness they can."

"Happiness!" scoffed Mrs. Colebrook, shifting the saucepan to the hob, "it all depends on what you call 'happiness.' I don't see much happiness in standing in a draughty shop taking money all day and adding up figures and stamping bills! Besides, look at the temptation. She meets all kind of people—"

"I think I'll go upstairs to my room, Mrs. Colebrook. I want to do a little work."

"You're a worker," said Mrs. Colebrook admiringly,"I'll call you when sup-per is ready."

"May I walk in to see Christina?" He asked permission in the same words every night and received the same answer.

"Of course you can; you need never ask, Mr. Sault. She'll be glad to see you."

At the head of the narrow stairway Sault knocked on a door and a cheerful voice bade him come in. It was a small room containing two beds. That which was nearest the window was occupied by a girl whose pallor was made more strangely apparent by a mop of bright red hair. Over her head, and hooked to the wall, was a kerosene lamp of unusual design and brilliance. She had been reading and one white hand lay over the open page of a book by her side. Sault looked up at the lamp, touched the button that controlled the light and peered into the flame.

"Working all right?"

"Fine," she said enthusiastically, "You're a brick, Ambrose, to make it. I had no idea you could do anything like that. Mother won't touch it; the thinks it will explode."

"It can't explode," he said, shaking his head. "Those vapor gas lamps are safe, unless you fool with them. Have it put outside the door in the morning and I'll fill it. Well, where have you been today, Christina?"

She showed her small white teeth in a smile. "To Etruria," she said solemnly. "It is the country that was old when Rome was young. I went on an exploring expedition. We left Croydon Aerodrome by airplane and stayed overnight in Paris. My fiancé is a French marquis and we stayed at his place in the Avenue Kleber. The next morning we went by special train to Rome. I visited the Col-iseum by car and saw the temples and the ruins. I spent another day at the Vat-ican and St. Peter's and saw the pope. Then we went on to Volsinii and Tarquinii and I found a wonderful old tomb full of glorious Etruscan ware plates and am-poras and vases. They must have been worth millions. There we met a magi-cian. He lived in an old, ruined house on the side of the hill. He had a flock of goats and gave us milk. It was magic milk, for suddenly we found ourselves in the midst of an enormous marble city full of beautiful men and women in to-gas and wonderful robes. The streets were filled with rich chariots drawn by lit-tle horses. The chariots shone like gold and were covered with figures of lions and hunters, and trees and scrolls—wonderful! And the gardens! They were beautiful. Flowers of every kind, heliotrope and roses and big, white trumpet lilies and the marble houses were covered with wisteria—oh dear!"

"Etruria?" repeated Sault thoughtfully. "Older than Rome? Of course, there must have been—people before the Romans, the sort of ancient Britons of Rome—"

Her eyes, fixed on his, were gleaming with merriment. "Of course. I told you about the marvelous trip I had to China? When I was the lovely concubine of

Yang-Kuei-Fee? And how the eunuchs strangled me? That was long after Rome, but China was two thousand years old then."

"I remember," he said soberly, "you went to China once before then—" His glance fell on the pages of the book and he picked it up, turning its meaningless leaves.

"It is all about Etruria," she said. "Evie borrowed it from the store. They have a circulating library at the store. Have you seen Evie?"

He shook his head. "Not for weeks," he said, "I am usually in my room when she comes home."

Christina Colebrook, invalid and visionary, puckered her smooth brows into a frown. She had emerged from her world of dreams and make-believe and was facing the ugliness of life that eddied about her bed.

"Evie is changed quite a lot," she said. "She is quieter and dresses more carefully. Not in the way you would notice, she always had good taste, but especially in the way of underclothes. All girls adore swagger underclothes. They live in dread that one day they will be knocked down by a motor-bus and taken to a hospital wearing a shabby camisole! But Evie—she's collecting all sorts of things. You might think she was getting together a trousseau. Has she ever spoken to you about anybody called 'Ronnie'?"

"No—she never speaks to me," said Ambrose.

"You know nobody called Ronnie?"

He signified his ignorance. At the moment he did not associate the name.

"She talks in her sleep," Christina went on slowly, "and she's spoken that name lots of times. I haven't told mother; what would be the good, with her heart as it is? 'Ronnie' is the man who is worrying her. I think she is in love with him, or what she thinks is love. And he is somebody in a good station of life, because once she called out in the middle of the night, 'Ronnie, take me in your car.'"

Sault was silent. This was the first time Christina had ever spoken to him about the girl.

"There is only one thing that can happen," said she wisely, "and that would break mother's heart. Mother has very narrow views. The people of our class have. I should feel that way myself if I hadn't seen the world," she patted the book by her side, "perhaps mother's view is right. She is respectable and the old Roman Emperor Constantine, when he classified the nobility, made the 're-spectable' much superior to the 'honorable.'"

"What do you mean—about Evie?"

"I mean that she'll come to me one night and tell me that she is in trouble. And then I shall have to get mother into a philosophical mood and try to make her see that it is better for a child to be illegitimate than not to be born at all."

"Good gracious!" said Ambrose, startled. "But it may be—just a friendship."

"Rats!" said Christina contemptuously. "Friendships between attractive shop girls and well-to-do young men! I've heard about 'em—platonic. Have you ever heard of Archianassa? She was Plato's mistress. He didn't even practice the kind of love that is named after him. Evie is a good girl and has really fine principles. I shock her awfully at times, I wish I didn't. I don't mean I wish I didn't say things that make her shocked, but that she wouldn't be shocked at all. You have to have a funny kink in your mind before you take offense at the woman and man facts. If you blush easily, you fall easily. I wish to God Evie wasn't so pretty. And she's a dear, too, Ambrose. She has great schemes for getting me away to a country where my peculiar ailment will dissolve under uninterrupted sunlight. Poor darling! It would be better if she thought more of her own dangerous sickness."

"Ronald Morelle," said Ambrose suddenly, "but it wouldn't be he."

"Who is Ronald Morelle?"

"He is the only Ronald I know. I don't even know him. He's a friend of a— a friend of mine."

"Rich—where does he live?"

"In Knightsbridge somewhere."

Christina whistled. "Glory be! Evie's shop is in Knightsbridge!"

At eleven o'clock that night Evie Colebrook came into the room, and, as she stooped over the bed to kiss her sister, Christina saw something.

"You've been crying, Evie."

Evie turned away quickly and began to unfasten her skirt. "I—I twisted my ankle—slipped off the sidewalk—I was a baby to cry!"

Christina watched her as she undressed rapidly. "You haven't said your prayers, Evie."

"Damn my prayers!" There was a little choke at the end. "Put out the light, Christina, I'm awfully tired."

Christina reached up for the dangling chain that Ambrose Sault had fixed to the lamp, but she did not immediately pull it. "Mr. Sault was talking about people he knew tonight," she said carelessly. "Have you ever heard of a man called Ronald Morelle?" There was no answer, then.

"Good-night, Christina."

Christina pulled the chain and the light went out.

V

Beryl Merville told herself, at least once a day, that the average girl did not give two thoughts about the source of her father's income. In her case, there was less reason why she should trouble her head.

Dr. Merville had retired from practice four years before. In his time, he was what is loosely described as "a fashionable physician," and certainly was regarded as one of the first authorities of cardiac diseases in the country. His practice, as a consultant, was an extensive one, and his fees were exceptionally high, even for a fashionable physician. When he retired he was indubitably a rich man. He sold his house in Devonshire Street and bought a more pretentious home in Park Place, but—the zest for speculation, repressed during the time he was following his profession, had occupied the hours of leisure which retirement brought to him. An active man, well under sixty, the emptiness of his days, after he had turned over his work, filled him with dismay. He had broken violently from the routine of twenty-five years and found time the heaviest of the burdens he had ever carried. He tried to find interests and failed. He was under an agreement to the doctor who had purchased his practice not to return to his profession, or he would have been back in Devonshire Street a month after he had left. He bought a few thoroughbreds and sent them to a trainer, but he had no love for the turf and, although he won a few respectable stakes, he quitted the game at the end of the first season.

Then he tried the stock market, made a few thousands in oil and grew more interested. A rubber speculation hurt him, but not so much that his enthusiasm was damped or his bank balance was seriously affected. He followed this loss with what might have been a disastrous investment in South African Mines. Then, at a nerve-racking moment, came Steppe, who held up the market and let out Merville, bruised and shaken, but not ruinously so. Here might have ended the speculative career of Dr. Merville, had he not been under an obligation to the South African. Within a month of their meeting, the doctor's name appeared on the prospectus of one of Steppe's companies—a mild and unromantic cold storage flotation which was a success in every sense. Merville had many friends in society; people who might look askance at the name of Jan Steppe, and be disturbed by the recollection of certain other companies which that gentleman had floated, accepted Dr. Merville's directorship as evidence of the company's stability and financial soundness. The issue was oversubscribed and paid a dividend from the first year.

This object lesson was not lost upon the big man. He followed the promotion with another. The East Rand Consolidated Deep was floated for three-quarters of a million. Applications came in for two millions. Dr. Merville was chairman of the board. Even Jan Steppe was surprised. Large as was the circle of Merville's acquaintances, neither his personal popularity nor his standing as a financial authority could account for this overwhelming success. Merville himself discounted his own influence, not realizing that in the twenty-five years of professional life, he had built up a national reputation. His name had been a household word since his treatment of a foreign royalty whose case had been regarded by native physicians as hopeless. This may not have been a complete explanation; probably the fact that the stock in the cold storage company stood at a premium had something to do with the rush for Consolidated Deeps.

The new company did not pay dividends, but long before the first was due, Mr. Steppe had launched two others. On paper Dr. Merville made a fortune; actually, he acquired heavy liabilities, not the least of which was his heavy participation in a private flotation which Mr. Steppe, with unconscious humor, labeled: "The Investment Salvage Syndicate." It was a stockholding company and in the main it held such stock as a general public declined to purchase. There are rules of behavior which normal people do not transgress. A gentleman does not search the overcoat pockets of his fellow clubmen, and confiscate such valuables as he may find; nor does he steal into the houses of people he does not know and remove their silver. A corporation man has a less rigid code. Dr. Merville found himself consciously assisting in the manipulation of a stock, a manipulation which could only be intended to deprive stockholders of their legitimate rights. There was one unpleasant moment of doubt and shame when Merville sought to disentangle his individuality from this corporative existence. He tried to think singly, applying the tests which had governed his life—he found it easier to divide his responsibility.

Somehow he felt less venal when only a fourteenth of the blame attached to him. This fraction represented his holding in Consolidated Deeps. Wealth is an effective narcotic. Rich and fearless men can find a melancholy pleasure in the contemplation of their past sins. But poverty and the danger of poverty acts as a microphone through the medium of which the still small voice of conscience is a savage roar.

Beryl thought he was unusually nervous when she went to find him in his study. He started at the sound of her voice.

"Ready—yes, dear. What time did Steppe say?"

"Eight o'clock. We have plenty of time, father—the car isn't here yet. Do you know whether Ronnie will be there?"

Dr. Merville was looking abstractedly at her; his mind, she knew, was very far away. "Ronnie? I don't know. John Maxton will be there. I saw him today. Steppe admires him and John is clever; he will be a judge one of these days. Yes—a judge." The little grimace he made was involuntary.

"One would think you expected to meet him in his official capacity," she laughed.

"Absurd of course—as to Ronnie? How do you feel about him, Beryl?" The maid tapped at the door to say the car had arrived.

Beryl answered: "Do you mean—I don't quite know what you do mean?"

"About the scandal. Do you remember a man who came to see you—why he should have come to you I don't know—with a story about his sister?"

"East was the name. Yes, Ronnie told me all about it. The man is a blackmailer and his sister was not much better. Ronnie had shown a kindness to the girl, he met her at some—some mission or other. Ronnie does queer things like that—and he gave her some money to go on a holiday. That was all."

"Humph—ready?"

"But, daddy, don't you believe Ronnie?" She was desperately anxious to consolidate her own faith.

"I don't know. Ronnie is a queer fellow—"

He was ready to go; his overcoat was over his arm and yet he lingered. She guessed he would say something more about Ronald Morelle and was stiffening to defend him, but she was mistaken.

"Beryl, you are twenty-two and very beautiful. I may be biased but I hardly think I am. I have seen many lovely women in my life and you could hold your own with any of them. Do you ever think of getting married?"

She tried hard to control herself, but the color in her face deepened and faded.

"I haven't thought much about it," she said. "There are two parties to a marriage, daddy."

"Are you fond of anybody? I mean are you, in your heart—committed to any one man?"

A pause, then: "No."

"I'm glad," said her father, relieved. "Very glad—you must look for something in a man which fellows like Ronnie Morelle can never give to a woman—power, fortune, mental strength and stability—come along."

She followed him to the car dumb with astonishment, but not at that moment apprehensive. She knew that he had been talking of Jan Steppe.

VI

Mr. Steppe had a house in Berkeley Square which he rented from its lordly owner. Beryl had dined there before, and it had been a baffling experience, for in no respect did the personality of the tenant find an opportunity of expressing itself. The furnishings and the color schemes of the landlord had been left as they had been found, and since the atmosphere of the place was late Victorian, Mr. Steppe was unconformable to his surroundings.

Beryl thought of him as a Sultan amidst samplers.

Sir John Maxton was talking to him when they were announced. One of the greatest advocates at the bar, Maxton was tall, slender, esthetic. His gentle manner had led many a confident witness into trouble. He had a reputation at the bar as a just and merciless man; a master of the art of cross-examination.

"The doctor told me you were likely to be here," he said, when she had escaped from Steppe's thunderous civilities. "I hoped Ronnie would have come—have you seen him lately?"

"Only for a few minutes on Monday. I met him in the park. I didn't know you were a friend of his, Sir John?"

Maxton's lips curled. Beryl wondered if he was trying to smile, or whether that twitch indicated something uncomplimentary to Ronnie.

"I'm more than a friend—and less. I was one of the executors of his father's will. Old Bennett Morelle was my first client and I suppose I stand in *loco parentis* to Ronnie by virtue of my executorship. I have not seen him for quite a year.

Somebody told me that he was scribbling! He always had a bent that way—it is a thousand pities he didn't take the law seriously—an occupation would have kept him out of mischief."

"Has Ronnie been called to the bar?" she asked in astonishment. Maxton nodded.

"Just before the war, but he has never practiced. I hope that the newspaper connection will keep him busy."

"But Ronnie works very hard," she asserted stoutly. "He has his company work, he is a director of several and chairman of one I believe." Maxton looked at her with the faintest shade of amusement in his eyes.

"Of course," he said drily, "that is an occupation." He lowered his voice. "Do you mind if I am ill-bred and ask you if you have known our host very long?"

"A few years." He nodded.

Beryl, glancing across at her father and Steppe, saw that the doctor was talking earnestly. She caught Steppe's gaze and looked back to Sir John.

"I have been fighting a case for him—rather a hopeless proposition, but we won. The jury was wrong, I think, in giving us a verdict. I can say this because the other side have entered an appeal which is certain to succeed."

Jan Steppe must have heard the last sentence.

"Huh? Succeed? Yes, perhaps—it doesn't matter very much. I had a verdict, a disqualified winner is still a moral winner, huh, doctor? You used to be a racing man, what do you think?"

Dinner was announced whilst the doctor was disclaiming any knowledge of the turf or its laws. The dinner was exquisite in its selection and brevity. Mr. Steppe had one special course which none of the others shared. He invited them and showed no regret when they refused. A footman brought a silver dish piled high with steaming mealy cobs. He took them in his hands and gnawed at the hot corn. It was probably the only way that mealies could be eaten, she told herself—no more inelegant an exhibition than the sword-swallowing manoeuvre which followed the serving of asparagus.

"Sault?" Mr. Steppe was wiping his fingers on his serviette. "You asked me once before, Beryl—where was it? In the park. No, I haven't seen him. I very seldom do. Strange man, huh?"

The butler had attended more frequently to Dr. Merville's wine glass than to any other of the guests. His gloom had disappeared and he was more like the cheerful man Beryl remembered.

"Sault is a danger and a menace to society," he said.

Steppe's brows lowered but he did not interrupt.

"At the same time he can exercise one of the most beneficent forces that nature has ever given into the care of a human being."

"You pique my curiosity," said Maxton, interested. "Is he psychic or clairvoyant—from your tone one would imagine that he had some supernatural power."

"He has," nodded Merville. "I discovered it some time ago. He lodges with a woman named Colebrook in a very poor part of the town. Mrs. Colebrook suffers from an unusual form of heart disease. She had a seizure one night and Sault came for me. You will remember, dear, when I was called out in the middle of the night—a year ago. The moment I examined the woman, who was unconscious, and in my opinion *in extremis*, I knew that nothing could be done. I applied the remedies which I had brought with me, and which I had thought, from his description of the seizure, would be necessary, but with no effect. Sault was terribly upset. The woman had two daughters, one bedridden. His grief at the thought that she would die without her daughter seeing her, was tragic. I think he was going upstairs to bring the girl down, when I said casually that if I could lend the patient strength to live for another hour, she would probably recover. What followed, seems to me even now as part of a fantastic dream."

Beryl's elbow was on the table, her chin in her palm and she was absorbed. Maxton lay back, his arm hanging over the back of his chair, weighing every word; Steppe, his hands clasped on the table, his head bent, skeptical.

"Sault bent down and took the inert hands of the woman in his—just held them. Remember this, that she was the color of this serviette, her lips gray. I wondered what he was doing—I don't know now. Only her face went gradually pink and her eyes opened."

"How long after he took her hands?" asked Maxton.

"Less than a minute I should think. As I say, she opened her eyes and looked around and then she nodded very slowly. 'What do you think of that, Dr. Merville?' she said."

"She knew you, of course?"

"She had never seen me in her life. I learned that afterwards. Sault dropped her hands and stood up. He was looking ghastly. Not a vestige of color. I said to him: 'Sault, what is the matter,' and he answered in a cockney whine, that was h-less and ungrammatical—Sault never makes an error in that respect—'It's me 'eart, sir, I get them attacks at times—haneurism.'"

"Sault?"

Steppe's face was puckered into a grimace of incredulity.

"Go on, please, father!" urged the girl.

"What came after was even more curious. Mrs. Colebrook got up quite unaided, sat down in a chair before the fire and fell fast asleep. Sault sat down, too. I gave him some brandy and he seemed to recover. But he did not speak again, not even to answer my questions. He sat bolt upright in a wooden chair by the side of the kitchen table—all this happened in the kitchen. He didn't move for a long time and then his hands began to stray along the table. There was a big work basket at the other side and presently his hands reached it and he drew it toward him. I watched him. He took out some garment, I think it was a night dress belonging to one of the girls. It was unfinished and the needle was sticking into it—he began to sew!"

"Good God!" cried Maxton. "Do you suggest that on touching of hands the two identities changed?"

"I suggest that—I assert that," said the doctor quietly, and drank his wine.

"Rubbish!" growled Steppe. "What did Sault say about it?"

"I will tell you. Exactly an hour after this extraordinary transference had been made, I saw Mrs. Colebrook going pale. She opened her eyes and looked at me in a puzzled way, then at the daughter, a pretty child who had been present all the time. 'I always 'ave these attacks, sir,' she said, 'a haneurism the doctors call it!'"

"And Sault?"

"He was himself again, but distressingly tired and wan."

"Did he explain?"

The doctor shook his head.

"He didn't understand or remember much. The next day out of curiosity I called at the house and asked him if he could sew. He was amused. He said that he had never used a needle in his life, his hands were too big."

Beryl sat back with a sigh. "It doesn't seem—human," she said.

The doctor had opened his mouth to reply when there was a crash in the hall outside and the sound of a high, aggressive voice. Another second and the door was thrown violently open and the man lurched in. He was hatless and his frock coat was covered with the coffee-colored stains of wet mud. His cravat was awry and the ends hung loose over his unbuttoned waist-coat. A stray lock of black hair hung over his narrow forehead. He strode into the center of the room and with legs apart, one hand on his hip and the other caressing his long, brown beard, he surveyed the company with a sardonic smile.

"Hail! Thieves and brother bandits!" he said thickly. He spoke with a slight lisp. "Hail! Head devil and chief of the tribe! Hail! Helen—"

Steppe was on his feet, his head thrust forwards, his shoulders bent. Maxton saw him and started. There was something feline in that crouching attitude. "You drunken fool! How dare you come here, huh!"

Mr. Moropulos snapped his fingers contemptuously. "I come, because I have the right," he said with drunken gravity, "who will deny the prime minister the right of calling upon the king?" he bowed and nearly lost his balance, recovering by the aid of a chairback.

"Go to my study, Moropulos, I will come out with you," Steppe had gained control of himself, but the big frame was trembling with pent rage.

"Study—bah! Here is my study! Hail, doctor, man of obnoxious draughts, hail, stranger, whoever you are—where's the immaculate Ronnie? Flower of English chivalry and warrior of a million flights—huh?"

He bellowed his imitation of Steppe's grunt and chuckled with laughter.

"Now, listen, confederates, I have done with you all. I am going to live honest. Why? I will tell you—"

"Moropulos!" Beryl turned quickly toward the door. She knew before she saw the stolid figure that it was Sault. Moropulos turned too.

"Ah! The faithful Ambrose—do you want me, Sault?" His tone was mild, he seemed to wilt under the steady gaze of the man in the doorway. Ambrose Sault beckoned and the drunken intruder shuffled out, shamefaced, fearful.

"Quite an interesting evening," said Sir John Maxton as he closed the car door on the Mervilles that night.

VII

Two days later Sir John Maxton made an unexpected call upon the doctor and it occurred to him that he might also have made an unwelcome appearance; for he interrupted a tête-à-tête.

"I thought I should find the doctor in. Well, Ronnie, how are you after all these years?"

Ronnie was relieved to see him—that was the impression which the lawyer received. And Beryl, although she was her sweet, equable self, would gladly have excused his presence. Maxton had an idea that he had surprised them in the midst of a quarrel. The girl was flushed and her eyes were unusually bright. Ronnie's countenance was clouded with gloom. Sir John was sensitive to atmosphere.

"No, I really won't stay, I wanted to have a chat with the doctor about the extraordinary story he told us the other night. I was dining with the Lord Chief and some other judges last night and, without mentioning names, of course, I repeated the story. They were remarkably interested, Berharn says that he had heard of such a case—"

"What is all this about?" asked Ronnie curiously. "You didn't tell me anything, Beryl. Who, what and where is the 'case'?"

"Mr. Sault," she said shortly.

"Oh, Sault! He is an extraordinary fellow—I must meet him. They say that he cannot read or write."

"Is that a fact?" Sir John Maxton looked at the girl.

"Yes—I believe so. Ronnie on the contrary is in the way of becoming a famous writer, Sir John."

"So I hear." He wondered why she had so deliberately and so abruptly brought the conversation into another channel.

Ronald Morelle, for his part, was not inclined to let the subject drift. "It is quaint how that coon intrigues you all," he said, "oh, yes, he is colored. You haven't seen him, John, or you wouldn't ask that question."

"I have seen him; it did not appear to me that he was colored—he has a striking face."

"At any rate, he seems to have struck you and Beryl all of a heap," said Ronnie smiling. "Really I must meet him. Are you going, Sir John?" Maxton was taking his farewell of the girl. "Because if you are, I'll walk a little way with you. 'Bye, Beryl."

"Goodbye, Ronnie," she said quietly.

Once in the street Maxton asked: "What is the matter with you and Beryl?"

"Nothing—Beryl is just a little grandmotherly. She went to the theatre last night with some people and she spotted me in a box."

"I see," said Sir John drily, "and of course you were not alone in the box."

"Why on earth should I be?" demanded the other. "Beryl is really unreasonable. She swore that my friend was a girl she had seen me with in the park."

"And who was it—is that a discreet question?"

"No it isn't," said Ronnie instantly. "I don't think one ought to chuck names about—it is most dishonorable and caddish. The lady was a very great friend of mine."

"Then I probably know her," said Sir John wilfully dense. "I know most of the people in your set, and I cannot imagine that you would be scoundrel enough to escort the kind of girl you couldn't introduce to me or Beryl or any other of your friends."

"I give you my word of honor," Ronnie was earnest, "that the lady was not only presentable, but is known personally to you. The fact is, that she had a row with her fiancé, a man I know very well, a Coldstreamer, and I was doing no more than trying to reconcile them—bring them together you understand. She was dreadfully depressed, and I got a box at the theatre with the idea of cheering her up. My efforts," he added virtuously, "were successful. Beryl said that it was a girl—the daughter of a dear friend of mine, she had seen me talking with in the park."

"What dear friend of yours was this?"

"I don't think you've met him," parried Ronnie.

"Did she have trouble with her fiancé, too?" asked Sir John innocently. "Really, Ronnie, you are coming out strong as a disinterested friend of distressed virgins! If I may employ the imagery and language of an American burglar whom I recently defended—Sir Galahad has nothing on you!"

"You don't believe me, John," said Ronnie injured.

"Of course I cannot believe you. I am not a child. You had some girl with you, some 'pick up,' innocent or guilty, God knows. I will assume her innocence. The sophisticated have no appeal for you. There was a girl named East—a chorus girl, if I remember rightly—"

"If you're going to talk about that disgraceful attempt to blackmail me, I'm finished," said Ronnie resigned.

"Why didn't you charge her and her brother with blackmail? They came to me—"

"Good lord, did they? I'll break that infernal blackguard's neck!"

"When will you meet him?" Ronnie did not answer.

"They came to me and I knew that the story was true. The brother, of course, *is* a blackmailer. He is levying blackmail now and you are paying him—don't argue, Ronnie, of course you are paying him. You said just now that you would break his neck, which meant to me that you see him frequently—when he comes to draw his blood money. If it were a case of blackmail, why did you not prosecute? The mere threat of the prosecution would have been sufficient to have sent him to ground—it struck me that the girl was acting under the coercion of her brother, and I do not think you would have had any trouble from her. Ronnie, you are rotten." He said this as he stopped at the corner of Park Lane and Piccadilly, and Ronnie smiled nervously.

"Oh come now, John, that is rather a strong expression."

"Rotten," repeated the lawyer. He screwed a monocle in his eye and surveyed his companion dispassionately. "Chorus girls—shop girls—the mechanics of joy who serve Madame Ritti—that made you jump, eh? I know quite a lot about you. They are your life. And God gave you splendid gifts and the love of the sweetest, dearest girl in this land."

"Who is this?" asked the young man slowly.

"Beryl. You do not need to be told that. Search the ranks of your light women for her beauty, Ronnie."

A girl passed them, a wisp of a girl on the borderline of womanhood. She carried a little bag and was hurrying home from the store where she was employed. Even as he listened to the admonition of his companion, Ronnie caught her eyes and smiled into them—she paused and looked round once—he was still watching her.

"I am afraid I must leave you, John, I've a lot of work to do, and you are quite mistaken as to my character—and Beryl." He left the lawyer abruptly and walked toward the gates of the park where the girl had stopped, ostensibly to tie a shoe-lace.

Sir John saw her pass leisurely into the park; a few seconds later Ronnie had followed. His time was his own, for Evie Colebrook was working that evening, the annual stocktaking was in progress, as she had told him when they were at the theatre on the previous night.

"Rotten!" repeated Maxton, and stalked gloomily to his club.

VIII

Mr. Ronald Morelle's flat was on the third floor of a block that faced busy Knightsbridge. His library was a large and airy room at the back and from the open casements commanded an uninterrupted view of the park. It was a pleasant room with its rows of bookshelves and its chintzes. The silver fireplace and the rich Persian rugs which covered the parquet were the only suggestions of luxury. There were one or two pictures which François had an order to remove when certain visitors were expected. The rest were decent reproductions with the exception of a large oil painting above the mantelpiece. It was a St. Anthony and was attributed to Titiano Vecellio. The austere saint loomed darkly from a sombre background and was represented as an effeminate youth; the veining of the neck and shoulders was characteristically Titian, so too was the inclination of a marble column which showed faintly in the picture. Titiano's inability to draw a true vertical line is well known and upon this column, more than upon other evidence, the experts accepted the picture as an early example of the fortunate painter's work.

Ronnie was indifferent as to the authenticity of the picture. The dawning carnality on Anthony's lean face, the misty shape of the temptress—Titian or his disciple had reduced to visibility the doubt, the gloating and the very thoughts of the Saint.

A black oak table stood in the center of the room and a deep Medici writing chair was placed opposite the black blotting-pad. It pleased Ronnie to imitate those ministers of state who employed this color to thwart curious-minded servants who, with the aid of a mirror, might discover the gist of outward correspondence.

It was nearing midnight when the sound of Ronnie's key in the lock sent his sleepy servant into the lobby. Ronnie stood in the hall tenderly stripping his gloves. "Has anybody been?"

"No, m'sieur."

"Letters?"

"Only one, m'sieur. An account."

He opened the library door and Ronnie walked in. He switched on the light of his desk lamp and sat down. "I have not been out all the evening, François."

"No, m'sieur."

"I came home after dinner and I have not left this room, do you understand?"

"Perfectly, m'sieur."

"Have we any iodine—look for it, damn you, don't gape!"

François hurried out to inspect the contents of the bath room locker, where were stored such first aid remedies as were kept in the flat. Ronnie looked at his hand and pulled back the cuff of his coat; three ugly red scratches ran from the wrist to the base of the middle fingers. His lips pursed angrily. "Little beast," he said. "Well?"

"There is a bottle—would m'sieur like a bandage?"

"It is not necessary—have you a cat in the flat? No, well get one tomorrow. You need not keep it permanently. I don't think there will be any trouble. Bring me a hand-mirror from my dressing-table—hurry."

He lifted the shade from the table lamp and, in the mirror, examined his face carefully. His right cheek was red, he imagined finger-marks, but the fine skin had not been torn.

"I have had a quarrel with a lady, François. A common girl—I'd not think she will make any further trouble, but if she does—she does not know me anyway."

Ronald's love-making had ended unpleasantly, and he had left the dark aisles of the park in a hurry, before the scream of a frightened girl had brought the police to the spot.

"I was expecting m'sieur to telephone me saying that I might go home," said François. He lodged in Kensington, and sometimes it was convenient for Ronnie, that he should go home early. Two women came in the morning to clean the flat and he usually arrived in time to carry in his master's breakfast from the restaurant attached to the building.

"No, I didn't telephone. Take this glass back and bring me the evening newspapers. That is all. You can clear out."

When the front door closed upon his valet, Ronnie got up and, walking to the window, pulled aside the curtains. The casement was open and he sat down on the padded window-seat, looking out into the darkness. He was not thinking of this night's adventure, being something of a philosopher. The sordidness and the vulgarity of it, would not distress him in any circumstances. He was thinking of Beryl and what John Maxton had said. He knew that she liked him, but he had made no special effort to foster her affection or to evolve from their relationship to one more intimate. By his code, she was taboo; lovemaking with Beryl could only lead to marriage, and matrimony was outside of his precarious plans. It pleased him to ponder upon Beryl—perhaps she was in love with him. He had not considered the possibility before. That women only differed by the hats they wore was a working rule of his; but it was strange that the influence he exercised was common to girls so widely separated by birth, education and taste as Beryl was from Evie Colebrook—and others.

Self-disparagement was the last weakness to be expected in Ronald Morelle, and yet, it was true to say that he had restricted his hunting for so long to one variety of game, that he doubted his ability to follow another.

His father had been an enthusiastic hawker, one of the remaining few who followed the sport of kings, and Ronnie invariably thought of his adventuring in terms of falconry. He was a hawk, enseamed, a hawk that swung on its rigid sails, waiting on until the quarry was sprung. Sometimes the quarry was not taken without talons to rend and tear at the embarrassed falcon—he felt the wounds on his hand gingerly. But a trained hawk respects the domestic fowl, even the folk of the dovecot may coo at peace whilst he waits on in the sky. Beryl—? She was certainly lovely. Her figure was delectable. And her mouth, red and full— a Rossetti woman should not have such lips. Was it Rossetti who painted those delicately featured women? He got up and found a big portfolio filled with prints. Yes, it was Rossetti, but Beryl's figure was incomparably more delicious than any woman's that the painter had drawn. He came back to the window, staring out into the night, until, in the gray of dawn, the outline of trees emerged from the void. Then he went to bed and to sleep. He did not move for five hours and then he woke with a horrible sense of desolation. He blinked round the room and at that instant the clock of a church began to strike—the quarters sounded—a pause.

"Toll—toll—toll—toll—toll—toll—toll—toll." Nine o'clock! With a scream of fear he leaped out of bed, sweating, panic-stricken, forlorn. Nine o'clock! "No—no—Christ—no!"

François, an early arrival, heard his voice and rushed in. "M'sieur," he gasped.

Ronald Morelle was sitting on his bed, sobbing into his bands.

"A nightmare, François—a nightmare—get out, blast you!" But he had had no nightmare, could recall nothing of dreams, though he strove all day, his head throbbing. Only he knew that to hear nine o'clock striking had seemed very dreadful.

IX

"I saw your friend Ronald Morelle today," said Moropulos, sending a writhing ring of smoke to the ceiling, Sprawling on a big morris chair, his slippered feet resting on the edge of a fender, he watched the circle break against the ceiling. A pair of stained gray flannel trousers, a silk shirt and a velvet coat that had once been a vivid green; these and an immense green silk cravat, the color of which showed through his beard, constituted his usual morning negligee.

Ambrose Sault, busy with the body of an unfinished safe, which in the rough had come from the maker's hands that morning, released the pressure of his acetylene lamp and removed his goggles before he replied.

He was working in shirt and trousers, and his sleeves were rolled up, displaying the rope-like muscles of his arm. He looked across to his indolent companion and wiped the perspiration from his forehead.

"Mr. Ronald Morelle is neither a friend nor an acquaintance, Moropulos. I don't think I have ever seen him. I have heard of him."

"You haven't missed much by not knowing him," Moropulos, "but he's a good-looking fellow."

He flicked the ash of his cigarette on to the tiled hearth. "Steppe is still annoyed with me." Sault smiled to himself.

"You think he is justified? Perhaps. I was terribly drunk, but I was happy. Some day, my dear brother, I shall get so drunk that even you will not hold me. I move towards my apotheosis of intoxication certainly and surely. Then I will be irresistible and I shall have no fear of those brute arms of yours." He sucked at the cigarette without speaking for a long time. Sault went back to his work.

"I have often wondered!" said Moropulos at last.

"What?"

"Whether it would have been better if I had followed the advice of my head man that morning I pulled you aboard the sloop. You remember Bob the Kanaka boy? He wanted to knock you on the head and drop you overboard; you were too dangerous, he said. If a government boat had picked us up and you had been found on board as well as—certain other illicit properties, I should have had a double charge against me. I said 'no' because I was sorry for you."

"Because you were afraid of me," said Sault calmly. "I knew you were afraid when I looked into your eyes. Why do you speak of the islands now—we haven't talked about the Pacific since I left the boat."

"I've been thinking about you," confessed Moropulos with a quick sly glance at the man. "Do you realize how—not 'curious'—what is the word?"

"Incurious!" suggested Sault, and Moropulos looked at him with reluctant admiration.

"You are an extraordinary *hombre,* Sault. Merville says you have the *vocabulaire*—that is English or something like it—of an educated man. But to return—do you realize how incurious I am? For example, I have never once asked you, in all our years of knowing one another, why you killed that man?"

"Which man?"

Moropulos laughed softly. "Butcher! Have you killed so many? I refer to the victim for whose destruction the French government sent you to New Caledonia."

Sault stood leaning his back against the table his eyes fixed on the floor. "He was a bad man," he said simply, "I tried to find another way of—stopping him, but he was clever and he had powerful friends, who were government officials. So I killed him. He hired two men to wait for me one night. I was staying at a little hotel on the Plassy Road. They tried to beat me because I had reported this man. Then I knew that the only thing I could do was to kill him. I should do it again."

Moropulos surveyed him from under his lowered brows. "You were lucky to escape 'the widow,' my friend," he said, but Ambrose shook his head.

"Nobody was executed in those days; capital punishment had not been abolished, but the Senate refused to vote the executioner his salary. It had the same effect. I was lucky to go to New Caledonia. Cayenne is worse."

"How long did you serve?"

"Eight years and seven months," was the reply.

Moropulos made a little grimace. "I would sooner die," he said and lit another cigarette. Deep in thought he smoked until Ambrose made a move to pick up his Crooke's glasses.

"Don't work. I hate to see you—and hate worse to hear you. What do you think of Morelle?"

"I don't know him; I have heard about him. He is not a good man."

"What is a good man?" Moropulos demanded contemptuously. "He is a lover of ladies, who isn't? He is a cur too. Steppe walks on him. He is scared of Steppe but then everybody is, except you and I." Ambrose smiled.

"Well, perhaps I am—he is such a gorilla. But you are not."

"Why should I be? I am stronger than he."

Moropulos looked at the man's bare arms. "Yes—I suppose it comes down to that. The basis of all fear, is physical. When will the safe be finished?"

"In a week. I am assembling the lock at home. I shall make it work to five letters. The only word I can spell. I shouldn't have known that, but I heard a man spell it once—on the ship that brought me home. He was a steerage passenger and he used to take his little child on the deck when it was fine, and the little one used to read Scripture stories to him. When she came to a hard word, he spelled it. I heard one word and never forgot it."

"I'll be glad when the thing is finished," the Greek meditated. "We have a whole lot of papers that we never want to see the light of day, Steppe and I. We could destroy them, but they may be useful, correspondence that it isn't safe to keep and it isn't wise to burn. You are an ingenious devil!"

In the Paddington directory, against "Moropulos, 49 Junction Terrace," were the words, "mining engineer." It was a courtesy status, for he had neither mined nor engineered. Probably the people of Junction Terrace were too occupied with their own strenuous affairs to read the directory. They knew him as one who at irregular periods was brought home in the middle of the night singing noisily in a strange language. Cicero's oration was Greek to Cassius; the melodious gibberish of Mr. Moropulos was Greek to Junction Terrace, though they were not aware of the fact. No. 49 was a gaunt, damp house with a mottled face, for the stucco had peeled in patches and had never been renewed. Moropulos bought it at a bargain price and made no contingency allowance for dilapidations. The windows of the upper floors were dingy and unwashed. The owner argued that as he did not occupy the rooms above, it would be a wicked waste of money to clean the windows. Similarly he dispensed with carpets in the hall and on the stairs.

His week-ends he spent in more pleasing surroundings, for he had a cottage on the borders of Hampshire where he kept hens and grew cabbage-roses and on Sundays loafed in his garden, generally in his pajamas, to the scandal of the neighborhood. He had a whimsical turn of mind and named his cottage, "The Parthenon," and supported this conceit by decorating his arcadian groves with plaster reproductions of the great figures of mythology, such figures as Phidias and Polycletus and Praxiteles chiselled. He added to this a wooden pronaos which the local builder misguidedly surmised was intended for the entrance to a new cinema. When they discovered that the erection had no other purpose than to remind Moropulos of departed Hellenic splendors, the grief of the villagers was pathetic.

Here he was kept, reluctantly, tidy. He owned a small American car which supplied him the transportation he required, and made his country home accessible. It was Friday, the day he usually left town, but he had lingered on, hoping to see some tangible progress in the construction of the safe.

"You never seem to get any further," he complained. "You have been fiddling with that noisy lamp for two hours, and, so far as I can see, you've done nothing. How long will it be before anything happens?" and then before Sault could reply he went on: "Why don't you come to my little Athens, Sault? You prefer to stay in town. And you are a man of brains! Have you a girl here, eh?"

"No."

"Gee! What a time that fellow Ronnie must have! But they will catch him some day—a mad father or a lunatic fiancé, and ping! There will be Ronnie Morelle's brains on the floor, and the advocates pleading the unwritten law!"

"You seem to know a lot about him?"

Moropulos ran his fingers through his beard and grinned at the ceiling. "Yes—I can't know too much. We shall have trouble with him. Steppe laughs at the idea. He has him bound to his heel—is that the expression, no? Well, he has him like that! But how can you bind a liar or chain an eel? His very cowardice is a danger."

"What have you to be afraid of?" asked Sault. "So far as I can make out, you are carrying on an honest business. It must be, or the doctor wouldn't be in it." His tone was sharp and challenging. Moropulos had sufficient *nous* not to accept that kind of challenge.

"I can understand that you have papers that you wish to keep in such a way that nobody but yourselves can get at them. All businesses have their secrets."

"Quite so," agreed the Greek and yawned.

"Ronnie will pay," he said, "but I am anxious that I should not be asked to contribute to the bill. I have had a great deal of amusement watching him. The other night I was in the park. I go there because he goes. I know the paths he uses. And there came with him a most pretty young lady. She did not know him."

"You guessed that?"

"I know, because later, when she complained, she did not know his name. Ronnie!" he mused. "Now I tell you what I will undertake to do. I will make a list, accurate and precise, of all his love affairs. It will be well to know these, because there may come a day when it will be good to flourish a weapon in this young man's face. Such men marry rich women."

Sault was working and only muttered his reply. He was not then interested in Ronnie Morelle.

X

He stayed on in the house long after Moropulos had dragged himself to his room and had dressed for the journey. So absorbed was he in his task that the Greek left without his noticing. At seven o'clock he finished, put away his tools in a cupboard, threw a cloth over the safe, and went out, locking the door behind him.

Both Steppe and Moropulos had urged him to live in the house, but though he had few predilections that were not amenable to the necessities of his friends, Sault was firm on this point. He preferred the liberty which his lodgings gave him. Possibly he foresaw the difficulties which might arise if he lived entirely with the Greek. Moropulos had a vicious and an uncertain tongue; was tetchy on some points, grotesquely so, on the question of Greek decadence, although he had lived so long away from his native country that English was almost his mother tongue. Sault could be tactful, but he had a passion for truth, and the two qualities are often incompatible.

A bus carried him to the end of the street where he lodged, and he stopped at a store on the corner and bought a box of biscuits for Christina. She was secretary and reader to him, and he repaid her services with a library subscription and such delicacies as she asked him to get for her. The subscription was a godsend to the girl, and augmented, as it was, by an occasional volume which Evie was allowed to bring from the store library by virtue of her employment, her days were brightened and her dreams took a wider range than ever. The driving force of learning is imagination. By imagination was Christina educated.

Evie sometimes said that she did not understand one half of the words that Christina used. To Mrs. Colebrook her daughter was an insoluble enigma. She associated education with brain fever and ideas above your station, and whilst she was secretly proud of the invalid's learning, she regarded Christina's spinal trouble as being partly responsible for the abnormality. Mrs. Colebrook believed in dreams and premonitions and the sinister significance of broken picture wires. It was part of her creed that people who are not long for this world possess supernatural accomplishments. Therefore she eyed Christina's books askance, and looked upon the extra library subscription as being a wild flight in the face of Providence. She expressed that view privately to Ambrose Sault.

"You have come at a propitious moment, Sault Effendi," said Christina solemnly as he came in. "I have just been taking my last look at the silvery Bosphorus. My husband, taking offense at a kiss I threw to the handsome young sultan as he rose beneath my latticed window, has decreed that tonight I am to be tied in a sack and thrown into the dark waters!"

"Good gracious," said Ambrose. "You *have* been in trouble today, Christina."

"Not very much. The journey was a lovely one. We went by way of Bergen—and thank you ever so much for that old Bradshaw you got for me. It was just the thing I wanted."

"Mr. Moropulos kindly gave it to me—yes—Bergen?"

"And then to Petrograd—the Czars were there, poor people—and then to Odessa, and down the Black Sea in—oh, I don't know. It was a silly journey today, Ambrose—I wasn't in the heart for a holiday."

"Is your back any worse?"

She shook her head. "No—it seems better. I nearly let myself dream about getting well. Do you think that other idea is possible? We can borrow a spinal carriage from the Institute but mother hasn't much time, and besides, I couldn't get down those narrow stairs without a lot of help. Yes—yes, yes! I know it is possible now. But the chariot, dear Ambrose?"

"I've got it!" He chuckled at her astonishment. "It will come tomorrow. It is rather like a motor-car for I have to find a garage for it. In this tiny house there is no room. But I got it—no, it didn't cost me a great deal. Dr. Merville told me where I could get one cheap. I put new tires on and the springs are grand. Christina, you will be—don't cry, Christina, please—you make me feel terrible!" His agitation had the effect of calming her.

"There must be something in this room that makes people weep," she gulped. "Ambrose—Evie is just worrying me to death."

"What is wrong?"

She shook her red head helplessly. "I don't know. She is changed—she is old. She's such a kid, too—such a kid! If that man hurts her," the knuckles of her clenched hand showed bone-white through the skin, "I'll ask you to do what you did for mother, Ambrose, give me strength for an hour—" her voice sank to a husky whisper, "and I'll kill him—kill him—"

Sault sat locking and unlocking his fingers, his eyes vacant. "She will not be hurt. I wish I were sure it was Ronald Morelle. Steppe has only to lift his finger—"

They heard the sound of Mrs. Colebrook's heavy feet on the stairs and Christina wondered why she was coming up. She had never interrupted their little talks before.

"Somebody to see you, Christina, and I'm sure it is too kind of you, miss, and please thank the doctor. I'll never be grateful enough for what he did—"

Ambrose Sault got up slowly to his feet as Beryl came into the room.

"I wonder if you really mind my coming—I am Beryl Merville."

"It is very good of you, Miss Merville," said Christina primly. She was ready to dislike her visitor; she hated the unknown people who called upon her, especially the people who brought jelly and fruit and last year's magazines. Their touching faith in the virtues of calves'-foot and fruit as a panacea for human ills, their automatic cheerfulness and mechanical good-humor, drove her wild. The church and its women had given up Christina ever since she had asked, in answer to the inevitable question; "Yes, there are some things I want; I'd like a box of perfumed cigarettes, some marron glacé and a good English translation of 'Liaisons Dangereux.'"

She loathed marron glacé and scented tobacco was an abomination. Her chief regret was that the shocked inquirer had never heard of "Liaisons Dangereux". Christina only knew of its existence from a reference in a literary weekly which came her way.

Beryl sensed the hidden antagonism and the cause. "I really haven't come in a district visitor spirit," she said. "I'm not frightfully sorry for you and I haven't brought you oranges—"

"Grapes," corrected Christina. "They give you appendicitis—mother read that on the back page of 'Health Hints.' Sit down, Miss Merville. This is Mr. Sault." She nodded to Ambrose.

"Mr. Sault and I are old acquaintances," she said. She did not look at him. "I have to explain why I came at all. I know that you are not particularly enthusiastic about stray visitors—nobody is. But my father was talking about you at lunch today. He has never seen you, but Mr. Sault has spoken about you and, of course, he does know your mother. And father said: 'Why don't you go along and see her, Beryl?' I said, 'She would probably be very annoyed—but I'll take her that new long wordy novel that is so popular. I'm sure she'll hate it as much as I.'"

"If it is *Let the World Go*, I'm certain I shall," said Christina promptly, "but I'd love to read it. Let us sneer together." Beryl laughed and produced the book.

It seemed an appropriate moment for Ambrose to retire and he went out of the room quietly; he thought that neither of the girls saw him go, but he was mistaken. Christina Colebrook was sensitive to his every movement, and Beryl had really come to the house to see him.

On her way home she tried to arraign herself before the bar of intelligence, but it was not until she was alone in her room that night that she set forth the stark facts of her folly. She loved Ronald Morelle, loved him with an intensity which frightened her; loved him, although he was, according to all standards by which men are judged, despicable. He was a coward, a liar, a slave to his baser appetites. She had no doubt in her mind, when she faced the truth, that the stories which had been told of him were true. The East girl—the pretty parlormaid who had begun an action against him.

And yet there was something infinitely pathetic about Ronald Morelle, something that made her heart go out to him. Or was that a case of self-deception too? Was it not the beautiful animal she loved, the sleek, lithe tiger—alive and vital and remorseless? To all that was brain and spirit in her, he was loathsome. There were periods when she hated him and was bitterly contemptuous of herself. And in these periods came the soft voice of Ambrose Sault, whispering, insinuating. That was lunacy, too. He was old enough to be her father; was an illiterate workman, an ex-convict, a murderer; when her father had told her he had killed a man she was neither shocked nor surprised. She had guessed, from his brief reference to New Caledonia, that he had lived on that island under duress. He must have been convicted of some great crime; she could not imagine him in any mean or petty rôle. A coarse-handed workman, shabby of attire—it was madness to dream and dream of him as she did. And dreams, so Freud had said, were the expressions of wishes unfulfilled. What did she wish? She was prepared to answer the question frankly if any answer could be framed. But she had no ultimate wish. Her dreams of Ambrose Sault were unfinishable. Their ends ran into unfathomable darkness.

"I wonder if he is very fond of that red-haired girl?" she asked her mirror. Contemplating such a possibility she experienced a pang of jealousy and hated herself for it.

Jan Steppe came back from Paris on the eve of her birthday. He called at the house the next morning, before she was down; and interviewed Dr. Merville; when Beryl went in to breakfast, two little packages lay on her plate. The first was a diamond shawl pin.

"You are a dear, daddy!" She went round the table and kissed him. "It is beautiful and I wanted one badly." She hurried back to her place. Perhaps Ronnie had remembered—?

She picked up the card that was enclosed and read it. "Mr. Steppe?"

Her father shot a quick glance at her. "Yes—bought it in Paris. He came in person to present it, but left when he found that you were not down—rather pretty." This was an inadequate description of the beautiful plaque that flashed and glittered from its velvet bed.

"It is lovely," she said, but without warmth. "Ought I accept—it is a very expensive present!"

"Why not? Steppe is a good friend of ours; besides, he likes you," said the doctor, not looking up from his plate. "He would be terribly hurt if you didn't take it—in fact, you cannot very well refuse."

She ran through her letters. There was a note from Ronnie, an invitation to a first night. He said nothing about her birthday.

"Oh, by the way, some flowers came. I told Dean to put them in your room. I have been puzzling my head to remember when I told him the date of your birthday. I suppose I must have done so, and, of course, he has the most colossal memory."

"Who, father?"

"Sault. He must have got up very early and gone to the market to get them. Very decent of him."

She went out of the room with an excuse and found her maid in the pantry. She had filled a big bowl with the roses. There were so many that only room for half of them had been found.

"The others I will put in the doctor's room, Miss," said the maid.

"Put them all in my room, every one of them," demanded Beryl.

She selected three and fastened them in her belt before she went back to the breakfast room. The doctor laughed.

"I've never seen you wearing flowers before—Sault would be awfully pleased."

This she knew. That was why she wore them.

XI

Evie Colebrook came home at an unusually early hour and the girl on the bed looked up in surprise.

"I heard mother talking to somebody, but I had no idea it was you, Evie. What is the matter—has your swain another engagement?"

"My swain, as you call him, is working tonight," said Evie, "and it is so hot that I thought I would come home and get into my pajamas."

"Mother has been talking about your eccentric tastes, with particular reference to pajamas," said Christina. "She thinks that pajamas are indelicate. In her young days girls weren't supposed to have legs."

"Father wore pajamas."

"Father also drank. Mother thinks that the pajamas had something to do with it. She also thinks that book reading was a contributary cause."

"What terrible jaw-breaking words you use, Christina. Father did read a lot, didn't he?"

"Father was a student. He studied, amongst other things, race horses. Do you know who father was?" Evie stared at her expectantly.

"He was a carpenter, wasn't he?"

"He was the youngest son of the youngest son of a lord. Take that look off your face, Evie; there is no possibility of our being the rightful heiresses of the old Hall. But it is true; he had a coat of arms."

"Then why did he marry mother?"

"Why do people marry anybody?" demanded Christina. "Why did grandfather marry grandmother? Besides, why shouldn't he have married mother? He was only a cabinet maker when he met her. She has told me so. And his father was a parson, and his mother the Honorable Mrs. Colebrook, the daughter of Lord Fanshelm. There is blue blood in your veins, Evie."

"But really, Christina," Evie's voice was eager and her eyes bright, "you are not fooling; is it true? It makes such an awful difference—"

Christina groaned. "My God, what have I said?" she asked dramatically.

"But really, Christina?"

"You are related so distantly to nobility that you can hardly see it without a telescope," said Christina. "I thought you knew. Mother used always to be talking about it at one time. My dear, what difference does it make?"

Evie was silent.

"A man doesn't love a girl any more because she has a fifth cousin in the House of Lords; he doesn't love her any less because her mother takes in laundry, and if her lowly origin stands in the way of his marriage, and he finds that really she is the great grandaughter of a princess, he cannot obliterate her intermediate relations."

"What's 'intermediate'?"

"Well, mother and father, and the parson who got into trouble through drinking, and his wife who ran away with a groom."

Evie drew a long sigh.

"Where is your swain?" she asked. "I don't like that word 'swain,' it sounds so much like 'swine.'"

"I hope you will never see the resemblance any clearer," said Christina. "My swain is working, too. I shouldn't take off that petticoat, if I were you, Evie; he may come in and you can see your knickers through that dressing-gown."

"Christina!"

"I hate mentioning knickers to a pure-minded girl," said Christina, fanning herself with a paper, "but sisters have no secrets from one another. Ambrose, if that is who you mean, is very busy these days."

"Do you call him Ambrose to his face?" asked Evie curiously, and her sister snorted.

"Would you call Julius Caesar 'Bill' or 'Juley' to his face; of course not. But I can't think of him as Ambrose Sault, Esquire, can I?"

"I don't understand him," said Evie. "He seems so dull and quiet."

"I'll get him to jazz with you the next time you're home early," said Christina sardonically.

"Don't be so silly. Naturally he isn't very lively being so old."

"Old! He is lively enough to carry me downstairs as though I were a pillow and wheel me for hours at a time in that glorious chariot he got for me! And he is old enough—but what is the good of talking to you, Evie?"

Presently her irritation passed and she laughed. "Tell me the news of the great world, Evie; what startling happenings have there been in Knightsbridge?"

"I can tell you something about Mr. Sault you don't know," Evie was piqued into saying. "He has been in prison." Christina turned on her side with a wince of pain.

"Say that again."

"He has been in prison." A long pause.

"I hoped he had," Christina said at last. "I believe in imprisonment as an essential part of a man's education—who told you?"

"I'm not going to say."

"Ronald Morelle—aha!" She pointed an accusing finger at the dumbfounded Evie.

"I know your guilty secret! The 'Ronnie' you babble about in your sleep is Ronnie Morelle!"

"Wh—what makes you—it isn't true—it is a damned lie—!"

"Don't be profane, Evie. That is the worst of druggists' shops, you pick up such awful language. Mother says you can't work amongst pills without getting ideas in your head."

"I never talk in my sleep—and I don't know Ronnie Morelle—who is he?"

Evie's ignorance was badly assumed. Christina became very thoughtful. She lay with her hand under her cheek, her gray eyes searching her sister's face.

"Would Ronnie be impressed by your distant relationship with nobility?" she asked quietly. "Would it make such an awful difference if he knew about the coat of arms in father's Bible? I don't think it would. If it did, he isn't worth worrying about. What is he?"

"Didn't Mr. Sault tell you?" asked Evie hotly. "He seems to spend his time gossiping about people who are a million times better than him—"

"Than he," murmured Christina, her eyes closed.

"He is a nasty scandal-mongering old man! I hate him!"

"He didn't say that Ronnie had been in prison," Christina's voice was gentle. "All that he said was that the only 'Ronnie' he knew was Ronald Morelle. He did not even describe him or give him a character."

"How absurd, Christina! As if old Sault could give Mr. Morelle 'a character'! One is a gentleman and the other is an old fossil!"

"Old age is honorable," said Christina tolerantly, "the arrogance of you babies!"

"You're half in love with him!"

"Wholly," nodded Christina. "I love his mind and his soul. I am incapable of any other kind of love. I never want a man to draw my flaming head to his shoulder and whisper, that until he met me, the world was a desert, and food didn't taste good. It is because Ambrose Sault never paws me or holds my hand or kisses me on the brow in the manner of a father who hopes to be something closer, that I love him. And I shall love him through eternity. When I am dead and he is dead. And I want nothing more than this. If he were to die tomorrow, I should not grieve because his flesh means nothing to me. The thing he gives me is everlasting. That is where I am better off than you, Evie. You have nothing but what you give yourself. You think he gives you these wonderful memories which keep you awake at nights. You think it is his love for you that thrills you. It isn't that, Evie. Your love is the love of the martyr who finds an ecstatic joy in his suffering."

Groping toward understanding, Evie seized this illustration. "God loves the martyr—it isn't one-sided," she quavered and Christina nodded.

"That is true, or it may be true. Does your god love you?"

"It is blasphemous to—to talk of Ronnie as God."

"God with a small 'g.'"

"It is blasphemous anyhow. Ronnie *does* love me. He hasn't silly and conventional ideas about—about love as most people have. He is much broader-minded, but he does love me. I know it. A girl knows when a man loves her."

"That is one of the things she doesn't know," interrupted Christina. "She knows when he wants her, but she doesn't know how continually he will want her. He is unconventional, too? And broad-minded? The broad-minded are usually people who take a generous view of their own shortcomings. Is he one of those unconventional souls who think that marriage is a barbarous ceremony?"

"Who told you that?" Evie was breathless from surprise.

"It isn't a unique view—broad-minded men often try to get narrow-minded girls to see that standpoint."

"You're cynical—I hate cynical people," said Evie, throwing herself on her bed, "and you have all your ideas of life out of books, and the rotten people who come in here moaning about their troubles. You can't believe writers—not some writers—there are some, of course, that give just a true picture of life—not in books, but in articles in the newspapers. They just seem to know what people are thinking and feeling, and express themselves wonderfully."

"Ah—so Ronnie writes for the newspapers, does he?"

Evie's indignant retort was checked by a knock on the door.

"That is Mr. Sault—can he come in?"

"I suppose so," answered Evie grudgingly. She got off the bed and tied her dressing-gown more tightly. "I don't really show my legs through this kimono do I, Christina?"

"Not unless you want to—come in!"

Ambrose Sault looked tired. "Just looked in before I went to my room," he said. "Good evening, Evie."

"Good evening, Mr. Sault."

Evie's dressing-gown was wrapped so tightly as to give her a mummified appearance.

"I saw the osteopath today and I've arranged for him to come and talk to you tomorrow," said Ambrose, sitting on the edge of the bed at the inviting gesture of Christina's hand.

"I will parley with him," she nodded. "I don't believe that he will make a scrap of difference. I've seen all sorts of doctors and specialists. Mother has a list of them—she is very proud of it."

"I'm only hoping that this man may do you some good," said Ambrose, rubbing his chin meditatively. "I have seen some wonderful cures—in America. Even Dr. Merville believes in them. He says that if you build a sky-scraper and the steel frame isn't true, you cannot expect the doors to shut or the windows to open. I'm sorry I am so late, but the osteopath was dining out, and I had to wait until he came back. He hurt his ankle too, and that took time. I had to give him a rubbing. He is the best man in London. Dr. Duncan More."

She did not take her eyes from his face. Evie noticed this and discounted Christina's earlier assertion.

"Will it cost a lot of money?" asked Christina.

"Not much, in fact very little. The first examination is free. He doesn't really examine you, you know. He will just feel your back, through your clothes. I asked him that, because I know how you dislike examinations. And if he doesn't think that you can be treated, and that there is a chance of making you better, he won't bother you any more."

"I don't believe in these quack doctors," said Evie decidedly. "They promise all sorts of cures and they only take your money. We have a lot of those kind of remedies at the store, but Mr. Donker, the manager, says that they are all fakes—don't tell me that an osteopath isn't a medicine. I know that. He's a sort of doctor, but I'll bet you he doesn't do any good."

"Cheer up, Job!" said Christina. "Faith is something. I suppose you mean well, but if I took any notice of you I'd give up the struggle now."

"I don't want to depress you, you're very unkind, Christina! But I don't think you ought to be too hopeful. It would be such an awful—what's the word, comedown for you."

"Reaction," said Sault and Christina together and they laughed.

Sault went soon after and Evie felt that a dignified protest was called for.

"There is no reason why you should make me look like a fool before Sault," she said hurt. "Nobody would be happier than I should be if you got well. You know that. I'm not so sure that Mr. Sault is sincere—"

"What?"

Christina leaned upon her arm and her eyes were blazing.

"You can say that he is old and ugly, if you like, and shabby and—anything. But don't dare to say that, Evie—don't dare to say that he isn't sincere!"

Evie lay awake for a long time that night. Christina was certainly a strange girl—and when she said she did not love Sault, she was not speaking the truth. That was just how she had felt, when Christina had hinted that Ronnie was not sincere. Only she had been too much of a lady to lose her temper. About old Sault, too! What did he do for a living? She must ask Christina.

XII

Mr. Jan Steppe sat astride of a chair, his elbows on the back-rest, his saturnine face clouded with doubt.

"It certainly looks like a very ordinary safe to me, Sault. Do you mean to say that an expert could not get inside without disturbing the apparatus, huh?"

"Impossible," replied Sault. "I have filled the top chamber with water and I have tried at least a thousand combinations and every time I put the combination wrong, the safe has been flooded."

He twisted the dials on the face of the unpretentious repository, until he brought five letters, one under the other, in line with an arrow engraved on the safe door. He was a long time doing this and Steppe and the Greek watched hm.

"Now!" said Sault.

He turned the handle and the door swung open. The contents were two or three old newspapers and they were intact.

"What is the code word?" Steppe peered forward. "Huh—why did you choose that word, Sault?"

"It is one of the very few words I can spell. Besides which, each letter is different."

"It is not an inappropriate word," said Moropulos amused, "and one easy to remember. I intend pasting a notice on the safe, Steppe, explaining frankly that unless the code word is used, and if any other combination of letters is tried, indeed, if the handle is turned, whilst the dial is set at any other word than the code word, the contents of the safe are destroyed. This may act as a deterrent to promiscuous burglars."

Steppe fingered his stubbly beard. "That will be telling people that we have something in the safe that we want to keep hidden, huh?" he said dubiously. "A fool idea!"

"Everybody has something in his safe that he wants to keep hidden," said the other coolly.

"Now let me try—shut the door, Sault, that is right." Steppe got out of the chair to spin the dials. "Now we will suppose that I am some unauthorized person trying to find a way of opening the safe. So!"

He turned the handle.

"Open it."

Sault worked at the dials and presently the door swung open. The newspapers were saturated and an inch of water at the bottom of the safe splashed out and into a bath-tub that Sault had put ready.

"How about cutting into the safe? Suppose I am a burglar, huh? I burn out the lock or the side, and don't touch the combination?"

"I have left a hole in one side of the safe," said Sault, and pointed to a rubber plug that had been rammed into a small aperture.

With a pair of pincers he pulled this out and a stream of water spurted forth and was mostly caught in the can he held.

"That has the same effect," he explained. "The water is pumped at a pressure into the hollow walls of the safe. The door is also hollow. When the water runs out, a float drops and releases the contents of the upper chamber. In the case of the door, the float operates the same spring that floods the safe when the handle is turned."

Steppe scratched his head. "Perfect," he said. "You have experimented with the acid?"

Sault nodded. "Both with sulphuric and hydrochloric," he said. "I think hydrochloric is the better."

Steppe turned to the Greek. "You had better keep it here," he said, and then: "Will it be ready today? I want to get those Brakpan letters out of the way. I needn't tell you, Sault, that the code word must be known only to us three, huh? I don't mind your knowing—but, you, Moropulos! You have got to cut out absinthe—d'ye hear? Cut it out—right out!" His growl became a roar that shook the room and Moropulos quailed.

"It is cut out," he said sulkily. "I am confining my boozing to the 'Parthenon.' I've got to have some amusement."

"You have it, if all I hear is true," said Steppe grimly. "Give Sault a hundred, Moropulos. It is worth it. What do you do with your money, Sault? You don't spend it on fine clothes, huh?"

"He goes about doing good," said Moropulos, with a good-natured sneer. "I met him in Kensington Gardens the other day, wheeling an interesting invalid. Who was she, Sault?"

"My landlady's daughter," replied the other shortly.

"No business of yours, anyhow," growled Steppe. "You've met Miss Merville, huh? Nice lady?"

"Yes, a very nice lady," said Sault steadily. He pushed back his long gray hair from his forehead.

"Pretty, huh?"

Sault nodded and was glad when his employer had departed.

"Steppe is gone on that girl," said Moropulos. "He'd have brained you, if you had said she wasn't pretty!"

"He wouldn't have brained me," said Sault quietly.

"I suppose he wouldn't. Even Steppe would have thought twice about lifting his hand to you. He's a brute though, I saw him smash a man in the face once for calling him a liar—at a directors' meeting. It was an hour before the poor devil knew what had happened. Yes, she is pretty. I see her riding some mornings, a young Diana—delicious. I'd give a lot to be in Steppe's shoes."

"Why?"

Moropulos rolled a cigarette with extraordinary rapidity and lit it. "Why? Well, if he wants her, he'll have her. Steppe is that kind. I don't suppose the doctor would have much to say in the matter. Or she, either."

Sault picked up an iron bar from the table. It was one of four that he had brought for the purpose of strengthening the safe, and it was nearly an inch in diameter.

"I think she would have something to say," he said, weighing the bar on the palms of his hands.

And then, to the Greek's amazement, he bent the steel into a V. He used no apparent effort; the bar just changed its shape in his hands as though it had been made of lead.

"Why did you do that?" he gasped.

"I don't know," said Ambrose Sault, and with a jerk brought the steel almost straight.

"Phew!"

Moropulos took the bar from his hand.

"I shouldn't like to annoy you seriously," he said. He did not speak of Beryl again.

XIII

Evie Colebrook had found a note awaiting her at the store on the morning of the day she came home early. It consisted of a few words scrawled on a plain card, and had neither address nor signature:

> *"Dearest girl*: I shall not be able to see you tonight. I have a long article to write and shall probably be working through the night, when your dear and precious eyes are closed in sleep. *Your lover."*

She had the card under her pillow when she slept.

"Are you sure you aren't too busy," said Beryl when she came down, a radiant figure, to the waiting Ronnie. "Now that you have taken up a literary career, I picture you as being rushed every hour of the day."

"Sarcasm is wasted on me," Ronnie displayed his beautiful teeth. "Unflattering though it be, I admit to a slump in my literary stock. I have had no commissions for a week."

"And I'm not taking you away from any of those beautiful friends of yours?"

"Beryl!" he murmured reproachfully. "You know that I have no friends—if by friends you mean girl friends."

"It is my mad jealousy which makes me ask these questions," she said quizzically. "C.ome along, Ronnie, we will be late."

What the play was about, Beryl never quite remembered. Ronnie, sitting in the shade of the curtains, was more interested in his companion. It was strange that he had known her ever since she was a child and he a schoolboy, and yet had never received a true impression of her beauty. He watched her through the first act, the tilt of her chin, the quick smile.

"Beryl, you ought to be painted," he said in the first interval. "I mean by a portrait painter. You look so perfectly splendid that I couldn't take my eyes off you."

The color came slowly and, in the dim light of the box, a man who had not been looking for this evidence of her pleasure, would have seen nothing.

"That is a little less subtle than the usual brand of flattery you practice, isn't it, Ronnie? Or is your artlessness really an art that conceals art?"

"I'm not flattering you—I simply speak as I feel. I never realized your loveliness until tonight." She straightened up and laughed.

"You think I'm crude—I suppose I am. You do not say that I am keeping my hand in, though you probably think so. I admit I have had all sorts of flirtations, in fact, I have been rather a blackguard in that way, and of course I've said nice things to girls—buttered them and played to their vanity. But if I were trying to make love to you, I should be a little more subtle, as you say. I should imply my compliments. It is just because my—my spasm is unpremeditated that I find myself at a loss for words. There is no sense in my making love to you, anyway, supposing that you would allow me. I can't marry—I simply won't marry until I have enough money and I haven't nearly enough. If in four years' time the money doesn't come—well then, I'll risk being a pauper, but the girl will have to know."

She said nothing. Here was an unexpected side to his character. He had some plan of life and a code of sorts. If she had been better acquainted with that life of his, which she so far suspected, she would have grown alert when Ronnie unmasked his way of retreat. She was surprised at his virtuous reluctance to make a woman share his comparative poverty—she should have been suspicious when he fixed a time limit to his bachelorhood. It was not like Ronnie to plan so far in advance, that she knew; it might have occurred to her that he was definitely excusing the postponement of marriage. As it was, she was seeing him in a more favorable light. Ronnie desired that she should. His instinct in these matters was uncannily accurate.

"It was worth coming out with you, if only to hear your views on matrimony," was all the comment she made.

"I don't know—" he looked gloomily into the auditorium, "in many ways I have been regretting it. That doesn't sound gallant, but I am not in a mood for nice speeches—you think I am? I did not mean to be nice when I said that you were lovely, any more than I wish to be nice to Titian when I praise his pictures. Beryl, I've been fond of you for years. I suppose I've been in love with you, though I've never wanted to be. That is the truth. I've recognized just how unfair it would be, to chain a woman like you to a rake—I'm not sparing myself— like me. God knows whether I could be constant. In my heart I know that if I had you, there could be no other woman in the world for me—an intimate knowledge of my own character makes me skeptical."

Beryl was spared the necessity for replying. The curtain went up on the second act just then. She knew he was looking at her, and turned in her chair to hide her face. Her heart was beating tumultuously. She was trembling. She was a fool—a fool. He meant nothing—he was a liar; lied as readily as other men spoke the truth. That frankness of his was assumed—he was acting. Versed in the weaknesses of women, he had chosen the only approach that would storm her citadel. She told herself these truths, her reason battling in a last desperate stand against his attack. And yet—why should he not be sincere? For the first time he had admitted the unpleasant charges which hitherto he had denied. He surely could not expect to make her love him more by the confession of his infidelities?

If he had followed up his talk, had made any attempt to carry on the conversation from the point where he left it, she would have been invincible. But he did not. When the curtain went down again, he was more cheerful and was seemingly interested only in the people he recognized in the stalls. He asked her if she would mind if he left her. He wanted to smoke and to meet some men he knew.

She assented and was disappointed. They had a long wait between these two acts, and as he had returned to the box after a shorter interval than she had expected, there was plenty of time, had he so wished, to have resumed his conversation. He showed no such desire, and it was she who began it.

"You puzzle me, Ronnie. I can't see—if you loved me, how you could do some of the things you have done. You won't be so commonplace as to tell me that you wanted to keep me out of your mind and that that form of amusement helped you to forget me."

"No," he admitted, "but, Beryl dear, need we discuss it? I don't know why I spoke to you as I did. I felt like it."

"But I am going to discuss it," she insisted. "I want my mind set in order. It is overthrown for the moment. What prevented you from keeping me as a friend all this time—a real close friend, if you loved me? Oh, Ronnie, I do want to be fair to you even at the risk of being shameless, as I am now. Why could you not have asked me? Even if it meant waiting?"

He looked down at the floor. "I have some sense of decency left," he said in a low voice. And then the curtain went up.

Beryl looked at her program. The play had four acts; there was another interval. He did not leave her this time; nor did he wait for her to begin.

"I'm going to be straight with you, Beryl," he said, "I want you—I adore you. But I cannot commit you to an engagement which may adversely affect your father and incidentally myself. I am being brutally selfish and mercenary, but I am going to say what I think. You'll be amused and perhaps horrified when I tell you that Steppe is very keen on you."

She was neither amused nor horrified; but on the other hand, if Ronnie Morelle realized that in his invention he had accidentally hit upon the truth, he would not have been amused and most certainly terror would have struck him dumb. If Beryl had only said what she was of a mind to say, that she had learned from her father that Steppe was in love with her, she might have silenced him. But she said nothing. Ronnie's explanation seemed natural—knowing Ronnie.

"I'd sooner see you dead than married to him," he said vehemently, "but none of us can say that now. We are in a very tight place. Steppe could ruin your father with a gesture—he could very seriously inconvenience me." Here he was much in earnest, and the girl, with a cold feeling at her heart, knew he spoke the truth.

"But that time will pass. We shall weather the storm which is shrieking round our ears—you don't read the financial papers—you're wise. You see what might happen, Beryl?"

Beryl nodded. She was ridiculously happy.

"A great play, don't you think so, Miss Merville?" It was Sir John Maxton who had pushed through the crowd in the vestibule.

"Splendid," she said.

"Ronnie, did you like it?"

"I never heard a word," said Ronnie, and somehow that statement was so consonant with his new honesty that it confirmed her in a faith which was as novel.

The car carried them through the crowded circus and into the quietude of Piccadilly.

"Oh, Ronnie—I am so happy—"

His arm slipped round her and his lips pressed fiercely against her red mouth.

"Why can't you sleep?" asked the drowsy Christina, as the girl lit her candle for the second time.

"I don't know—I'm having such beastly dreams," said Evie fretfully.

BOOK THE SECOND

I

The step of Ambrose Sault was light and there was a buoyancy in his mien when he came into Mrs. Colebrook's kitchen, surprising that good lady with so unusual an appearance at an hour of the day when she was taking her afternoon siesta.

"Lord, how you startled me!" she said. "The ostymopat came this morning. A stout gentleman with whiskers. Very nice, too, and American. But bless you, Mr. Sault, he'll never do any good to Christina, though I wish he could, for I'm up and down those blessed stairs from the moment I get up to the moment I go to bed. He'll never cure her. She's had ten doctors and four specialists, and she's been three times to St. Mary's hospital; to say nothing of the Evelyna when she was a child and fell out of the perambulator that did it. Ten doctors and four specialists—they're doctors, too, in a manner of speaking, so you might say fourteen."

Sault never interrupted his landlady, although his forbearance meant, very often, a long period of waiting.

"Can I see Christina, Mrs. Colebrook?" he begged.

"Certainly you can, you needn't ask me. She'll be glad to see you," said Mrs. Colebrook conventionally. "I thought of going up myself, but she has always got those books. Do you think so much reading is good for her—?"

"I'm sure it is."

"But—well, I don't know. I've never read anything but the Sunday papers, and they've got enough horrors in 'em—but they actually happened. It isn't guesswork like it is in books. I never read a book through in my life. My husband—! Why, when he passed away, there was enough books in the house to fill a room. He'd sooner read than work at any time. He was a bit aristocratic in his way."

Sault had come to understand that "aristocratic" did not stand, as Mrs. Colebrook applied the word, for gentleness of birth, but for a loftiness of demeanor in relation to labor.

He made his escape up the stairs. Christina was not reading. She lay on her back, her hands lightly folded, and she was inspecting the end bed-rail with a fixity of gaze that indicated to Ambrose how far she was from Walter Street and the loud little boys who played beneath her window.

"I have nothing for you today—I haven't been baking."

She patted the bed and he sat down.

"The osteopath has been, I suppose mother told you? She has the queerest word for him, 'ostymopat.' Yes, he came and saw, or rather, he prodded in a gentle, harmless kind of way, but I fancy that my spine has conquered. He didn't say very much, but seemed to be more interested in the bones of my neck and shoulders than he was in the place where it hurts. He wouldn't tell me anything, I suppose he didn't want to make me feel miserable. Poor, kind soul—after all the uncomplimentary things that have been said about my spinal column!"

"He told me," said Ambrose, and something in his face made her open her eyes wide.

"What did he say—please tell me—was it good?"

He nodded and a beatific smile lightened his face.

"You can be cured; completely cured. You will walk in a year or maybe less. He thinks it will take six months to manipulate the bones into their place; he talked about 'breaking down' something, but he didn't mean that he would hurt you. He just meant that he would have to remove—I don't know what it is, but it would be a gradual process and you would feel nothing. He wants your mother to put you into a sort of thin overall before he comes."

He lugged a parcel from his pocket. "I bought one—a smock of thick silk. I thought you had better have silk. He works at you through it, and it makes his work easier for him and for you if—anyhow, I got silk, Christina."

Her eyes were shining, but she did not look at him. "It doesn't seem possible," she said softly, "and it is going to cost a lot of money—cost you. The silk overall is lovely, but I wouldn't mind if I wore sackcloth. You great soul!"

She caught his hand in both of hers and gripped it with a strength that surprised him.

"Evie is quite sure that I am in love with you, Ambrose—I lied to her when I said I never called you Ambrose. And, of course, we are in love with one another, but in a way that poor Evie doesn't understand. If I was normal, I suppose I'd love you in her way—poor Ambrose, you would be so embarrassed."

She laughed quietly.

"Love is a great disturbance," said Ambrose. "I think Evie means that kind."

"Were you ever in love that way? I have never been. I think I love you as I should love my child, if I had one. If you say that you love me as a mother, I shall be offended, Ambrose. Do you think it will really happen—will it cost very much?"

"A pound a visit, and he is coming every day except Sunday."

Christina made a calculation and the immensity of the sum left her horror-stricken.

"A hundred and fifty pounds!" she cried. "Oh, Ambrose—how can you? I won't have the treatment. It is certain to fail—I won't, Ambrose!"

"I've paid a hundred on account. He didn't want to take it, but I said I would only let him come on those terms. I wasn't speaking the truth—I'd have let him come on any terms. So you see, Christina, I've paid, and you *must* be treated!"

"Hold my hand, Ambrose—and don't speak a word. I'm going for a long walk—I haven't dared walk before."

She resumed her gaze upon the bed-rail and he sat in silence whilst she dreamed.

Evie returned at ten o'clock that night and heard Christina singing as she mounted the stairs. "Enter, sister, has mother told you that I am practically a well woman?"

"Don't put too high hopes—"

"Shut up! I'm a well woman I tell you. In a year I shall walk into your medicine shop and sneer at you as I pass. Have you brought home any candy? 'Sweets' is hopelessly vulgar, and I like the American word better. And you look bright and sonsy. Did you see the god?"

"I wish you wouldn't use religious words, Christina, just when we are going to bed, too. I wonder you're not afraid. Yes, I saw my boy."

"Have you a boy?" in simulated surprise. "Evie, you are a surprising child. Whom does he take after?"

"Really, I think you are indecent," said her sister, shocked. "You know perfectly well I mean—Ronnie."

"Oh, is he the 'boy'? To you girls everything that raises a hat or smokes a cheap cigar is strangely boyish. Well, is he nearly dead from his midnight labors?"

"I'd like to see you write a long article for the newspapers," said Evie witheringly.

"I wish you could. You may even see that. Tell me about him, Evie. What is he like—what sort of a house has he?" She waited.

"He lives in a flat, and, of course, I've never seen it. You don't imagine that I would go into a man's flat alone, do you?"

Christina sighed. "There are points about the bourgeoisie mind which are admirable," she said. "What does 'bourgeoisie' mean? The bourgeoisie are the people who have names instead of numbers to their houses; they catch the nine twenty-five to town and go home by the five seventeen. They go to church at least once on Sunday and their wives wear fascinators and patronize the dress circle."

"You talk such rubbish, Christina. I can't make head or tail of it half the time. I don't see what it has got to do with my not going in to Ronnie's flat. It wouldn't be respectable."

"Why didn't I think of that word?" wailed Christina. "Evie."

"Huh?" said Evie, her mouth full of pins and in an unconscious imitation of one who, did she but know it, held her soul in the hollow of his hands.

"Where do you meet your lad—I simply can't say 'boy'?"

"Oh, anywhere," said Evie vaguely. "We used to meet a lot in the park. As a matter of fact, that is where I first saw him, but now he doesn't go to the park. He says the crowd is vulgar and it is you know, Christina; why I've heard men addressing meetings and saying that there wasn't a God! And talking about the king most familiarly. It made my blood boil!"

"I don't suppose the king minds, and I'm sure God only laughed."

"Christina!"

"Well, why not? What's the use of being God if He hasn't a sense of humor? He has everything He wants, and that is one of the first blessings He would give Himself. Where do you meet Ronnie, Evie?"

"Sometimes I have dinner with him, and sometimes we just meet at the tube station and go to the pictures." Christina pinched her chin in thought.

"He knows that girl who came to see you, Miss Merville. I told him about her visit, and he asked me if she knew that I was a friend of his, and whether she had seen me. She rather runs after him, I think. He doesn't say so, he is too much a gentleman. I can't imagine Ronnie saying anything unkind."

"But he sort of hinted," suggested Christina.

"You *are* uncharitable, Christina! Nothing Ronnie does is right in your eyes. Of course he didn't hint. It is the way he looks, when I speak about her. I know that he doesn't like her very much. He admitted it, because, just after we had been talking about her, he said that I was the only girl he had ever met who did not bore him—unutterably. His very words!"

"That was certainly convincing evidence," said Christina, and her sister arrested the motion of her hair brush to look suspiciously in her direction. You could never be sure whether Christina was being nice or unpleasant.

II

Ronald Morelle had once been the victim of a demoralizing experience. He had awakened in time to hear the church clock strike nine, and for the space of a few seconds, he had suffered the tortures of hell. Why, he never discovered. He had heard the clock strike nine since then, in truth he had been specially wakened by François the very next morning, in the expectation that the tolling of the bell would recall to his mind the cause of his abject fear. But not again did the chimes affect him. He had made a very thorough examination of his mind in the Freudian method, but could trace no connection between his moments of terror and the sound of a bell. "A nightmare, as an unpleasant dream is called, may be intensively vivid, yet from the second of waking leaves no definite memory behind it," said a lesser authority.

He had to rest content with that. He had other matters to think about. Steppe, an unusual visitor, came to his flat one morning. Ronnie was in his dressing-gown, reading the morning newspapers, and he leaped up with a curious sense of guilt when the big man was announced.

You dabble in press work, Morelle, don't you?" Ronnie acknowledged his hobby.

"Do you know anybody in Fleet Street—editors and such like?"

"I know a few—Why, Mr. Steppe?"

Steppe lit a cigar and strolling across the room looked out of the window. He carried the air of a patron to such an extent that Ronnie felt an interloper, an uncomfortable feeling to a man still in pajamas.

"Because we've got to beat up a few friendly press criticisms," said Steppe at last. "The financial papers are raising merry hell about the Klein River diamond flotation and we have to get our story in somehow or other. You don't want to be called a swindling company promoter, huh? Wouldn't look good, huh?"

"I don't see how I come into it," said Ronnie.

"You don't, huh? Of course you don't! Have you ever seen anything but a shop girl's ankles? You—don't see! You're a director, so is Merville. You've drawn directors' fees. I'm not a director—it doesn't matter a damn to me what they say."

The name of Jan Steppe seldom appeared amongst the officers or directors of a company. He had his nominees who voted according to the orders they received.

"What makes it so almighty bad is that I was floating the Midwell Traction Corporation next week. We'll have to put that back now, but it will keep. What are you going to do?"

"I don't know exactly what to do," said Ronnie. It was the first time he had ever been called upon to justify his directors' fees. "I know a few men—but I doubt if I can do anything. Fleet Street is a little rigid in these things."

"Get an article in somewhere," ordered Steppe peremptorily. "Take this line: That we bought the Klein River Mine on the report of the best engineer in South Africa. We did. There's no lie about that. Mackenzie—he's in a lunatic asylum now. And the report was in his own handwriting, so there won't be a copy. And you needn't mention that he is in a lunatic asylum, most people think he is dead."

"Didn't he write to us complaining that we only put an extract from his report into the prospectus?"

"Never mind about that!" snarled Steppe. "I didn't come here for a conversation. He did write; said that we'd published a sentence away from the context.

He didn't think I was going to put the worst into the prospectus, did he? What he said was, that the Klein River Mine would be one of the richest in South Africa if we could get over difficulties of working, which he said were insuperable. He was right. They are. The only way to work that mine is with deep sea divers! Now, have this right, Morelle, and try to forget Flossie's blue eyes and Winnie's golden hair. This is business. Your business. You've got to take that report (Moropulos will give it to you, but you mustn't take it from the office) and extract all that is good in it. At the general meeting you have to produce your copy and read it. If anybody wants to see the original, refer 'em to Mackenzie. You've got to make Klein River look alive and you haven't to defend it, d'ye hear me? You've got to handle that mine as though you wished it was yours, huh? No defence! The hundred-pound shares are at twelve; you've got to make 'em look worth two hundred. And it is dead easy if you go the right way about it. Ask any pickpocket. The easiest way to steal a pocketbook is to go after the man that's just lost his watch. Make 'em think that the best thing they can do is to buy more Klein Rivers and hold them, huh? You've got to think it, or you won't say it. Get this meeting through without a fuss, and there's a thousand for you."

"I'll try," said Ronnie.

Yet, it was in no confident mood that he faced a hall-full room of enraged stockholders a week later. The meeting was described as "noisy"; it ended in the passing of a vote of confidence in the directors. Ronnie was elated; no other man but Steppe could have induced him to present a forged document to a meeting of critical stockholders, and when Klein Rivers rose the next day to seventeen, he was not as enthusiastic as Dr. Merville, who 'phoned his congratulations on what was undoubtedly a remarkable achievement.

He spoke of nothing else that day, and Beryl basked in reflected approval. Her father knew nothing. He wondered why Ronnie, whom he did not like overmuch, called with greater frequency. He had too large an experience of life to harbor any misconception as to his second cousin's private character, although he would, in other circumstances, have passively accepted him as a son-in-law. Men take a very tolerant view of other men's weaknesses. The theory that the world holds a patch of arable land reserved for young men to put under wild oats, and that without exciting the honest farmers whose lands adjoin, is a theory that dies hard as the cultivated fields increase in number.

He did not regard Ronnie as a marrying man, and with the exception of a few moments of uneasiness he had had when he noted Beryl's preference for his associate's society, he found nothing objectionable in the new interest which Ronnie had found. But he wished he wouldn't call so often.

Dr. Merville might, and did, dismiss Ronnie's errant adventures with a philosophical *sua cuique voluptas*—he found himself taking a more and more lenient view of Ronald Morelle's character. A man is never himself until he is idle. Successions of nurses, schoolmasters and professors shepherd him into the service of his fellows, and the conventions of his profession, no less than a natural desire to stand well with the friends and clients he has acquired in his progress, assist him in maintaining something of the appearance and mental attitude which his tutors have formed in him. Many a man has gone through life being some other man who has impressed him, or some great teacher who has imparted his personality into his plastic pupil.

The first instinct of a man lost in the desert is to discard his clothes. The doctor, wandering in this financial waste, began to discard his principles. He was unconscious of the sacrifice. If, in the course of his professional life he had made a mistaken diagnosis, or blundered in an operation, he would have known. If at school he had committed some error, he would have been corrected. Now, though this he did not realize, he was, for the first time in his life, free from any other authority than his own will and conscience. He fell into a common error when he believed, as he did, that standards of honor and behavior are peculiar to the trades in which they are exercised and that right and wrong are adaptable to circumstances.

"Ronnie is coming to dinner tonight, isn't he? You know I shall not be here, my dear? I promised Steppe I would spend the evening with him. I wish you would tell Ronnie how pleased we all are at his very fine speech. I never dreamed that he had it in him—Steppe talks of making him chairman of the company."

"I thought he was that."

"No—er—no. The chairman is a man named Howitt—a very troublesome fellow. Steppe bought him out before the meeting. Ronnie was only acting chairman."

"I thought you were a director, daddy?" She was curious on this point and had waited an opportunity of asking him why he had not been present at the meeting.

"I am, in a sense—but my nerves are in such a state just now, that I simply couldn't bear the strain of listening to a crowd of noisy louts jabbering stupid criticism. The company is in a perfectly sound position. You can see that from the way the stock has jumped up in the past few days. These city people aren't fools, you know."

She wondered if it was the "city people" who were buying the stock or were responsible for the encouraging rise in Klein River Diamonds. More likely, she thought, the buyers were the people who knew very little about stock exchange transactions.

Ronnie arrived as the doctor was going out, and they met in the street before the door. "It was nothing," said Ronnie modestly, "they were rather rowdy at first, but after I had had a little talk with them—you know how sheep-like these fellows are. I discovered from Steppe who was likely to be the leader of the opposition, and I saw him before the meeting. Of course, he was difficult and full of threats about appointing a committee of investigation. However—"

"Yes, yes, you did splendidly—you'll find Beryl waiting for you. Er—Ronnie."

"Yes?"

"Don't unsettle her—she is in an enquiring mood just now, especially about the companies and things. I shouldn't talk too much about Klein Rivers. She is a very shrewd girl. Not that there is anything about Klein Rivers that is discreditable."

"I never talk business to Beryl," said Ronnie. Which was nearly true.

He found her in the drawing-room and took her into his arms. She was so dear and fragrant. So malleable in his skilled hands now that the barrier of her suspicion had been broken down.

III

In the middle of the night, Ambrose Sault turned in his narrow bed and woke. He was a light sleeper and the party walls of the tiny house were thin.

He got out of bed, switched on the light of a portable electric lamp which stood within reach of his hand and, thrusting his feet into slippers, opened the door. The house was silent, but a crack of light showed under Christina's door.

"Are you awake, Christina?" he asked softly. "Is anything wrong?"

"Nothing, Mr. Sault."

It was not Christina. There was no hint of tears in her voice. Ambrose went back to his bed, and to sleep. He knew that he had not been mistaken either as to the sound that had awakened him or the direction from whence it came. For one terrific moment he had thought it was Christina and that the new treatment which had already commenced was responsible for the loud sobs which had disturbed his sleep. He was sorry for Evie. He was easily sorry. A cat writhing in the middle of the street, where a too swift motor-car had passed, wrung his heart. A child crying in pain made him sweat. When he saw a man and a woman quarrelling in this vile neighborhood, he rushed from the scene lest the woman be struck.

"What did he get—up for," whispered Evie, "he is always—interfering."

"The wonder to me is that the whole street isn't up," said Christina. "What is the matter, Evie?"

"I don't know— I'm miserable." Evie flounced over in her bed. "I just had to cry. I'm sorry."

Christina was very serious; she too had been awakened by the hysterical outburst. It carried a meaning to her that she had the courage to face.

"There is nothing wrong, is there, Evie?" No answer.

"I can't be all the help to you that I should like, darling, and I am a pig to you at times. But I get tetchy myself, and it is a bore lying here day after day. You would tell me if there was anything wrong, wouldn't you?"

"Yes," whispered the girl.

"I mean, really wrong. If it was anything that—affected your health. Nothing would make you wrong in my eyes. I should just love you and help you all I could. You know that. It isn't wise to keep some secrets, Evie, not if you know that there is somebody who loves you well enough to take half your burden from you."

"I don't know what you're driving at," said Evie in a fret. "You don't mean—? I'm a virgin, if that is what you mean," she said crudely.

Christina snorted. "Then what in hell are you snivelling about?" she demanded savagely. She was not unreasonably irritated.

"I haven't—seen—Ronnie—for a week!" sobbed the girl.

"I wish to God you'd never seen him," snapped Christina and wished she hadn't, for the next minute Evie was in bed with her, in her arms.

"I'm so unhappy—I wish I hadn't met him, too—I know that it isn't right, Chris—I know it isn't—I know I shall never be happy. He is so much above me—and I'm so ignorant—such—a—such a shop girl."

Christina cuddled the slim figure and kissed her damp face. "You'll get over that, Evie," she said soothingly.

"But I love him so!"

"You don't really—you are too young, Evie—you can't test your feelings. I was reading today about some people who live in Australia, natives, who think that a sort of sour apple is the most lovely fruit in the world. But it is only because they haven't any other kind of fruit. If you go to a poor sort of store to buy a dress, you get to think the best they have in stock is the best you can buy anywhere. It takes a lot of courage to walk out of that shop and find another. After a while you are sure and certain that the dress they show you is lovely. It is only when you put it against the clothes that other women have bought from the better shops, that you see how old-fashioned and tawdry and what an ugly color it is." She waited for an answer, but Evie was asleep.

Ambrose came home early the next day. Every other afternoon he took Christina to Kensington Gardens. He kept the long spinal carriage in a stable and spent at least half an hour in cleaning and polishing the wheels and lacquered panels of the "chariot."

"Shut the door, Ambrose." He obeyed.

"You heard Evie crying? It was nothing. She hasn't seen her man for a week and she was a little upset. I promised her to tell you that it was all your imagination, if you asked. Poor Evie doesn't know that you wouldn't ask anyhow."

"Is it Ronald Morelle, Christina?"

She nodded and, seeing his face lengthen, she asked: "Is he a good man, Ambrose? Do you think there is any danger to Evie?"

"I don't know him personally," Ambrose was speaking very slowly. "No, I don't know him. Once or twice I have seen him but I have never spoken. Moropulos says he is rotten. That was the word he used. There have been one or two nasty incidents. Moropulos likes talking about that sort of thing—what was that word you told me, Christina? It is not like me to forget? It describes a man with a bad curiosity."

"Prurient?"

"That is the word. Moropulos has that kind of mind. He has books—all about beastly subjects. And pictures. He says that Ronald Morelle is bad. The worst man he has ever met. He wasn't condemning him, you understand. In fact, he was admiring him. Moropulos would."

Christina was plucking at her underlip pensively.

"Poor Evie!" she said. "She thinks she is in love with him. He is a beautiful dream to her, naturally, because she has never met anybody like him. I wish he had made the mistake of thinking she was easy, the first time he met her. That would have ended it. What I am afraid of, is that he does understand her, and is wearing down her resistance gradually. What am I to do, Ambrose?"

Years before, when he was working in a penal settlement, Ambrose Sault had bruised and cut his chin. He had been working in tapioca fields, and the prison doctor had warned him not to touch the healing wound with his hand for fear of poisoning it. From this warning he had acquired a curious trick. In moments of doubt he rubbed his chin with the knuckle of a finger. Christina had often seen him do this and had found in the gesture sure evidence of his perplexity.

"You can't advise me?" she said, reading the sign. "I didn't think you would be able to."

"I can go to Morelle and warn him," suggested Saul, "but that means trouble—here. I don't want to make mischief."

She nodded. "Evie would never forgive us," she said with a sigh. "I'm ready, Ambrose."

He stooped and lifted her from the bed, as though, as she once described it, she were of no greater weight than a pillow.

Mr. Jan Steppe was dressing for dinner when Sault was announced. "Tell him to wait—no, send him up."

"Here, sir?" asked the valet.

"Where else, you fool, huh?"

Sault came into the dressing-room and waited until his employer had fixed a refractory collar.

"Don't wait, you." The valet retired discreetly

"Well, Sault, what do you want?"

"The daughter of the woman I lodge with knows Morelle," said Ambrose Sault briefly. "She's a pretty child and I don't want anything to happen to her that will necessitate my taking Morelle and breaking his neck."

Steppe looked round with a scowl. "'Necessitate'? You talk like a damned professor. I'm not Morelle's keeper. It is enough trouble to keep him up to the scratch in other matters. As to breaking his neck, I've got something to say to that, Sault, huh?" He faced the visitor, a terrifying figure, his attitude a threat and a challenge.

"You might have to identify him," said Sault thoughtfully, "that is true."

Steppe's face went red. "Now see here, Sault. I've never had a fight with you and I don't want to, huh? You're the only one of the bunch that is worth ten cents as a man, but I'll allow nobody to dictate to me—nobody, whether he is a girl-chasing dude or an escaped convict. Get that right! I've smashed bigger men and stronger men than you, by God!"

"You'll not smash me," said Sault coolly, "and you needn't smash Morelle. I'm telling you that I won't have that girl hurt. A word from you will send Morelle crawling at her feet. I don't know him, but I know of him. He's that kind."

Steppe glared. "You're telling me, are you?" he breathed. "You think you've got me because you're indispensable now that you know about the safe. But I'll have another safe and another word. D'ye hear? I'll show you that no damned lag can bully me!"

The other smiled. "You know that the code is safe with me. That's my way. I would break Morelle or you for the matter of that—kill you with my hands before your servant could come—but the code would be with me. You know that too." He met, had not feared to meet, the fury of Steppe's eyes and presently the big man turned away with a shrug.

"You might," he said, speaking more to himself than to Ambrose Sault. "One of these days I'll try you out. I'm not a weakling and I've beaten every man that stood up to me." He looked round at the visitor and the anger had gone from his face.

"I believe you about the safe. You're the first man or woman I've ever believed in my life. Sounds queer, huh? It is a fact. I'm not frightened of you—nobody knows that better than you." Sault nodded.

"About Morelle—I'll talk to him. What is this girl—you're not in love with her yourself, huh? Can't imagine that. All right, I'll speak to Morelle—a damned cur. Anything more?"

"Nothing," said Ambrose and went out.

Steppe stared at the closed door. "A man," he said and shivered. No other man breathing had caused Steppe to shiver.

He saw Ronnie at a club late that night. "Here, I want you," he jerked his head in the direction of a quiet corner of the smoking room, and Ronnie followed him, expecting compliments, for they had not met since the meeting.

"You've got a parcel of women in tow, huh?" said Steppe.

"I don't quite understand—" began Ronnie.

"You understand all right. One of them is a friend of Sault's—Colebrook, I think her name must be. Go steady. She is a friend of Sault's. He says he'll break your neck if you monkey around there, do you get that, huh? Sault says so. He'll do it."

Ronnie did not know Ambrose Sault any better than Ambrose knew him. The threat did not sound very dreadful and he smiled.

"You can grin; maybe I'll see the same grin when I come to look at you on the mortuary slab. Sault is a hell of a bad man to cross. He has had his kill once and that will make the second seem like blowing bubbles. That's all."

Ronnie was annoyed, but not greatly impressed. He only knew Sault as a sort of superior workman, who did the dirty work of the confederacy. Sometimes he used to wonder how Steppe employed him, but then he also speculated upon the exact standing of Moropulos whose name never appeared on a prospectus and who had, apparently, no particular duties.

Threats did not greatly distress Ronnie Morelle. He had been threatened so often; and it was his experience that the worst was over when the threat came. He was free of the park now. Walking down Regent Street, one Saturday afternoon, he had come face to face with The Girl Who Had Screamed. She was with a tall, broad-shouldered young man and she had recognized him. After he had passed them, Ronnie, from the tail of his eye, saw the couple stop and the girl point after him. The man looked as though he were going to follow, but The Girl Who Screamed caught his arm. And that was the end of it.

The man might hate him, but would not make a fuss. The offense was comparatively old, and men did not pursue other people's stale vendettas. The beginning and end of vengeance was a threatening gesture. He knew just what that broad-shouldered man was saying, and thinking. He was a scoundrel, he deserved flogging. If he had been on hand when the girl squealed, he would have torn the heart out of the offender. But he wasn't there; and the girl had shown both her purity and her intelligence by preferring his gentle courtship to the violent love-making of Ronnie Morelle. In a sense the incident was subtly flattering to the broad-shouldered young man.

Ronnie was not seeing Evie in these days, he was more pleasingly engaged. The new game was infinitely more intriguing, an opponent better armed for the fight and offering a more glorious triumph.

But Steppe's warning piqued him. Sault! His lips curled in derision. That nigger! That half-caste jail-bird! He wrote to Evie that night making an appointment.

IV

"You don't know how happy I was when I found your letter at the store this morning. The manager doesn't like girls to get letters, he is an awful fossil, but he's rather keen on me. I told him your letters were from an uncle who isn't friends with mother."

"What a darling little liar you are!" said Ronnie amused. "My dear, I've missed you terribly. I shall have to give up my writing, if it is going to keep me from my girl." She snuggled closer to his side as they walked slowly through the gloom to her favorite spot. She did not tell him how she had sat there every evening, braving the importunities of those less attractive ghouls who haunt the park in the hours of dusk.

"There have been times," said Ronnie when they had found chairs and drawn them to the shadow of a big elm, "when I felt that I could write no more unless I saw you for a moment. But I set my teeth and worked. I pretend sometimes that you are sitting on the other side of the table and I look up and talk to you."

"You are like Christina," said the delighted girl, "she makes up things like that. Would you have liked to see me really walk into the room and sit down opposite to you?"

He held her more tightly. "Nine-tenths of my troubles would vanish," he said fervently, "and I could work—by heaven, how I should work if I had the inspiration of your company! I wish you weren't such a dear little puritan. I'm half inclined to engage a housekeeper if only to chaperon you."

He waited for a rejoinder, but it did not come.

"You have such queer ideas about how people should behave," he said. "In fact you are awfully old-fashioned, darling."

"Am I—I suppose I am."

"Why, the modern girl goes everywhere, bachelor parties and dances—chaperons are about as much out of date as the dodo."

"What is a dodo?"

"A bird—a sort of duck."

She gurgled with laughter. "You funny boy—"

"You know Sault, don't you? Isn't he a great friend of yours?"

She struggled up out of his arms. "Friend! Of course not. He is a great friend of Christina's but not of mine. He is so old and funny-looking. He has gray hair and he is quite dark—When I say dark, I mean he is not a negro, but—well, dark."

"I understand. Not a friend of yours?"

"Of course not. There are times when I can't stand him! He doesn't read or write, did you know that? Of course you do—and he has been in prison, you told me that, too. If mother knew she would have a fit. Why do you talk about him, Ronnie?"

"I've no special reason, only—"

"Only what, has he been talking about me?"

"Not to me, of course—he told a friend of mine that he didn't like you to know me. It was a surprise to me that he was aware we were friends. Did you tell him?"

"Me—I? Of course not. I never heard of such nerve! How dare he!"

"S-sh—don't get angry, darling. I'm sure he meant well. You have to do something for me, Evie dear."

"Talking about me—!"

"What is the use?" He bent his head and kissed her. "It will be easy for you to say that you've only met me once or twice—and that you are not seeing me any more."

"But you—you *will* see me, Ronnie?"

"Surely. You don't suppose that anything in the world will ever come between us, do you? Not fifty Saults."

"It is Christina!" she said. "How mean of her to discuss me with Sault! And I've done so much for her; brought her books from the store and given her little things—I do think it is deceitful of her."

"Will you do as I ask?"

"Of course, Ronnie darling. I'll tell her that I've given you up. But she is terribly sharp and I must be careful. I sleep in the same room, ours is a very small house. I used to have a room of my own until Sault came—the horrid old man. He is in love with Christina. It does seem ridiculous, doesn't it, a man like that? Christina says she isn't, but really—she is so deceitful."

"Will you tell her what I suggest?" he insisted.

"Yes—I'll tell her. As for Mr. Sault—"

"Leave me to deal with Mr. Sault," said Ronnie grandly.

Evie reached home, her little brain charged with conflicting emotions. Her relief at meeting the man again, the happiness that meeting had brought, her resentment at Sault's unwarranted interference, her hurt from Christina's supposed duplicity and breach of confidence, each contended for domination and each in turn triumphed.

"I have given up Ronnie and I am not going to meet him again," she said as she entered the room.

She was without finesse and Christina, instantly alert, was not impressed. "This is very sudden. What has happened?"

"I've given him up!" Evie slammed her hat down on a rickety dressing-table. She had no intention of letting the matter rest there. Her annoyance with Sault must be expressed.

"If a girl cannot have a friendship without her own sister and her sister's beastly friends making up all sorts of beastly stories about her and breaking their sacred word, too, by telling beastly people about their private affairs, then she'd better give up having friendships," she said a trifle incoherently.

"I want to sort that out," said Christina, frowning, "the only thing I'm perfectly sure about is that somebody is beastly. Do you mean that people have been talking about you and your—Ronnie?"

Evie glowered at her. "You know—you know!" she blurted tremulously. "You and Sault between you, trying to interfere in my—interfering in my affairs."

"Oh," said Christina, "is that all?"

"Is that all! Don't you think it enough, parting Ronnie and I? Breaking my heart, that is what you're doing!" she wailed. "I'll never speak to Sault again. The old murderer—that's what he is, a murderer! I'm going to tell mother and have him chucked out of the house. We're not safe. Some night he'll come along with a knife and cut our throats. A nigger murderer," she screamed. "He may be good enough to be your fancy man, but he's not good enough for me!"

"Open the window and tell the street all about it," suggested Christina. "You'll get an audience in no time. Go along! Open the window! They would love to hear. Every woman in this street screams her trouble sooner or later. The woman across the road was shouting 'murder' all last night. Be fashionable, Evie. Ronnie would love to know that you made a hit in Walter Street."

Evie was weeping now. "You're horrible and vulgar, and I wish I was dead! You've—you've parted Ronnie and I—you and Sault!"

"I don't think so," said Christina quietly, "my impression is that you are saying what Ronnie told you to say."

"I swear—" began Evie.

"Don't swear, Evie, screech. It is more convincing. Ronnie told you to say that you had given him up. What did Ambrose Sault do?"

"He went to a friend of Ronnie's with a lot of lies—about me and Ronnie. And you must have told him, Christina. It was mean, mean, mean of you!"

"He didn't want telling. He heard you the other night when you were having hysterics and yelling 'Oh, Ronnie, Ronnie!' at the top of your voice. You did everything except give Ronnie's address and telephone number. Apart from that I did tell him. I wanted to know the kind of man you're raving about. And your Ronnie is just dirt."

"Don't dare to say that—don't dare!"

"If mother didn't sleep like a dormouse she'd hear you—some people think they can make black white if they shout 'black' loudly enough. Ronald Morelle has a bad reputation with girls. I don't care if you foam at the mouth, Evie, I'm going to say it. He is a blackguard!"

"Sault told you! Sault told you!" Evie's voice had a shrill thin edge to it. "I know he did—a murderer—a nigger murderer, that is what he is. Not fit to live under the same roof as me—I shall tell Ronnie what he said—I'll tell him tomorrow, and then you'll see!"

"As you are permanently parted, I don't see how you will have an opportunity of telling him," said Christina. "I could have told him myself, today. I saw him."

"Saw him, how?" Evie was surprised into interest.

"With my eyes. Mr. Sault took me into Kensington Gardens and I saw him—he pointed him out to me."

Evie smiled contemptuously. "That is where you and your damned Sault were wrong," she said in triumph. "Ronnie has been working in his flat all the afternoon! He was writing an article for *The Statesman!*"

"He didn't seem to be working very hard when I saw him," said Christina unmoved, "unless he was dictating his article to Miss Merville. They were driving together. Mr. Sault said: 'There is Morelle'—"

"He should have said 'Mister.'"

"And I saw him. He is good-looking; the best looking man I have ever seen."

"It wasn't Ronnie—I don't mean that Ronnie isn't good looking. He's lovely. But it couldn't have been him. Besides, he hates that Merville girl, at least he doesn't like her. You are only saying this to make me jealous. How was he dressed?"

"So far as I could see, he wore a long-tailed coat—he certainly had a top hat. Mr. Sault said that he thought he had been to Lady Somebody-or-other's garden party. Mr. Steppe was going, but couldn't get away."

"Now I know it wasn't Ronnie! He was wearing a blue suit—no, he *hadn't* changed his clothes. He told me he didn't dress until an hour before he met me. Sault is a—he must have been mistaken."

Before she went to bed she came over to say "good night."

"I'm sorry I lost my temper, Chris."

"My dear, if you lose nothing else, I shall be happy."

"I hate your insinuations, Christina! Some day you will find out what a splendid man Ronnie is—and then you'll be surprised."

"I shall," admitted Christina, and later, when Evie was dropping into sleep, "Who did Ambrose kill?"

"Eh—? I don't know. Somebody in Paris—" Another long silence.

"He must have been a terrible villain!"

"Who, Sault?"

"No, the man he killed," said Christina.

She lay awake for a long time. It was two o'clock when she heard his key in the lock. She raised her head, listening to the creaking of the stairs as he came up. He had to pass her room and she whispered: "Good night, Ambrose!"

"Good night, Christina."

She blew a kiss at the door.

V

Mr. Steppe, with a gardenia in his buttonhole, leaned out of the window of his car and waved his yellow glove in greeting and Beryl, who was just about to enter her own machine, stepped back upon the sidewalk and waited. She felt a little twinge of impatience, for she was on her way to the Horse Show and Ronald.

"Is the doctor in—good! He can wait—where are you off to, Beryl, huh? Looking perfectly lovely too. I often wonder what those old back-veld relations of mine would say if they ever saw a girl like you. Their women are just trek-oxen—mustn't say 'cows,' huh? Are you in a great hurry?"

"Not a great hurry," she smiled, "but I think father is expecting you."

"I know. But he'll not be worried if I'm late. Drive me somewhere. I want to talk."

She jumped at the opportunity of placing a time-limit on the conversation.

"Drive to Regents Park, round the inner circle and back to the house," she ordered, and Mr. Steppe handed her into the car.

"I want to have a little chat about your father," he said, greatly to her surprise. He had never before spoken more than two consecutive sentences in reference to Dr. Merville.

"What I tell you, Beryl, is in confidence," he said. "I'm not sure whether I ought to tell you at all, but you're a sensible girl, huh? No nonsense. That is how a woman should be. The doctor has lost a lot of money you know that?"

"I didn't know," she answered in alarm, "but I thought father confined his investments to your companies?"

"Yes—so he has. He has taken up a lot of shares—against my advice. He is carrying—well I wouldn't like to tell you the figure. He bought them—against my advice. Most of my stock is only partly paid up. He is carrying nearly a million shares in one concern or another. That is all right. You can carry millions, always providing there is a market, and that you can sell at a profit, or else that there isn't any need to call up the remainder of the capital. That need has arisen in the case of two companies in which he is heavily involved. Now, Beryl, you are not to say a word about what I have told you."

"But—I don't quite follow what you have said. Does it mean that father will be called upon to pay large sums of money?" He nodded.

"Or else—?"

"There is no 'or else,'" said Steppe. "The capital has to be called in, in justice to the shareholders and the doctor must pay. Somebody must pay. In fact, I am going to pay. That was the reason I was calling on him today."

"He has been very worried lately," said Beryl in a troubled tone. "I don't know how to thank you, Mr. Steppe. Is it a big sum?"

"It runs to hundreds of thousands," said Steppe. "Very few can lay their hands on that amount, huh? Jan Steppe! They know me in the city, hate me, would slaughter me, but they don't despise me. I can sign cheques for a million and they'd be honored."

"But father must make some arrangement to pay you, Mr. Steppe—" she began.

"That is nothing. The shares may rise in value—there is no telling what may happen with the market in an optimistic mood. But I thought I would let you know. Steppe isn't a bad fellow, huh?"

She heaved a long sigh. "No—you are kind, most kind. I wish father wouldn't touch the stock market. Temperamentally, he is unfitted for a gambler. He is so easily depressed. Can't you persuade him, Mr. Steppe?"

"If you say the word, I'll stop him," said Steppe. "There is nothing I wouldn't do for you, Beryl." She was silent.

"I'm grateful," she said, as the car was heading for the house. "I cannot put myself under any bigger obligation—father must do as he wishes. But if you could help him with advice—?"

It occurred to her then, that if he could, at a word, arrest the speculative tendencies of Dr. Merville, why had he contented himself with "advice" when her father had made his disastrous investments?

Saying good-bye to him at the door of the house, Beryl drove on to Olympia a disturbed and anxious girl. Steppe watched the car out of sight before he mounted the steps and rang the bell.

"You saw us, huh? Yes, I wanted to talk to Beryl and I knew that you wouldn't mind waiting. I've got to call up the unpaid capital of Brakpan Mines and Toledo Deeps."

The doctor moved uneasily. "Couldn't you wait a little while?" he asked nervously. "The shares are moving. They went up a fraction yesterday—which means that there are buyers."

"I was the buyer," said Steppe. "I took a feeler at the market. I bought five hundred—and I could have had five hundred thousand at the price. They were falling over one another to sell. No, I'm afraid I've got to make a call and you'll have to take up your shares, huh? Well, I'm going to let you have the money."

"That is good of you—"

"Not at all. I must keep your name sweet and clean, Merville. I am going to marry Beryl."

The doctor opened a silver box and took out a cigar with a shaking hand. "Beryl is a very dear girl," he said. "Have you spoken to her?"

"No, there is plenty of time. I don't want to scare her—let her get used to me, Merville, huh? That's that. You are crossing with me tonight, huh? Good, I hate the Havre route, but you can sleep on board and that saves time. Abrahams is coming from Vienna with the Bulgarian concession. I'm inclined to float it."

Ronnie was waiting in the main entrance when the girl arrived. In some respects he was a model escort. He never expected a woman to be punctual and had trained himself in the art of patient waiting.

"No, really, I haven't been here very long," he replied to her apology, "and you, of all women, are worth waiting for."

"You are a dear. I don't believe you, but still you are a dear. I'm so sick of life today, Ronnie—don't ask me why. Amuse me."

"How is the doctor?" he queried, as they were shown into their seats.

"He is going to Paris tonight with Mr. Steppe," she said. "I'm rather glad. Two or three days abroad will do him a lot of good. There aren't many people here this afternoon, Ronnie."

"Most of the swells are at Ascot," he explained, "the night séance is crowded. Gone to Paris, eh?" The news made him thoughtful.

She drove him back to the house to tea. Dr. Merville was out and was not returning to dinner. The maid said he had left a letter in his study. Beryl found it to be a note saying he was unlikely to see her before he went; his bag would be called for, he added.

"My hard-hearted parent has gone without saying goodbye," she said. "Take me out to dinner, Ronnie. After, I would like to see a revue. I feel un-intellectual today; I'm in the mood when I want to see people with red noses and baggy trousers. And I want to be in a box. I love boxes, since—"

Ronald Morelle walked home from Park Crescent stopping at a messenger office to scribble a note.

"It is at a drug store in Knightsbridge," he said. "I want the boy to give it to the young lady in the pay desk. Perhaps he had better make a purchase—a cake of soap, if that is the boy," he smiled upon the diminutive messenger, "and let him hand the letter to the lady when he puts in his bill."

He came to the flat to find François laying out his dress clothes.

"Finish what you are doing and go home. I shall not want you this evening," he said. "Stay—have a bottle put on ice. You can lay the small table. You might have bought some flowers. I hate flowers, but—get some. You can throw them away tomorrow."

"Yes, m'sieur," said his imperturbable man, "for how many shall I lay supper?"

"For three," answered Ronnie.

It was a convention that he invariably entertained two guests, but François had never had to wash more than two used glasses.

VI

Beryl was still in the drawing-room and the tea table had not been cleared when Ambrose Sault came for the doctor's bag. She heard the sound of his voice in the hall and came to the head of the stairs.

"Is that you, Mr. Sault? Won't you come up for a moment?"

The doctor had telephoned to Moropulos, he explained, asking him to take the grip to his club. She gathered that it was usual for Ambrose to carry out these little commissions.

"How is Miss Colebrook? —has she forgiven me for acting the part of district visitor? She is a nice girl and her hair is such a wonderful color."

"The osteopath says she will get well," replied Ambrose simply, "and when I went in to see her this morning she told me she really thought that she felt better already. She has the heart of a lion, Miss Merville."

"She is certainly brave." Beryl knew she was a brute because she could not work up an enthusiastic interest in Christina Colebrook.

"It will be wonderful if she is cured." Sault's voice was hushed. "I daren't let myself think about it—in fact, I shall be more bitterly disappointed than she, if the treatment does not succeed."

"You are very fond of her?" She had been examining his face as he spoke, wondering what there was in him that she had seen at their first meeting which reminded her of Ronnie. There was not a vestige of likeness between them. This man's face, for all its strength, was coarse; the eyes were the only fine features it possessed. And the skin—there was a yellow-brown tinge in it. She remembered her father saying once that people who had negro blood in their veins betrayed their origin even though they were quite white, by a dark half-moon on their finger-nails. Whilst he was speaking, he moved his hands so that his nails were discernible. They were ugly nails, broad and ragged of edge—yes, there it was—a brown crescent showing against the deep pink.

"Yes, I'm fond of her. She is lovable. I haven't met anybody like Christina before."

Why was she annoyed? Perhaps "annoyed" hardly described her emotion. She was disappointed in him. Her attitude toward Sault was enigmatical—it was certainly capricious. She was a little nauseated and was glad when he went.

Sault carried the suitcase to the club and left it with a porter. He wished he had an excuse for calling every day at the house—the sight of her exalted him, raised him instantly to a higher plane.

He saw Evie walking home in front of him; she saw him, stopped and became interested in a shop window. She always avoided him in the street and would not dream of walking with him. In the kitchen, to which she followed him, she condescended to speak.

"You were looking very pleased with yourself when I saw you in High Street, Mr. Sault," she said.

"Was I—yes, I was feeling good. You're home early tonight, Evie."

Mrs. Colebrook had a washing day and was at her labors in the scullery, and Evie could flare up without reproof.

"I'm so glad you notice when I come in, and go out!" she said. "It is nice to know that all your movements are watched. I suppose I ought to ask your permission when I stay out late? We always like to please the lodger!"

He looked down into the pretty flushed face and smiled gently. "I believe you are trying to be cross with me, Evie," he said good-naturedly, "and I don't feel like being cross with anybody. My dear, it is no business of mine—"

"Don't call me 'my dear,' if you please! You have a nerve to 'my dear' me! A man like you!"

Sault's knuckle touched his chin awkwardly. "I didn't mean to be offensive—"

"You are offensive! You are the most beastly offensive person I know! You go prying and spying into my business and telling lies about gentlemen whose boots you're not fit to blacken."

"Hello, hello!" Mrs. Colebrook stood in the kitchen doorway, wiping her soapy hands on her apron. "What's this, Evie? Telling lies about you? Mr. Sault would not tell a lie to save his life. What gentleman? He'd have to be a pretty good gentleman for Mr. Sault to blacken his boots."

Evie wilted before her mother's fiery gaze and, turning, slammed from the room.

"It is nothing, Mrs. Colebrook," smiled Ambrose. "I made her angry—something I said. It was my fault entirely. Now what about those blankets?"

"You're not going to wash any blankets," said Mrs. Colebrook, "and Evie has got to say she is sorry."

"I washed blankets before you were born, Mrs. Colebrook, or soon after, at any rate. I promised you I'd come home and help you."

He went with her to the little scullery with its copper and wash tub, she protesting.

"I didn't think you meant it," she said, "and I can't let you do it. You go into the kitchen and I'll make you a cup of tea."

"Blankets," said Ambrose, rolling up his sleeves.

Evie burst into her room, red with anger. She hated Sault more than ever. She said so, flinging her hat wildly on the bed.

"Oh—was that you who was strafing?" asked Christina.

"I gave him a piece of my mind," said Evie with satisfaction.

"That was generous, considering the size of it." Christina bent outward and laid down the paper and stylograph she had been using.

"I couldn't have done that a few days ago," she said, "and what has poor Ambrose done?"

"He had the cheek to tell me I was home very early, as if he was the lord of the house!"

"Aren't you home early?"

"It is no business of his, the interfering old devil!"

Christina eyed her critically. "You came home in a bad temper," she said. "I suppose giving up Ronnie has got on your nerves."

"I haven't given him up!" Evie snapped, "only he's busy tonight."

Christina chewed a toffee ball reflectively. "That man is certainly industrious," she said. "They will have to bring out new papers to print all he writes. Does he find time to eat?"

Evie lifted her nose scornfully.

"What did you say to my Ambrose?"

"I told you."

"You said that you gave him a piece of your mind—that doesn't mean anything to me. Did you call him a murderer?"

"Of course I didn't—I hope I'm a lady."

"I've often hoped so, and maybe one of these days my hopes will be realized. So you didn't call him a murderer? You lost a great opportunity. Don't be offensive to him again, Evie," she said quietly.

Evie did not reply. When Christina spoke in that tone of voice she was frightened of her.

"What is Ambrose doing now?"

"I don't know—in the kitchen, I suppose, guzzling food. And I'm starving! But I won't sit down at the same table as a black man, I won't!"

"Don't be a fool, Evie. Go down and get some food. You can bring it up here and eat it. And, Evie—Ambrose is a very dear friend of mine and I dislike hearing you call him a 'black man.' He is almost as white as you and I. His great grandfather was an Indian."

"If you don't like to hear me say unpleasant things about your friends, don't say them about mine."

Here, Evie thought, not without reason, that she had a point which was worth laboring. She was astonished when Christina surrendered without firing another shot.

"Perhaps you are right, dear. Go and get something to eat."

Evie returned almost immediately with the news that the kitchen was empty and that she had seen one whom she was pleased to describe as "the enemy" bending over a washtub, his arms white with lather.

"Do you think he is making up to mother?" she asked, as that interesting possibility presented itself.

Christina choked. "Don't say funny things when I'm eating candy," she begged.

VII

The revue had reached its seventh scene before Beryl and her escort were shown into the big stage box of the Pavilion. She had hardly taken her seat before she saw a familiar face in the stalls.

"Isn't that Mr. Moropulos?" she asked, and following the direction of her eyes he nodded. The Greek did not appear to have noticed them. He was conspicuous as being the only man in that row of the stalls who was not wearing evening dress.

"Yes, that is Moropulos. Don't let him see you, Beryl."

Apparently Mr. Moropulos did not identify the pair, for though he turned his head in their direction he showed no sign of recognition. Half-way through the last part of the revue, he disappeared and they did not see him again.

"And now home. It has been a jolly afternoon and evening," said Beryl as they came out.

Ronnie was looking round for his car. "What a fool I am," he said. "I told Parker not to wait—for some extraordinary reason I imagined your car would be here. We'll have to take a taxi."

The cab had hardly started before he tapped at the window and leaning out, gave a fresh direction.

"Come home and have some supper. I've just remembered that I told François I was bringing a couple of men home—told him early this morning."

She hesitated. "I can't stay very long," she said. "No—nobody is waiting up for me. My maid never does—it spoils my enjoyment of a dance if I think that

I am keeping some poor girl out of her bed. I'll come in for five minutes, dear."

His arm came round her, her head drooped toward him.

"Ronnie—I'm so glad all this has come about, darling—I've run after you—I know I have. But I don't care—four years seems such an awful long time to wait."

"An eternity," he breathed.

"And marriage is, as you say—in your immoral way—only a third party sanction—it is silly." He kissed her.

An automatic lift carried them to the third floor and Ronnie went in switching on the lights.

"I wonder whether father will be angry," she asked, "if your man—"

"He sleeps out," Ronnie helped her off with her wrap. "He's never here after nine. This is my own room, Beryl—but you saw it when the doctor brought you here to dinner."

She walked over to the big black table and sat down.

"Here genius broods," she laughed quietly, "what a humbug you are, Ronnie! I don't believe you write a thousand words a month!"

He smiled indulgently.

"And there is your wicked Anthony! He looks worse by artificial light. Now, Ronnie, I really must go."

"Go?" incredulously, "with foie-gras sandwiches and a beautifully dry wine?"

The door into the dining-room was open and he pointed. "It is the last bottle of that wine. Jerry will be furious when he comes to breakfast in the morning and finds it gone."

Ronnie had a friend, one Jeremiah Talbot, a man after his own heart. Beryl had met him once, a languid loose-lipped man with a reputation for gallantry.

"Well—I'll eat just a little—and then you must take me home. You shouldn't have paid off the cab."

He was too busy at the wine bucket to listen. She sat on the edge of one of the window chesterfields and let her eyes rove around the room, and after a while he brought a plate and a filled glass.

She put her lips to the wine and handed it back to him. "No more, dear."

A sudden panic had taken possession of her, and she was shaking. "No—!" And yet it was so natural and so comforting to let him hold her. She relaxed, unresisting.

"I shouldn't be here, Ronnie," she murmured between his kisses, "let me go, darling—please." But he held her the tighter and she did not deny his greedy lips.

VIII

Ronnie woke with a start, stared at the window and cursed. Pulling on a dressing-gown he slipped from the room and at the sight of him the woman who was dusting the sideboard paused in her labors.

"I don't want you here today—where is your friend?"

"In the pantry, sir."

"Well, take her with you—ah, François, listen. Turn these women out and then go out yourself—go to the city—and get—buy anything you like, but don't come back before eleven—no twelve."

He waited until the flat was empty and returned to his room. Beryl was lying with her head in the crook of her arm. She was not asleep—nor crying, as he had feared.

"I'm dreadfully sorry, darling—I must have fallen asleep."

"What is the time?" She did not turn but spoke into the pillow.

"Eight—curse it! You can't go home in evening dress."

"Why not?"

She struggled up, her face averted.

"It is the best way," she said, "will you get me a cab?"

When he came up again, she was tidying her hair at the mirror. "It was very foolish," she remarked without emotion.

"There is nobody below, and, thank God, there was an Albert Hall ball last night," said Ronnie, "and it is only eight—shall I come down with you?"

She shook her head. "No—just show me how to work the elevator. An Albert Hall ball? Where could I have been after that finished? You lie better than I, Ronnie."

"Having breakfast—lots of people make a special function of breakfast after those shows."

"All right—show me how the elevator works."

To her maid a quarter of an hour later: "I'm going to bed, Dean, and if Mr. Morelle rings up, will you tell him that I am very sorry I cannot see him this morning. You can bring me a cup of chocolate—yes, I've had breakfast, but bring me some chocolate."

She was standing by the window in a silk wrap when the maid brought the tray. Beryl did not look round.

"Put it down, Dean—I will ring when I want you."

She walked across the room and locked the door. Then she came to the mirror and looked for a long time at herself. "Yes—Beryl—it is you! I was hoping it was somebody else!"

IX

That same morning Mr. Moropulos asked a question of Ambrose Sault.

"What exposure should you give to a photograph taken, say, soon after eight o'clock in the morning?"

"What sort of a morning?"

"This morning."

Ambrose glanced out of the window.

"You could get a snap shot on a twenty-fifth of a second," he said.

Mr. Moropulos produced a folding Kodak from his pocket. "Would this stop be wide enough?"

Ambrose took the camera in his hand. "Yes," he said. "What were you taking, a scene or a figure?"

"A figure," said Mr Moropulos, "a lady in evening dress."

Ambrose smiled. "Eight o'clock is a funny time to photograph a lady in evening dress," he said.

"An amusing time—if one hadn't been waiting up all night to take it. I was here at five. Yes—I came back for the camera. I took a chance of missing the lady, but even if I had it wouldn't have mattered. But eight o'clock!" he laughed gleefully, "how very obliging. Sault, my Ambrosial man, I am going to sleep."

"I think you need it," said Ambrose.

He did all the work of the house, even to making Mr. Moropulos' bed and he was glad of the opportunity to "spring-clean" the sitting-room. He only interrupted his labors to cut a crust of bread and a slice of cheese for his lunch.

At five o'clock in the afternoon the telephone bell rang for the first time that day. "Is that Mr. Moropulos—is that you, Mr. Sault?"

"Yes, lady."

He recognized her voice instantly and his heart leaped within him.

"I'm so glad—will you come to the house please?"

"Yes—I'll come right away." He hung up the receiver as Moropulos strolled in yawning.

"He-e! Who was the caller?"

"A friend of mine," said Sault.

"Didn't know you had any friends—are you going? Make me some coffee before you go, Sault."

"Make it yourself," said Ambrose.

Moropulos grinned after him. "I'd give a lot of money to stick a knife into that big chest of yours, my good Ambrose," he said pleasantly.

Marie opened the door to the untidy visitor, showing him straight to the drawing-room and Beryl came halfway to him, taking his hand in both of hers.

"I'm so glad you've come—I had to send for you—do you mind? I want to talk to you—about nothing in particular—I'm nervy. Can't you tell from my hand?"

The hand in his was shaking, he felt the quiver of it. And she looked pale. Why had she sent for him? She was amazed at herself. Perhaps it was his strength she wanted; a rock on which she might rebuild the shattered fabric of her reason. She had been thinking of him all the afternoon. Ronnie never came to her mind. He was incidental—reality lay with the coarse-featured man whom she had likened to a Caesar.

"I don't want you to do anything for me, except be here. Just for a little while." She was pleading like a frightened child.

"I am here—I will stay here until you want me to go," said Ambrose, and smiled into her eyes.

"Mr. Sault, I do so wish to talk about something. It won't hurt you will it?" She had only released his hands to pull a chair forward. Opposite to him she sat, this time both of her hands in his. Why? She gave up asking the question.

"You killed somebody, is it true—I knew it was true before I asked you. Did it injure you—make you think less of yourself—did you loathe the man you killed because he made you do it? You are looking at me so strangely—you don't think I am mad, do you?"

"I don't think you are mad. No, I didn't even hate the man. He deserved death. I did not wish to kill him, but there was no other way. There must be that definite end to some problems—death. There is no other. I believe implicitly in it—destruction. A man who is so vile that he kills in his greed or his lust! Who takes an innocent and a helpful life—helpful to the world and its people—you must destroy him. The law does this, so that the brain behind his wicked hands shall not lead him to further mischief. If you have a sheep-dog that worries sheep you shoot him. There is no other way. Or he will breed other sheep dogs with the same vice. Most problems are soluble by various processes. Some of them drastic, some of them commonplace. A few, a very few, can only be ended that way. My man was one of these. I won't tell you the story—he was a bad man and I killed him. But I didn't hate him, nor hate myself. And I think no less of myself—and no more. I did what I thought was right—I've never regretted it, but I've never been proud of it."

She listened, fascinated. The hands in his were quiet now, there was a hue in her cheeks.

"How fine to feel like that—to detach yourself—but why should you regret? You injured no one. Except the man and—was he married?"

He nodded. "I didn't know at the time. She came forward afterwards and paid the expenses of my defense—she hated him—it was very sad."

They were quiet together until she lifted her head and spoke. "Mr. Sault—I'm going to ask you another strange question. Have you, in all your life, ever been in love?"

"Yes," he said instantly.

"With a woman, just because she is a woman? As I might love a man because he has all the outward attractions of a man? Have you loved her just for her beauty and despised her mean soul and her vicious mind, and—and despising—still loved?"

She hung upon his words, and when he said "no" her heart sank.

"No—no, I couldn't do that. That would be—horrible!"

He shuddered. She had made Ambrose Sault shudder! Ambrose Sault who spoke calmly of murder, had shuddered at something, which, to him, was worse than murder! The fragrance of sin which had held to her and supported her through the day, was stale and sour and filthy. She shrank away from him, but he held her hands tightly.

"Let me go, please," her voice sounded faint.

"In a moment—look at me, lady."

She raised her eyes to his and they held them.

"I am going to say something to you that I never dreamed I would say; I never thought the words would come to me. Look at me, lady, a rough man—old— I'm more than fifty, ugly, with an old man's shape and an old man's hands. Illiterate—I love you. I shall never see you again—I love you. You are beautiful— the most beautiful lady I have seen. But it isn't that. There is something in you that I love—I don't know what—soul—spirit—individuality. I hope I haven't revolted you—I don't think I have."

"Ambrose!" She clutched at the hands he was drawing away. "I must tell you—there is nothing to love but what you see, there is no soul—no soul— nothing but weakness and a pitiful cowardice. I love a man who is like that, too. Foul, foul! But beautiful to look at—and, Ambrose, I have given him all that he can take."

Not a muscle of his face moved.

"I have given him everything—this very day—that is why I sent for you. There must be something in what you say—a spirit in me responds to you— oh, Ambrose, I love him!"

She was sobbing against the stained and raveled coat. There was a scent of some pungent oil—turpentine. But he did not speak. His big hand touched her head lightly, smoothing her hair.

"You think I'm—what do you think I am?" she asked.

"You know," he patted her shoulder gently. "I suppose you are wondering what I am feeling? I will tell you this—I am not hurt. I can't be hurt, for you have lost nothing which I prize. If you were different, you wouldn't like me to say that."

He took her face between his rough hands and looked into her eyes. "How very beautiful it is!" he said.

She shut her eyes tight to keep back the tears.

"I said I wouldn't see you again. Perhaps I won't—but if you want me send for me."

She dried her eyes. "I'm a weakling—I wish I was wicked and didn't care—I don't care, really. What has happened is—" she shrugged, "it is the discovery of my own rottenness that has shocked me—nearly driven me mad. You are going now, Ambrose—that is so lovely in you—you even know when to go!"

She laughed nervously and laid her two hands on his shoulder. She did not want to kiss or be kissed. And she knew that he felt as she did.

"Come to me when I want you—I shall be busy inventing lies for the next few days. Good-bye, Ambrose." When he had gone she realized that no man's name had been mentioned. Perhaps he knew.

X

For the first time in his life Ronald Morelle was regretting an adventure. All day long he had been trying to write, with the result that his wastepaper basket was full of torn or twisted sheets, even as the silver ash-tray on the table was heaped with cigarette ends. He had gone half a dozen times to the telephone to call up Merville's house and had stopped short of giving the number. Then he tried to write her a note. He could think of nothing to say beyond the flamboyant beginning. What was the use of writing? And what was she thinking about it all? He wished—and he wished again. He had made a hopeless fool of himself. Why had he done it? For the truth unfolded as the hours passed, that an end must be found to this affair. In other cases *finis* had been written at his discretion, sometimes cheerfully, sometimes with tears and recriminations. There had been instances that called for solid compensations. Beryl was not to be ended that way. Besides, he had half-promised her—he grew hot at the very thought of matrimony and in the discomfort of the prospect, the pleasant irresponsibilities of bachelorhood and the features that went to the making of his life, seemed too good to lose.

In such a mood, he thought of Evie Colebrook. How perfectly attractive she was; he could admire her virtue and coldbloodedly compare her with Beryl—to Beryl's disparagement. He was hemmed in by his new responsibility; ached to be free from fetters that were still warm from the forge. Late at night he wrote two letters, one to Beryl, the other and the longer to Evie.

Beryl had hers with her morning tea, saw who it was from the moment the maid pulled aside the curtains and let in the morning sunlight. She turned it over in her hand—now she knew. So that was how she felt about a letter from Ronnie. Not so much as a tremor, not a quicker pulsation of heart.

She opened the envelope and read:

> "*My very dearest*: I don't know what to write to you or how. I adore the memory of you. I am shaken by the calamity—for you. Command me, I will do as you wish. I will not see you again though it breaks my heart."

It was written on a plain card, unsigned. She sent him a wire that morning: "Come to tea."

In answer came a hurried note by special delivery.

> "I cannot: I dare not trust myself. I am overwhelmed by the sense of my treachery. That I should have brought a second's unhappiness to you!"

Unsigned. Ronnie never signed or dated such epistles.

She read the note and laughed. Yes, she could laugh.

On the third evening, her father returned in a most cheerful frame of mind. He had carried through a business deal, he and Steppe. And he had enjoyed the trip, having met a number of French medical men who had entertained him.

"They were charming, and the new Pasteur laboratories were most fascinating. We feared you would have had a dull time, Beryl. I hope Ronnie didn't desert you!"

"I am afraid he didn't," she said, and the doctor beamed. "You're not too fond of him, I am glad of that for he is rather a rascal. I suppose young men, some young men, are like that—conscienceless."

"Did you have a good crossing?" she asked, and turned the conversation into a more pleasant way.

"Sault was to have met us at the station but he did not turn up. Perhaps Moropulos is drinking. One never knows when Moropulos will break out. He is afraid of Steppe."

"Who isn't?" she asked with a grimace.

The doctor scratched his cheek meditatively. "I don't know—I'm not afraid of him. Naturally, I shouldn't like a rough and tumble with him, physically or verbally. Ronnie, of course, is in the most abject terror of him. The only man who isn't—er—reluctant to provoke him, is Sault." He chuckled.

"Steppe told me that he had a row with Sault over some girl that Ronnie had been carrying on with—the daughter of the woman Colebrook, my dear. Apparently, Sault went to our friend Jan and told him to put a stop to it, and Steppe was naturally annoyed, and do you know what Sault said?" Her eyes were shining.

"He told Steppe that in certain contingencies he would kill him, before his servant could reach him; to his face!"

"What did Mr. Steppe think of it?" she found her voice to ask.

"Amused—and impressed, too. He says Sault wouldn't tell a lie, wouldn't do a mean thing to save his soul. That is something of a testimonial from a man like Steppe who, I am sorry to say, is inclined to be a little uncharitable."

Beryl folded her serviette; she looked to be absorbed in the operation.

"He was telling me that Sault was one of the finest mathematicians in the country. And he doesn't read or write! Of course, he writes figures and symbols perfectly. He attends every lecture that he can get to; a remarkable personality."

"Very."

"I thought you rather liked him?"

She started from her reverie. "Who—Ambrose?"

"Ambrose!"

"That is his name, isn't it?"

"But, my dear," smiled the doctor indulgently, "you wouldn't call him by his Christian name! I think he would be rather annoyed to be treated like a servant."

"I wasn't thinking of him as a servant."

They got up from the table together and she went with him as far as his study door.

"What have you been doing with yourself—theatres?"

"Yes, and a ball. An all-night affair. I came home at eight."

"Humph—bad for you, that sort of thing."

She was sure it was. It was bad to lie, too, but she was beyond caring. Ambrose never lied. He would lie for her. Ronnie also would lie—for himself. She mused and mused, thinking of Sault—Ambrose Sault. And the red-haired invalid. And this sister of hers whom Ambrose had gone to Steppe about—she laughed quietly. She would have loved to have seen that contest of giants. Could Steppe be browbeaten? It seemed impossible, and yet Ambrose had cowed him.

She dreamed that night that she saw Ronald and Sault fighting with reaping hooks—she woke up with a shiver. For in her dream their heads had been exchanged, and Ronnie's face smiled at her from Sault's broad shoulders. It was growing light, she found, when she peeped through the curtains. She went to bed again, but did not sleep any more.

It was a coincidence that Ronald Morelle was also awake at that hour. His new responsibility was weighing on him like a leaden weight. She would never let him go. Her wire had terrified him. "There's no end to it!" he said with a groan, "no end."

He did not love Beryl; he loved nobody, but there were some girls whom he wanted to see again and again. Evie was one of that kind. He did not want to see Beryl. He pictured himself chained for life to a woman who was now wholly without attraction. To this misery was added a new and unbelievable horror.

Steppe called just as Ronald was going out to lunch. At any time Steppe was an unwelcome visitor. In the state of Ronnie's nerves, he felt it impossible that he could support the strain of the big man's company for five minutes. He wished Steppe wouldn't barge in without warning. It was not gentlemanly.

"I'm awful glad to see you, Mr. Steppe; when did you get back?"

"Last night—I won't keep you a minute. I'm on my way to make a call on that swine Moropulos," he growled. "I want to see you about Beryl."

Ronald Morelle's heart missed a beat. Had she told? He turned white at the thought. Luckily Steppe was striding up and down the room, hands in pockets, bearded chin on chest.

Ronnie's mouth had gone dry and he had a cold sinking feeling inside him. "Yes—about Beryl," he managed to say.

"You're a great friend of hers, huh? Known her for a long time?"

Ronnie nodded.

"You have some influence with her?"

"I—I hope so—not a great influence—"

"I am going to marry Beryl. The doctor has probably hinted to you that I have plans in that quarter, huh?"

Ronnie swallowed. "No," he said, "I didn't know—my congratulations."

"Keep 'em," said the other shortly, "they're not wanted yet. You're a great friend of hers, huh? Go about with her a great deal? I suppose it is all right. I'd pull the life out of you if it wasn't—but Beryl is a good girl—what I want you to do is this; give me a good name. If you have any influence, use it. Get that?"

"Certainly," Morelle found voice to say, "I'll do what I can."

"That's all right. And, Morelle, when I'm married you won't be asked to spend a great deal of time at my house. You'll come when I invite you. That's straight, huh? So long."

Ronald shut the door on him.

XI

What a mess! What a perfect hell of a mess he was in. He stood by the window, biting his nails. Suppose Beryl told? He wiped his forehead. Girls had queer ideas about their duty in that respect. He knew of cases. One of those threatening gestures which had come his way was the result of such a misguided act of confession on the part of a girl whom he had treated very handsomely indeed. A baser case of ingratitude it would be difficult to imagine. Beryl might. She had principles. Phew!

He heard the trill of the telephone in François' pantry.

"Mr. Moropulos," said François, emerging from his room.

Ronnie scowled. "Tell him—no, put him through." He laid down his walking stick and gloves.

"Yes, Moropulos—good morning—lunch? Well, I was going out to lunch with some people."

Moropulos said that his business was important.

"All right—oh, anywhere—one of those little places in Soho." He slammed down the instrument viciously. But this was a time to consolidate his friends and their interests. Not that Moropulos was a friend, but he was useful and might be more so.

The Greek arrived at the restaurant to the minute and was looking more spruce than usual.

"Have you seen Steppe?" was his first question.

"I understood he was on his way to see you—he seemed angry," said Ronnie.

"Our dear Steppe is always angry," answered the Greek coolly. "This time, however, he has no cause. If he has gone to my house, he will not see me."

"What is the trouble?"

Moropulos shrugged. "He has been informed by evil-minded people that during his absence I was—well, not to put too fine a point on it, very drunk."

"And were you?"

"On the contrary, at the very hour, when his spies informed him I was dancing on a table in a low part of the east end, and shouting that the Mackenzie report was a forgery—"

Ronnie went pale. "Good God! You never said that?" he gasped.

"Of course not. If I had, it would be a serious thing for me. I, Paul Moropulos, tell you, Ronald Morelle, that it would be a disastrous thing for me. Just now my relations with dear Jan are—er—strained. I do not wish a breach."

"But surely if Steppe's men say—"

"'Let them say,'" quoted Moropulos, "it is what I say, and you say, and somebody else says, that counts, for at the very moment I was supposed to be misbehaving," he emphasized his words, "I was dining with you and the lovely Miss Merville in your flat."

"What! Why, that is a lie!"

"What is one lie worse than another? Observe I give you the date; it was one day before the charming Miss Merville spent the night with you alone in your very beautiful flat." Had the floor collapsed, Ronald Morelle could not have received a worse shock.

"I recognize your embarrassment and sympathize with you," said Moropulos, "but it is essential for my happiness and ultimate prosperity, that both you and Miss Merville should testify that I dined with you on the previous night."

Ronnie had nothing to say. He had not yet realized the tremendous import of the man's threat.

"I will save you a lot of trouble by telling you that I followed you from the Pavilion to Knightsbridge. I spent the whole of the night outside, wondering when she would come out, and I photographed her as she got into the cab. The photograph, an excellent one, is now in a secret place. Steppe, I hope, will never see it," he added, looking at his *vis-à-vis* from under his eyelids. "Steppe is angry with me; how unjust! It was impossible that I could have been making a fool of myself, at the very hour we three together were talking of—what were we talking of?—Greece, let us say, the academies. Steppe would not believe you, of course, but he would believe Miss Merville and a great unpleasantness would be avoided. I am sorry to make this demand upon you, but you see how I am situated? I swear to you that I had no intention of using my knowledge. It was an amusing little secret of my own."

Ronald found his voice. "Am I to tell—Miss Merville that you know? That you have a photograph?"

Moropulos spread his hands. "Why should she know? It is not necessary."

Ronnie was relieved. It was something to be spared the scene which would follow the disclosure that a third person was in their secret. He asked for no proofs that Moropulos knew, and any thought of the girl and what this meant to her, never entered his head. If Steppe knew! He grew cold at the thought. Steppe would kill him, pull his life out of him. Ronald Morelle was prepared to go a long way to keep his master in ignorance.

"I will see Miss Merville," he said, and then feeling that a protest was called for: "You have behaved disgracefully, Moropulos—to blackmail me. That is what it amounts to!"

"Not at all. It was a simple matter to tell Steppe that on the night in question I was waiting soberly outside your flat, watching his interests. He is immensely partial to Beryl Merville. A confusion of dates would not have been remarked; he would be so mad that the lesser would be absorbed in the greater injury. He, he would forgive—you—"

Ronald shuddered.

In the afternoon he made his call. "It is lucky finding you alone, dear," he began, awkwardly for him, "you'll never guess what I've been through during the past few days—"

She was very calm and self-possessed. A shade paler, perhaps, but she was of a type that pallor suited. And she met his eyes without embarrassment. That made matters more difficult for Ronald. He plunged straight away into the object of his visit.

"Where were you on Tuesday night, Beryl?"

She was puzzled. "Tuesday—? I forget, why?"

"Try to think, dear," he urged.

"I was dining at home. Father was out, I think. I'm not sure. I went to a concert after with the Paynters. Yes, that was it—why?"

"You were dining with Moropulos and I."

She stared at him. "I don't understand."

"Moropulos is in trouble with Steppe. He has been drinking and some of Steppe's watchers have reported that be made an ass of himself, gave away some business secrets, and that sort of thing. Steppe is naturally furious and Moropulos wants to prove an alibi."

"That he was dining with us, how absurd! Where?"

"In my flat."

She surveyed him steadily. He was unusually excited. She had never seen Ronnie like that before. Nothing ever ruffled him.

"Of course, I can't tell such a lie, even to save your friend," she said. "I was dining at home, although father has such a wretched memory that he won't be sure whether I was here or not."

"Where did you meet the Paynters, did they call for you?" he asked eagerly and she shook her head.

"No, I met them at Queens Hall. I was late and they had gone into the hall. But that is beside the point. I am not helping you in this matter."

"But you must, you must," he was frenzied. "Moropulos knows—he saw you come into the flat—and come out."

There was a dead silence. "When—on that night?"

She walked across the room, her hands clasped behind her. Ronnie had expected hysteria—he marveled at her calm.

"Very well," she said at last. "I dined with you and Moropulos. You had better invent another lady. Let us be decent, even in our inventions. And Mr. Moropulos entertained us with talk about—what?"

"Anything," nervously, "I know that you think I'm a brute—I can't tell you what I think about myself."

"I can save you the trouble. You think you are in danger and you are hating me because I am the cause."

"Beryl!"

She smiled. "Perhaps I am being uncharitable. The complex of this situation doesn't allow for very clear thinking. I may take another view next week. Will you post this letter for me as you go out?"

He went down the stairs dumbfounded. Her quietness, the unshaken poise of her, staggered him. "Will you post this letter!"—as if his visit had been an ordinary call. He glanced at the envelope. It was addressed to a Bond Street milliner, and on the back flap was scribbled: "Send the blue toque also."

"H'm," said Ronnie as he dropped the letter into the post box. He felt in some indefinable way that he was being slighted.

XII

Mrs. Colebrook acclaimed it as a miracle and discovered in the amazing circumstance the result of her industrious praying.

"Every night I've said: 'Please God, make Christina well, amen.'"

The osteopath, a short, bearded man, who perspired with great freedom, grunted his grudging satisfaction. Christina was not well by any means, but for the first time in her life she stood upon her own two feet. Only for a few seconds, with Mrs. Colebrook supporting her on the one side and the bone doctor on the other, but she stood. "Yes—not bad after a month's work," said the osteopath. "You must have massage for those back muscles, they are like wool. If you don't mind a man doing it, you couldn't do better than persuade Mr. Sault. He is an excellent masseur—I found this out by accident. The evening he came to engage me, I'd been dining out and sprained my ankle getting out of a cab—young lady, I observe your suspicion. I am an abstainer and have not touched strong wines for twenty years. I came in feeling bad and I was not inclined to discuss spines with him or anybody. But he insisted on massaging the limb—said he had learned the art in a hospital somewhere—yes, ask him. Otherwise it will cost you half a guinea a day."

Evie heard all this early in the afternoon. It was early closing day and she came home to lunch. She flew up the stairs and literally flung herself upon Christina.

"You darling. Isn't it wonderful! Mother says you stood up by yourself. Oh, Chris, didn't it feel splendid!"

"Mother is a romancer," smiled Christina. "I certainly did stand on my feet, with considerable assistance, and it felt like hell!—pardon the language—physically. Spiritually and intellectually it was a golden moment of life. Oh, Evie, I'm gurgling with joy inside and the prospect of Ambrose rubbing my back fills me with bliss."

"Ambrose—Mr. Sault?"

Christina inclined her head gravely.

"But not your *bare* back?"

"I fear so," said Christina. "I knew this would be a shock to you."

"Don't be silly, Chris—it is all right I suppose," and then with a happy laugh, "of course it is all right. I'm wrong. I think I must have an unpleasant mind. You've always said I had—well, you've hinted. I'd even let him rub my back if it would do you good."

"You Lady Godiva," murmured Christina admiringly, "quo vadis?"

"That means where am I going? I always mix it up with that other one, 'the sign of the cross.' I am going to a matinee with a girl from the shop. She had tickets sent to her by a gentleman who knows the manager. It will be a bad play; you can't get tickets for a success. How is your Ambrose? I haven't seen him for weeks. Ronnie says that there has been an awful lot of trouble at the office—"

"Oh! Has he an office?"

"I don't know—some office Ronnie is connected with. He's a director, my dear. I saw his name in the paper—Ronnie, I mean."

"Has Ambrose been in trouble?"

"No, some other man, I forget his name. It is foreign and he drinks. But it has all blown over now."

Christina sighed. "I don't see how Ambrose came into it, even after your lucid explanation."

"Ambrose, that is to say Mr. Sault, is supposed to look after—whatever his name is. It sounds like the name of a cigarette. He is supposed to stop him drinking. And he found this—Moropulos, that's the name, in a bar and hauled him out and Moropulos fought him. I don't know the whole story but I do know that there was a row."

"Is the cigarette person still able to walk about?" asked Christina incredulously.

"Yes, but they are very bad friends. Moropulos says he'll get even with

Sault."

"Unhappy man," said Christina. "Ronnie is getting quite communicative, isn't he?"

"We're real friends," answered the girl enthusiastically, "we're just pals! I sometimes feel—I don't know whether I ought to tell you this. But I will. I sometimes feel that I really don't want to marry Ronnie at all. I feel that I could be perfectly happy, married to somebody else, if I had him for a friend. Isn't that queer?"

Christina thought it was queer and wondered if this attitude of mind was Evie's very own or whether it had grown by suggestion. But she had evidently done Ronnie an injustice in this instance.

"I've never told Ronnie this," said Evie. "I don't fancy that he would understand, but I did ask him whether he thought that he could be friends with Beryl Merville if she married somebody else. I only asked him for fun, just to hear what he would say. My dear, how he loathes that girl! I could tell he was sincere. He was so furious! He said that if she married, he would never visit her house and he wished he had never seen her."

Christina made no response. It was on the tip of her tongue to say that Beryl Merville must know the man very well to have excited such hatred, but she observed the truce.

When Ambrose put in an appearance late in the evening she learned that he had heard from the osteopath. His large smile told her that even before he spoke.

"Now, Ambrose, did he say anything about massage?"

Ambrose nodded. "I'll do it if you'll let me," he said simply. "My hands aren't as awkward as they look."

Later her mother, who had been an interested spectator of the treatment, spoke a great truth. "It seems natural for Mr. Sault to be rubbing your back, Christina. He's just like a—a soul with hands—sounds ridiculous I know, but that is what I felt. He wasn't a man and he wasn't a woman. It seemed natural, somehow—how did you feel about it?"

"Mother, I begin to feel that I got my genius from you," said Christina, patting a rumpled sheet into place, "I couldn't have bettered that; 'a soul with hands'!"

Mrs. Colebrook blinked complacently. "I've always been a bit clever in describing people," she said. "Do you remember how I used to call Evie 'spitfire'?"

"Don't spoil my illusions mother—'a soul with hands' entitles you to my everlasting respect. And don't tell Evie, or she'll talk about his feet. He has big feet, I admit, though he makes less noise than Evie. And he snores, I heard him last night."

XIII

There came a day when Christina put her feet to the grimy pavement of the street and walked slowly but without assistance to Dr. Merville's car, borrowed through Beryl, for the afternoon.

It was a cold, clear day in January, the wind was in the east and the gutters of Walter Street were covered with a thin film of ice.

A momentous occasion, for in addition to other wonders, Christina was wearing her first hat! Evie had chosen and bought it. The woolen costume was one from Mrs. Colebrook's wash-tub. Ambrose had provided a gray squirrel coat. It had appeared at the last moment. But the hat was a joy. Christina had worn it in bed all the morning, sitting up with pillows behind her and a mirror in her hand.

"Lend me that powder-puff of yours, Evie," she said recklessly. "My skin is perfect. I admit it. But I can't appear before the curious eyes of the world wearing my own complexion. It wouldn't be decent."

"If you take my advice," suggested the wise Evie, "you'll put a dab of rouge on your cheeks. Nobody will know."

"I am no painted woman," said Christina, "I am poor but I am respectable. Ambrose would think I had a fever and send for the osteopath. No, a little powder. My eyes are sufficiently langorous without eyeblack, I think. It must be powder or nothing."

Ambrose did not accompany them, and Evie and Mrs. Colebrook were her attendants in the drive to Hampstead.

Beryl saw them; she had arranged with Ambrose and the chauffeur that the car should go past the house and she watched from behind a curtained window.

So that was Evie; it was the first time she had seen her—no, not the first time. She was the girl to whom Ronnie had been speaking that holiday morning when she had passed them in the park. She was very pretty and petite—the kind Ronnie liked. She lingered at the window long after they had passed, loath to face an unpleasant interview.

She knew it would be unpleasant; her father had been so anxious to please her at lunch; his nervousness was symptomatic. He wanted to have a little talk with her that afternoon, he said; she guessed the subject set for discussion.

Sitting before the drawing-room fire she was reading when he came in rubbing his hands, and wearing a cheerful smile which was wholly simulated.

"Ah, there you are, Beryl. Now we can have a chat. I get very little time nowadays."

He poked the fire vigorously and sat down. "Beryl—" he seemed at some loss for an opening, "I had a talk with Steppe the other day—we were talking about you."

"Yes?"

"Steppe is very fond of you—loves you," Dr. Merville cleared his throat. "Yes, he loves you, Beryl. A fine man, a little rough, perhaps, but a fine man and a very rich man."

"Yes?" said Beryl again and he grew more agitated.

"I don't know why you say 'Yes, yes,'" he said irritably. "A young girl doesn't as a rule hear such things without displaying some—well, some emotion. How do you feel about the matter?"

"About marrying Mr. Steppe? I suppose you mean that? I can't marry him: I don't wish to."

"I'm sure you would learn to love him, Beryl."

She shook her head. "Impossible. I'm sorry, father, especially if you wished me to marry him. But it is impossible."

The doctor stared gloomily into the fire. "You must do as you wish. I cannot conscientiously urge you to make any sacrifice—he is a rough sort, and I'm afraid he will take your refusal badly. I don't mind what he does—really. I've made a hash of things—it was madness ever to invest a penny. I had a hundred and fifty thousand when I came into this house. And now—!"

She listened with a cold feeling in her heart. "Do you mean—that you depend upon the good will of Mr. Steppe—that if you were to break your connection with him and his companies, your position would be affected—?"

He nodded. "I am afraid that is how matters stand," he said, "but I forbid you to take that into consideration." Yet he looked at her so eagerly, so wistfully, that she knew his lofty statements to be so many words by which he expressed principles, long since dead. The form of his vanished code showed dimly through the emptiness of his speech.

"I am a modern father—I believe that a girl's heart should go where it will. Girls do not marry men to save their families, except in melodrama, and fathers do not ask such a ghastly sacrifice. I should have been glad if you had thought kindly of Steppe. It would have made my course so much more smooth. However—" He got up, stooped to poke the fire again, hung the poker tidily on the iron and straightened himself.

"Let me think it over," she said, not looking at him. Not until he was out of the room did he feel uncomfortable.

She had been prepared for this development. Steppe had been a constant visitor to the house and his rare flowers filled the vases of every room except hers. And her father had hinted and hinted. That Dr. Merville was heavily in the debt of her suitor she could guess. Steppe had told her months before that he had to come to the rescue of the doctor. Only she had hoped that so crude an alternative would not be placed before her, though she knew that such arrangements were not altogether confined to the realms of melodrama. At least two friends of hers had married for a similar reason. A knightly millionaire bootmaker had married Lady Sylvia Frascommon and had settled the Earl of Farileigh's bills at a moment when that noble earl was dodging writs in bankruptcy. She could look at the matter more calmly because she had come to a dead end. There was nothing ahead, nothing. She did not count Ambrose Sault's love amongst the tangibilities of life. That belonged to herself. Steppe would marry that possession. It was as much of her, as hands and lips, except that it was beyond his enjoyment. In the midst of her examination, her father came in.

"There is one thing I forgot to say, dear—Ronnie, who is as fond of you as any of us, thinks that you ought to marry—he says he'll be glad to see you married to Steppe. I thought it was fine of Ronnie."

"Shut the door, father, please; there's a draught," said Beryl.

Dr. Merville returned to his study shaking his head. He couldn't understand Beryl.

So Ronnie approved! She sat, cheek in hand, elbow on knee, looking at the fire. Steppe did not seem so impossible after that. Ronnie! He would approve, of course. What terrors he must have endured when he discovered that Steppe was his rival! What mental agonies! An idea came to her.

She went down to the hall where the telephone was and gave his number.

"Hello—yes."

"Is that you, Ronnie?"

"Yes—is that you, Beryl?" his voice changed. She detected an anxious note. "How are you—I meant to come round yesterday. I haven't seen you for an age."

"Father says that you think I ought to marry Steppe."

There was an interval. "Did you hear what I said?" she asked.

"Yes—of course it is heartbreaking for me—I feel terrible about it all—but it is a good match, Beryl. He is one of the richest men in town—it is for your good, dear."

She nodded to the transmitter and her lips twitched. "I can't marry him without telling him, can I, Ronnie?" She heard his gasp.

"For God's sake, don't be so mad, Beryl! You're mad! What good would it do—it would break your father's heart—you don't want to do that, do you? It would be selfish and nothing good could come of it—"

She was smiling delightedly at her end of the wire, but this he could not know.

"I will think about it," she said.

"Beryl—Beryl—don't go away. You mustn't, you really mustn't—I'm not thinking about myself—it is you—your father. You won't do such a crazy thing, will you? Promise me you won't—I am entitled to some consideration."

"I'll think about it," she repeated and left him in a state of collapse.

XIV

It happened sometimes that Mr. Moropulos had extraordinary callers at his bleak house in Paddington. They came furtively, after dark, and were careful to note whether or not they were followed. Since few of these made appointments and were unexpected, it was essential that the Greek should be indoors up to ten o'clock. Therefore, he failed in his trust when his unquenchable thirst drew him away from business. He was maintained in comfort by Jan Steppe to receive these shy callers. Mr. Moropulos was not, as might be supposed, engaged in a career of crime, as we understand crime. The people who came and whom he interviewed briefly in his sitting-room, were respectable persons who followed various occupations in the city and would have swooned at the thought of stealing a watch or robbing a safe. But it was known in and about Threadneedle Street, Old Broad Street and in various quaint alleyways and passages where bareheaded clerks abound, that information worth money could be sold for money. A chance-heard remark, the fag-end of a conversation in a board room, heard between the opening and closing of a door; a peep at a letter, any of these scraps of gossip could be turned into solid cash by the bearded Greek.

It was surprising how quickly his address passed round and even more surprising how very quickly Moropulos had organized an intelligence service which was unique as it was pernicious. He paid well, or rather Steppe paid, and the returns were handsome. A clerk desiring to participate in a rise of value which he knew was coming, could buy a hundred shares through Moropulos and that, without the expenditure of a cent. Moropulos knew the secrets of a hundred offices; there were few business amalgamations that he did not hear about weeks in advance. When the Westfontein Gold Mines published a sensational report concerning their properties, a report which brought their stock from eight to nothing, few people knew that Moropulos had had the essential part of the report in his pocket the day after it arrived in London. It cost Steppe three thousand pounds, but was worth every penny. The amount of the sum paid was exaggerated, but it was also spread abroad. And in consequence, Mr. Moropulos was a very busy man.

He was in his sitting-room on that shivering winter night. A great fire roared in the chimney, a shaded lamp was so placed, that it fell upon the book and the occupant of the sofa could read in comfort. On a small eastern table was a large tumblerful of barley water. From time to time Mr. Moropulos sipped wryly.

It was nearing ten and he was debating within himself whether he should go to bed or test his will by a visit to a café where he knew some friends of his would be, when he heard the street door slam and looked over his shoulder. It could only be Sault or—

The door opened and Jan Steppe came in, dusting the snow from the sleeve of his coat. It was a handsome coat, deeply collared in astrachan and its lining was sealskin, as Moropulos did not fail to observe.

"Alone, huh?" said Steppe. He glanced at the barley water by the Greek's side and grinned sardonically. "That's the stuff, not a headache in a bucketful!"

"Nor a cheerful thought," said Moropulos. "What brings you this way, Steppe?"

"I want to put some things in the safe."

Sault's invention stood on a wooden frame behind a screen.

"Have to be careful about this word—give me some more light," said Steppe at the dial.

Moropulos rose wearily and turned a switch.

"That's better—huh. Got it!"

The door swung open and, taking a small package from his pocket, the big man tossed it in.

"Got something here, huh?"

He pulled out an envelope. There was a wax seal on the back.

"'The photograph,'" he read and frowned at the other.

"It is mine," said Moropulos.

"Nothing to do with the business?"

"Nothing."

Steppe threw it hack and turned the dial.

"Nothing new, huh?"

He glanced at the barley water again.

"Where's Sault?"

"He goes home early. I don't see him again unless one of your hounds sends for him."

Steppe's smile was half sneer.

"You don't like Sault—a good fellow, huh?"

Moropulos wrinkled his nose like an angry dog. His beard seemed to stiffen and his eyes blazed.

"Like him—he's not human, that fellow! Nothing moves him, nothing. I tried to smash him up with a bottle, but he took it away from me as if I were a child. I hate a man who makes me feel like that—if he hadn't got my gun away I'd have laid him out. It would be fine to hurt the devil—and he is a devil, Steppe. In-human. Sometimes I give him a newspaper to read—just for the fun of it. But it never worries him."

"Don't try. He's a bigger man than you. You want to rouse him, huh? The day you do, God help you! I don't think you will. That's how I feel about him. He's cold. Chilly as a Druid's hell. He is dangerous when he's quiet—and he's always quiet."

"He is no use to me. It is a waste of money keeping him. I'll give you no more trouble."

Steppe pursed his lips until his curling black moustache bristled like the end of a brush. It was a grimace indicative of his skepticism. He had reason.

"Leave it. Sault will not give you any bother. I don't want strangers here, huh? Cleaners who are spying detectives."

Moropulos took his book again as his employer went out. But he did not read. His eyes looked beyond the edge of the page, his mind was busy. Detestation of Ambrose Sault was not assumed, as he had simulated so many likes and dislikes. Sault's maddening imperturbability, his immense superiority to the petty annoyances with which his daily companion fed him, his contempt for the Greek's vulgarity, these things combined to the fire of the man's hatred. They were incompatibles—it was impossible to imagine any two men more unlike.

Moropulos was one whose speech was habitually coarse; his pleasures fleshly and elemental. He delighted to talk of his conquests, cheap enough though they were. He had collected from the Levant the pictures that hawkers and dragomen show secretly, and these were bound up in two huge volumes over which he would pore for hours. So it pleased him, beyond normal understanding, to bring Beryl Merville into the category of easy women. He had never doubted that she was bad. There were no other kind of women to Moropulos. Suspecting, before there were grounds for suspicion, he had watched and justified his construction of the girl's friendship with Ronnie Morelle. He was certain when he watched her come out of the Knightsbridge flat that if he had been fortunate, he would have seen her there before, perhaps the previous night. Beryl was no less in his eyes than she had been. She was bad. All women were bad, only some were more particular than others in choosing their partners in sin.

He had reason to meet Ronald Morelle the next morning and returning he brought news.

Ambrose was clearing the snow from the steps and path before the house when he arrived.

"Come in," he was bubbling over with excitement, "I've got a piece of interesting information." Ambrose in his deliberate fashion put away broom and spade before he joined the other.

"You know Beryl Merville, don't you? Steppe is marrying her."

He had no other idea than to pass on the news, and create something of the sensation which its recital had caused him. But his keen eyes did not miss the quick lift of Sault's head or the change that came to his face. Only for the fraction of a second, and then his mask descended again.

"What do you think of it, Sault? Some girl, eh?"

He added one of his own peculiar comments. "Who told you?"

"Ronald Morelle. I don't suppose he minds—now. Lucky devil, Steppe. God! If I had his money!" Ambrose walked slowly away, but his enemy had found the chink in his armor. He was certain of it. It was incredible that a man like Ambrose Sault would feel that way, but he would swear that Ambrose was hurt. Here he was wrong. Ambrose was profoundly moved; but he was not hurt.

That day Moropulos said little. It was on the second and third days that he went to work with an ingenuity that was devilish to break farther into the crevice he had found.

Ambrose made little or no response. The slyest, most outrageous innuendo, he passed as though it had not been spoken. Moropulos was piqued and angry. He dare not go farther for fear Sault complain to Steppe. That alone held him within bounds. But the man was suffering. Instinctively he knew that. Suffering in a dumb, hopeless way that found no expression.

On the Friday night Ambrose returned to his lodging looking very tired. Christina was shocked at his appearance. "Ambrose—what is the matter?"

"I don't know, Christina—yes, I know. Moropulos has been very trying. I find it so much more difficult to hold myself in. I suppose I'm getting old and my will power is weakening."

She stroked the hand that lay on the arm of the chair (for she was sitting up) and looked at him gravely.

"Ambrose, I feel that you have given me some of your strength. Do you remember how you gave it to mother?"

He shook his head. "No, not you—I purposely didn't. I've a loving heart for you, Christina. I shall carry you with me beyond life."

"Why do you say that tonight?" she asked with an odd little pain at her heart.

"I don't know. Steppe wants me to go down with Moropulos to his place in the country. Moropulos has asked me before, but this time Steppe asked me. I don't know—"

He shook his head wearily. She had never seen him so depressed. It was as if the spirit of life had suddenly burned out.

"I hope it will be as you say, Ambrose, but, my dear, you are overtired; we oughtn't to discuss souls and eternities and stuff like that. It is sleep you want, Ambrose."

"I'm not sleepy."

He bent over her, his big hand on her head. "I am glad you are well," he said.

She heard him go downstairs and out of the house, late as it was. A few minutes afterwards Evie came in.

"Where is Sault going?" she asked. "I saw him stalking up the street as though it belonged to him. And oh, Chris, *what* do you think Ronnie says! Mr. Steppe is marrying that girl who came here—Beryl Merville!"

"Fine," said Christina absently.

She knew now and her heart was bursting with sorrow for the man who had gone out into the night.

XV

"The Parthenon" occupied an acre of land that had once been part of a monastery garden. Until Mr. Moropulos with his passion for Hellenic nomenclature had so named it, the old cottage and its land was known by the curious title: "Brothergod Farm," or as it appeared in ancient deeds, "The Farmstead of Brother-of -God."

For Mr. Moropulos there was a peculiar pleasure in setting up in the monastery land such symbols of the pantheistic religion of ancient Greece as he could procure.

The house itself consisted of one large kitchen-hall on the ground floor and two bedrooms above. A more modern kitchen had been built on to the main walls by a former tenant. The cottage was well furnished, and unlike his home in Paddington, the floors were carpeted, a piece of needless extravagance from the Greek's point of view, but one which he had not determined, for he had bought the cottage and the furniture together, the owner being disinclined to sell the one without the other.

The garden was the glory of the place in the summer. It had a charm even on the chill afternoon that Ambrose deposited his bag at the white gate. A wintry sun was setting redly, turning to the color of wine the white face of the fields. In the hollows of the little valley beyond the Cottage, the mists were lying in smoky pools. His hands on the top of the gate, he gazed rapturously at such a sun set as England seldom sees. Turquoise—claret—a blue that was almost green.

Drawing a long breath he picked up his bag and walked into the house.

"Go down and look after Moropulos. He is weakening on that barley water diet—he told me himself."

Thus Steppe. His servitor obeyed without question, though he knew that the shadow of death was upon him.

Moropulos was stretched in a deep mission chair, his slippered feet toward the hearth. And he had begun his libations early.

On the floor within reach of his hand, was a tumbler, full of milky white fluid. There was a sugar-basin—a glass jug half filled with water and a tea strainer. Ambrose need not look for the absinthe bottle. The accessories told the story.

"Come in—shut the door, you big fool—no you don't!" Moropulos snatched up the tumbler from the floor and gulped down its contents. "Ha-a! That is good, my dear—good! Sit down!" he pointed imperiously to a chair.

"You'll have no more of that stuff tonight, Moropulos," Ambrose gathered up the bottle and took it into the kitchen. The Greek chuckled as he heard it smash. He had a store—a little locker in the tool-shed; a few bottles in his bedroom.

"Come back!" he roared. "Come, you big pig! Come and talk about Beryl. Ah! What a girl! What a face for that hairy gorilla to kiss!"

Sault heard, but went on filling a kettle and presently the shouts subsided.

"When I call you, come!" commanded Moropulos sulkily as Ambrose returned with a steaming cup of tea in his hand.

"Drink this," said Ambrose.

Moropulos took the cup and saucer and flung them and their contents into the fireplace. "For children, for young ladies, but not for a son of the south—an immortal, Sault! For young ladies, yes—for Beryl the beautiful—"

A hand gripped him by the beard and jerked his head up. The pain was exquisite—his neck was stretched, a thousand hot needles tortured his chin and cheek where the beard dragged. For the space of a second he looked into the gray eyes, fathomless. Then Ambrose broke his grip and the man staggered to his feet mouthing, grimacing, but silent. Nor did Ambrose speak. His eyes had spoken, and the half-drunken man dropped back into his chair, cowering.

When Sault returned to the room, after unpacking his bag, Moropulos was still sitting in the same position. "Do you want anything cooked for your dinner?"

"There is—fish—and chops. You'll find them in the kitchen."

He sat, breathing quickly, listening to the sizzle and splutter of frying meat. Ambrose Sault shut the door that led into the kitchen and the Greek stood up listening. From beneath a locker he produced a bottle, quietly he took up the water-jug and sugar and stole softly up to his room. He locked the door quietly, put down his impedimenta and opened a drawer of an old davenport. Underneath an assortment of handkerchiefs and underwear, he found an ivory-handled revolver, a slender-barrelled, plated thing, that glittered in his hand. It was loaded; he made sure of that. His hatred of Ambrose Sault was an insensate obsession. He had pulled him by the beard, an intolerable insult in any circumstances. But Sault was a nigger—he sat down on the only chair in the room and prepared a drink.

"Are you coming down? I've laid the table and the food is ready," Ambrose called from the bottom of the stairs.

"Go to hell!"

"Come along, Moropulos. What is the sense of this? I am sorry I touched you."

"You'll be more sorry," screamed the Greek. His voice sounded deafeningly near for he had opened the door. "You dog, you—"

Mr. Moropulos had a wider range of expletives than most men. Ambrose listened without listening.

Pulling out a chair from the table, he sat down and began his dinner. He heard the feet of the drunkard pacing the floor above, heard the rumble of his voice and then the upper door was flung violently open and the feet of Moropulos clattered down the stairs. He had taken off his coat and his waistcoat. His beard flowed over a colored silk shirt, beautifully embroidered. But it was the thing in his hand that Ambrose saw, and, seeing, rose.

The man's face was white with rage; an artery in his neck was pulsating visibly. "You pulled my beard— You ignorant negro— You nigger thing— You damned convict! You're going on your knees to lick my boots—my boots, not Beryl's, you old fool—"

Ambrose did not move from the position he had taken on the other side of the table.

"Down, down, down!" shrieked Moropulos, his pistol waving wildly.

Sault obeyed, but not as Moropulos had expected. Suddenly he dropped out of view behind the edge of the white cloth and in the same motion he launched himself under the table, toward the man. In a second he had gripped him by the ankles and thrown him—the pistol dropped almost into his hands.

Moropulos stumbled to his feet and glared round at his assailant. "I hope to God you love that woman; I hope to God you love her—you do, you old fool! You love her—Ronald Morelle's mistress! I know! She stayed a night at his flat—other nights too—but I saw her as she came out—I photographed her!"

"You photographed her as she came out?" repeated Ambrose dully.

A grin of glee parted the bearded lips.

"I've hurt you, damn you! I've hurt you! And I'm going to tell Steppe and tell her father and everybody!"

"You liar." Sault's voice was gentle. "You filthy man! You saw nothing!"

"I didn't, eh? Oh, I didn't! Morelle admitted it—admitted it to me. And I've got the photograph in a safe place, with a full account of what happened!"

"In the safe!"

Moropulos had made a mistake, a fatal mistake. He realized it even as he had spoken.

"And you—and Morelle—have her in your cruel hands!"

So softly did he speak that it seemed to the man that it was a whisper he heard.

Sault held in his hands the pistol. He looked at it thoughtfully. "You must not hurt her," he said.

Moropulos stood paralyzed for a moment, then made a dart for the door. His hand was on the latch when Ambrose Sault shot him dead.

BOOK THE THIRD

I

Ambrose looked a very long time at the inert heap by the door. He seemed to be settling some difficulty which had arisen in his mind, for the gloom passed from his face and pocketing the revolver slowly, he walked across to where Paul Moropulos lay. He was quite dead.

"I am glad," said Ambrose.

Lifting the body, he laid it in the chair; then he took out the pistol again and examined it. There were five live cartridges. He only needed one. In the kitchen he put on the heavy overcoat he had been wearing when he arrived. Returning, he lit the candle of a lantern and went out into the back of the house where Moropulos had erected a small army hut to serve as his garage. He broke the lock and wheeled out the little car. Ambrose Sault was in no hurry: his every movement was deliberate. He tested the tank, filled it, put water in the radiator; then started the engines and drove the car through the stable gates on to the main road, before, leaving the engines running, he paid another visit to the house and blew out the lamp.

As he reached the dark road again he saw a man standing by the car. It proved to be a villager.

"Somebody heard a shot going off up this way. I told 'un was only Mr. Moropuly's old car backfiring."

"It was not that," said Ambrose as he stepped into the car. "Good night."

He drove carefully, because his life was very precious this night. He thought of Christina several times, but without self-pity. Christina would get well—and her love would endure. It was of the quality which did not need the flesh of him. Ronald Morelle must die. There was no other solution. He must die, not because he had led the woman to his way; that was a smaller matter than any and, honestly, meant nothing to Ambrose. Ronald's offense was his knowledge. He knew: he had told. He would tell again.

A policeman stopped him as he drove through Woking. He was asked to produce a license and, when none was forthcoming, his name and address were taken. Ambrose gave both truthfully. It was a lucky chance for the policeman. Afterwards he gave evidence and became important: was promoted sergeant on the very day that Steppe sneered at a weeping man. That was seven weeks later—in March, when the primroses were showing in Brother-of-God Farm.

Ambrose knew Ronald's flat. He had gone there once with Moropulos, and he had waited outside the door whilst Moropulos was interviewing Ronnie.

Nine o'clock was striking as the car drew up before the flat—Ronnie heard it through the closed casement.

Nine o'clock? He dropped his pen and leaned back in his chair. What was the cause of that cold trickling sensation—his mouth went dry. He used to feel like that in air raids.

A bell rung.

"François—" Louder, "François!"

"Pardon, m'sieur." François came out of his pantry half awake.

"The door." Who was it, thought Ronnie—he jumped up.

"What do you want, Sault?"

Ambrose looked round at the waiting servant. "You," he said. "I want to know the truth first—that man should go."

Ronnie flushed angrily. "I certainly cannot allow you to decide whether my servant goes or remains. Have you come from Mr. Steppe?"

Ambrose hesitated. Perhaps it was a confidential message from Steppe, thought Ronnie. This uncouth fellow often served as a messenger.

"Wait outside the door, François—no, outside the lobby door."

"I haven't come from Steppe."

Suddenly Ronnie remembered. "Steppe said you had gone to the country with Moropulos—where is he?"

"Dead."

Ronnie staggered back, his pale face working. He had a horror of death.

"Dead?" he said hollowly, and Sault nodded.

"I killed him."

A gasp. "God—! Why!"

"He knew—he said you had told him. He knew because he was outside your flat all night and photographed her as she went out."

The blood of the listener froze with horror. "I—I don't know what you're talking about—who is the 'she'?"

"Beryl Merville."

"It is a lie—absurd—Miss Merville—! Here?"

He found his breath insufficient for his speech. Something inside him was paralyzed: his words were disjointed.

"It is true—she was here. She told me."

"You—you're mad! Told you! It is a damned lie. She was never here. If Moropulos said that, I'm glad you've killed him!"

"He took a photograph and wrote a statement; you know about that because he spoke to you and you admitted it all."

"I swear before God that Moropulos has never spoken to me. I would have killed him if he had. The story of the photograph is a lie—he invented it. That was his way—where is this picture?"

Ambrose did not answer. Was this man speaking the truth? His version was at least plausible. He must go at once to the house in Paddington and get the envelope—it must be destroyed. How would he know if Ronnie was speaking the truth? Ronald Morelle, his teeth biting into his lip, saw judgment wavering. He was fighting for his life; he knew that Sault had come to kill him and his soul quivered.

"Where is that picture? I tell you it is an invention of that swine. He guessed— Even to you I will not admit that there is a word of truth in the story."

He had won. The hand that was thrust into the overcoat pocket returned empty.

"I will come back," said Sault.

When he reached the street he saw a man looking at the number plate of his car. He took no notice, but drove off. He had to break a window to get into the house at Paddington. He had forgotten to bring his keys. That delayed his entrance for some while. He was in the room, and his fingers on the dial of the combination, when three men walked through the door.

He knew who they were. "I have a revolver in my pocket, gentlemen," he said. "I have killed Paul Moropulos, the owner of this house." They snapped handcuffs upon his wrists.

"Do you know the combination of this safe, Sault?" asked the tall inspector in charge. He had been reading a typewritten notice affixed to the top.

"Yes, sir," said Ambrose Sault.

"What is it?"

"I am not at liberty to say."

"What is in it—money?"

No answer. The officer beckoned forward one of the uniformed men who seemed to fill the hall.

"This safe is not to be touched, you understand? By anybody. If you allow the handle to be turned, there will be trouble. Come along, Sault."

The handcuffs were unnecessary. They were also inadequate. In the darkness of the car—

"I am very sorry, inspector—I have broken these things—I was feeling for a handkerchief and forgot."

They did not believe him, but at the police station they found that he had spoken the truth. The bar of the cuff had been wrenched open, the steel catch of the lock torn away.

"I did it absentmindedly," said Ambrose shamefaced. They put him into a cell where he went instantly to sleep. The handcuffs became a famous exhibit which generations of young policemen will look upon with awe and wonder.

II

Sunday morning, and the bells of the churches calling to worship. Fog, thin and yellow, covered the streets. All the lamps in Jan Steppe's study were blazing, he had the African's hatred of dim lights and there was usually one lamp burning in the room he might be using, unless the sun shone.

He paced up and down the carpet, his hands thrust deep into his pockets, his mind busy. He was too well-equipped a man to see danger in any other direction than where it lay. In moments of peril, he was ice. He could not be cajoled or stampeded into facing imaginary troubles, nor yet to turn his back upon the real threat. All his life he had been a fighter and had grown rich from his victories. Struggle was a normal condition of existence. Nothing had come to him that he had not planned and worked for, or to gain which he had not taken considerable risks. The risks now were confined to Ambrose Sault and his fidelity to the trust which had been forced upon him by circumstances. He was satisfied that Ambrose would not speak. If he did—

Steppe chewed on an unlighted cigar.

The removal of Moropulos meant an inconvenience Sault scarcely counted. The Greek was a nuisance and a danger, whilst his extravagance and folly had brought his associates to the verge of ruin. When the police arrested Ambrose Sault they took possession of the house in which he had been found. Amongst other things seized, was the safe upon which Moropulos had pasted a typewritten notice in his whimsical language:

TO BURGLARS AND ALL WHOM
IT MAY CONCERN

———————————————

CAUTION

Any attempt to open this safe, except by the employment of the correct code word, will result in the destruction of the safe's contents.
DON'T TURN THE HANDLE

Steppe had seen the notice but had not read it. If it had not been affixed! One turn of the handle and every paper would have been reduced to a black pulp. He tried to remember what was stored in the cursed thing. There were drafts, memoranda, letters from illicit agents, a record of certain transactions which would not look well—the Mackenzie report! Later he remembered the photograph in the sealed envelope. Why had Sault gone to the safe? The report he had had from the police—they had been with him for the best part of the morning—was to the effect that Sault had been arrested at the moment he was swinging the dials. What was Sault after? He could not read: only documents were in the safe.

A footman appeared. "Who?—Morelle—show him in."

Ronnie was looking wan and tired. He had not recovered from his fright.

"Well? I got your 'phone call. Don't 'phone me, d'ye hear—never! You get people listening in at any time; just now the exchanges will be stiff with detectives. What were you trying to tell me when I shut you up?"

"About Sault—he came to me last night."

"Huh! Fine thing to talk about on the 'phone! Did you tell the police?"

"No, and I've ordered François to say nothing. After Sault went, I sent François to—to Moropulos' house. I knew Sault was going there."

"How did you know? And why did he come to you anyway?"

The answer Ronnie had decided upon after much cogitation. "Oh—a rambling statement about Moropulos. I couldn't make head or tail of it. He said he was going to the house; I was afraid of trouble, so I sent François."

"You knew Moropulos was in Hampshire—I told you they were both there."

"I'd forgotten that. I don't want to come into this, Steppe—"

"What you 'want,' matters as much to me as what your François wants. If Sault says he came to your flat—but he won't. He'll say nothing—nothing."

He looked keenly at the other. "That was all he said, huh? Just a rambling statement? Not like Sault that, he never rambles. Did he tell you that he killed Moropulos?"

Ronnie hesitated.

"He did! Try to speak the truth, will you? So he told you he had killed the Greco?"

"I didn't take him seriously. I thought he must be joking—"

"Fine joke, huh? Did Sault ever pull that kind of joke? You're not telling me the truth, Morelle—you'd better. I'm speaking as a friend. What did he come to talk to you about, huh? He never even knew you—had no dealings with you. Why should he come to you after he'd committed a murder?"

"I've told you what happened," said Ronnie desperately.

Again the quick scrutiny. "Well—we shall see."

Ronald waited for a dismissal.

"That sounds like the doctor's voice," he said suddenly.

Steppe strode to the door and opened it.

"Why, Beryl, what brings you out? Good morning, doctor—yes, very bad news."

Beryl came past him and went straight to Ronald. "Did you see him, Ronnie—did he come to you?"

"To me—of course not. I hardly knew him."

"Don't lie," said Steppe impatiently, "we're all friends here. What makes you think he went to Morelle, Beryl?"

"I wondered."

"But you must have had some reason?"

She met the big man's eyes coldly. "Must I be cross-examined? I had a feeling that he had been to Ronnie. I don't know why—why does one have these intuitions?"

"We saw it in the morning papers," explained the doctor. "I am fearfully worried; poor Moropulos, it is dreadful."

Steppe smiled unpleasantly. "He is the least troubled of any of us," he said callously, "and the next least is Sault. I saw the detective who arrested him. He said Sault went straight to sleep the moment they put him into the cell, and woke this morning cheerful. He must have nerves of iron."

"Can anything be done for him, Mr. Steppe?"

"He shall have the best lawyer—that Maxton fellow. He ought to be retained. As far as money can help, I'll do everything possible. I don't think it will make a scrap of difference."

"Mr. Steppe, you knew what an evil man Moropulos was: you know the provocation he offered to Ambrose Sault, isn't it possible that the same cause that made him kill this man, also sent him to the safe?"

"What safe is this—was that in the newspapers too?"

"Yes: he was not a thief, was he? He would not be trying to open the safe for the sake of getting money? He came to get something that Moropulos had."

"I wonder—" Steppe was impressed. "It may have been the photograph."

Ronnie checked the exclamation that terror wrung. He was livid.

"Do you know anything about a photograph?" asked Steppe with growing suspicion.

"No." Here Beryl came to the rescue.

When he saw her lips move, Ronnie expected worse.

"Whatever it was, I am sure that the safe holds the secret: Ambrose would not kill a man unless—unless there was no other solution. Won't you open the safe, Mr. Steppe?"

"I'll be damned if I do!" he vociferated violently. "There is nothing there which would save him."

"Or justify him—or show the Greek as being what he was?"

Steppe could not answer this: he had another comment to offer. His attitude toward her had changed slightly since the big diamond had blazed upon her engagement finger: a reminder of obligations past and to come.

"You're taking a hell of an interest in this fellow, Beryl?"

"I shall always take a hell of an interest in every matter I please," she said, eyeing him steadily. "Unless you satisfy me that nothing has been left undone that can be done for Ambrose, I shall go into the witness box and swear to all that I know."

"My dear—" Her father's expostulation she did not hear.

Steppe broke into it. "There is something about this business which I don't understand. You and Moropulos and this fellow dined together once—or didn't you? Sounds mighty queer, but I won't enquire—now."

"You'll open the safe?"

"No!" Steppe's jaw set like a trap. "Not to save Sault or any other man! There is nothing there to save him, I tell you. But if there was—I wouldn't open it. Get that into your mind, all of you."

She regarded him thoughtfully, and then Ronnie. He looked in another direction.

"I am taking the car, father."

Even Steppe did not ask her where she was going.

III

Christina had known in the middle of the night when the police came to search Sault's room. A detective of high rank had been communicative; she heard the story with a serenity which filled the quaking Evie with wonder. If her face grew of a sudden peaked, a new glory glowed in her eyes.

Mrs. Colebrook wept noisily and continued to weep throughout the night. Christina meditated upon an old suspicion of hers, that her mother regarded Ambrose Sault as being near enough the age of a lonely widow woman, to make possible a second matrimonial venture. This view Evie held definitely.

"Oh, Chris—my dear, I am so sorry," whimpered the younger girl, when the police had taken their departure. "And I've said such horrid things about him. Chris, poor darling, aren't you feeling awful—I am."

"Am I feeling sorry for Ambrose? No." Christina searched her heart before she went on. "I'm not sorry. Ambrose was so inevitably big. Something tremendous must come to him: it couldn't be otherwise."

"I was afraid something might happen." Evie shook her head wisely. "This Greek man was very insulting. Ronnie told me that. And if poor Ambrose lost his temper—"

"Ambrose did not lose his temper," Christina interrupted brusquely. "If Ambrose killed him, he did it because he intended doing it."

"In cold blood!" Evie was horrified.

"Yes: Ambrose must have had a reason. He tells me so—don't gape, Evie, I'm not delirious. Ambrose is here. If I were blind and deaf and he sat on this bed he would be here, wouldn't he? Presence doesn't depend on seeing or hearing or even feeling. He'd be here if he was not allowed to touch me. Go back to bed, Evie. I'm sleepy and I want to dream."

Beryl arrived soon after eleven. Evie was out and Mrs. Colebrook, red-eyed, brought her up to the bedroom. Christina was sure the girl would come and had got up and dressed in readiness.

Some time went by before they were alone. Mrs. Colebrook had her own griefs to express, her own memories to retail. She left at last singultient in her woe.

"Do you think you are strong enough to come to the house?" asked Beryl. "I could call for you this afternoon. Perhaps you could stay with me for a few days. I feel that I want you near to me."

This, without preliminary. They were too close to the elementals to pick nice paths to their objectives. They recognized and acknowledged their supreme interests as being common to both.

"Mother would be glad to get rid of me for a day or two," said Christina.

"And I am sending my father abroad," nodded Beryl, with a faint smile. "When shall I come?"

"At three. You have not seen him?"

Beryl shook her head.

"They are taking him into the country. We shall never see him again," she said simply. "He will not send for us. I am trying to approach it all in the proper spirit of detachment. He is a little difficult to live up to—don't you feel that?"

"If I say 'no' you will think I am eaten up with vanity," said Christina with a quick smile. "I am rather exalted at the moment, but the reaction will come perhaps, in which case I shall want to hang on to your understanding."

At three o'clock the car arrived. Mrs. Colebrook saw her daughter go without regret. Christina was unnatural. She had not shed a tear. Mrs. Colebrook had heard her laughing and had gone up in a hurry to deal with hysteria, only to find her reading Stephen Leacock. She was appalled.

"I am surprised at you, Christina! Here is poor—Mr. Sault in prison—" Words failed her, she could only make miserable noises.

"Mother has given me up," said Christina, when she was lying on a big settee in Beryl's room, her thin hand outstretched to the blaze. "Mother is a sort of female Hericletos—she finds her comfort in weeping."

Beryl was toasting a muffin at the fire.

"I wish it were a weeping matter," she said, and went straight to the subject uppermost in her mind. "Moropulos took a photograph of me coming from Ronald Morelle's flat. I had spent the night there." She looked at the muffin and turned it. "Moropulos was—nasty. He must have told Ambrose that he knew."

Christina stirred on the sofa. "Did Ambrose know?"

"Yes: I told him. Not the name of the man, but he guessed, I think—I know the photograph was in the safe. He went to Ronnie. Perhaps to kill him. I imagine Ronnie lied for his life. The police were looking for Ambrose. The—killing of Moropulos was discovered by a man who heard the shot and the car had just passed through Woking after the police had been warned. A detective saw the car outside Ronnie's flat and followed it. I don't know all the details. Father has seen the inspector in charge of the case. Do you like sugar in your tea?"

"Two large pieces," said Christina, "I am rather a baby in my love of sugar. Do you love Ronnie very much, Beryl—you don't mind?"

"No—please. Love him? I suppose so: in a way. I despise him, I think he is loathsome, but there are times when I have a—wistful feeling. It may be sheer ungovernable—you know. Yet—I would make no sacrifice for Ronnie. I feel that. I have made no sacrifice. Women are hypocrites when they talk of 'giving': they make a martyrdom of their indulgence. Some women. And it pleases them to accept the masculine view of their irresponsibility. They love sympathy. For Ambrose I would sacrifice—everything. It is cheap to say that I would give my life. I have given more than my life. So have you."

Christina was silent.

"I have faced—everything," Beryl went on. She was sitting on a cushion between Christina and the fire, her tea cup in her hands. "You have also—haven't you, Christina?"

"About Ambrose? Yes. He has passed. The law will kill him. He expects that. I think he would be uncomfortable if he was spared. He told me once, that all the way out to New Caledonia, he grieved about the people who had been guillotined for the same offense as he had committed. The unfairness of it! He never posed. Can you imagine him posing? I've seen him blush when I joked about that funny little trick of his; have you noticed it? Rubbing his chin with the back of his hand?"

Beryl nodded.

"He said he had tried to get out of the habit," Christina continued. "No, Ambrose couldn't pretend, or do a mean thing; or lie. I'm getting sentimental, my dear. Ambrose was distressed by sentimentality. Mother kissed his hand the day I stood for the first time. He was so bewildered!"

They laughed together.

"Are you marrying Steppe?" asked Christina. She felt no call to excuse the intimacy of the question.

"I suppose so. There are reasons. At present he is rather impersonal. As impersonal as a marriage certificate or a church. I have no imagination perhaps. I shall not tell him. You don't think I should—about Ronnie, I mean?"

Christina shook her red head. "No. As I see it, no. If you must marry him, you are doing enough without handing him another kind of whip to flog you with."

"I told Ambrose: that was enough," said Beryl. "My conscience was for him. Steppe wants no more than he gives."

The clock chimed five.

Ambrose at that moment was passing through the black gates of Wechester County Prison and Ronald Morelle was taking tea with Madame Ritti.

IV

Madame lived in a big house at St. John's Wood. A South American minister had lived there, and had spent a fortune on its interior adornment. Reputable artists had embellished its walls and ceilings, and if the decorations were of the heavy florid type, it is a style which makes for grandeur. The vast drawing-room was a place of white and gold, of glittering candelabras and crimson velvet hangings. How Madame had come to be its possessor is a long and complicated story. The minister was recalled from London on the earnest representations of the Foreign Office and a budding scandal was denied its full and fascinating development.

Madame had many friends, and her house was invariably full of guests.

Some stayed a long time with her. She liked girls about her, she told the innocent vicar who called regularly, and might have been calling still, if his wife had not decided that if Madame required any spiritual consolation, she would put her own pew at her disposal. Her object (confessed Madame) was to give her guests a good time. She succeeded. She gave dances and entertained lavishly. She made one stipulation: that her visitors should not play cards. There was no gambling at Alemeda House. The attitude of the police authorities toward Madame Ritti's establishment was one of permanent expectancy. Good people, people with newspaper names, were guests of hers: there was nothing furtive or underhanded about her parties. Nobody had ever seen a drunken man come or go. The guests were never noisy only—Madame's girl guests were many. And none of the people who came to the dances were women.

Madame was bemoaning the skepticisms of the authorities to Ronnie.

She was a very stout woman, expensively, but tastefully dressed. Her lined face was powdered, her lips vividly red. A duller red was her hair, patently dyed. Dyed hair on elderly women has the effect of making the face below seem more fearfully old. She wore two ropes of pearls and her hands glittered.

Ronnie always went to Madame Ritti in his moments of depression; he had known her since he was little more than a schoolboy. She had a house in Pimlico then, not so big or so finely furnished, but she had girl guests.

"You know, Ronnie, I try to keep my house respectable. Is it not so? One tries and tries and it is hard work. Girls have so little brain. They do not know that men do not really like rowdiness. Is it not so? But these policemen—oh, the dreadful fellows! They question my maids—and it is so difficult to get the right kind of maid. Imagine! And the maids get frightened or impertinent," she laid the accent on the last syllable. She was inclined to do this, otherwise her English was perfect.

The door opened and a girl lounged in. She was smoking a cigarette through a holder—a fair, slim girl, with a straight fringe of golden hair over her forehead.

Ronnie smiled and nodded.

"Hello, Ronnie—where have you been hiding?"

Madame snorted. "Is it thus you speak? 'Hello, Ronnie,' my word! And to walk in smoking! Lola, you have to learn."

"I knew nobody else was here," replied the girl instantly apologetic, "I'm awfully sorry, Madame."

She hid the cigarette behind her and advanced demurely. "Why, it is Mr. Morelle! How do you do?"

"That is better, much better," approved Madame, nodding her huge head. "Always modesty in girls is the best. Is it not so, Ronnie? To rush about, fla— fla—fla!" Her representation of gaucherie was inimitable. "That is not good. Men desire modesty. Especially Englishmen. Americans, also. The French are indelicate. Is it not so? Men wish to win; if you give them victory all ready, they do not appreciate it. That will do, Lola."

She dismissed the girl with a stately inclination of her head.

"What have you been doing? We have not seen you for a very long time. You have other engagements? You must be careful. I fear for you sometimes," she patted his arm. "You will come tonight? You must dress, of course. I do not receive men who are not in evening dress. Grand habit, you understand? The war made men very careless. The smoking jacket—tuxedo—what do you call it? And the black tie. That is no longer good style. If you are to meet ladies, you must wear a white bow and the white waistcoat with the long coat. I insist upon this. I am right, is it not so? All the men wear grand habit nowadays. What do you wish, Ronnie?"

"Nothing in particular; I thought I would come along. I am feeling rather sick of life today."

She nodded. "So you come to see my little friends. That is nice and they will be glad. All of them except Lola; she is going out to dinner tonight with a very great friend. You know your way: they are playing baccarat in the little salon. It amuses them and they only play for pennies."

Ronnie strolled off to seek entertainment in the little salon.

He was rung up at his flat that evening four times. At midnight Steppe called him up again.

"M'sieur, he has not returned. No, M'sieur, not even to dress."

Madame Ritti, for all the rigidity of her dress regulations, made exceptions seemingly.

Ronald was sleeping soundly when Steppe strolled into his room and let up the blind with a crash.

"Hullo?" Ronnie struggled up. "What time is it?"

"Where were you last night?" Steppe's voice was harsh, contumelious. "I spent the night ringing you up. Have the police been here?"

"Police, no. Why should they?"

"Why should they!" mimicked the visitor, "because Sault stopped his car before the entrance of these flats. Luckily, they are not sure whether he went in or not. The detective who saw the car did not notice where Sault had come from. They asked me if there was anybody in Knightsbridge he would be likely to visit, and I said 'no,' d'ye hear? No! I can't have you in their hands, Morelle. A cur like you would squeal and they would find out why he came. And I don't want to know."

The dark eyes bent on Ronnie were glittering.

"You hear? I don't want to know. Moropulos is dead. In a week or two Sault will be dead and Beryl will be married. Why in hell do you jump?"

Ronnie affected a yawn and reached out for his dressing gown.

"Of course I jumped," he was bold to say, even if he quaked inwardly. "You come thundering into my room when I'm half asleep and talk about police and Moropulos. Ugh! I haven't your nerve. If you want to know, Sault came here to ask me where you were. I thought he was a little mad and told him you were out of town."

"You're a liar—a feeble liar! Get up!"

He stalked out of the room slamming the door behind him, and when Ronnie joined him, he was standing before the mantelpiece scowling at the Anthony.

"Now listen. They will make enquiries and it is perfectly certain that they will trace you as being a friend of Moropulos. I want to keep out of it, and so do you. At present they cannot connect me with the case except that I had dealings with Moropulos. So had hundreds of others. If they get busy with you they will turn you inside out; I don't want you to get it into your head that I'm trying to save you trouble. I'm not. You could roast in hell and I'd not turn the hose on to you! I'm thinking of myself and all the trouble I should have if the police got you scared. Sault didn't come here, huh? Was anybody here beside you?" he asked quickly.

"Only François."

"Your servant!" Steppe frowned. "Can you trust him?"

Ronnie smiled.

"François is discreet," he said complacently.

A shadow passed across Steppe's dark face.

"About the women who come here, yes; but with the police? That is different. Bring him in."

"I assure you, my dear fellow—"

"Bring him here!" roared the other.

Ronnie pressed a bell sulkily.

"François, you were here in the flat on Saturday night, huh?"

"Yes, M'sieur."

"You had no visitors, huh?"

François hesitated.

"No visitors, François: you didn't open the door to Sault—you know Sault?" The man nodded.

"And if detectives come to ask you whether Sault was here, you will tell them the truth—you did not see him. Your master had no visitors at all; you saw nobody and heard nobody."

He was looking into a leather pocketbook as he spoke, fingering the notes that filled one compartment.

François' eyes were on the note case, too.

"Nobody came, M'sieur. I'll swear. I was in the pantry all evening."

"Good," said Steppe, and slipped out four notes, crushing them into a ball.

"Do you want to see me, today?" asked Ronnie, and his uncomfortable guest glared.

"Not today. Nor tomorrow, nor any day. Where were you last night?"

François retired in his discretion.

"I went to Brighton—"

"You went to Ritti's—that—!"

He did not attempt any euphemism. Madame Ritti's elegant establishment he described in two pungent words.

"God! You're—what are you? I'm pretty tough, huh? Had my gay times and known a few of the worst. But I've drawn a line somewhere. Sault in prison and Moropulos dead—and you at Ritti's! What a louse you are!"

He stalked into the hall, shouted for François and dropped the little paper ball into his hand. François closed the door on him respectfully.

"A beast—!" said Ronnie, disgusted.

V

Instructed by Steppe to defend him, a solicitor interviewed Ambrose Sault in his airy cell. He expected to find a man broken by his awful position. He found instead, a cheerful client who, when he was ushered into the cell, was engaged in covering a large sheet of paper with minute figures. A glance at the paper showed the wondering officer of the law that Sault was working out a problem in mathematics. It was, in fact, a differential equation of a high and complex character.

"It is very kind of Mr. Steppe, but I don't know what you can do, sir. I killed Moropulos. I killed him deliberately. Poor soul! How glad it must have been to have left that horrible body with all its animal weaknesses! I was thinking about it last night: wondering where it would be. Somewhere in the spaces of the night—between the stars. Don't you often wonder whether a soul has a chemical origin? Some day clever men will discover. Souls have substance, more tenuous than light. And light has substance. You can bend light with a magnet: I have seen it done. The ether has substance: compared with other unknown elements, ether may be as thick as treacle. Supposing some super-supernatural scientist could examine the ether as we examine a shovel full of earth? Is it not possible that the soul germ might be discovered? For a soul has no size and no weight and no likeness to man. Some people think of a soul as having the appearance of the body which it inspires. That is stupid. If death can cling to the point of a needle and life grows from a microscopic organism, how infinitesimal is the cell of the soul! The souls of all the men and the women of the world might be brought together and be lost on one atom of down on a butterfly's wing!"

The lawyer listened hopefully. Here was a case for eminent alienists. He saw the governor of the jail as he went out.

"I should very much like this man to be kept under medical observation," he said. "From my conversation with him, I am satisfied that he isn't normal."

"He seems sane enough," replied the governor, "but I will speak to the doctor: I suppose you will send specialists down?"

"I imagine we shall; he isn't normal. He practically refuses to discuss the crime—occupied the time by talking about souls and the size of 'em! If that isn't lunacy, then I'm mad!"

Steppe, to whom he reported, was very thoughtful.

"He isn't mad. Sault is a queer fellow, but he isn't mad. He thinks about such things. He is struggling to the light—those were the words he used to me. Yes, you can send doctors down if you wish. You have briefed Maxton?" The lawyer nodded.

"He wasn't very keen on the job. It is a little out of his line. Besides, he'll be made a judge in a year or two, and naturally he doesn't want to figure on the losing side. In fact, he turned me down definitely, but I was hardly back in my office—his chambers are less than five minutes walk away—before he called me up and said he'd take the brief. I was surprised. He is going down to Wechester next week."

Steppe grunted.

"You understand that my name doesn't appear in this except to Maxton, of course. I dare say that if I went on to the witness stand and told all I knew about Moropulos and what kind of a brute he was, my evidence might make a difference. But I'm not going and your job is to keep me out of this, Smith."

Steppe's attitude was definite and logical. Sault, in a measure, he admired without liking. He saw in him a difficult, and possibly a dangerous, man. That he had piqued his employer by his independence and courage did not influence Steppe one way or another. It was, in truth, the cause of his admiration. Sault was a man in possession of a dangerous secret. The folly of entrusting two other men with the combination word of the safe had been apparent from the first. He had been uneasy in his mind, more because of the unknown reliability of Moropulos, than because he mistrusted Sault, and he had decided that the scheme for the storage of compromising documents possessed too many disadvantages. Without telling either of his associates, he had arranged to transfer the contents of the safe to his own custody when the disaster occurred. The safe was in the hands of the curious police. And the more he thought about the matter, the more undesirable it seemed that the safe should be opened. It contained, amongst other things, the draft of a prospectus which had since been printed—the shares went to allotment two days before the murder. The draft was in his own hand, a dozen sheets of pencilled writing, and it described in optimistic language certain valuable assets which were in fact non-existent. The financial press had remarked upon the fact, and not content with remarking once, had industriously continued to remark. Steppe had made a mistake, and it was a bad mistake. The cleverest of company promoters occasionally overstep the line that divides the optimistic estimate from misrepresentation. Fortunately, his name did not appear on the prospectus; most unfortunately, he had preserved the draft. He had put it aside after Dr. Merville had copied the document. He had a reason for this. Jan Steppe seldom appeared in such transactions: even his name as vendor was skilfully camouflaged under the title of some stock-holding company. He was a supreme general who issued his orders to his commanders: gave them the rough plan of their operations, and left them to lick it into shape. It sometimes happened that they deviated from his instructions, generally to the advantage of the scheme they were working: occasionally they fell short of his requirements and then his draft proved useful in emphasizing their error. And this was only one of the safe's contents. There were others equally dangerous.

Steppe believed that his servant would die. To say that he hoped he would die would be untrue. Belief makes hope superfluous. It was politic to spend money on the defense of a man who, being grateful, would also be loyal. He could accept Sault's death with equanimity, and without regret. With relief almost. Evidence could be given which would show Moropulos in an unfavorable light. The Greek as a drunkard: his reputation was foul: he was provocative and quarrelsome. The weapon was his own (Sault had once taken it away from him) and a plea of self-defense might succeed—always providing that Mr. Jan Steppe would submit himself to cross-examination, and the reflected odium of acquaintance with the dead man and his killer.

And Mr. Jan Steppe was firmly determined to do nothing of the kind. Sault would carry his secret to the grave unless—suppose this infernal photograph which Moropulos had put into the safe—suppose Sault mentioned this to the lawyers: but he would be loyal. Steppe, having faith in his loyalty, decided to let him die.

Sir John Maxton had changed his mind on the question of defending Sault as a result of an urgent request which had reached him immediately after the solicitor had left his chambers.

He called on Beryl Merville on his way home. She was alone. Christina had returned to her mother, and Dr. Merville was at Cannes, mercifully ignorant of the comments which the financial newspapers were passing upon a company of which he was president.

"I will undertake the defense, Beryl, though I confess it seems to me a hopeless proposition. I had just that moment refused the brief when you rang through. If I remember aright, I have met Sault—wasn't he that strong looking man who came to Steppe's house the night we were dining there? I thought so. And Moropulos—who was he? Not the drunken fellow who made such a fool of himself? By jove I hadn't connected them—I have only glanced at the brief and I am seeing Sault on Friday. Fortunately, I am spending the week-end in the country, and I can call in on my way. Smith is attending to the inquest and the lower Court proceedings. I saw Smith (he is the solicitor) this afternoon: he tells me that Steppe is paying for the defense. That is a professional secret, by the way. He also surprised me by expressing the view that Sault is mad."

"He is not mad," she said quietly, "why does he think so?"

Sir John humped his thin shoulders: a movement indicative of his contempt for the lawyer's opinion on any subject.

"Apparently Sault talked about souls as though they were microbes. Smith, being a God-fearing man, was shocked. To him the soul stands in the same relationship to the body as the inner tube of a tire to the cover. He is something of a spiritualist, and spiritualism is the most material of the occult sciences—it insists that spirits shall have noses and ears like other respectable ghosts. From what he said, I couldn't make head or tail of Sault's view."

"Ambrose is not mad," said the girl, "he is the sanest man I have ever met, or will meet. His view is different: he himself is different. You cannot judge him by any ordinary standard."

"You call him 'Ambrose,'" said Sir John in surprise, "is he a friend of yours?"

"Yes."

She said no more than that, and he did not press the question. It was impossible to explain Ambrose.

VI

A call at the Colebrook's in the afternoon or evening had become a regular practice since Christina had stayed with her. Evie had very carefully avoided being at home when Beryl called.

"I'm sorry I don't like your aristocratic friend, and I know it is a great comfort to have somebody to speak to, about poor Mr. Sault, but I simply can't stand her. Ronnie says that he quite understands my dislike. Christina, do you think Miss Merville is a—you won't be offended, will you? Do you think she is a good girl?"

"Good? Do you mean, does she go to church?"

"Don't be silly. Do you think she is a—virtuous girl? Ronnie says that some of these society women are awfully fast. He says it wouldn't be so bad if there was love in it, because love excuses everything, and the real wicked people are those who marry for money."

"Like Beryl," said Christina, "and love may excuse everything—like you—he hopes."

Evie sighed patiently.

"Do you know what I think about Ronnie?" asked Christina.

"I'm sure I don't want to know," snapped Evie, roused out of her attitude of martyrdom.

"I think he is a damned villain!—shut up, I'm going to say it. I think he is the very lowest blackguard that walks the earth! He is—"

But Evie had snatched up her coat and fled from the room.

Christina's orders from the osteopath were to go to bed early. She was making extraordinary progress and had walked unassisted down the stairs that very day—she was lying dressed on the bed when Beryl arrived.

"I suppose you'll liken me to the squire's good wife visiting the indigent sick," she said, "but I've brought a basket of things—fruit mostly. Do you mind?"

"I've always wanted to meet Lady Bountiful," said Christina. "I thought she never stepped from the Christmas magazine covers. Did you meet Evie?"

"No, I thought she was out."

"She's hiding in the scullery," said Christina calmly.

"She doesn't like me. Ronnie, I suppose?"

Christina nodded. "Ronnie at first hand may be endurable: as interpreted by Evie he is—there is only one word to describe him—I promised mother that I would never use it again. Any news?"

Beryl nodded. "I had a letter—"

"So did I!" said Christina triumphantly, and drew a blue envelope from her blouse.

"Written by the prison chaplain and dictated by Ambrose. Such a typical letter—all about the kindness of everybody and a minute description of the cell intended, I think, to show how comfortable he is."

Christina had had a similar letter.

"Sir John Maxton is defending him," said Beryl. "That is what I have come to tell you. He is a very great advocate."

They looked at one another, and each had the same thought.

"The best lawyer and the kindest judge and the most sympathetic jury would not save Ambrose," said Christina, and they looked for a long time into one another's eyes and neither saw fear.

Beryl did not stay long. They ran into a blind alley of conversation after that: a time of long quietness.

Jan Steppe was waiting in the drawing-room when she returned. The maid need not have told her: she sensed his presence before the door was opened. She had seen very little of Steppe, remembering that she had engaged herself to marry him. She did not let herself think much about it: she had not been accurate when she told Christina that she had no imagination. It was simply that she did not allow herself the exercise of her gift. The same idea had occurred to Jan Steppe—he had seen little of her. He was a great believer in clearing up things as he went along. An unpleasant, but profitable, trait of his.

"Been waiting for you an hour: you might leave word how long you'll be out, huh, Beryl?"

A foretaste, she thought, of the married man, but she was not offended. That was just how she expected Steppe would talk: probably he would swear at her when he knew her better. Nevertheless—

"I go and come as I please," she said without heat. "You must be prepared to put me under lock and key if you expect to find me in any given place, at any given time. And then I should divorce you for cruelty."

He did not often show signs of amusement. He smiled now.

"So that's your plan. Sit down by me, Beryl, I want a little talk."

She obeyed: he put his arm about her, and looking down, she saw his big hairy hand gripping her waist.

"Why are you shaking, Beryl? You're not frightened of me, huh?" he asked, bending his swarthy face to hers.

"I—I don't know." Her teeth were chattering. She was frightened. In a second all her philosophy had failed and her courage had gone out like a blown flame. Every reserve of will was concentrated now in an effort to prevent herself screaming. Training, education, culture, all that civilization stood for, crashed at the touch of him. She was woman, primitive and unreasoning: woman in contact with savage mastery.

"God! What's the matter, huh? You expect to be kissed, don't you? I'm going to be your husband, huh? Expect to be kissed then, don't you? What is the matter with you?"

She got up from the sofa, her legs sagging beneath her. Looking, he saw her face was colorless: Steppe was alarmed. He wanted her badly. She had the appeal which other women lacked, qualities which he himself lacked. And he had frightened her. Perhaps she would break off everything. He expected to see the ring torn from her trembling hand and thrown on the floor at his feet. Instead of that:

"I am very sorry, Mr. Steppe—foolish of me. I've had rather a trying day." She was breathless, as though she had been running at a great pace.

"Of course, Beryl, I understand. I'm too rough with you, huh? Why, it is I who should be sorry, and I am. Good friends, huh?"

He held out his hand, and shivering, she put her cold palm in his.

"Doctor coming back soon? That's fine. You haven't sent him on any newspapers, huh? No, he could get them there."

Other commonplaces, and he left her to work back to the cause of her fright.

With reason again enthroned (this was somewhere near four o'clock in the morning) she could find no other reason than the obvious one. She was afraid of Steppe as a man. Not because he was a man, but because he was the kind of man that he was. He was a better man than Ronnie, she argued. He had principles of sorts. Ronnie had none. Perhaps she would get used to him: up to that moment it did not occur to her to break her engagement, and curiously enough, she never thought of her father. Steppe was sure in his mind that he held her through Dr. Merville. That was not true. Neither sense of honor nor filial duty bound her to her promise, nor was marriage an expiation. She must wear away her life in some companionship. After, was Ambrose Sault, in what shape she did not know or consider. She never thought of him as an angel.

VII

Sometimes the brain plays a trick upon you. In the midst of your everyday life you have a vivid yet elusive recollection of a past which is strange to you. You see yourself in circumstances and in a setting wholly unfamiliar. Like a flash it comes and goes; as swiftly as the shutter of a camera falls. Flick! It is gone and you can recall no incident upon which you can reconstruct the vision of the time-fraction. Beryl saw herself as she had been before she came upon a shabby gray-haired man studying the wallpaper in the hall of Dr. Merville's house. Yet she could never fix an impression. If the change of her outlook had been gradual, she might have traced back step by step. But it had been violent: catastrophic. And this bewildering truth appeared: that there had been no change so far as Ronnie was concerned. He had not altered in any degree her aspect of life. It worried her that it should be so. But there it was.

She had a wire from her father the next morning to say that he was returning at once. Dr. Merville had seen certain comments in the newspaper and was taking the next train to Paris.

She did not go to the station to meet him and was not in the house when he arrived. Even in the days that followed she saw little of him, for he seemed to have pressing business which kept him either at Steppe's office or Steppe's house. One night she went to dinner there. It was a meal remarkable for one circumstance. Although Sault was coming up for trial the following week, they did not speak of him. It was as though he were already passed from the world. She was tempted once to raise his name, but refrained. Discussion would be profitless, for they would only expose the old platitudes and present the conventional gestures.

In the car as they drove home the doctor was spuriously cheerful. His lighter manner generally amused Beryl; now her suspicions were aroused, for of late, her father's laborious good humor generally preceded a request for some concession on her part.

It was not until she was saying good night that he revealed the nature of his request.

"Don't you think it would be a good idea if you cut your engagement as short as possible, dear?" he asked with an effort to appear casual. "Steppe doesn't want a big wedding—one before the civil authorities with a few close friends to lunch afterwards—"

"You mean he wants to marry at once?"

"Well—not at once, but—er—er—in a week or so. Personally, I think it is an excellent scheme. Say in a month—"

"No, no!" she was vehement in her objection, "not in a month. I must have more time. I'm very sorry, father, if I am upsetting your plans."

"Not at all," said his lips. His face told another story.

Possibly Steppe had issued peremptory instructions. She was certain that if she had accepted his views meekly, the doctor would have named the date and the hour. Steppe may have expressed his desire, also, that she should be married in gray. He was the sort of man who would want his bride to wear gray.

Jan Steppe, for all his wealth and experience, retained in some respects the character of his Boer ancestors. His dearest possession was a large family Bible, crudely illustrated, and this he cherished less for its message (printed in the *taal*) than for the family records that covered four flyleaves inserted for the purpose. He liked wax fruit under glass shades and there hung in his library crayon enlargements of his parents, heavily framed in gold. He was a member of the Dutch Reformed Church and maintained a pew in the kirk at Heidelberg where he was born and christened. He believed in the rights of husbands to exact implicit obedience from their wives. The ultimate value of women was their prolificacy; he might forgive unfaithfulness; sterility was an unpardonable offense. Springing, as he did, from a race of cattle farmers, he thought of values in terms of stock breeding.

Instinctively Beryl had discovered this: on this discovery her repugnance was based, though she never realized the cause until long afterwards.

The day of the trial was near at hand. Sir John Maxton had had two interviews with his client. After the second, he called on her.

"I haven't seen you since I met him, have I? Your Sault! What is he, in the name of heaven? He fascinates me Beryl, fascinates me! Sometimes I wish I had never taken the brief—not because of the hopelessness of it—it is hopeless, you know—but—"

"But?" she repeated, when he paused, puzzling to express himself clearly.

"He is amazing: I have never met anybody like him. I am not particularly keen on my fellows, perhaps I know them too well and have seen too much of their meannesses, their evilness. But Sault is different. I went to discuss his case and found myself listening to his views on immortality. He says that what we call immortality can be reduced to mathematical formulae. He limited the infinite to a circle, and convinced me. I felt like a fourth form boy listening to a 'brain' and found myself being respectful! But it wasn't that—it was a sweetness, a clearness—something Christlike. Queer thing to say about a man who has committed two murders, both in cold blood, but it is a fact. Beryl, it is impossible to save him, it is only fair to tell you. I cannot help feeling that if we could get at the character of this man Moropulos, he would have a chance, but he absolutely refuses to talk of Moropulos. 'I did it,' he says, 'what is the use? I shot him deliberately. He was drunk: I was in no danger from him. I shot him because I wanted him to die. When I walked over to where he lay, he was dead. If he had been alive I should have shot him again.' What can one do? If he had been anybody else, I should have retired from the case.

"There is a safe in this case, probably you have read about it in the newspapers. It was found in the Greek's house, and is a sort of secret repository. At any rate, it cannot be opened except by somebody who knows the code word. I suspected Sault of being one who could unlock the door and challenged him. He did not deny his knowledge but declined to give me the word. He never lies: if he says he doesn't know, it is not worth while pressing him because he really doesn't know. Beryl, would your father have any knowledge of that safe?"

She shook her head. "It is unlikely, but I will ask him. Father says that Ronnie is going to the trial. Is he a witness?"

Sir John had, as it happened, seen Ronnie that day and was able to inform her. "Ronnie is writing the story of the trial for a newspaper. What has Sault done to him? He is particularly vicious about him. In a way I can understand the reason if they had ever met. Sault is the very antithesis of Ronnie. They would 'swear,' like violently different colors. I asked him if he would care to stay with me—I have had the Kennivens' house placed at my disposal, they are at Monte Carlo—but he declined with alacrity. Why does he hate Sault? He says that he is looking forward to the trial."

Beryl smiled. "For lo, the wicked bend the bow that they may shoot in the darkness at the upright heart," she quoted.

VIII

Ronald Morelle also found satisfaction in apposite quotations from the Scriptures. When he was at school the boys had a game which was known as "trying the luck." They put a Bible on the table, inserted a knife between the leaves, and whatever passage the knife-point rested against, was one which solved their temporary difficulties.

Ronnie had carried this practice with him, and whenever a problem arose, he would bring down The Book and seek a solution. He utilized for this purpose a miniature sword which he had bought in Toledo, a copy of the Sword of the Constable. It was a tiny thing, a few inches in length. Its handle was of gold, its glittering blade an example of the best that the Fabrica produced.

"It is really wonderful how helpful it is, Christina," said Evie, to whom he had communicated the trick. "The other day, when I was wondering whether you would be better for good, or whether this was only, so to speak, a flash in the pan—because I really *don't* believe in osteopaths, they aren't proper doctors— I stuck a hat pin in the Bible and what do you think it said?"

"Beware of osteopaths?" suggested Christina lazily.

"No, it said, 'Make me to hear joy and gladness, that the bone which Thou hast broken may rejoice!'"

"My bones were never broken," said Christina, and asked with some curiosity: "How do you reconcile your normal holiness with playing monkey tricks with the Bible?"

"It isn't anything of the sort," replied Evie tartly, "the Bible is supposed to help you in your difficulties."

"Anyway, my bones rejoice to hear that Ronnie is such a Bible student," said Christina.

Evie knew that to discuss Ronald Morelle with her sister would be a waste of time. Ronnie was to her the perfect man. She even found, in what Christina described as a "monkey trick," a piety with which she had never dreamed of crediting him. Christina was unjust, but she hoped in time to change her opinions. In the meantime, Ronald Morelle was molding Evie's opinions in certain essentials pertaining to social relationship, and insensibly, her views were veering to the course he had set. She had definitely accepted his attitude toward matrimony. She felt terribly advanced and superior to her fellows and had come to the point where she sneered when a wedding procession passed her. So far, her assurance, her complete plerophory of Ronnie's wisdom rested in the realms of untested theory.

But the time was coming when she must practice all that Ronnie preached, and all that she believed. She was no fool, however intense her self-satisfaction. She was narrow, puritanical, in the sense to which that term has been debased, and eminently respectable. He might have converted her to devil worship and she would have remained respectable. Ronnie was going abroad after the trial. He had made money, and although he was not a very rich man, he had in addition to the solid fortune he had acquired through his association with Steppe, a regular income from his father's estate. He intended breaking with Steppe and was in negotiation for villas in the south of France and in Italy. Evie knew that she would accompany him, if he insisted. She knew equally well that she would no longer be accounted respectable. That thought horrified her. To her, a wedding ring was adequate compensation for many inconveniences. The fascinations of Ronnie were wearing thin: familiarity, without breeding contempt, had produced a mutation of values. The "exceedingly marvelous" had become the "pleasantly habitual." And she had, by accident, met a boy she had known years before. He had gone out to Canada with his parents and had returned with stories of immense spaces and snow-clad mountains and cozy farms, stories that had interested and unsettled her. And he had been so impressed by her, and so humble in the face of her imposing worldliness. Ronnie was, of course, never humble, and though he called her his beloved, she did not impress him, or make him blush, or feel gauche. She had more of the grand lady feeling with Teddy Williams than she could ever experience in the marble villas of Palermo. And Teddy placed a tremendously high value upon respectability. Still—he could not be compared with Ronnie.

She had consented to pay a visit to Ronnie's flat. She was halfway to losing her respectability when she reluctantly agreed, but the thrill of the projected adventure put Teddy Williams out of her mind. The great event was to be on the day after Ronnie came back from Wechester.

In the meanwhile, Ronnie, anticipating a dull stay at the assize town, made arrangements to fill in his time pleasantly.

The day before he left London he called on Madame Ritti and Madame gave a sympathetic hearing to his proposition.

"Yes, it will amuse Lola, but she must travel with her maid. One must be careful, is it not so? One meets people in such unlikely places and I will not have a word spoken against my dear girls."

IX

The case of the King against Ambrose Sault came on late in the afternoon of the third assize day. The assizes opened on the Monday and the first two and a half days were occupied by the hearing of a complicated case of fraudulent conversion; it was four o'clock in the afternoon when Sault, escorted by three warders, stepped into the pen and listened to the reading of the indictment.

It was charged against him that "He did wilfully kill and murder Paul Dimitros Moropulos by shooting at him with a revolving pistol with intent to kill and murder the aforesaid Paul Dimitros Moropulos."

He pleaded "Guilty," but by the direction of the Court, a technical plea of "Not Guilty" was entered in accordance with the practice of the law. The proceedings were necessarily short, the reading of the indictment, the swearing in of the jury, and the other preliminaries were only disposed of before the Court rose.

Wechester Assize Court dates back to the days of antiquity. There is a legend that King Arthur sat in the great outer hall, a hollow cavern of a place with vaulted stone roof and supporting pillars worn smooth by contact with the backs of thirty generations of litigants waiting their turn to appear in the tiny court house.

"I knew I was going to have a dull time," complained Ronnie. "Why on earth didn't they start the trial on Monday?"

"Partly because I could not arrive until today," said Sir John. "The judge very kindly agreed to postpone the hearing to suit my convenience. I had a big case in town. Partly, so the judge tells me, because he wanted to dispose of the fraud charges before he took the murder case. Are you really very dull, Ronnie?" He looked keenly at the other.

"Wouldn't anybody be dull in a town that offers no other amusement than a decrepit cinema?"

"I thought I caught a glimpse of you as I was coming from the station, and, unless I was dreaming, I saw you driving with a lady—it is not like you to be dull when you have feminine society."

"She was the daughter of a very old friend of mine," said Ronnie conventionally.

"You are fortunate in having so many old friends with so many pretty daughters," said Sir John drily.

Ronnie was in court at ten o'clock the following morning. The place was filled, the narrow public gallery packed. The scarlet robed judge came in, preceded by the High Sheriff, and followed by his chaplain; a few seconds later came the sound of Ambrose Sault's feet on the stairway leading to the dock.

He walked to the end of the pen, rested his big hands on the ledge and bowed to the judge. And then his eyes roved round the court. They rested smilingly upon Sir John, bewigged and gowned, passed incuriously over the press table and stopped at Ronald Morelle. His face was inscrutable: his thoughts, whatever they were, found no expression. Ronald met his eyes and smiled. This man had come to him with murder in his heart: but for Ronnie's ready wit and readier lie, his name, too, would have appeared in the indictment. That was his thought as he returned the gaze. Here was his enemy trapped: beyond danger. His smile was a taunt and an exultation. Sault's face was not troubled, his serenity was undisturbed. Rather, it seemed to Sir John, who was watching him, that there was a strange benignity in his countenance, that humanized and transfigured him.

Trials always wearied Ronnie. They were so slow, so tedious: there were so many fiddling details, usually unimportant, to be related and analyzed. Why did they take the trouble? Sault was guilty by his own confession, and yet they were treating him as though he were innocent. What did it matter whether it was eight or nine o'clock when the policeman stopped the car in Woking and asked Sault to produce his license? Why bother with medical evidence as to the course the bullet took—Moropulos was dead, did it matter whether the bullet was nickel or lead?

From time to time sheer ennui drove him out of the court. He had no work to do—his description of Sault in the dock, his impression of the court scene, had been written before he left his hotel. The verdict was inevitable.

Yet still they droned on, these musty lawyers; still the old man on the bench interjected his questions.

Sir John, in his opening speech, had discounted his client's confession. Sault felt that he was morally guilty. It was for the jury to say whether he was guilty in law. A man in fear of his life had the right to defend himself, even if in his defense he destroyed the life of the attacker. The revolver was the property of Moropulos, was it not fair to suppose that Moropulos had carried the pistol for the purpose of intimidating Sault, that he had actually threatened him with the weapon? And the judge had taken this possibility into account and his questions were directed to discovering the character and habits of the dead man.

Steppe, had he been in the box, would have saved the prisoner's life. Ronnie Morelle knew enough to enlighten the judge. Steppe had not come, Ronnie would have been amused if it were suggested that he should speak.

The end of the trial came with startling suddenness.

Ronnie was out of court when the jury retired, and he hurried back as they returned.

The white-headed associate rose from behind his book-covered table and the jury answered to their names.

"Gentlemen of the jury, have you considered your verdict?"

"We have."

The voice of the foreman was weak and almost inaudible.

"Do you find the prisoner at the bar guilty or not guilty?"

A pause.

"Guilty."

There was a sound like a staccato whisper. A quick explosion of soft sound, and then silence.

"Ambrose Sault, what have you to say that my lord should not condemn you to die?"

Ambrose stood easily in the dock: both hands were on the ledge before him and his head was bent in a listening posture.

"Nothing."

His cheerful voice rang through the court. Ronnie saw him look down to the place where Sir John was sitting, and smile, such a smile of encouragement and sympathy as a defending lawyer might give to his condemned client; coming from the condemned to the advocate, it was unique.

The judge was sitting stiffly erect. He was a man of seventy, thin and furrowed of face. Over his wig lay a square of black silk, a corner drooped to his forehead.

"Prisoner at the bar, the jury have found the only verdict which it was possible for them to return after hearing the evidence." He stopped here, and Ronnie expected to hear the usual admonition which precedes the formal sentence, but the judge went on to the performance of his dread duty. "The sentence of this court is, and this court doth ordain, that you be taken from the place whence you came, and from thence to a place of execution, and there you shall be hanged by the neck until you are dead, and your body shall afterwards be buried within the precincts of the prison in which you were last confined. And may God have mercy upon your soul."

Ambrose listened, his lips moving. He was repeating to himself word by word the sentence of the law. He had the appearance of a man who was intensely interested.

A warder touched his arm and awoke him from his absorption. He started, smiled apologetically, and, turning, walked down the stairs and out of sight.

"Good-bye, my friend—I shall see you once again," said Ronnie.

He had decided to leave nothing undone that would authorize his presence at the execution.

Going into the hall to see the procession of the judge with his halberdiers and his trumpet men, he saw Sir John passing and his eyes were red. Ronnie was amused.

"Are you traveling back to town tonight, Ronnie?"

"No, Sir John. I leave in the morning."

Sir John wrinkled his brows in thought.

"You saw him? Did you ever see a man like him? I am bewildered and baffled. Poor Sault, and yet why 'poor'? Poor world, I think, to lose a soul as great as his."

"He is also a murderer," said Ronnie with gentle sarcasm. "He has brutally killed two men—"

"There is nothing brutal in Ambrose Sault," Sir John checked himself. "I go back by the last train. I am dining with the judge in his lodgings and he told me I might bring you along."

"Thank you, I've a lot of work to do," said Ronnie so hastily that the other searched his face.

"I suppose you are alone here?"

"Quite—the truth is, I promised to drive with a friend of mine."

"A man?"

Lola came through the big doors at that moment.

"I was looking for you, Ronnie—my dear, I am bored to tears—"

Sir John looked after them and shook his head.

"Rotten," he said. That a man could bring his light o' love to this grim carnival of pain!

X

Late in the afternoon Christina received a note delivered by hand.

"Mother, would you mind if I spent the night with Miss Merville?"

Mrs. Colebrook shook her head without speaking. In these days she lived in an atmosphere of gloom, for she had adopted the right of chief griever.

"Nobody else seems to care about poor Mr. Sault," she had said many times. "I really can't understand you, Christina, after all he has done for you. I won't say that you're heartless, because I will never believe that about a child of mine. You're young."

"Do you think Mr. Sault would like to know that you go weeping about the house for his sake?" asked Christina patiently.

"Of course he would! I would like somebody to grieve over me and I'm sure he'd like to know that somebody was dropping a silent tear over him."

On the whole, Mrs. Colebrook preferred to be alone that night. The late editions would have the result of the trial. Evie would be out, too. She was going to a theatre with Teddy Williams. That, Mrs. Colebrook thought, was heartless, but Evie had an excuse. Mr. Sault had done nothing for her: had even quarreled with her.

So Christina went gladly to her new friend. She saw the doctor for a minute in the hall and in his professional mood, Dr. Merville was charming.

"You open up vistas of a new career for me, Miss Colebrook," he laughed. "With you as a shining example, I am almost inclined to take up osteopathy in my old age! Really, you have mended wonderfully."

In Beryl's little room she heard the news.

"We expected it, of course," she said. "Did Sir John wire anything about Ambrose—how he bore it?"

"Yes, here is the telegram."

Christina read: "Sault sentenced to death. He showed splendid courage and calmness."

"Naturally he would," said Christina quietly. "I am glad the strain is over, not that I think it was a strain for him. Beryl, I hope we are going to be worthy disciples of our friend? There are times when I am very afraid. It is a heavy burden for a badly equipped mind like mine. But I think I shall go through without making a weak fool of myself. I almost wish that *I* was marrying Jan Steppe. The prospect would take my mind off—no it wouldn't. And it doesn't in your case."

"I don't want to have my mind relieved of Ambrose," said Beryl. "We can do nothing, Christina. We never have been able to do anything. Ambrose could appeal, but of course, he won't do anything of the sort. I had a mad idea of going to see him. But I don't think I could endure that."

Christina shook her head.

She saw him every day. He never left her; he was sitting there now with his hands folded, silent, thoughtful. She avoided saying anything that would hurt him. In moments when Evie annoyed her, as she did lately, the thought that Ambrose would not approve, cut short her tart retort. She confessed this much and Beryl agreed. She felt the same way.

Beryl had had another bed put in her own room and they talked far into the night. There was nothing that Ambrose had ever said which they did not recall. He had said surprisingly little.

"Did he ever tell you in so many words that he loved you, Beryl?"

Only for a second did Beryl hesitate. "Yes," she said.

"You didn't want to tell me that, did you? You were afraid that I should be hurt. I'm not. I love his loving you. I don't grudge you a thought. He ought to love somebody humanly. I always think that the one incompleteness of Christ was his austerity. That doesn't sound blasphemous or irreverent, does it? But he missed so much experience because he was not a father with a father's feelings. Or a husband with a husband's love. I suppose theological people can explain this satisfactorily. I am taking an unlearned view—"

Evie was very nervous, thought Christina, when she saw her the next afternoon. Usually she was self-possession itself. She snapped at the girl when she asked her how she had enjoyed the play, although she was penitent immediately.

"Mother has been going on at me for daring to see a play the night poor Ambrose was sentenced," she said. "I'm sure nobody feels more sorry than I do. You're different to mother. I ought to have known that you weren't being sarcastic."

"How is Teddy? I remember him when he was a tiny boy. Do you like him, Evie?"

Evie pursed her red lips. "He's not bad," she granted. "He's very young and—

well, simple."

"You worldly old woman!" smiled Christina. "You make me feel a hundred!"

Yes, Evie was nervous. And she took an unusual amount of trouble in dressing.

"Where are you going tonight—all dolled up?"

Evie was pained. "That is an *awfully* vulgar expression, Chris: it makes me feel like one of those street women. I am going to meet a girl friend."

"Where are you going, Evie?" Christina quietly insisted.

"I am going to see Ronnie, if you want to know. You make me tell lies when I don't want to," snapped Evie. "Why can't you leave me alone?"

Christina sighed. "Why don't I, indeed," she agreed wearily. "What is to be, will be: I can't be responsible for your life, and it is stupid of me to try. Go ahead, Evie, and good luck."

A remark which considerably mystified Evie Colebrook. But, as she told herself, she had quite enough to try her without worrying about Christina and her morbid talk. The principal cause of her worry was an exasperating lapse of memory. In the agitation of the proposal, she had forgotten whether Ronnie had asked her to meet him in the park at the usual place, or whether she had agreed to go straight to the flat. An arrangement had been made one way or the other, she was sure. She decided to go to the flat.

Beryl came to the same decision.

"Steppe and I are going to Ronnie's place tonight," said Dr. Merville. "It will be a sort of—er—board meeting as Jan is leaving London tomorrow. I haven't had a chance of asking him about a matter which affects me personally. You do not read the financial newspapers, do you, Beryl? You haven't heard from the Fennings, or any of the people you know—er—any unpleasant comment?"

She shook her head again.

"Jan was asking me again about—you, Beryl. I can't get him to talk about anything else. I think you will have to decide one way or the other." He was pulling on his gloves, an operation which gave him an excuse for looking elsewhere than at her. "It struck me that he was growing impatient. You are to please yourself—but the suspense is rather getting on my nerves."

She made no answer until, accompanying him to the door, she made a sudden resolve.

"How long will you be at Ronnie's?" she asked.

"An hour, no longer, I think, why?"

"I wondered," she said.

It was lamentably, wickedly weak in her; a servile surrender to expediency. She knew it, but in her desperation she seized the one straw that floated upon the inexorable current which was carrying her to physical and moral damnation. Ronnie must save her: Ronnie, to whom she had best right of appeal. It was a bitter, hateful confession, that, despising him, she loved him. She loved the two halves of the perfect man. Sault and Ronnie Morelle were the very soul and body of love. She loathed herself—yet she knew it was the truth. Ronnie must help. He might not be so vile as she believed him to be: there might be a spirit in him, a something to which she could reach. The instinct of honor, some spark of courage and justice transmitted to him by the men and women who bred him. Anything was better than Steppe, she told herself wildly, anything! She dreamed of him, terrible dreams that revolted her to wakefulness: by day she kept him from her mind. And then came night and the unclean dreams that made her very soul writhe in an agony of shame, lest, in dreaming, she had exposed a foulness which consciously she had seen in herself.

If Ronnie failed—

("Ronnie will fail: you know he will fail," whispered the voice of reason.)

She could but try.

XI

A foreign-looking servant opened the door to Evie Colebrook.

"Mr. Morelle is out, Mademoiselle, is he expecting you?"

She was in a flutter, ready to fly on the least excuse. "Yes—but I will come back again."

François opened the door wide. "If Mademoiselle will wait a little—perhaps Mr. Morelle will return very soon."

François was an ugly, bullet-headed little man, and his name was a war creation. It was in fact "Otto," and he was a German Swiss.

She came timidly into the big room and was impressed by the solid luxury of it. She would not sit, preferring to walk about, delighted with the opportunity of making so leisurely an inspection of a room hallowed by such associations. So this was where Ronnie worked so hard. She laid her hand affectionately upon the big black table. François watched her a little sadly. He had a sister of her age and, in his eyes at least, as pretty. Moreover, François had grown tired of his employer. Men servants were in demand and he would have no difficulty in finding another job. Except for this: Ronald paid extraordinarily good wages.

He saw her pick up a framed photograph. "This is Mr. Morelle's portrait, isn't it? I don't like it."

Evie felt on terms with the man. It seemed natural that she should. She had wondered if François would be at Palermo, too.

"Yes, Mademoiselle, that is his portrait."

Evie frowned critically at the picture. "It is not half good looking enough."

"That is possible, Mademoiselle," said François, without enthusiasm.

He had never done such a thing before. He marveled at his own temerity, even now.

"Mademoiselle, you will not be angry if I say somethings?" he asked, and as he grew more and more agitated, his English took a quainter turn.

Evie opened her eyes in astonishment. "No, of course not."

"And you must promise not to tell Mr. Morelle."

"It depends," hesitated the girl, and then, "I promise."

"Mademoiselle," said François a little huskily, "I have a little sister so big as you in Switzerland. Her name is Freda, and, Mademoiselle, when I see you here, I think of her, and I say, I will speak to this good young lady. Mademoiselle, I do not like to see you here!" He said this dramatically.

Evie went crimson. "I don't know what you mean."

"I have make you cross," said François, in an agony of self-reproach. "You think I am silly, but I speak with a good heart."

There was only one way out of this awkward conversation. Evie became easily confidential. She spoke as a woman of the world to a man of the world.

"Of course you did," she said. "I appreciate what you say, François. If I saw a girl—well—compromising herself, I mean a girl who hadn't my experience of the world, I'd say the same as you, but—"

A knock at the outer door interrupted her. François shot an imploring glance in her direction, and she nodded.

"There you are, Ronnie—didn't you say I was to come straight here?"

"Hello, Evie," he seemed a little annoyed. "I told you I would meet you at the Statue."

Evie was abashed. "Oh, I am sorry," she began, but he went on.

"Any letters, François?"

"Yes, M'sieur, on the desk."

"All right, clear out."

But François lingered. "M'sieur."

"Well?" asked Ronnie, turning with a scowl.

François was ill at ease.

"Tomorrow my brother is coming from Interlaken, may I have an evening for myself, M'sieur?"

Ronald was angry for many reasons: he was not in the mood to grant favors.

"You have Sundays and you have your holidays. That's enough," he said.

François went out crestfallen.

"I suppose you think I'm unkind," said Ronnie with a laugh, as he helped take off her coat. "But if you give that sort of people an inch, they'll take the earth."

He dropped his hands upon her shoulders and looked into her eyes.

"It is lovely to have you here. You're two hours too soon—"

"Am I?" she asked in alarm. "I was so upset last night that I don't know what you said."

"I said ten o'clock, but it doesn't matter. Only François would have been gone by then. How lovely you are, Evie! How slim and straight and desirable!"

Suddenly she was in his arms, his face against hers. She struggled, pushing him away, escaping at last, too breathless for speech.

"You smother me," she gasped. "Don't kiss me like that, Ronnie. Let's talk.

You know I oughtn't to be here," she urged. "But I did so want to see your beautiful house."

He did not take his eyes from her. "You are going to do what I asked you?"

She nodded, shook her head, her heart going furiously. "I don't know—Ronald, I do love you, but I'm so—so frightened."

He drew her down to him and she sat demurely on the edge of the deep lounge chair he occupied.

"And I'll take you—where shall I take you?" he bantered.

"Somewhere in Italy, you said."

"Palermo! Glorious Palermo—darling, think of what it will be, just you and I. No more snatched meetings and disagreeable sisters, eh?"

Evie was thinking: he did not break in upon her thoughts. She was good to see. More attractive in her silence, for she had the slightest of cockney twangs.

"I wish Christina could come," she said at last; a note of defiance was in her tone. "A change like that would be splendid for her, and I've always planned to give her one."

"Christina? Good lord! Come with us? You mad little thing, I'm not running a sanatorium."

He laughed, leaning back in the chair to look up at her. "Ronnie, I know it is awful nerve on my part—but if you love me—"

He expected this. The philosophies he imparted seldom survived the acid test which opportunity applied.

"I suppose," she went on nervously, "it would be too much of a come-down to think of—of marrying me?"

"Marriage!" His voice was reproving, his manner that of a man grievously hurt.

"You know what I think—what we both think about marriage, Evie?"

"It is—it is respectable anyway."

"Respectable!" he scoffed. "Who respects you? Who thinks any worse of you if you aren't married? People respect you for your independence. Marriage! It is a form of bondage invented by professional Christians who make a jolly good living out of it."

"Well, religion is something. And the Bible—"

Ronnie jumped up.

"We'll try the luck, Evie!" He went to a shelf and took down a book.

Evie was a dubious spectator. The fallibility of the method seemed open to question when such enormous issues were at stake. Yet she accepted a trifle reluctantly, the little sword he handed to her, and thrust it between the pages of the closed book.

She opened it at the passage the sword had found.

"'Woe unto you—'" she began, but he snatched the book from her hands.

"No, silly," he said, and read glibly. "'There is no fear in love: perfect love casteth out fear!'"

Evie was skeptical.

"You made it up!" she accused. "I mean, you only pretended it was there. I know that passage. I learned it at school—it is in John."

He chuckled, delighted at her astuteness. "You little bishop," he said, and kissed her. "Now sit and amuse yourself. I want to speak to François."

He was on his way to the pantry to dismiss François to his home when the bell sounded. He stopped François with a gesture.

XII

"Don't open the door for a minute," he said in a low voice. "Evie, will you come tomorrow night—no not tomorrow. Today is Monday, come on Friday."

"Yes, dear." She was glad to escape.

"Through there," he pointed. "François, let mademoiselle out by the pantry door after you have answered the bell."

Who was the visitor? People did not call upon him except by invitation—except Steppe. And Jan Steppe came slowly and suspiciously into the hall. Ronnie scarcely noticed the doctor who followed him.

"Why were you keeping me waiting?" he growled.

"François could not have heard the bell," answered Ronnie easily.

"That's a lie." He looked round the room and sniffed. "You had a woman here, as usual, I suppose?"

Ronnie looked injured.

"M'm. Some shop girl," insisted the big man. "One of your pickups, huh?"

"I tell you I have been alone all the evening," said Ronnie, resigned. "François, isn't that so?"

Jan Steppe saved the servant from needless perjury.

"He's as big a liar as you are. You'll burn your fingers one of these days." He had a deep, harsh laugh, entirely without merriment. "You had a little trouble about one last year, didn't you?"

Merville, impatient and fretful, broke in. "Let him alone, Steppe. I want to get this business over."

Steppe stared at him. "Oh, you want to get it over, do you? We'll hurry things up for you, doctor!"

Ronnie was interested. He had never heard Steppe speak to Merville in that tone. There had been a marked change in Jan's attitude, even in the past few days. However, Ronnie was chiefly concerned in considering all the possible reasons for this call. The doctor explained and Ronnie breathed again.

"We'll sit here," said Steppe.

He sat down in Ronnie's library chair and taking a bundle of documents from his inside pocket, he threw them on the table.

"Here are the papers you want, Merville—and by the way!" He turned in his chair and glowered at Ronnie. "Do you remember we pooled the Midwell Traction shares, Morelle?" His voice was ominous.

"Er—yes—of course," said Ronnie, quaking.

"We undertook to hold the stock until we mutually agreed as to the moment we should unload, huh?" Steppe demanded deliberately.

Ronald made an ineffectual attempt to appear unconcerned.

"And we undertook not to part with a share until the stock reached forty-three. Do you remember, huh?"

"Yes," said Ronnie, and the big man's fist crashed down on the table.

"You're sure you remember?" he shouted. "You sold at thirty-five. Do that again, and d'ye know what I'll do?"

"I'm sure Ronald wouldn't—" began Merville, but was silenced.

"You shut up! It didn't matter so much that Traction slumped. But you broke faith with me, you rat!"

"Don't lose your temper, Steppe," said the other sulkily, "it was a mistake, I tell you. My broker sold without authority."

"Whilst we are on the subject of the Traction shares, I want to ask about the statement I filed in regard to the assets of the company. Was it right?" For a week the doctor had been trying to put this question. "Of we three, I'm the only director—you're not in it and Ronnie isn't in it, if there is anything wrong, I should be the goat?"

Steppe's voice was milder. Here was a topic to be avoided.

"Huh! You're all right. What are you frightened about?"

"I'm not frightened, but you had the draft?"

"It is in the safe," said Steppe with some satisfaction.

"Steppe, how do we stand there?" asked the doctor urgently. "I know Moropulos was doing work for you of a sort. What was his position and Sault's? Is that the safe which Sault made? He told me about it some time ago."

Steppe turned his head again in Ronald's direction.

"You went to the trial! You saw him! You've seen him before—what do you think of him—clever, huh?"

"Well, I don't know—"

"Of course he's clever, you fool," said the other contemptuously. "If you had his brains and his principles, you'd be a big man. Remember that—a big man."

"I am attending the execution," said Ronnie, "the under sheriff is admitting three press reporters, and I am to be one of them."

Steppe eyed him gloomily, groping after the mind of the man who could fear him, yet did not fear to see a man done to death.

"I'll tell you men all about Moropulos and Sault because you're all tarred with my brush. This is the big pull of Sault. A pull he's never used. Moropulos and I had business together. He was on one side of a wall called 'Law,' huh? I was on the other. The comfortable side. And he used to hand things over. That put me a bit on his side. There were letters and certain other documents which we had to keep, yet were dangerous to keep. But you might always want 'em. I was scared over some shares that—well, I oughtn't have had them. And that's how Sault came to make the 'Destroying Angel,' that's a good name! I christened it. There was a combination lock, the word being known only to Moropulos, Sault and myself. If you used the wrong combination—any combination but the right one, the acids are released and the contents of the safe destroyed. If you try to cut through the sides—the water runs out, down drops a plunger with the same result. When Moropulos was killed I tried to get at it, but the police were there before me. There was a typewritten note pasted on the top of the safe, telling exactly what would happen if they monkeyed with it. They haven't dared to touch it. It's in the Black Museum today with enough stuff inside to send me—well, a hell of a long way."

"Suppose this man tells?" asked Merville fearfully.

"He won't tell. That kind of man doesn't squeal. If it had been Ronald Morelle, I'd have been on my way to South America by now. A word from Sault and I'm—" he snapped his fingers, "but do you think it worries me? I can sleep and go about my work without a second's fear. That's the kind of man I am. No nerves—look at my hand." He thrust out his heavy paw stiffly. "Steady as a rock, huh? Good boy, Sault!"

"I met him once—" began Ronnie.

"I've met him more than once," said the grim Steppe. "A man with strange compelling eyes, the only fellow that ever frightened me!" He looked at Ronald curiously. "It is unbelievable that a white-livered devil like you can see him die. It would make me sick. And yet you, whose nerves ought to be rags considering the filthy life you live, can stand calmly by—ugh! I don't know how you can do it! To see a man's soul go out!"

Ronnie laughed quickly. "Sault's rather keen on his soul. Boyle, the governor, says he recited Henley's poem on his way to the cells."

But Steppe did not laugh. "Soul? H'm. He made me believe in something—soul or spirit or—something. He dominated me. Do you believe in the soul, Merville?"

"Yes, I do. A transient x that only abides in the body at the will of its host."

Ronnie groaned wearily. "Oh, God, are you going to lecture?" he asked and Jan Steppe roared at him.

"Shut up! Go on, Merville. Do you mean that it leaves the body before—death?"

"I think so," said Merville thoughtfully. "I've often stood by the side of a patient desperately sick, and suddenly felt in my body his despair and weakness, and seen him brighten and flush with my strength."

"Really?" Steppe's voice was intense. "Do you mean that your spirits have exchanged themselves?"

Dr. Merville flicked the ash of his cigar into the fireplace. "Call it 'spirit,' 'soul,' 'X,' anything you like—call it individuality. There has been a momentary exchange."

"How do you explain it?"

"Science doesn't explain everything," said Merville. "Science accepts a whole lot of what we call 'incommensurables.'"

"H'm," Steppe pushed away the papers and rose. "H'm. That'll do for the night. Keep those papers, you fellows, and digest them. You going out, Morelle?"

"No, would you like me to go anywhere with you?" Ronnie was eager to serve.

"No," shortly. "Merville, I'm dining with you tomorrow. And I hope Beryl won't have a headache this time. I've got a box at the Pantheon."

The doctor was obviously embarrassed.

"She—well, she isn't very bright just now."

"Let her be bright enough to come to dinner tomorrow night," said Steppe.

The door banged and Ronnie drew a deep breath.

"Thank God," he said piously.

XIII

François went after them, not unhappy to detach himself from a tense and threatening atmosphere, his resentment against his employer somewhat modified when he reached home, by a letter from his visiting brother announcing the postponement of his departure from Switzerland.

Therefore it was Ronnie who answered the sharp ring of the bell. When he saw the girl his jaw dropped.

"Really, Beryl! You place me in a most awkward position. Whatever made you come? Steppe was here—suppose he came back? Why didn't you bring somebody with you?"

He was flustered and scared. Steppe might return at any moment.

"I'm sorry I have outraged the proprieties," said Beryl with a little smile. "Did that child from the druggist's have a chaperon?"

"Eh?" Ronnie was startled.

"I saw her come in and I saw her go out. I've been waiting for an opportunity of seeing you. She's pretty, but, oh, Ronald, she's only a baby!"

Ronnie made a quick recovery from his surprise. If she had seen Evie, she had also seen Steppe and must be sure that he had gone. She would probably know from her father what were their plans for the night.

"I give you my word of honor, Beryl," said he earnestly, "that she merely came to see me about her sister—you know her, Christina, I think she is called. Evie is very anxious that I should help send her abroad. As far as Evie is concerned, you can put your mind at rest. I give you my solemn word of honor that I have never as much as held her hand."

She knew he was lying, but tonight of all nights she must accept his word. She was in a fever: it was almost painful to hold fast to the last shreds of her failing reserve.

"Ronald." Her voice was tremulous and he braced himself for a scene. "You don't want me to marry Steppe?"

So that was it. And he had thought she had accepted the position so admirably.

"Ronald, you know it would be—death to me—worse than death to me. Can't you—can't you use your imagination?"

Her eyes avoided his: that alone helped to restore a little of his poise. She had come as a suppliant, and would not be difficult to handle. The old Beryl, polished, cynical mistress of herself and her emotions, might have beaten him down; induced God knows what extravagant promises.

"I don't want to talk about what has happened. I am not reproaching you or appealing to any sense of duty but—"

She stood there, her eyes downcast, twisting her gloves into tight spirals. He said nothing, holding his arguments in reserve against her exhaustion.

"You make it hard, awfully hard for me, Ronnie. You do know—Steppe wants to marry me?"

He nodded.

"Do you realize what that means—to me, Ronnie?"

"He's not a bad fellow," protested Ronnie. "Really, Beryl, I never dreamed you were going to take this line. Is it decent?"

"He's—he's awful, Ronnie, you know he's awful. He's hideous, he's just animal all through. Animal with reasoning powers, gross—horrible. You liked me, Ronnie," she was pleading now. "Why—why don't you marry me? I love you—I must have loved you. I could learn to respect you so easily. They say you're rotten, but you're of my own kind. Ronnie, don't you know what it means to me to say this—don't you know?"

She was gripping his arm with an intensity which made him wince. Hysteria—suppose Steppe did come back? He went moist at the thought.

"Ronnie, why don't you?" she breathed. "It would save me. It would save father, too. He would accept the accomplished fact, and be relieved. Ronnie, it would save my soul and my body. I'd serve you as faithfully as any woman ever served a man, I would Ronnie. I'd be—I'd be as light as the lightest woman you know—don't you realize what I am saying—?"

"My dear girl," he said, thoroughly alarmed, "I couldn't oppose Steppe, he's a good fellow, really he is; I'm sure you'd be happy. I'm awfully fond of you—"

"Then take me away! Go with you tonight—now, now! Take me. Ronnie, I'll go—now—this very minute and I'll bless you. He wouldn't want me then. I know him."

"I—I wish you wouldn't talk such rot," he quavered.

"Take me," she urged desperately. "There is a train tonight for Ostende, take me. Take me, Ronald, I could love you—I could love you in gratitude—save me from this gross man."

Ronnie, in a flurry of fear, pushed her away. "You don't know what you're talking about," he said shrilly. "Steppe would kill me. Beryl, I'm fond of you, but I can't cross Steppe."

That was the end, her last throw in the game. Ronnie was Ronnie. That was all. She was very calm now; but for her pallor and the uncontrollable tremor of her hands, her old self.

That she had humiliated herself did not bring her a moment's regret. Stampeded—she had been stampeded by sheer physical fear.

"I think I'll go," she said, taking up her furs. "You need not get me a cab—this time. And Moropulos cannot photograph me. I might have forced you to do what I wished, playing on your fears. I couldn't do that. What a coward—but I won't reproach you, Ronnie."

She held out her hand and he held it reluctantly. This time he took no risks. He gave her a minute's start and then he, too, went out. Madame Ritti was ever a place of refuge to Ronnie when his nerves were jangled.

XIV

How quickly the days flew past! Beryl had a letter from Sir John Maxton one Saturday:

"I have seen our friend for the third time since the sentence; you know that on Tuesday he 'goes the way'—those are his own words. What can I tell you of him, Beryl, that you do not know? He has become one of my dearest friends. How strange that seems, written! Yet it is true and when he asked me if I would come and see him on the morning, I agreed. In France it is the custom of the defending advocate to be present—I am glad it is not necessary in England. Yet I shall go and I pray that I may be as fearless as he.

"He spoke of you yesterday and of 'Christina'—that is Miss Colebrook, isn't it? But so cheerfully!

"The officers of the prison are fond of him and even the chief warder, a hard-bitten Guardsman, who was the principal flogger at Pentonville for many years, speaks of him affectionately. Completely untroubled—that is how I should describe Ambrose. He has been allowed the privilege of a reader, one of the warders, an educated man who acts as librarian to the prison. He has chosen Gibbon's 'Roman Empire' and on my suggestion, he is concentrating on the chapters dealing with the creation of the Byzantine Empire. The story of Belesarius fascinates him; Belesarius is a character after his own heart, as I knew would be the case.

The chaplain sees him frequently and Ambrose is politely attentive. It is rather like a village schoolmaster strutting Newton in astronomy. Ambrose is so far advanced that the good man's efforts to bring him to an understanding are just a little pathetic. 'I can't understand Mr. Pinley's God,' he said to me when I called immediately after the clergyman's visit. 'He is a slave's conception of a super-master—the superstition of a fighting tribe.' Ambrose holds to his own faith, which is comprehended in Henley's poem 'Out of the dark which covers me.' He recites this continuously.

"I said that he spoke of you and Christina. I asked him if he would like to see you both, knowing that if he did you would face the ordeal. But he said that it was unnecessary."

On the Monday evening Christina came to the house. They did not sleep that night.

"I suppose we're neurotic, but I never felt saner," said Beryl, "or more peacefully minded. And yet if it were somebody I did not know, some servant with whom I was just on nodding terms, I should be a bundle of nerves. And it is Ambrose! Christina, are we just keyed up, over-strained—shall we collapse? I have wondered."

"I shall not break," said Christina, "I have been worrying about you—"

Yet it was Christina on whom the chimes of the little French clock on the mantelpiece fell like the knell of doom.

"—six—seven—eight—nine!" counted Beryl, tense, exalted.

It was over. Ambrose Sault bad gone the way.

"Goodbye, Ambrose!"

Christina's voice was a wail. Before Beryl could reach her, she had slipped to the floor in a dead faint.

XV

Ronald Morelle came down the carpeted stairs of the House of Shame, and there was a half smile on his lips, as though the echoes of laughter were still vibrating through this silent mansion and he must respond.

The hall was in darkness except for the light admitted by a semi-circular transom. Turning his head, he saw that the door of the salon was ajar, and he hesitated. He had never seen the salon by daylight, only at night, when the soft lights were burning and silver chandeliers glowed with tiny yellow globes.

He pushed open the door. The darkness here had been relieved by somebody who had opened one window and unshuttered two others. The room was in disorder, chairs remained where the sitters had left them, and the cold gray light of morning looked upon tarnished gilding and faded damask, and the tawdry litter of the night before. Merciless, pitiless, contemptuous was the sneer of the clean dawn.

Ronald's smile deepened. And then he caught a reflection of himself in one of the long mirrors. He looked pale and drawn. He shivered. Not because the mirror gave back the illusion of a sick man—he knew well enough he was healthy—but because he glimpsed the something in his eyes, the leering devil that sat behind the levers and turned the switches of desire.

A car was waiting for him at the end of the slumbering street. Madame did not like cars at the door in the early hours of the morning, and he stepped in, wrapping his coat about him.

The sun had not yet risen and Wechester was a two hours' run with a clear road.

Sault was in Wechester Gaol awaiting the dread hour, and from somewhere in Lancashire, a gaunt-faced barber who had marked in his diary the date of an engagement, had taken a train to Ronald's destination, carrying with him the supple straps that would bind the wrists of the living and be slipped from the wrists of the dead.

The clear sky gave promise of a perfect winter day, but the morning air was cold. He pulled up the windows of the car and wished he had bought a newspaper or book to wile away the time. In two hours the soul of Ambrose Sault—

The soul! What was the soul? Was it Driesh's "Entelechy"; that "innnermost secret" of animation? Was there substance to the soul? Was it material? A flame, Merville had once called it, a flame from a common fire. Could the flame leap at will from a man's body and leave him—what? A lunatic, a madman, a beast without reason? Ronald shrugged away the speculation, but the scholar in him was uneasy and insensibly he came back to the problem.

The promise of fair weather was belied as the car drew nearer to Wechester. A mist, thin and white, lay like a blanket on the streets, and Ronald's car "hawked" its way into the still thicker mist which lay on Wechester Common. The car drew up at the prison gates, and he looked at his watch. It wanted a quarter of nine.

Ronnie saw a thin man, thinly clad, walking up and down outside. His hair was long and fell over his coat collar, his nose was red with the cold, and now and again he stopped to stamp his feet. Ronnie wondered who he was.

A wicket opened at his ring, and he showed his authority through the bars before, with a clang and a clatter of turning locks and the thud of many bolts, the door swung open and he found himself in a square stone room furnished with a desk, a high stool and one chair.

The warder took his authority and read it, made an entry in the book, and rang a bell. It was a cheerless room, in spite of the fire, thought Ronald. Three sets of handcuffs garlanded above the chimney piece; a suggestive truncheon lay on brackets near the warder's desk, and within reach of his hand, and a framed copy of Prison Regulations only served to emphasize the bareness of the remaining wall.

Again the clatter and click of the lock and another warder came in.

"Take this gentleman to the governor's room," said the doorkeeper.

Ronald was amused because the second warder put his hand on his arm as though he were a prisoner, and did not remove his hand even when he was unlocking the innumerable gates, doors and grilles which stood between liberty and the prisoners.

The governor's room was scarcely more cheerful than the gatekeeper's lodge. There was a desk piled with papers, a worn leather armchair and an office smell which was agreeable and human.

The governor shook hands with the visitor, whom he had met before, and Ronald nodded to the two other pressmen who were waiting.

Then they took him out into the yard.

The warder led the way, and the doctor followed, then came the governor and last, save for the warder who brought up the rear, went Ronald Morelle, without a single tremor of heart, to the house of doom.

To a great glass-roofed hall with tier upon tier of galleries and yellow cell doors, and near at hand (that which was nearest to them as they came in) one cell, door ajar. Outside three blankets neatly folded were stacked one on each other. They were the blankets in which the condemned man had slept.

Here was a wait. A nerve-racking wait to those with nerves. Ronald had none. A small door opened into the yard and he strolled through it and found himself in a small black courtyard. Twenty paces away was a little building which looked like a tool house. There were two gray-black sliding doors and these were open. All he could see was a plain clean interior with a scrubbed floor, and a yellow rope that hung from somewhere in the roof. He was joined by an officer whom he took to be the chief warder.

Physically Ronald was a coward. He admitted as much to himself. He feared pain, he shrank from danger. In his questionable business transactions he guarded himself m every way from unpleasant consequences, employing two lawyers who checked one another's conclusions.

Yet he could watch the pain of others and never turn a hair. He had witnessed capital operations and had found stimulus in the experience which the hospital theatre brings to the enthusiastic scientist. He had seen death administered by the law in England, America and France. Once he stood by the side of a guillotine in a little northern town of France and watched three shrieking men dragged to "the widow" and was the least affected of the spectators, until the blood of one splashed his hand. And then it was only disgust he felt. He himself was incapable of violent action. He might torture the helpless, but he would have to be sure they were helpless.

"Chilly this morning, sir," said the chief warder conversationally, and said that he did not know what was happening to the weather nowadays. "Is this the first time you've been inside?"

"In a prison? Oh lord, no," said Ronnie.

"Ah!" The warder jerked his head toward the door. "On this kind of job?"

"Yes, twice before."

The officer looked glum.

"Not very pleasant. It upsets all the routine of the establishment. Can't get the men out for exercise till after it is over. They sit in their cells and brood— we always have a lot of trouble afterwards."

"How is he going to take it?" asked Ronald.

"Who, the prisoner?" Mr. Marsden smiled. "Oh, he's going to take it all right. They never give any trouble—and he—he'll go laughing, you mark my words. We like him, here—that's a funny thing to say, isn't it? But I assure you, I've had to take three men off observation duty—they are the warders who sit in the cell with him—they got so upset. It is a fact. Old fellows who'd prison service for years. Here's the deputy."

A tall man in a trench coat had come through the grille.

"Good morning, Morelle, have you seen the governor?"

Ronnie nodded.

"He won't be here for the—er—event," said Major Boyle. "Between ourselves, he said he couldn't stand it. An extraordinary thing. Have you seen Sir John Maxton?"

"No, is he here?" asked Ronnie interested.

"He's in the cell with the man—there he is."

Sir John's face was gray: he seemed to have shrunken. He had not expected to see Ronnie, but he made no comment on his presence.

"Good morning, Boyle. Good morning, Ronnie. I have just said goodbye to him."

"Aren't you staying?"

"No—he understands," said Sir John briefly. Then he seemed to be conscious of Ronnie's presence. The deputy had gone back to the hall.

"Ronnie, how could you come here this morning—and meet the eyes of this man so soon to face God?" he asked in a hushed voice.

Ronnie's lips curled.

"I suppose you feel in your heart that it is a great injustice, that your noble-minded murderer should go to a shameful death, whilst a leprous but respectable member of society like myself walks free through that gate!"

"I would wish no man this morning's agony," said the other.

"Suppose you were God—"

"Ronnie, have you no decency!"

"Oh, yes—but suppose you were: would you transfer the soul and the individuality of us two, Ambrose Sault and Ronnie Morelle?"

"God forgive me, I would, for you are altogether beastly!"

Ronnie laughed again.

There was the sound of a slamming door and a man came into the yard, squat, unshaven, a little nervous. A derby hat was on the back of his head, and in his hands, clasped behind him, was a leathern strap.

"There's the hangman," said Ronnie. "Ask him what he thinks of murderers' souls! What is death, Sir John? Look at those tablets on the wall—just a few initials. Yet they sleep as soundly as the great in the Abbey under their splendid monuments. Though they were hanged by the neck until they were dead. You would like God to change us. One of those changes which Merville talked about the other night—it was a pity you weren't there."

Sir John said nothing: he walked to the grille and a warder unlocked the steel door. For a second he stood and then, as the hangman went into the hall, he passed out through the opened gate.

Presently two warders came from the hall and then another two, walking solemnly in slow step, and then a bound man; a great rugged figure who overshadowed the clergyman by his side. The drone of the burial service came to Ronald Morelle and he took off his hat.

Sault was reciting something. His powerful voice drowned the thin voice of the minister:

"It matters not how straight the Gate—"

He paced in time to the metre.

"How charged with punishment the scroll,

"I am the master of my fate—"

Nearer, and yet nearer, and then their eyes met!

The debonair worldling, silk hat in hand, his hair brushed and pomaded, his immaculate cravat set faultlessly—and the other! That big gray-faced man with the mane of hair, his rough clothes and his collarless shirt!

They looked at one another for a fraction of a second, eye to eye, and Ronald felt something was drawing at him, tugging at his very heart strings. The eyes of the man were luminous, appealing, terrible. And then with a crash the world stood still—all animate creation was frozen stiff, petrified, motionless, and Ronald swayed for a moment.

Then a firm hand on his arm pushed him forward. He stepped forth mechanically. He had a curious, almost painful feeling of restriction. And then he realized, with a half-sob, that his hands were bound behind him, strapped so tightly that they were swollen and tingling, and warders were holding his arms. He tried to speak, but no sound came, and looking up he saw—!

Once more he was looking into eyes, but they were the eyes of himself! Ronald Morelle was standing watching him with sorrow and pity. Ronald Morelle was watching himself! And then again the urgent hand pressed him forward and he paced mechanically.

"—I know that my Redeemer liveth—"

The little clergyman was walking by his side, reading tremulously. Ronald looked down at himself, his shoe was hurting him, somebody had left a nail there and he cursed François: but those were not his shoes he was looking at, they were great rough boots and his trousers were old and frayed and there was a shiny patch on his knee.

"—Man that is born of a woman hath but little time upon this earth, and that time is filled with misery."

He walked like one in a dream into the shed and felt the trap sag under him. The executioner—it must be the executioner, he thought, stooped and strapped his legs tightly. Ronald wondered what would happen. It was an absurd mistake, of course, rather amusing in a way—François had not been paid his month's salary, and François was meeting his brother today from Interlaken, Interlaken in the Oberland.

The man put a cloth over his face—it was linen, unbleached and pungent. When the executioner passed the elastic loops behind his ears, he released one too quickly and it stung.

"It is not me, it is not me," said Ronald numbly, "it is the body of Ambrose Sault—the gross body of Ambrose Sault! I'm standing outside watching! It is Sault who is being hanged—Sault! I am Morelle—Morelle of Balliol—Major Boyle," he screamed aloud. "Major Boyle—you know me—I am Morelle—"

Yet his body was huge—he felt its grossness, its size, the strength of the corded muscles of the arm; the roaring fury of the life which surged within him. He heard a squeak—the lever was being pulled—

With a crash the trap gave way and the body of Ambrose Sault swung for a second and was dead, but it was the soul of Ronald Morelle that went forth to the eternal spaces of infinity.

The prison clock struck nine.

BOOK THE FOURTH

I

A warder came round the edge of the pit with his arms extended as the executioner, reaching out his hand, steadied the quivering rope. The prison doctor looked down the pit.

"He's all right," he said vaguely.

The tremulous clergyman was the last to go; backing out of the death chamber he watched the warders close and lock the doors.

The body of Ronald Morelle settled its top hat firmly on its shapely head and looked down at the little parson. There were tears in that good man's eyes.

"He was not bad, he was not bad," he murmured shakily. "I wish he had repented the murder."

"There was nothing to repent," said Ronald quietly, "if repentance were possible, the murder was unnecessary."

His voice was strangely deep and rich. Hearing himself, he wondered.

The minister looked up at him in surprise.

"He said exactly the same thing to me this morning," he said, "and in almost identical words; the poor fellow expressed his thoughts in language which seemed unnatural remembering his illiteracy."

"Poor soul," said Ronnie thoughtfully. "Poor lonely, lonely soul!"

He took the minister's arm in his and they walked back to the prison hall. There was a surplice to be shed, devotional books to be packed in a little black bag.

The condemned cell was being turned out by two men in convict's garb. One was using a broom, sweeping with long, leisurely strokes, and his face had a suggestion of sadness. The other was carrying out the remainder of the bedding and washing the utensils which the dead man had used. All this Ronald noticed with a curiously detached interest.

Shepherded back again to the governor's office, there was a form to be signed, testifying that he had witnessed the execution which had been carried out in a proper and decorous manner. Ronald took the pen and hesitated a second before he signed. The appearance of his signature on paper interested him—it was unfamiliar.

"You've seen these executions before, Mr. Morelle?" said the under-sheriff.

"Oh, yes," said Ronald quietly. "I do not think I shall come again. The waste of it, the malice of it!"

"An eye for an eye and a tooth for a tooth," said the under-sheriff gruffly and Ronald smiled sadly.

"The Old Testament is excellent as literature but in parts diabolical as a code of morals," he said, and went through the porter's lodge to the world.

There was a small crowd, some twenty or thirty people grouped at a distance from the gate. Their interest was concentrated upon the kneeling figure that confronted Ronnie as he walked out of the lodge.

"He comes here every time we have a hanging," said the gateman in Ronnie's ear.

It was the thin man in the threadbare coat; he knelt bareheaded, his blue hands clasped, his voice hoarse with a cold.

"—let him be the child of Thy mercies—pardon, we beseech Thee, O Lord our God, this our brother who comes before Thy seat of Judgment—"

Ronnie listened to the husky voice. Presently and with a final supplication, the man got up and dusted his knees.

"For whom are you praying?" asked Ronnie gently.

"For Ambrose Sault, brother," answered the man.

"For Ambrose Sault?" repeated Ronnie absently; "that is very sweet." He looked thoughtfully at the man and then walked away.

Following the Common road that would have taken him to Wechester, he heard a car coming behind him and presently the glittering bonnet moved past him and stopped.

"Excuse me, sir."

Ronnie looked round. He did not know the chauffeur who was touching his cap. And yet he had seen his face.

"I thought you may have missed the car—I had to park away from the prison."

Of course! He breathed a heavy sigh as the problem was solved. It was his own car and the chauffeur's name was Parker.

"I haven't the slightest idea where I was going," he laughed. "You look cold, Parker. We had better stop in Wechester and get breakfast."

Parker could only gape.

"Yes, sir," he stammered, "but don't worry about me, sir. I shall be all right."

Ronnie was puzzling again. Then he had it. The Red Lion! There was an inn just outside of Wechester; he had stopped there before. Apparently Parker expected some such directions.

They left the mists behind them at Wechester and came to the Red Lion.

A pretty girl waitress at the hotel saw Ronnie and tossed her head. Her manner was cold. He couldn't remember.

That was the oddness of it. He had lost some of his memories. They were completely blotted out from his mind. Why was this pretty girl so cross? He was to learn. Finishing his breakfast he strolled out into the big yard where the car was garaged. The chauffeur was at his breakfast.

"Hi! I want to have a talk with you!"

A man was approaching. He looked like a groom, wearing gaiters as he did, and he was in his shirtsleeves. Moreover, his style and appearance was hostile.

"You're the man who was staying here for the trial!" challenged the newcomer.

"Was I—I suppose so."

"Was you!" sneered the groom savagely. "Yes, you was! Staying here with a young woman and you went and interfered with my young woman. Yes, interfered—said things to her."

His voice went up the scale until he was shouting. There was a stir of feet and men and women came to the doors of outhouses and kitchens.

"Doesn't it strike you that you are making the young lady feel uncomfortable—if she is here," said Ronnie seriously. "You are shouting what should be whispered—no, no, Parker, please do not interfere."

"I'll tell you what does strike me," bellowed the groom, rolling up his sleeves, "that I'm going to give you the damnedest lacing you ever had—put 'em up!"

He lunged forward, but his blow did not get home. A hand gripped him by one shoulder and swung him round—crash! He fell against a stable door. Happily there was a wall for Parker to lean against. He was openmouthed—incredulous.

Phew! Morelle who was ready to drop from terror at a threat, was standing, hands on hips, surveying the bewildered fire-eater.

"I'm extremely sorry you made me do that," he said almost apologetically, "but you really must not shout—especially about unpleasant things. If I—if I behaved disgracefully to the lady, I am sorry."

All this in a voice that did not reach beyond his adversary. Parker heard the low music of it and scratched his head. Morelle's voice had changed.

Later, when Ronnie was preparing to depart, Parker ventured to offer felicitations.

"I never saw a man go through it like that fellow did—and they think something of him as a fighter in these parts."

"It was nothing," said Ronnie hastily, "a trick—I learned it in New Caledonia from a Japanese who was in the same prison."

Parker blinked.

"Yes, sir," he said, and then Ronnie laughed.

"What on earth am I talking about? I think we will go home, Parker."

"Yes, sir," said Parker, breathing hard. He had never seen his master drunk before, and drunk he undoubtedly was, for not only had he fought, but he was civil. Parker hoped he would keep drunk.

In his pocket Ronnie found a gold cigarette case, a pocketbook, a watch and chain, a small billcase and a gold pencil. In his trousers pocket were a few silver coins and some keys. He found them literally; the seat of the car was strewn with his discoveries. Whose were they? The cigarette case was inscribed: "To Ronnie from Beryl." Ronnie—Beryl? Of course they were his own properties. He chuckled gleefully at his amusing lapse.

"No, I shan't want you again. Parker—how do I get into touch with you if—? Yes, of course, I 'phone you at the garage. Good morning."

"Good morning." Parker was too dazed to return the politeness.

Ronnie shook his head smilingly when the porter opened the gate of the automatic elevator. He would walk, he said, and went up the stairs two at a time. This exercise tired him slightly. And usually he felt so strong, nothing tired him. That day he lifted Moropulos and flung him on his bed. Moropulos had hated him ever since.

II

"What am I thinking about?" said Ronnie Morelle aloud.

François was not in. Ronnie had expected him to be there and yet would have been surprised had he seen him. There was a letter lying on the table. Ronnie saw it when he entered the room. He did not look at it again for some time. Strolling aimlessly round the library, hands in pockets, he stopped before the Anthony over the mantelpiece—ugly and a little unpleasant. He made a little grimace of disgust. Out of the tail of his eye he saw the letter. Why did people write to him, he wondered, troubled? They knew that he couldn't read, he made no secret of his ignorance. Yet, picking up the envelope, he read his own name and was unaware of his inconsistency. The letter was from François. His brother had arrived. He had gone to the station to meet him and would return instantly. Would Monsieur excuse? It was unlikely that monsieur would return before him, but if he did, would he be pleased to excuse. He wrote "excuse" three times and in three different ways, and they were all wrong. Ronald laughed softly. Poor François! Poor—

His face became grave and slowly his eyes went back to the Anthony, that lewd painting.

Poor soul! His eyes filled with tears. They rolled with the curious leisure of tears down his face, and dropped on the gray suede waistcoat.

Poor soul! Poor weak, undeveloped soul!

Ronnie was sitting on the Chesterfield to read the letter. François, coming in hurriedly, saw a man crying into the crook of his arm and stood petrified.

"M'sieur!"

Ronnie looked up. His eyes were swollen, his smooth skin blotchily red in patches.

"Hello, François. I'm being stupid. Get me a glass of water, please."

His hand was shaking so that he could hardly hold the glass to his chattering teeth.

François watched and marvelled.

"Did you meet your brother?" Ronnie was drying his eyes and smiling faintly at the valet's grotesque dismay.

"Yes, M'sieur. I hope that M'sieur was not inconvenienced—"

Ronnie shook his head.

"No—make me something. Coffee or tea—anything—have you brought your brother here?"

"Oh, no, M'sieur."

"You will want to see him, François. You may take the rest of the day off."

"Certainly, M'sieur," said François, recovering himself. His services were seldom dispensed with until later in the day. Possibly his employer had excellent reason.

Ronnie did not hear the bell ring and until he caught the click of the lock and the sound of voices in the lobby, he had no idea that he had a caller.

François came in alone, secretive, low-voiced.

"It is Mister East, M'sieur: Yesterday was the day, but m'sieur forgot," he said mysteriously.

"Yesterday was—what day?" Ronnie rubbed his chin with a knuckle. How stupid of him to forget!

"Ask him to come in please."

François hesitated, but went, returning with a thin young man whose face seemed all angles and bosses. He was well dressed, a little too well dressed. His plastered hair was parted and one fringe curled like a wave of black ink that had been petrified just as it was in the act of breaking on the yellow beach of his forehead.

He had a way of holding back his head so that he looked down his nose in whatever direction his gaze was turned. "Morning," he said coldly and cleared his throat.

"Good morning?" Ronnie's tone was polite but inquisitive.

"I called yesterday but nobody was in," said Mr. East, gently stern.

"Why did you call at all?" asked Ronnie.

A look of amazement toning to righteous anger from Mr. East.

"Why did I call at all?" he repeated. "To give you a chance of actin' the man; to collect what is due to a poor girl that was—"

"To commit blackmail, in fact?" smiled Ronnie. (He was quick to smile today.)

"Eh?"

"I remember—I have given you money every week, ostensibly for your sister. Tell her to come and see me."

"What! Her come to see you? In this, what I might term, den of iniquity? No! I don't allow you to see the poor girl. And as for blackmail, didn't you, of your own free will, offer to pay?"

Mr. East had grown red in the face, he was indignant, hurt, and soon would be pugnacious.

Ronnie got to his feet and the listening François heard the door open.

"Get out, please," said Ronnie pleasantly. "I don't wish to hurt you but get out."

The man was speechless.

"I am going to a lawyer," he blustered, "I won't soil my hands with you."

"I think you are very wise," said Ronnie and closed the door on him.

On the mat outside, Mr. East stood for at least five minutes thinking, or trying to think.

"He's been drinking!" he said hollowly, and, had he consulted Parker, his suspicions would have received support.

François heard his employer's summons and came from his tiny compartment.

"I am going out," said Ronnie.

"I will telephone for the car, M'sieur," but Ronnie shook his head.

"I will walk," he said. "You need not wait, François. Have I a key?"

"Yes, M'sieur," wonderingly, "it is on the chain of m'sieur."

Ronnie pulled a bunch from his pocket.

"Which is it—this?"

"Certainly, M'sieur."

"You need not wait," said Ronnie again. "I do not know when I shall be in."

"Good, M'sieur."

Well might François wonder, for Ronnie was speaking in French, the French of a man who had lived with French people. And Ronald Morelle, though he had a knowledge of that language, never spoke it, or if he did, his accent was bad and his vocabulary limited.

It was eight o'clock at night when Ronnie returned. The flat was in darkness and was chilly. He turned on the lights before he closed the door and had a difficulty in finding the switch. It took him a longer time to locate the controls of the electric stove in the fireplace. They were skilfully hidden.

In the kitchenette he lit a gas-ring and filling a copper kettle, set the water to boil.

François, in his hurry to meet his brother that morning, had forgotten to dust the black writing table. Ronnie found a duster and remedied his man's neglect.

By the time he had finished, the kettle was boiling. The tea was in a little wooden box; the sugar he found on another shelf—there was no milk. Ronnie put on his coat and with a jug in his hand, went out to find a dairy. The hall porter saw a man in a silk hat and wasp-waisted overcoat passing his lodge, and came out hurriedly.

"Excuse me, Mr. Morelle. Is there anything I can do for you?"

"I want some milk," said Ronnie simply, "but please don't trouble; there is a dairy in the Brompton Road, I remember seeing the place."

"They will be closed now, sir," said the porter. "If you give me the jug, I'll get some for you."

He took the vessel and made a flat-to-flat canvass and was successful in his quest.

When Ronnie opened the door to the porter, Ronnie was in his shirt-sleeves and he had a broom in his hand. He explained pleasantly that he had upset a can of flour. François occasionally prepared an omelette for his master.

"If you'll let me sweep it up—" began the porter, but Ronnie declined the offer.

With a cup of tea and a slice of bread and butter he made a meal, cleared away the remnants of the feast and washed and dried the utensils.

Then he sat down to pass the evening. The book-shelves were bewilderingly interesting. He took out a book. Greek! Of course, he read Greek and this was the Memorabilia; its margins covered with pencil notes in his own handwriting!

Presently he replaced the book and tried to reduce the events of the day to some sort of order. The execution! What happened outside the execution shed?

He had looked into the eyes of the condemned man and suddenly the placid current of his mind had been disturbed as by a mighty wind. And standing there he had watched something being taken into the death house; whose uncouth body was it that hung strapped and strangled in the brick pit? Ambrose Sault's?

He remembered a second of painful experience when he had a confused memory of strange people and places, queer earthquake memories. He recollected having been flogged by a red-haired brute of a man who wielded a strap; he recalled a dim-lit cell and the pale blue eyes of a clergyman who was pleading with him; of a woman, dark-faced and thick-lipped—his mother?—

he remembered the past of Ambrose Sault! He had been Ambrose Sault in those ten seconds, with all the consciousness of Sault's life, all the passion of Sault's faith. And then the weighted traps had fallen with a thunderous clap and he was Ronald Morelle again—only different.

Yet he was not wholly conscious of the difference. What a strange business it was! How was humanity served by that ritual of death? His heart melted within him as in a vivid flash he saw the blank despair of the trussed victim of the law shuffling forward to annihilation. He was being weak—but, oh God, how sad, how unutterably sad! He sobbed into his hands and was pained at the futility of his grief. Poor soul! Poor, mean, smirched soul! How vilely it had served the beautiful body which was its habitation!

He looked up frowning, his tear-stained face puckered in perplexity. Beautiful body? Ambrose Sault was gross, uncouth. And by all accounts a good man. Even Steppe admired his principles. Why should principles be admired? It was natural to be honest and clean.

He had left the door of the pantry ajar; the shrill sound of the bell brought him to his feet.

He waited to wipe his face and the bell rang again impatiently.

"My friend, you must wait," said Ronnie.

A third time the bell rang before he opened the door. Steppe filled the doorway, the expanse of his shirt-front showed like a great white heart, against the gloom of his evening dress.

"Hello. You're in, huh? Long time answering the bell—I suppose you've got somebody here."

He looked around. The only light in the room was the shaded table-lamp. Ronnie had extinguished the others before he sat down.

"The wicked love the darkness, huh, huh!" Steppe chuckled, and then looking past him, Ronnie saw that he was not alone. Beryl waited at the door and behind her was Dr. Merville.

"Get dressed and come out," commanded Steppe noisily. "What's the matter with all you people, huh? Come along. We're going to a theatre. You're as bad as Beryl, sitting in the dark. You overbred people think too much."

"May we come in, Ronnie?" asked Beryl.

It was very likely that Steppe's crude suggestion was justified. She had no illusions about Ronnie.

"Come in? Of course you can come in," said Steppe scornfully. "Now hurry, Morelle. We'll give you ten minutes—and put some lights on."

"There is enough light."

Ronnie's voice was calm and deep. Steppe, turning to find the switch, swung back again and peered at his face.

"What's that?" he asked sharply. "I said there wasn't—what have you done to your voice? Here!"

He walked across the room and ran his hand down the three switches.

Ronnie screwed up his eyes to meet the painful brilliance.

He saw Beryl's look of surprise, met the stare of the big man.

"He's been crying!" bellowed Steppe in delight. "Huh, huh! Look at him, Beryl, sniveling!"

"Mr. Steppe—Jan! How can you!"

"How can I? By God, he's been sniveling! Look at his face, look at his eyes!" Steppe slapped his thigh in an ecstasy of joy. "So it got you, huh? I couldn't understand how a fellow like you could see it, without curling up!" His coarseness, the malignity, the heartlessness of the man sickened Beryl Merville. But Ronnie—! He was serene, unmoved by the other's taunts, meeting his eyes steadily.

"It was dreadful—so dreadful, Steppe. To see that poor shrieking thing thrust forward, struggling—"

"What!" shouted Steppe, and the girl gasped.

"Ambrose Sault—shrieking in fear—"

"You lie!" snarled Steppe. "Sault wasn't that kind. I've seen Maxton and he says he was without fear. You're dreaming, you fool. If it had been you—yes. You'd have squealed—by God! You would have raised Cain! But Ambrose Sault—he was a man. D'ye hear, a man. He's dead and I'm glad. But he was a man."

He held himself in with an effort.

"Get dressed and come out," he ordered roughly.

"I'm so sorry, Ronnie," the girl had come to him, pity and sympathy in her sad face. "It was dreadful for you."

He nodded. "Yes—it was dreadful. I am not coming out tonight, Beryl."

She squeezed his arm gently. "Poor Ronnie!"

"Poor fiddlesticks!" sneered Steppe. "Hurry, cry-baby. I'm not going to wait here all night. What are you afraid of? You shouldn't have seen the damned thing, if you were going to snivel about it. You should have 'Tried the luck'!"

He chuckled as at a joke as he saw the swollen eyes of his victim wander to the bookshelf.

"The luck!" said Ronnie. He was speaking to himself, as he moved to the bookcase.

Beryl saw him take down a worn volume and lay it on the table. He seemed like a man walking in his sleep. Mechanically he took up a miniature sword from a pin tray and held it for a moment in his hand.

"Try the luck!" scoffed Steppe. "Shall I go to the play, shan't I go to the play—dear Lord!"

For the space of a second their eyes met and Beryl, watching, saw the big man start. Then the sword was thrust between the pages and the book opened.

Ronnie looked gloomily at the close-set type—frowned. Then he read slowly, sonorously:

"I will take away from thee the desire of thine eyes with a stroke; yet neither shalt thou mourn nor weep; neither shall thy tears fall down."

The clock on the mantelpiece struck nine.

A silence, painful and intense, so profound that Beryl's quick breathings were audible.

"I will take away the desires of thine eyes with a stroke—"

"Don't read it again!" cried Steppe harshly. "I'm going—listening to this fool—come on, Beryl."

Turning at the door she saw him still standing at the table. His face was in shadow, his hands white and shapely, outspread upon the leather-covered top; the open book between them.

"He's drunk," said Steppe and she made no reply. Jan Steppe was very preoccupied all that evening, but not so completely oblivious of realities that he did not bargain with the doctor for certain shares in the Klein River Mine. Just before he had left his house Steppe had received a coded cable from Johannesburg.

III

On the morning of Ambrose Sault's execution, Evie found a letter awaiting her at the drug store. Whatever natural unhappiness of feeling she may have had when she left her weeping mother, vanished in the perusal of Ronnie's long epistle. The envelope bore the St. John's Wood postmark, but this she would not have regarded as significant, even if she had noticed it, which she did not.

Not a love letter in the strictest sense; it was too precise and businesslike for that. It gave her certain dates to be cherished, certain instructions to be observed. It went to the length of naming Parisian dressmakers where she might be expeditiously fitted. She was to bring nothing, only a suitcase with bare necessities. A week's stay in Paris would give her all the time she needed to equip herself. It was a trial to her that she would not see Ronnie for a month, not until the great day—she caught her breath at the thought. But he had stipulated this. Ronnie was too keen a student of women to give her the opportunity of changing her mind. His letters could not be argued with, or questioned.

And the month would quickly pass. Teddy Williams was a faithful attendant and, although he could not be compared in any respect with Ronnie, it was pleasant and flattering to extend her patronage to one who hung upon her words and regarded her as an authority upon most subjects.

She had imparted her views on marriage to Teddy, and that young man had been impressed without being convinced.

Ronnie's letter was to be read and re-read. She expected another the next day and, when it did not come, she was disappointed. Yet he had not promised to write; in his letter he had said: "Until you are my very own, I shall live the life of an anchorite."

She looked up "anchorite" and found that it meant "one who retires from society to a desert or solitary place to avoid the temptations of the world and to devote himself to religious exercises," and accepted this as a satisfactory explanation, though she couldn't imagine Ronnie engaging himself in religious exercises.

Life ran normally at home, now that Mr. Sault was dead. Evie had felt very keenly the disgrace of having a lodger who was a murderer. Only the fact that Ronnie knew him, too, and to some extent shared in the general odium, prevented her from enlarging upon the scandal to her mother and Christina. Beyond her comprehension was her sister's remarkable cheerfulness. Christina didn't seem to care whether Mr. Sault was alive or dead. She was her own caustic self and the shadow of her proper woe failed to soften or sadden her.

A week of her waiting had passed before Christina even mentioned the name of Ambrose Sault, and then it was in connection with the disposal of his room. Apparently he had paid his rent for a long period in advance, and Mrs. Colebrook refused to let the room again until the tenancy had expired.

"Mother is being sentimental over Ambrose and his room," said Christina, "but there is no reason why you shouldn't have the room, Evie. You've been aching for privacy as long as I can remember."

Evie shuddered.

"I couldn't sleep there, I'd be afraid he'd haunt me."

"I should be afraid he wouldn't," said Christina, with a little smile. "If you don't like the idea, I will have my bed put in there."

"No, no, please don't, Christina," begged the girl urgently. "I—I prefer to sleep here if you don't mind. I want to be with you as much as I can and I'm out all day."

"And home much earlier. Is it Ronnie or Teddy?"

"I'm seeing a lot of Teddy," replied Evie primly, "he is quite a nice boy."

"And Ronnie?"

"Leave Ronnie alone," Evie turned a good-humored smile to her. "He is too busy to meet me so often."

"Loud cheers," said the ironical Christina. "Evie—why don't you ask him to call here? I should enjoy a chat with him."

"Here?" Evie was incredulous. "How absurd! Ronnie wouldn't dream of coming here."

Christina laughed.

"I won't tease you any more, Evie. Does he ever say anything about Ambrose? He was in the prison when Ambrose was executed."

Evie writhed.

"I wish you wouldn't talk about it, Christina—in such a cold-blooded way—ugh!"

"Does he?"

"I haven't seen him since that—that awful day," she said, "and I'm sure he wouldn't talk about it." Evie hesitated. "Do you think much about Mr. Sault, Chris?"

Christina put down her knitting in her lap and nodded.

"All the time," she said, "he isn't out of my thoughts for a second. Not his face, I mean, or his awkward-looking body, but the real. Do you remember, Evie, how embarrassed I used to make him sometimes, and how he'd rub his chin with the back of his hand? I always knew when Ambrose was troubled. And how he used to sit on my bed and listen so seriously to all my wails and whines?"

Evie looked for some evidence of emotion, but Christina's eyes were dry— she appeared to be happy.

"Yes—Chris, do you think I ought to take these stockings back to the store? They laddered the first time I put them on and I paid a terrible price for them."

Christina took the stockings from the girl and there all talk of Ambrose Sault came to an end.

A few afternoons later, returning from her early walk, she was met at the door by her agitated mother.

"There's a gentleman called to see you, Christina, he's in the kitchen,"

"A gentleman?"

"A gentleman" might mean anything by Mrs. Colebrook's elastic description. "He's a friend of Miss Merville's named Mr. Morelle."

"What?" Christina could hardly believe her ears. Ronnie Morelle? Had Evie conveyed her joking request to him? Even if she had, it was not likely he would call for the pleasure of seeing her.

Mrs. Colebrook hustled her into the kitchen and closed the door on them. She had all the respect of her class for the sanctity of private conversation.

Ronnie was sitting in the chair where Ambrose had so often sat, as Mrs. Colebrook reminded her at least three times a day. He rose as she entered and stood surveying her.

It was the first time she had seen him close at hand, and her first impression was one of admiration. She had never met so good-looking a man and instantly she absolved Evie for her infatuation. He did not offer his hand at first, and it was not until she was about to speak that it came out to her shyly. It was a strong hand and the warmth of the grip surprised her.

"Christina!" he said softly and she felt herself go red.

"That is my name. You are Ronnie Morelle? I have heard a great deal about you from Evie."

"From Evie?—yes, why of course! Your mother is looking well. She works very hard—too hard I think. Women ought not to do such heavy work."

She sat, tongue-tied, could only point to the chair from which he had risen.

"I had to come to see you—but I have been rather occupied and selfish. I have been reading a great deal—a sheer delight. You will understand that? And poor François has had a lot of trouble, his brother developed appendicitis. We have had an anxious time."

Ronnie Morelle! And he was talking gravely of the anxious time he had had because the brother of his servant—it was incredible.

She never dreamed that he was this kind of man; all her preconceived ideas and more than half of her prejudice against him, were swept away in a second. He was sincere; she knew it. Absolutely sincere. This was no pose of his.

"You haven't seen Evie—oh, yes, you have! She told you I wanted to see you, Mr. Morelle. I do, although I was only joking when I suggested your coming. Are you very fond of Evie?"

"Yes, she is a nice child. A little thoughtless and perhaps a little selfish. Young girls are that way, especially if they are pretty. I am fond of young people, all young things have an appeal for me. Kittens, puppies, chicks—I can watch them for hours."

This was Ronnie Morelle. She had to tell herself all the time. He was the man whom Ambrose Sault had described as "foul" and Ambrose was so charitable in his judgments; the man who had taken Beryl Merville.

"I am glad you spoke of Evie," he went on. "She must not be hurt. At her age men make a profound impression and color the whole of after-life. It is so easy to sour the young. It is hard to improve on the old texts," he smiled. "I wonder why I try. 'As the twig is bent, so is the tree inclined.' I never think that it is wise to reason with a girl in love—fascinated is a better word. *Aegrescit mendeno!* The disease thrives on remedies. I don't know where I picked up that phrase—it is Latin, isn't it?"

He went red again, was painfully embarrassed.

She fell back against the wall, white as death. Only by an effort of will did she arrest the scream that arose in her throat.

In his distress he was rubbing his chin with his knuckle! "Oh, my God!" cried Christina, wide-eyed. Springing up she took both his hands and looked into his face.

"Don't you *know!*" she breathed.

A smile dawned slowly in the handsome face of Ronnie Morelle.

"I know it is very good to see you, Christina," he said.

"Don't you—know? Look at me—Ronnie!"

Then as suddenly she released his hands and held on to the table.

"Get me some water, please."

She watched him as he went unerringly into the scullery. There were two taps, one connected with a rain-water cistern that her father had made; the other was the drinking water.

He turned the right tap, found a glass where it was invariably hidden on a shelf behind a cretonne curtain, and brought it back to her.

She drank greedily.

"Sit down—Ronnie. I want you to tell me something. You went to the execution—I know it hurts you, my dear, but you must tell me. How did he die?"

She waited, holding her breath.

"It was—terrible," he said in a low voice, "he was so afraid!"

"Afraid!" she whispered.

"I don't remember much. Every thought seemed to have gone out of my mind. Afterwards I was so numbed—why, I didn't even recognize my own car or know that I had a car."

"Did you touch him—look at him, then, did you, Ronnie?"

Ronald Morelle answered with a gesture.

"Did you—?"

"I looked at him, but only for a second. He was reciting a poem. Henley's. I was reading it today, trying to recall things. That was all, I just looked into his eyes and I was feeling hateful toward him, Christina. And that was all. He began to moan and cry out. I was terribly distressed."

She said no more. She wanted to be alone with her mad thoughts. When he rose to go, she was glad.

"I'll come again on Wednesday," he said, but corrected his promise. "No, Wednesday is wash day. Your mother will not want me here."

"How do you know, Ronnie, that it is mother's washday?" she was addressing him as if he were a child from whom information must be coaxed.

"I don't know. Evie may have told me—of course it is Wednesday, Christina!"

She nodded.

"Yes, it is Wednesday."

Mrs. Colebrook, consonant with her principles, had effaced herself so effectively that Christina had to seek her in her hiding-place. She was sitting in Sault's room and sniffed suspiciously when the girl called her.

"Mother, you have often told me about something Ambrose did when you were very ill. Will you tell me again?"

Mrs. Colebrook was happy to tell, embellishing the story with footnotes and interpolations descriptive of her own impressions on that occasion.

"Thank you, Mother."

"What did he want? I didn't like to come down whilst he was here—not in this old skirt. Did he know poor Mr. Sault? A la-di-da sort of fellow, but very polite. He quite flustered me, he was so friendly."

She relieved the girl from the necessity for replying by supplying her own answers.

At the foot of the stairs Mrs. Colebrook heard the snick of a key as Christina locked the door of her room. Mrs. Colebrook sighed. Christina was getting more and unsociable.

IV

Did Beryl know—should she know? Suppose she went to her and told her the crazy theory she had? Beryl would doubt her sanity. No, no good would come of precipitancy. She must be sure, thought Christina, lying on her bed, her hand at her mouth as though she feared that she might involuntarily cry her news aloud.

No particulars of Ambrose Sault's death had appeared in the press. The longest notice was one which, after a brief reference to the execution, went on to give details concerning the crime. Practically the references to the execution were similar:

> "Ambrose Sault was executed at Wechester Jail yesterday morning for the murder of Paul Moropulos. The condemned man walked with a firm step to the gallows and death was instantaneous. He made no statement. Billet was the executioner."

The hangman always received his puff. When she had been staying with Beryl, she had met Sir John Maxton; he had returned on the morning of the execution and had come straight to the house. He had said nothing that gave her any impression except that Ambrose had died bravely. Would he have heard anything later? She made up her mind, dressed and went out. There was a telephone a block away and she got through to Sir John's chambers in the Temple. To her relief he answered the telephone himself.

"Is that you, Sir John? It is Christina Colebrook—yes—I'm very well. Can I see you, Sir John? Any time, now if you wish. I could be with you in twenty minutes—oh, thank you—thank you so much."

A bus dropped her in Fleet Street and she walked through the Temple grounds to the ugly and dreary buildings where he rented chambers. They were on the ground floor, happily; Christina was still a semi-invalid.

"You've come to ask me about Sault!" he said as soon as she was announced.

"Why do you think that?" she smiled.

"I guessed. I suppose Ronnie has told everybody about the ghastly business. It seems impossible, impossible that he could have shown the white feather as he did," said Sir John. "I can hardly believe it is true, and yet when I got into touch with the deputy governor, he told me very much the same story—that one moment Sault was calm and literally smiling at death; the very next instant he was—pitiful, blubbering like a child. I hate telling you this, because I know you were such dear friends, but—you want to know?"

She inclined her head.

"Nothing else happened?"

"Nothing—oh, yes, there was one curious circumstance. In the midst of his amazing outburst Sault cried: 'Ronald Morelle of Balliol!' Did he know that Ronnie was at Balliol? I can only imagine that by this time he hadn't any idea at all what he was talking about."

She rose.

"Thank you, Sir John," she said quietly, "you have saved my reason."

"In what way?" His curiosity was piqued.

"There was something I had to believe—or go mad. That is cryptic, isn't it? But I can't be plain, for fear you think I've lost my reason already!"

Sir John was too polite to press her, too much of a lawyer to reveal his curiosity. He went on to talk of Sault.

"He was certainly the best man I have met in my life. By 'best' I particularly refer to his moral character, his ideals, his sense of divinity. His courage humbled me, his philosophy left me feeling like a child of six. I must believe what I am told, so I accept the story about his having made a scene on the scaffold, without question. But there is an explanation for it, that I'll swear, and an explanation creditable to Ambrose Sault."

Christina went home with a light heart, convinced.

She had begun a letter to Beryl and was debating halfway through whether she would as much as hint her peculiar theory, when Evie burst into the room cyclonically, her eyes blazing.

"He's been here! Mother said so—you were talking to him for a long time! Oh, Chris, what did he say—wasn't it wonderful of him to come? Don't you think he is handsome, Chris? Own up—isn't he a gorgeous man? Did he ask after me, was he very disappointed when he found I was out—?"

"I'll take your questions in order," said Christina, solemnly ticking them off on her finger. "He *has* been here, if he is Ronnie; he said a lot of things. It was certainly wonderful for me that he came. He asked after you, but didn't seem to be cast down to find you were out. Was that the lot? I hope so."

"But Christina!" she was quivering with excitement. "What do you think of him?"

"I—think—he—is—sublime!"

Evie glanced at her resentfully, suspecting sarcasm; saw that her sister was in earnest, and seeing this, was confounded.

"He is very nice," she said less enthusiastic, "yes—a dear—did you really get on with him, Chris? How queer! And after all that you've said about him! Didn't your conscience prick you—?"

Christina sent her red locks flying in a vigorous head-shake.

"No, it wasn't conscience," she said.

Evie, from being boisterously interested, became quietly distrait.

"Of one thing I am certain," volunteered Christina, "and it is that he will never behave dishonorably or give you, or for the matter of that, mother and me, one hour's real pain.''

"No—I'm sure he won't,'' said Evie awkwardly, the more awkward, because she was trying so hard not to be.

"Such a man couldn't be mean. I am certain of that,'' Christina went on. "Evie, I am not scared about you any more—and I was, you know. Just scared! Sometimes when you came back from seeing Ronnie, I dared not look at you for fear—I didn't exactly know what I feared. Now—well, I feel that you are in good hands, darling, and I shall not be thinking every time you go out: 'I wonder if she will come back again?'''

Evie's face was burning. If she had spoken, she would have betrayed herself. She became interested in the contents of a hanging cupboard and hummed a careless tune, shakily.

"Are you singing or is it the hinge?'' asked Christina.

"You're very rude—I was singing—humming.''

"There must be music in the family somewhere,'' said Christina, "probably it goes back to our lordly ancestor—''

"I told Teddy about that, about Lord Fransham—''

"Did you tell Ronnie?''

Evie wondered if she should say. Christina was so excellently disposed toward him that it would be a pity to excite her resentment.

"Yes—he laughed. He said everybody has a lord in his family if he only goes back far enough. Teddy thought it was wonderful and he said—you'll laugh?''

"I swear I won't.''

"Well—he said that he knew that I had aristocratic blood by my instep, it is so arched. And it is you know, Chris, just look!''

"Shurrup!'' said Christina vulgarly.

"Well—he did. Teddy isn't half the fool you think him. I don't exactly mean you, Chris, but people. His father has a tremendous farm, miles and miles of it. He sent Teddy over here for six months. What do you think for?''

Christina couldn't think.

"To find a wife!'' said Evie. "Isn't it quaint? And do you know that Teddy is staying at the Carlton-Grand. I thought he was living with his aunt in Tenton Street and I only discovered by accident that he was staying at a swagger hotel. He said he would write and tell his father about our lord.''

She sighed heavily.

"I like Teddy awfully. He is so grateful for—well, for anything I can do for him, such as putting his tie straight and telling him about things.''

"Why don't you marry Teddy?''

A few weeks ago Evie would have snorted scornfully. Now she was silent for a long time. She sighed again.

"That is impossible. I'm too fond of Ronnie and I believe in keeping—in keeping my word. Teddy's father is building a beautiful little house for him. And Teddy says that he has a quiet horse that a girl could ride. He believes in rid-

ing astride, so do I. I've never ridden, but that is the way I *should* ride—
through the corn for miles and miles. You can see the mountains from Teddy's
farm. They are covered with snow, even in the summer. There is a place called
Banff where you can have a perfectly jolly time, dances and all that. In the winter, when it is freezingly cold, Teddy goes to Vancouver, where it is quite
warm. He has an orange-farm somewhere."

For the third time she sighed. Christina in her wisdom, made no comment.

V

Evie usually had her breakfast alone. Christina was late and Mrs. Colebrook
breakfasted before her family came down and was, moreover, so completely occupied in supplying the needs of her youngest daughter, that it would have been
impossible to settle herself down to a meal.

Evie was generally down by a quarter to eight; the post came at eight o'clock.
Until recently Evie had no interest in the movements of that official. Very few
letters came to the house in any circumstances and of these Evie's share was neg-
ligible.

Teddy brought a new interest to the morning for he was a faithful correspondent, and the girl would have known long before, that he was an inmate
of a superior caravanserie, had not the youth, in his modesty, written on the
plainest of notepaper. Not then, nor at any other time, did the mail have any
thrill for Mrs. Colebrook. She had a well-to-do sister living in the north who
wrote to her regularly every six months. These letters might have been published as a supplement to the Nomenclature of Diseases, for they constituted
a record of the obscure ailments which inflicted the writer's family. She had a
sister-in-law living within a mile of her, whom she seldom saw and never
heard from. Whatever letters came to the house were either for Christina or
Evie, generally for Christina.

Ambrose Sault had once presented Christina with five hundred postal cards.
It was one of the freakish things that Ambrose did, but behind it, there was a
solid reason. Christina enjoyed a constant supply of old magazines and out-of-
date periodicals. Evie collected them for her from her friends. And in these pub-
lications were alluring advertisements, the majority of which begged the reader,
italically, to send for Illustrated Catalogue No. 74, or to write to Desk H. for a
beautiful handbook describing at greater length the wonders of the articles ad-
vertised. Sometimes samples were offered, samples of baby's food, samples of
fabric, samples of soap and patent medicine, and other delectable products.

Christina had expressed a wish that she could write, and Ambrose had supplied the means. Thereafter Christina's letter-bag was a considerable one. She
knew more about motor-cars, their advantages over one another, their super-
excellent speeds and economies, than the average dealer. If you asked her what

car ran the longest distance on a can of petrol, she would not only tell you, but would specify which was the better of the gases supplied. She knew the relative nutritive qualities of every breakfast food on the market; the longest-wearing boots and the cheapest furniture.

Evie had finished her meal when the postman knocked.

"A letter from Teddy and a sample for Christina, I suppose," speculated Mrs. Colebrook, hurrying to the door. She invariably ran to meet the postman having a confused idea that it was an offence, punishable under the penal code, to keep him waiting.

There was no mail for Christina.

"Here's your letter."

Evie took the stout and expensive looking envelope, embossed redly with the name of the hotel.

"Who's writing to me?" asked Mrs. Colebrook. She turned the letter over, examined the handwriting, critically deciphered the post-mark—finally tore open the flap of the envelope.

"Well, I never!" said Mrs. Colebrook. She looked at the heading again. "Who is 'Johnson and Kennett'?" she asked.

"The house agents? There is a firm of that name in Knightsbridge. What is it, mother?"

Mrs. Colebrook read aloud.

> *"Dear Madam:* We have been requested to approach you in regard to work which we feel you would care to undertake. A client of ours has a small house on the continent, for which he is anxious to secure a housekeeper. Knowing, through Dr. Merville, that you have a daughter who is recovering from an illness, he asks me to state that he would be glad if your daughter accompanied you. There is practically no work, three servants, all of whom speak English, are kept, and our client wishes us to state that the grounds are extensive and pretty, and hopes that you will make the freest use of them, and the small car which he will leave there. He himself does not expect to occupy the house, so that you will be practically free from any kind of supervision."

The salary was named. It was generous.

Mrs. Colebrook looked over her glasses at the wondering Evie.

"Mother! How perfectly splendid!"

But Mrs. Colebrook was not so enthusiastic. Change of any kind was anathema. She had acted as housekeeper in her younger days, so that the work had no terrors for her, but—abroad!

Foreign countries meant peril. Foreigners to her were sinister men who carried knives, and were possessed of homicidal tendencies. They spoke a language expressly designed to conceal their evil intentions, and they found their recreation in plotting in underground chambers. There was a cinema at the end of Walter Street.

"There is something written on the other side," said Evie suddenly.

Mrs. Colebrook turned the sheet.

"The invitation extends to your younger daughter, if she would care to accompany you."

"Well!" said Evie, and flew up the stairs to Christina's room.

"Christina! What do you think! Mother has had a letter from a house agent offering—"

"Don't tell me!" Christina interrupted, "let me guess! They've offered her a beautiful house in the country rent free—no? Then they've offered—let me think—a house in a nice warm climate where I can bask in the sunshine and watch the butterflies flirting with the roses!" Evie's jaw dropped.

"Whatever made you think—?"

Christina snatched the letter and read, her eyes bright with excitement.

"Oh, golly!" she said and laughed so long that Evie grew alarmed.

"No, I'm not mad, and I'm not clairvoyant. Mother, what do you think of it?"

Mrs. Colebrook had followed her daughter upstairs.

"I don't know what to think," she said. She was one of those people who welcome an opportunity to show their indecision. Mrs. Colebrook liked to be "persuaded," though she might make up her mind irrevocably, it was necessary that argument round and about should be offered, before she yielded her tentative agreement.

Nobody knew this better than Christina. She drew a long sigh of relief, recognising the signs.

"We'll talk it over after Evie has gone to her pill-shop," she said, and for once Evie did not contest a description of her place of business, which usually provoked her to retort.

"I only want to say, mother, that you need not worry about me. I can get lodgings at one of the girl's hostels. I don't think I want to go abroad. In fact, I know that I don't. But it would be fine for Christina. It is my dream come true. I've always had that plan for her—a place where she could sit in the sunshine and watch the flowers grow."

Christina's smile was all loving-kindness; she took the girl's fingers in her hand and pinched them softly.

"Off to your workshop, woman," she ordered. "Mother and I want to talk about the sunny south."

"I'm not sure that I can take it," said Mrs. Colebrook dismally, "I don't like the idea of living in a foreign place—"

"We'll discuss that," said Christina in her businesslike way. "Did those linoleum patterns come?"

VI

There was no letter for Evie when she arrived at the store. Curiously enough she was not as disappointed as she expected to be. There was a chance that Ronnie would have written after his visit to the house, but when she found her desk bare, she accepted his neglect with equanimity.

Her love for Ronnie was undiminished. She faced, with a coolness which was unnatural in her, the future he had sketched, and if at times she felt a twinge of uneasiness, she put the less pleasant aspect away from her. It would not be honorable to go back on her word, even if she wanted to do so. And she did not. As to the more agreeable prospect, she did not think about that either. It was easier to dismiss the whole thing from her mind. She told herself she was being philosophical. In reality, she was solving her problem by the simple process of forgetting it.

Leaving the store at midday to get her lunch, she saw Ronnie. He was driving past in his big Rolls and apparently he did not see her. Why was she glad— for glad she was? That thought had to be puzzled out in the afternoon, with disastrous consequences to her cash balance, for when she made her return that night, she was short the price of a hot-water bottle.

But Ronnie had seen her, long before she had seen him. He was on his way to lunch with a man he knew but toward whom he had for some reason conceived a dislike. It was rather strange, because Jerry Talbot was the one acquaintance he possessed who might be called "friend." They had known one another at Oxford, they had for some time hunted in pairs, they shared memories of a common shame. Yet when Jerry's excited voice had called him on the telephone that morning and had begged him to meet his erstwhile partner at Vivaldi's, Ronnie experienced a sense of nausea. He would have refused the invitation, but before he could frame the words, Jerry had rung off.

Vivaldi's is a smart but not too smart restaurant, and had been a favorite lunching place of Ronnie's. It was all the more unreasonable in him, that he should descend beneath the glass-roofed portico with a feeling of revulsion.

Mr. Talbot had not arrived, said the beaming *maître de hotel*. Yes, he had booked a table. Ronnie seated himself in the lounge and a bellboy brought him an evening newspaper which he did not read. Had he done so, he would not have waited.

Half an hour passed and Ronnie was feeling hungry. Another quarter of an hour.

"I am going into the restaurant—when Mr. Talbot comes, tell him I have begun my lunch."

He was shown to the table and chose a simple meal from the card. At any rate, Jerry's unpardonable rudeness gave him an excuse for declining further invitations.

He had finished his lunch and had signalled for his bill when, looking round, he recognized two men at one of the window tables. He would not have approached them, but Sir John Maxton beckoned.

Dr. Merville would gladly have dispensed with his presence, thought Ronnie, and wondered if he had intruded into an important conference.

"Come and sit down, Ronnie. Lunching alone? That is rather unusual, isn't it?"

"My friend disappointed me," said Ronnie and he saw the doctor's lip curl.

"Did she—too bad," said Maxton.

"It was a 'he,'" corrected Ronnie, and knew that neither man believed him. He noticed Sir John glancing at his companion.

"Ronnie, I wonder if you can help us. Do you remember the flotation of that Traction Company of Steppe's?"

"I don't think it is much good asking Ronnie," the doctor broke in with a touch of impatience. "Ronnie's memory is a little too convenient."

"I remember the flotation—in a way," admitted Ronnie.

"Do you remember the meeting that was held at Steppe's house when he produced the draft of the prospectus?" Ronnie nodded.

"Before we go any farther, John," interrupted Merville, "I think it will be fair to Ronnie, if we tell him that there is trouble over the prospectus. Some of the financial papers are accusing us of faking the assets. The question is, was I responsible, by including properties which I should not have included, or did Steppe, in his draft, give me the facts as I published them? I don't think Ronnie will remember quite so vividly if he knows that he may be running counter to Steppe."

Ronnie did not answer.

"You see what I am driving at," Sir John went on. "There may be bad trouble if the Public Prosecutor takes these accusations seriously—which, so far he hasn't. We want to be prepared if he does."

"I cannot remember very clearly," said Ronnie. "I am not a member of the Board. But I do recall very clearly Steppe showing a draft and not only showing it, but reading it."

"Do you remember whether in that draft he referred to the Woodside Repairing Sheds; and if he did, whether he spoke of those as being the absolute property or leased property of the company?"

"The absolute property," said Ronnie. "I remember distinctly because the Woodside Repairing Shops are on the edge of a little estate which my father left me—you remember, John? And naturally I was interested."

Merville was dumbfounded. Never in his most sanguine moments did he suppose that Ronnie would assist him in this respect. Ronnie, who shivered at a word from Steppe, whose sycophantic servant he had been!

"This may come to a fight," said Sir John, "and that would mean putting you in the box to testify against Steppe. Have you quarrelled with him?"

"Good gracious, no!" said Ronnie in surprise. "Why should I quarrel with him? He doesn't worry me. In a way he is amusing, in another way pathetic. I feel sometimes sorry for him. A man with such attainments, such powers and yet so paltry! I often wonder why he prefers the mean way to the big way. He uses his power outrageously, his strength brutally. Perhaps he didn't start right—got all his proportions wrong. I was working it out last night—the beginnings of Steppe—and concluded that he must have had an unhappy childhood. If a child is treated meanly, and is the victim of mean tyrannies, he grows up to regard the triumph of meanness as the supreme end in life. His whole outlook is colored that way, and methods which we normal people look upon as despicable are perfectly legitimate in his eyes."

"Good God!" said Sir John aghast. It was the man, not the arguments which startled him.

"Children ought not to be left to the chance training which their parents give them," Ronnie went on, full of his subject, "but here, I admit, I am postulating a condition of society which will never be realized. Some day I will start my Mother College. It is a queer sounding title," he said apologetically, "but you will understand I want a great institution where we can take the illegitimate children of the country, the unwanted children. They go to baby farmers and beasts of that kind now. I want a college of babies where we will teach them and train them from their babyhood up to think and feel goodly, not piously. That doesn't matter. But bigly and generously. To have high ideals and broad visions; to—"

He stopped and blushed, conscious of their interest and stupefaction; squirmed unhappily in his chair, and rubbed his chin nervously with the knuckles of his hand.

Sir John Maxton leaned back in his chair, his face twitching.

A waiter was passing.

"Bring me a brandy," he said hoarsely, "a double brandy."

Christina had only wanted water.

VII

"What flabbergasts me is Ronnie's willingness to go against Steppe," said the doctor, just before he dropped Sir John at his chambers.

He had done most of the talking since they left Vivaldi's and Maxton had been content that he should.

"I can only suppose that Ronnie has had a row with Jan."

"Tell me this, Merville," said Sir John, leaning his arms on the edge of the door and speaking into the car, "if you believe that Steppe is the rascal I pretty well know him to be, why are you allowing Beryl to marry him?"

An awkward question for the doctor.

"Oh, well—one isn't sure. I may be in error after all. Steppe is quite a good fellow."

"Do you owe him money?" asked Maxton quietly.

Close friendship has its privileges.

"A little—nothing to speak of. You don't think I would sacrifice Beryl—?"

"I don't know, Bertram—I don't know. Why ever you took up with that crowd is beyond me."

"By the way," said the doctor, anxious to switch to another subject, "that isn't an original idea of Ronnie's—the Mother College, or whatever he calls it. Poor Ambrose Sault had exactly the same dream. I never heard the details from him, but he has mentioned it. Funny that Ronnie is taking it up?"

"Yes," Sir John waved his hand and went into the building.

He rang for his clerk.

"Do you remember a young lady coming to see me a few days ago? A Miss Colebrook—have we any record of her address?"

"No, Sir John."

"H'm—put me through to Dr. Merville's house in Park Place—I want to speak to Miss Merville."

A minute later:

"Yes—John Maxton speaking, is that you, Beryl? I want to know Miss Colebrook's address—thank you," he scribbled on his blotting pad. "Thank you—no, my dear, only I may have to get in touch with her."

He remembered after he had hung up the telephone, that Ambrose Sault had propounded a will in which the address had appeared, but the will was in the hands of Sir John's own lawyers. Ambrose had left very little, so little that it was hardly worth while taking probate. But the recollection of the will gave him the excuse he wanted.

"Sir John rang me up, father, he asked for Christina's address. Do you know why?"

"No, dear. I wonder he didn't ask me. I have been lunching with him—and Ronnie. Rather, Ronnie joined us after lunch was through—he was loquacious and strange. H'm—"

"How strange?"

"Beryl, did you notice the other night—I agree with you, Steppe was brutal—how deep his voice had grown? Boys' voices change that way when they reach an age, but Ronnie isn't a boy. Changed—*and* his views on affairs. He held John spellbound whilst he delivered himself volubly on illegitimate children and the future of the race. And the curious thing is that Ronnie hates children. Loathes them; he makes no secret of that. Says that they are irresponsible animals that should be kept on the leash."

"He said that today?"

"No—oh, a long time ago. Now he wants a big institution where they can be trained—maybe it is a variation of his leash and cage theory. How did you get on?"

Steppe had been to lunch and was in the hall about to take his departure when Sir John rang.

"He came," she said indifferently, "it was a—pleasant lunch. I think he enjoyed it. I had mealies for him and he wrestled with them happily."

"Did you discuss anything?"

"The happy day?" she said ironically. "Yes, next Tuesday. Quietly. We go to Paris the same night. He wants the honeymoon to be spent in the Bavarian Alps, and he is sending his car on to Paris. I think that is all the news."

Her indifference bothered him.

"Steppe, I am sure, is a man who improves on acquaintance," he said encouragingly.

"I am sure he does," she agreed politely, "will you tell Ronnie, or shall I write to him?"

"I will tell Ronnie," said the doctor hastily. "I don't think I should encourage a correspondence with him, if I were you, Beryl. Jan doesn't like it. He was furious about you insisting upon Ronnie coming out with us the other night."

"Very well," said Beryl.

"I think—I only think, you understand, that Steppe is under the impression that you were once very fond of Ronnie, or that you had an affair with him. He is a very jealous man. You must remember that, Beryl."

"It almost seems that I am going to be happily married," she said with a queer smile.

She did not write to Ronnie. There was nothing to be gained by encouraging a correspondence—she agreed entirely with her father on that point. Steppe she dismissed from her thoughts just as quickly as she could.

Why had Sir John asked for Christina's address? There was no reason why he should not. Perhaps Ambrose left a message—but that would have been delivered long ago. And—if Ambrose had left any message, it would be to her. The will perhaps. The doctor had told them both that Ambrose had left his few possessions to Christina. She was glad of that. Yes, it must be the will.

This served at any rate to explain Sir John's call.

The appearance of a title at her front door, caused Mrs. Colebrook considerable qualms. It was her fate never to be wearing a skirt appropriate to the social standing of distinguished visitors.

Christina was lying down. She had had an interview with the osteopath in the morning and he had insisted upon twenty-four hours of bed.

"Show him up, mother. He won't faint at the sight of a girl in bed—lawyers have a special training in that sort of thing."

"He doesn't look like a lawyer," demurred Mrs. Colebrook, "he's a sir."

She conducted the counsel upstairs with many warnings as to the lowness of roof and trickiness of tread. Mrs. Colebrook was resigned to the character and number of Christina's visitors and, in that spirit of resignation, left them.

"We have met," said Sir John and looked around for a chair.

"Sit on the bed, Sir John," she laughed, "Evie broke the leg of the chair last night."

He obeyed her, looking at her quizzically.

"I saw Ronald Morelle at lunch today," he said, "I thought it best to see you— first. And let me get the will off my mind. It has been proved and there is a hundred or so to come to you. Ambrose was not well off, his salary in fact was ridiculously small. That, however, is by the way. I saw Ronnie."

She returned his steady searching gaze.

"Did you talk to Ronnie?"

"I talked to Ronnie," he nodded, "and Ronnie talked to me. Have you ever seen a man who had the odd habit of rubbing his chin with the back of his hand? I see that you have. Ronnie for example? Yes, I thought you would have noticed it."

"How did you know that he had been to see me?"

His thin hard face softened in a smile.

"Who else would he have come to see?"

"Beryl," she answered promptly and he looked surprised.

"Beryl? I know nothing of how he felt in that quarter. Beryl! How remarkable! I knew he would come here; if you had told me that you had not seen him, I should have thought I was—"

She nodded.

"That is how I felt, Sir John. I had to shake myself hard. It was like the kind of dream one has where you see somebody you know with somebody else's face. Yes, he came here. I had to have a glass of water."

"*I* had brandy," said Sir John gravely. "As a rule I avoid stimulants—brandy produces a distressing palpitation of heart. Perhaps water would have been better for me. That is all, I think, Miss Christina," he picked up his hat. "I had to see you."

"Do you think anybody knows or ought to know?" she asked.

It was the question that had disturbed her.

"They must find out. I have a reputation for being a hard-headed Scotsman. Why the heads of Scotsmen should be harder than any other kinds of heads I do not know. What I mean is, that I cannot risk my credit as a man of truth or my judgment as a man of law or my status as one capable of conducting his own affairs without the assistance of a Commissioner in Lunacy—people must find out. I think they will, the interested people. Beryl you say? Was he—fond of her? How astounding! She is to be married very soon, you know that?"

"Should she be told—she may not have an opportunity of discovering for herself, Sir John?"

"What can you tell her?" he asked bluntly.

She was silent. She had been asking herself that. Having ushered the visitor from the premises, Mrs. Colebrook joined her daughter, for immediately following Sir John had come a grimy little boy with a grimy little package. Mrs. Colebrook had spent an ecstatic five minutes in her kitchen revelling in the fruits of authorship.

"I've got something to show you, Christina." She held the something coyly under her apron. "It was my own idea—I didn't expect them so soon—came just after I'd left you and Sir What's-his-name."

"What is it, mother?"

Mrs. Colebrook drew from its place of concealment a double-leafed card. It was edged with black and heavy black Gothic type was its most conspicuous feature Christina read:

> In loving memory of Ambrose Sault,
> Who departed this life on March 17, 19—
> at the age of fifty-three
> Mourned by all who knew him
>
> *"We ne'er shall see his gentle smile,*
> *Or hear his voice again,*
> *Yet in a very little while,*
> *We'll meet him once again."*

Christina put down the card.

"I made that up myself," said Mrs. Colebrook proudly, "all except the poetry, which I copied from poor Aunt Elizabeth's funeral card. I think that verse is beautiful."

"I think it is prophetic," said Christina, and added inconsequently, as Mrs. Colebrook thought, "I wonder if Ronnie is coming today?"

VIII

Ronnie had some such idea when he parted from Maxton and the doctor. He went home to collect the bundle of books he had packed ready to take to Christina, and there discovered the reason why his absent-minded host had forgotten to put in an appearance.

Mr. Jerry Talbot was stretched exhaustedly in a lounge chair. He was a sallow young man with a large nose and a microscopic moustache. He had bushy eyebrows, arched enquiringly. Only one eyebrow was now visible, the other and the greater part of his slick head was hidden under black silk bandages. Looking at him, Ronnie wondered what he had ever seen in the man.

"'Lo, Ronnie," he greeted the other feebly, "I tried to 'phone you but you were gone. I had a sort of faint after I spoke to you this morning, that's why I didn't turn up; so sorry. But look at me, old boy, look at me!"

"How did this happen?" asked Ronnie.

"Lola!"

Ronnie frowned. Lola? Who—? Yes, yes, Lola. He remembered.

"We had rather a hot time at my house last night, and Madame sent some of the girls along. Lola got tight and after some argument about a brooch that one of my guests had lost, Lola picked up a champagne bottle and—there you are!"

"Where is she?"

"In quod," said Mr. Jerry Talbot viciously. "I gave her in charge, and, Ronnie, she *had* the brooch! They found it at the police station. So I was right when I called her a thieving little—whatever it was I called her. It is an awkward business for me, old thing, but of course I'm swearing blue-blind that I never invited her and that she came in without—sort of drifted in from the street. Madame put me up to that. She's fed up with Lola and so are the other girls."

"Just wait a moment," said Ronnie frowning, "do I understand that Madame is going to disown this girl, this, what is her name—?"

"Lola," scoffed Mr. Talbot, "good heavens, you're not pretending that you don't know her! And you took her to Wechester with you—"

"Yes, of course I did," agreed Ronnie. "It is rather terrible work—straightening out the ravel of life—yes, I know her."

"Madame is disowning her, and so are the other girls. Between ourselves, Ritti has cleared out everything of Lola's and sent her trunks to a baggage office. None of her maids will talk, and naturally, none of the people who go to Ritti's. Lola has had a tip to shut up about Madame's, and if she is wise, she'll admit she's a street girl who had the cheek to walk into the party. I had to tell you, Ronnie, in case this infernal girl mentions you. She is being brought before the magistrate this afternoon."

And so came Lola from the dingy cells with her evening finery looking somewhat bedraggled, and standing in the pen, pale and defiant, heard the charge of assault preferred against her.

"Have you any witnesses to call?"

"None. All my witnesses have been standing on the box committing perjury," sobbed the girl, broken at last.

"I was invited. Mr. Talbot sent for me—he sent to Madame Ritti's—"

"Madame Ritti says that she hardly knows you. That with the exception of a few days last year, when you were staying with her, you have never been to the house," said the patient magistrate. "She made you leave her, because she found you were an undesirable."

"Your worship, there is a gentleman here who wishes to give evidence," said the usher.

Ronald Morelle stepped to the stand, smiled faintly at the open-mouthed surprise of Jerry Talbot, at the shocked amazement of Madame Ritti, and bowed to the magistrate.

He gave his name, place of living, and occupation.

"Now, Mr. Morelle, what can you tell us?" demanded the magistrate benevolently.

"I know this girl," he indicated the interested prisoner, "her name is Lola Pranceaux, or rather, that is the name by which she is known. She is an inmate of a house," he did not say "house," and Madame Ritti almost jumped from her seat at his description, "maintained by Madame Ritti. I can also assure your worship that she is very well known to the prosecutor, Mr. Talbot, and to me. I have taken her away to the country on more than one occasion. To my knowledge she was invited last night to Mr. Talbot's house. There is no reason why she should steal a trumpery brooch. She has jewels of her own. I myself gave her the solitaire ring she is now wearing."

The magistrate glared at Jerry Talbot.

"Are you pressing this charge?"

"No—no, your honor—worship," stammered Jerry. The man of law wrote furiously upon a paper. "You may go away, Pranceaux, you are discharged. I have heard a considerable amount of perjury in this case and I have heard the truth—not very pleasant truth, I admit. Mr. Morelle has testified for the accused with great frankness which I can admire. His habits and behavior are less admirable. Next case!"

Ronnie was the last of the party to leave the court. Lola came hurriedly across the waiting room to clasp his hand.

"Oh, Ronnie, you—pal! How lovely of you! I never thought you were such a brick! Madame looked like hell—she's pinched all my jewelry and now she'll have to give it up. Ronnie, how can I thank you?"

"Lola—come to my flat, I want to talk to you."

François who opened the door to them was not surprised. After all, one could not expect Ronald Morelle to improve in every respect. It was a pleasure to work for him, he was so considerate. Lola settled herself in the most comfortable corner of the settee and waited for François to go.

"You will have some tea?" Ronnie gave the order to a servant who was no less surprised than Lola.

"What have you done with that picture that was over the mantelpiece?" asked the girl, seeing a blankness of wall.

"I've burned it," said Ronnie.

"But it was worth thousands, Ronnie! You told me so."

"It was worth a few hundreds. If it had been a Titian I would not have destroyed it—it had its use in a gallery. But it was not. Worth a few hundreds perhaps. I burned it. François cut it into strips and we burned it in the furnace fire. François and I had a great day. He did not think the picture was pretty."

"It was your favorite?"

"*Was* it?" He was astonished. "Well, it is burned. It was too ugly. The subject—no the figures were a little ugly. Now, Lola, what are you going to do?"

She had half made up her mind.

"I shall take a flat—"

He shook his head.

"In a way, I have a recollection that you told me you had relations in Cornwall. Was I dreaming? And you said that when you had saved enough money you were going to buy a farm in Cornwall and raise hackneys. Was that a dream?"

She shook her head.

"No, that is my dream," she said, "but what is the use of talking about that, Ronnie. It would cost a small fortune."

"Could you do it on five thousand?" he asked.

"With my money and five thousand—yes."

"I will lend you three thousand free of all interest, and I will give you two thousand. I won't give it all to you, because I want a hold on you. Easy money spends itself. Will you go to Cornwall, Lola?"

François, entering, saved him from her hectic embrace.

"You're just—wonderful," she dabbed her eyes. "I know you think I'm dirt and I am—"

"Don't be silly. Why should I think that? I am not even sorry for you. Are you sorry for the train that is derailed? You put it back on the track. That is what I am doing. I am one of the derailers. It amused me, it hurt you—oh, yes, it did. I know I was not 'the first,' there would be an excuse for me in that event. We are all dirt if it comes to that—dirt is matter in the wrong place. I want to put you where you belong."

She was incoherent in her gratitude, awed a little by his seriousness and detachment, prodigiously surprised that François remained on duty.

When on her way to the hotel which was to shelter her, she read the evening newspaper, she could appreciate more fully just what Ronnie had done.

"Read this!" said Evie tragically.

Christina took the newspaper from her hands.

"'A curious case'—is that what you mean?"

The report was a full one, remembering how late in the day the charge had come up for hearing.

"Well?" said Christina, when she had finished reading.

"I shall write to Ronald." Evie was very stiff, very determined, sourly virginal. "Of course, you can't believe all that you read in the newspapers, but there is no smoke without fire."

"And every cloud has its silver lining," said Christina. "Let us *all* be trite! What is worrying you, Evie? I think it was fine of Ronnie to look after the girl."

"And they drove away from the court together!" wailed Evie.

"Why not? It is much better to go together than by taking separate routes and pretending they weren't meeting when all the time they were."

"I shall write to Ronnie, I must have an explanation," Evie was firm on this point.

Christina read the account again.

"I don't see what other explanation you can ask," she said. "He has said all that is fit for publication."

"What is this woman Lola to him?" demanded Evie furiously. "How dare he stand up—shamelessly—and admit—oh, Chris, it is *awful!*"

"It must be pretty awful for Lola, too," said Christina.

"That sort of girl doesn't mind—she likes to have her beastly name in the paper."

"You don't know," said Christina. "I won't descend to slopping over her poor mother, and her innocent sisters, and I'd die before I'd remind you that once she was like the beautiful snow. Ambrose always said that there was a lot of sympathy wasted over sinners. It is conceivable that she was quite a decent sort until somebody came along who held artistic views about marriage; most of these girls start that way, their minds go first. They get full of that advanced stuff. Some of 'em go vegetarian and wear sandals, some of 'em go on the streets. Generally speaking, the street girls are better fed. But that is how they start: they reach the streets in their own way. Some get into the studio party set. They bob their hair and hate washing. They know people who have black wallpaper and scarlet ceilings and one white rose rising from a jade vase. Evie, I have been laying on the flat of my back ever since I can remember, and I've had a procession of sinners marching around my bed—literally. Mother let people come because I was dull. I don't know Lola. She is a little above us, but Lola's kind are bred around here by the score, pigging four and five in a room; they have no reticences, there are no mysteries. All the processes of life are familiar to them as children. Then one fine day along comes Mrs. So-and-So and sits on the end of this bed and weeps and weeps until mother turns her out. There was a woman in this road who broke her heart over her daughter's disgrace. And when they came to bury the good lady they found she had never been married herself! All this weeping and wailing and talking about 'disgrace' doesn't mean anything in this neighborhood. It is conventional, expected of them, like deep mourning for widows and half mourning for aunts. We haven't produced many celebrities. We had a chorus girl who was in a divorce case, and there is a legend that Tota Belindo, the great Spanish dancer, came from this street. We turn out the tired old-looking girls that you never see up west. The Lolas come from families that care. Nice speaking people who haven't been taught to write by a sign-writer. I've heard about them and met one. She used to drink, that is how she came to Walter Street. That kind of a girl only pretends she doesn't care. She isn't like the hardy race of prostitutes we raise in Walter Street."

"I think your language is terrible, Christina! I ought to know you would defend this perfectly awful girl. You take a very lax view, Chris, it is a good thing I have a well-balanced mind—"

"You haven't," said Christina. "It isn't a month ago that you were sneering about marriage. I believe in marriage: I'm old-fashioned. Marriage is a wonderful bridge; it carries you over the time when, if you're not married, you are getting used to a strange man and comparing him unfavorably with your last. Besides, it is easier to divorce a man than to run away from him. Divorce is so easy that there is no excuse for remaining single."

"I don't know whether you're being decent or not, Christina. But there are some people who have never married all their lives, and they've been *perfectly* happy—of course, I can't tell you who they are, it is absurd to ask me. Only I know that there have been such people—in history, I mean. I believe in marriage, but it is much worse to be married to somebody you don't love than to be living with a man you do love."

"There are times when you remind me of *Uncle Tom's Cabin*," mused Christina. "I wonder why—oh, yes, little Eva who said such damnably true things so very truly. She died. The book had to have a happy ending anyway. Eva—Evie, I mean, I should write to your slave master and demand an explanation. I'll bet you won't, though!"

"Won't I?" Evie stiffened. "I have my self-respect to consider, Christina, and my friends. I hope Teddy hasn't read the case."

She wrote a letter, many words of which were underlined, and notes of exclamation stood up on each page like the masts of docked shipping.

Ronnie's answer was waiting for her next night.

"Will you come to the flat, Evie?"

Evie did not consult her sister; she took a lank young man into her confidence. Would he escort her and wait in the vestibule of the flats until she came out? Evie had discovered the need for a chaperon.

IX

François opened the door, and Evie walked hesitatingly into the lobby.

Ronnie was at his table and he was writing. He got up at once and came to meet her with outstretched hand. "It was good of you to come, Evie."

She started. His voice was so changed—his expression, too. Something had come into his face that was not there before. A vitality, an eagerness, a good humor. She was startled into beginning on a personal note.

"Why, Ronnie, dear, you *have* changed!"

She did not recognize how far she had departed from a certain program and agenda she had drawn up. Item number one was "not to call Ronnie, 'dear.'"

"Have I?" He flashed a smile at her as he pushed a chair forward and put a cushion at her back.

"Your voice even, have you had a cold?"

"No. I am getting old," he chuckled at the jest. Ronnie did not as a rule laugh at himself. "I had your letter about Lola. I thought it best that you should come. Yes, Evie, all that was in the paper was true. I know Lola."

"And she has been—all that you said, to you?"

"Yes." His voice was a little dreary. "Yes—all that."

She sat tight-lipped, trying to feel more angry than she did ("Be very angry" was item two on the agenda).

"I'm sorry that you had to know, you are so young and these things are very shocking to a good woman. Lola has gone back to her people. Naturally, I did not wish to appear in a police court, but there was a conspiracy to send this girl to prison. A late friend of mine was in it. I had to go to the court and tell the truth."

"I think it was very fine of you," she echoed Christina's words, but was wanting in Christina's enthusiasm.

"Fine? I don't know. It was a great nuisance. I have an unpleasant feeling about courts."

He rubbed his chin; Evie saw nothing remarkable in the gesture.

"Of course, Ronnie," she began, laboring under the disadvantage of calmness, for she could not feel angry, "this makes a difference. I was prepared to sacrifice everything—my good name and what people thought about me—it was horrible of you, Ronnie—to take that girl into the country when—when you knew me. I can't forgive that, Ronnie."

He stood by his table, his white hand drumming silently.

"Did you come alone?" he asked.

She hesitated.

"No, I brought a friend. A gentleman. I used to know him when I was a child."

Ronnie looked at her searchingly. His eyes were soft and kind.

"Evie, I will tell you something. From the day I first met you I intended no good to you. When I arranged that we should go to Italy, to Palermo, I knew in my wicked mind that you would grow tired of me."

He put it that way, though he was loath to tell even so small a lie.

"Since—since I saw you last, I have been thinking of you, thinking very tenderly of you, Evie. I have always liked you; Christina and I have discussed you by the hour—"

"But you have never seen Christina until this week, Ronnie!"

Ronnie's hand went to his chin.

"Haven't I?" He was troubled. "I thought—let me say I have dreamed of these discussions. I dream a great deal nowadays. Queer ugly dreams. I woke this morning when the clock was striking nine—I felt so sad."

He seemed to forget her presence, for he did not speak for a time. He had seated himself on the edge of the desk, one polished boot swinging, and he was looking past her with an intensity of gaze that made her turn to see the thing that attracted him.

Her movement roused him, and he stammered his apologies.

Taking courage from his confusion, Evie delivered herself of the predication which she had not had the courage to rehearse.

"Ronnie, I think we've both made a great mistake. I like you awfully. I don't think I could like a friend more. But I don't feel—well, you can see for yourself that we're not the same way of thinking. Don't imagine I'm a prude. I'm very broad-minded about that sort of thing, but you can see for yourself—"

He saw very clearly for himself and held out his hand.

"Friends?" he asked.

She experienced a thrill of one who creditably performs a great renunciation without any distress to herself.

"Friends!" she said solemnly.

Ronnie walked round to his writing chair and sat down. She found satisfaction in the tremor of the hand that opened a portfolio on his desk.

"And you're not hurt?" he asked anxiously.

"No, Ronnie."

"Thank God for that," said Ronald Morelle. He was looking in the black case: presently he pulled out half a dozen photographs and passed them across to her.

"How perfectly lovely!" she said.

"Yes; in some respects more lovely than Palermo. And there are no earthquakes and no rumblings from old Etna."

She was looking at the photographs of a white villa that seemed to be built on the side of a hill. One picture showed a riotous garden, another a lawn with great shady trees and deep basket chairs.

"That is my house at Beaulieu," said Ronnie, "I want you to help me with that."

She looked at him, ready to reprove.

"Your mother is the very woman to run that house and the garden was made for Christina."

Her mouth opened.

"Not you!" she gasped. "You aren't the man who wants a housekeeper. Oh, Ronnie!"

"I haven't photographs of the Palermo villa. I have sent for some. An ideal place for a honeymoon, Evie."

He came round to the back of her chair and dropped his hand on her shoulder lightly.

"When you marry a nice man, you shall go there for your honeymoon. God love you!"

She took his hand and laid it against her cheek.

For the fraction of a second—

"I like Beaulieu, Ronnie, the house is a beauty—perhaps if I hurried I could go there before mother."

In the hall below Mr. Teddy Williams discussed Canada with the hall porter.

It was one of the two subjects in which he was completely interested.

The other came down by the elevator, importantly, and they went out into Knightsbridge together.

"I've been a long time, Teddy," she snuggled her arm in his, "but—well, first of all, my answer is 'Yes.'"

He paused, and in the view of revolted passersby, kissed her.

"And—and, Teddy, we'll go to Beaulieu afterwards. Mr. Morelle has promised to let us have his house."

"Isn't that grand!" said Teddy. "We've got a town called Beaulieu in Saskatchewan."

X

"Wasn't it just like Christina not to get excited with the great news? But really Evie was to blame, because she kept the greater news to the last."

"I can't believe it. That young man who called on Christina? I really can't believe it," said Mrs. Colebrook, who could, and did, believe it.

"Why don't you yell, Chris!" demanded her indignant sister.

"I *am* yelling," said Christina placidly. "I've been yelling longer than you, for I knew that it was Ronnie's house when the letter came."

But the announcement of Evie's engagement had an electrifying effect.

"That is the first time I have ever seen Christina cry," said Mrs. Colebrook with melancholy satisfaction. "There's a lot more in Christina than people think. If she'd only showed a little more nice feeling over poor Mr. Sault, I'd have liked it better. But you can't expect everything in these days, girls being what they are. Well, Evie, you're the first to go. I don't suppose Christina will ever marry. She's too hard. Canada won't seem so far if I'm in Bolo, Boole—whatever they call it."

Evie was sitting with her mother in the kitchen; from Christina's room came crooning.

> "My dear, oh my dear,
> Have ye come from the west—"

"Why Christina sings those old-fashioned songs when she knows 'Swanee' and 'The Bull Dog Patrol '—'Bull Frog,' is it?—I can't understand."

A rat-tat at the door made Evie jump.

Mrs. Colebrook's eyes went to the faded face of a clock on the mantelshelf. Allowing for day to day variation, to which the timepiece was subject, she made it out to be past eleven.

"Don't open the door," she said. "It may be those Haggins; they've been fighting all day."

Evie went to the door.

"Who is there?"

"Beryl Merville."

Evie opened the door and admitted the girl. Outside she glimpsed the tail lamps of a car.

"You are Evie, aren't you?" Beryl was breathless. "Have you any idea where I can find Ronnie?"

"Is that Beryl?"

It was Christina's voice; she came down in her dressing gown.

"I want to find Ronnie—I have been to his flat, he is not at home. I must see him."

She was wild with fear, Christina saw that; something had happened which had thrown her off her balance and had driven her, frantic, to Ronnie Morelle.

"Come up to my room, Beryl," she said gently.

Mrs. Colebrook looked at Evie as the sound of a closing door came down.

"It looks to me like a scandal," she said profoundly.

Evie said nothing. She was wondering whether she ought not to have been indignant at the suggestion that she knew the whereabouts of Ronnie Morelle. She wished she knew Beryl better—then she might have been asked upstairs to share the secret. After all, she knew Ronnie better than anybody.

"Perhaps I am better out of it, Mother," she said. "I am not sure that Teddy would like me to be mixed up in other people's affairs."

Christina pushed the trembling girl on to the bed.

"Sit down, Beryl. What is wrong?"

Beryl's lips were quivering.

"I must see Ronnie—oh, Christina, I'm just cornered. That man—Talbot, I think his name is, he is a friend of Ronnie's, has written to father—the letter came by hand, marked 'Urgent,' whilst daddy was out, and I opened it."

She fumbled in her bag and produced a folded sheet and Christina read:

> *"Dear Dr. Merville*: I think it is only right that you should know that your daughter spent a night at Ronald Morelle's flat.
>
> Miss Merville, at Morelle's suggestion, told you that she had been to a ball at Albert Hall. I can prove that she was never at the Albert Hall that night. I feel it is my duty to tell you this, and I expect you to inform Mr. Steppe, who, I understand, is engaged to your daughter."

"How did he know?"

Beryl shook her head wearily.

"Ronald told him—about the ball. When the elevator was going down, the morning I left the flat, I saw a man walking up the stairs. He must have seen me.

Ronnie told me the night before that Jeremiah Talbot was coming to breakfast with him. I just saw him as the lift passed him—he had stopped on the landing below Ronnie's and probably recognized me. Christina, what am I to do? Father mustn't know. It seems ever so much more important to me now."

"When do you marry, Beryl?"

"The day after tomorrow. I know Ronnie has quarreled with this man. I read that story in the newspapers. It was splendid of Ronnie, splendid. It was a revelation to me."

Christina bit her lip in thought.

"I will see Ronnie—tonight. No, I will go alone. I have been resting all day. You must go home. Have you brought your car? Good. I will borrow it. Give me the letter."

Beryl protested, but the girl was firm.

"You must not go—perhaps I am wrong about Ronnie, but I don't think so. Sir John Maxton has the same mad dream."

"What do you mean?"

Christina smiled. "One day I will tell you."

The vision of her daughter dressed for going out temporarily deprived Mrs. Colebrook of speech. Before she could frame adequate comment, Christina was gone.

She dropped Beryl at her house and drove to Knightsbridge. The porter was not sure whether Mr. Morelle was in or out. It was his duty to be uncertain. He took her up to Ronnie's floor and waited until the door opened.

"My dear, what brings you here at this hour?"

He had been out, he told her. A Royal Society lecture on Einstein's Theory had been absorbing. He was so full of the subject, so alive, so boyish in his interest that for a while he forgot the hour and the obvious urgency of her call.

"I love lectures," he laughed, "but you know that. Do you remember how I was so late last night that your mother locked me out—no, not your mother— it must have been François." He frowned heavily. "How curious that I should confuse François with your dear mother."

She listened eagerly, delightedly, forgetting, too, the matter that brought her. The phenomenon had no terror for her, tremendous though it was. He was the first to recall himself to the present.

"From Beryl?" he said quickly. "What is wrong?"

She handed him the letter and he read it carefully.

"How terrible!" he said in a hushed voice. "How appallingly terrible! He says she is marrying Steppe! That can't be true, either. It would be grotesque—"

She was on the point of telling him that the marriage was due for the second day, when he went abruptly into his room. He returned, carrying his overcoat, which he put on as he talked.

"The past can only be patched," he said, "and seldom patched to look like new. Omar crystallizes its irrevocability in his great stanza. We can no more 'shatter it to bits,' than 'remould it nearer to our heart's desire.'"

"Ronnie, Beryl is to be married the day after tomorrow."

"Indeed?"

He looked at her with a half smile and then at the clock. It was a minute past midnight.

"Tomorrow?"

She nodded.

"Where are you going?"

"To see Talbot. He acted according to his lights. You can't expect a cockerel to sing like a lark. There is no sense in getting angry because things do not behave unnaturally. I made him feel very badly toward me yesterday. I think he can be adjusted. Some problems can be solved: some must be scrapped. Have you a car—Beryl's—good. Will you drop me in Curzon Street?"

She asked him no further questions and when in the car he held her hand in his, she felt beautifully peaceful and content.

"Good night, Christina. I will see Beryl tomorrow."

He closed the car door softly and she saw him knocking at No. 703 as she drove away.

The door was opened almost immediately.

"Is Mr. Talbot in, Brien?"

The butler stared.

"Why—why, yes, Mr. Morelle," he stammered.

He had not waited at table these past two days without discovering that Ronald Morelle was a name to be mentioned to the accompaniment of blasphemous et ceteras.

"He is in bed. I was just locking up. Does he expect you, Mr. Morelle?"

"No," said Ronnie. "All right, Brien, I know my way up."

He left an apprehensive servant standing irresolutely in the hall.

Jeremiah was not in bed. He was in his dressing gown before a mirror and his face was mottled with patches of gray mud—a cosmetic designed to remove wrinkles from tired eyes.

Ronnie he saw reflected in the mirror.

"What—what the devil do you want?" he demanded hollowly. "What are you doing?"

"Locking the door," said Ronnie, and threw the key on to the pillow of a four-poster bed.

"Damn you open that door—you sneaking cad!"

Mr. Talbot experienced a difficulty in breathing, his voice was a little beyond his control. Also the plaster at the corner of his mouth made articulation difficult.

"I've come to see you on rather a pressing matter," said Ronnie evenly. "You wrote a letter to Dr. Merville making a very serious charge against my friend, Miss Merville. I do not complain and I certainly do not intend abusing you. I may kill you: that is very likely. I hope it will not be necessary. If you shout or make a noise, I shall certainly kill you, because, as you will see, being an intelligent man, I cannot afford to let you live until your servants come."

Mr. Talbot sat down suddenly, a comical figure, the more so since the dried mud about his eyes and the corner of his mouth made it impossible that he should express his intense fear. As it was, he spoke with difficulty and without opening his mouth wider than the mud allowed.

"You shall pay for thish, Morelle—my God!"

"I want you to write me a letter which I shall give to Miss Merville apologizing for your insulting note to the doctor—"

With a gurgle of rage, Talbot sprang at him. Ronnie half turned and struck twice.

The butler heard the thud of a falling body; it shook the house. Still he hesitated.

"Get up," said Ronnie. "I am afraid I have dislocated your beauty spots, Jerry, but you'll be able to talk more freely."

Mr. Talbot nursed his jaw, but continued to sit on the floor. His jaw was aching and his head was going round and round. But he was an intelligent man.

When he did get up he opened a writing bureau and, at Ronnie's dictation, wrote.

"Thank you, Jerry," Ronnie pocketed the letter. "Perhaps when I have gone you will regret having written and will complain to the police; you may even write a worse letter to the doctor—who hasn't seen your first epistle, by the way. I must risk that. If you do, I shall certainly destroy you. I shall be sorry because—well, because I don't think you deserve death. You can be adjusted. Most people can. Will you put a stamp on the envelope, Jerry?"

At the street door: "Perhaps you will lose your job because you have admitted me, Brien. If that happens, will you come to me, please?"

The dazed butler said he would.

Ronnie stopped at a pillar box to post the letter and walked home.

XI

Jan Steppe was an early riser. He was up at six; at seven o'clock he was at his desk with the contents of the morning newspapers completely digested. By the time most people were sleepily inquiring the state of the weather, he had dealt with his correspondence and had prepared his daily plan.

In view of his early departure from London he had cleared off such arrears of work as there was. It was very little, for his method did not admit of an accumulation of unsettled affairs. A man not easily troubled, he had been of late considerably perturbed by the erratic behavior of certain stocks. He had every reason to be satisfied on the whole, because a miracle had happened. Klein River

Diamonds had soared to an unbelievable price. A new pipe had been discovered on the property and the shares had jumped to one hundred and twelve, which would have been a fortunate development for Dr. Merville who once held a large parcel, had not Steppe purchased his entire holding at fifteen. He did this before the news was made public that the pipe had been located. Before Steppe himself knew—as he swore, sitting within a yard of the code telegram from his South African agent that had brought him the news twenty-four hours before it was published. So that the doctor was in this position; he owed money to Steppe for shares which had made Steppe a profit.

Ronnie had had a large holding. He was deputy chairman of the company. The day following the execution of Ambrose Sault, Steppe sent him a peremptory note enclosing a transfer and a cheque. Ronnie put cheque and transfer away in a drawer and did not read the letter. For some extraordinary reason on that day he could not read easily. Letters frightened him and he had to summon all his will power to examine them. Nearly a week passed before he got over this strange repugnance to the written word.

In the meantime Jan Steppe had not seen his lieutenant. He never doubted that the transfer, signed and sealed, was registered in the books of the company. Ronnie was obedient: had signed transfers by the score without question.

On this morning of March, Mr. Steppe was delayed in the conduct of his business by the tardy arrival of the mail. There had been a heavy fog in the early hours and letter distribution had been delayed, so that it was well after half-past eight before the mail came to him.

Almost the first letter he opened was one from the secretary of Klein River. He read and growled. The writer was sorry that he could not carry out the definite instructions which he had received. Apparently Mr. Steppe was under a misapprehension. No shares held by Mr. Morelle had been transferred. There was a postscript in the secretary's handwriting:

> "I have reason to believe that Mr. Morelle has been selling your stocks very heavily. He is certainly the principal operator in the attack upon Midwell Tractions which you complained about yesterday."

Jan Steppe, dropping the letter, pushed his chair back from the desk. A thousand shares in Klein River were at issue, he could not afford to tear bullheaded at Ronnie Morelle. So this was the bear—the seller of stock! Ronnie had done something like this before, and had been warned. Steppe let his fury cool before he got Merville on the wire. When, in answer to the summons, Merville arrived, Steppe was pacing the floor, his hands deep in his trousers pockets.

"Huh, Merville? Seen Ronald Morelle lately?"

"No: he hasn't been to the house for a very long time."

"Hasn't, huh? Like him?"

The doctor hesitated.

"Not particularly: he is a distant cousin of mine. You know that."

Steppe nodded. He was holding himself in check and the effort was a strain.

"He's selling Midwell Tractions: you know that?" he mimicked savagely. "I'll break him, Merville! Smash him! The cur, the crafty cur!"

He gained the upper hand of his tumultuous rage after a while.

"That doesn't matter. But I sent him a cheque and a transfer—one minute!"

He seized the telephone and shouted a number.

"Yes, Steppe. Has a cheque been passed through payable to Ronald Morelle—I'll give you the number if you wait."

He jerked out a drawer, found the stub of a cheque book and turned the counterfoil.

"There? March seventeenth. Cheque number L.V. 971842."

He waited at the telephone, scowling absentmindedly at the doctor.

"Huh? It hasn't been presented—all right." He smashed the receiver down on the hook.

"If he had paid in the cheque I would have got him—the swine! But he hasn't. I sent orders to transfer his Klein Rivers. I thought I was doing him a good turn—just as I thought I was doing one for you, Merville."

"And he refused to allow you to make the sacrifice," said the doctor drily.

"I don't like that kind of talk, Merville," Steppe's face was dark with anger. "I want you to come with me. I'm going to see this—this thing. And I'm going to get the transfer! Make no mistake about that! Call up the filthy hound and tell him you are coming round. Don't mention me. It will give him a chance of getting rid of his women."

He listened to the telephone conversation that followed.

"What was he saying?"

"He asked me if there was anything wrong. It struck me that he was anxious—he asked me twice."

"That fellow has an instinct for trouble," said Steppe.

Ronnie was dressed, which was unusual for him, at this early hour. And the doctor noticed, could hardly help noticing, that the library was gay with flowers. This also was remarkable, for Ronnie disliked to have flowers in a room. There were daffodils, *pierce-niege*, bowls of violets, and through the open casement with its curtains fluttering in the stiff breeze, Merville saw new window boxes ablaze with tulips.

"You're admiring my flowers, Bertram," smiled Ronnie. "I had to buy them ready-grown and the gentleman who owns the flat has misgivings as to the wisdom of flower boxes—he thinks they may fall on to somebody's head. Good morning, Steppe, you look happy."

Mr. Steppe was looking and feeling quite the reverse. He forced his face into a contortion intended to be a smile.

"Good morning, Ronnie. I thought I'd come along and see you about the transfer I sent to you. You forgot to fill it up."

"Did I?" Ronnie was genuinely surprised. "I remember I had a letter from you—"

He took a heap of papers from a drawer and as he turned them over, Steppe's eyes lit up.

"That's it," he said, and offhandedly, "put your name against the seal."

Ronnie took up a pen—and paused.

"I am transferring a thousand shares in the Klein River Diamond Mining Corporation—at twelve. They are worth more than that surely? I thought I saw them quoted at a hundred and something?"

"They were twelve when I sent you the transfer," said Steppe.

"Why did you send it? I don't remember expressing a wish to sell."

Here Steppe made a fatal mistake. He had but to say, "You agreed to sell," and Ronnie would have signed. There were some incidents in his past life that he could not remember. But the temper of the big man got the better of him.

"You're not expected to ask!" he roared, bringing his big fist down on the table with a crash. "You're expected to do as you're told! Get that, Morelle! I sent you the transfer and a cheque—"

"This must be the cheque," said Ronnie. He looked at the oblong slip and tore it into four pieces before he dropped the scraps into the waste basket.

Steppe was purple with rage, inarticulate.

Then the transfer followed the cheque.

"Don't let us have a scene," said Dr. Merville nervously. "You must meet Steppe in this, Ronnie."

"I'll meet him with pleasure. I have a thousand shares apparently; he wants them—good! He can pay me the market price."

"You dog!" howled Steppe, his face thrust across the table until it was within a few inches of Ronnie's. "You damned swindler! You're going straight to the office of the Klein River Company and sign another transfer. D'ye hear?"

"How could I not hear," said Ronnie, getting up, "as to signing the transfer, I will do so, on terms—if you are civil."

"If I'm civil, huh? If I'm civil! I'll break you, Morelle! I'll break you! There's a little document in my safe that would get you five years. That makes you look foolish!"

"Take it out of your safe," said Ronnie coolly, "which I understand the police have. They will be glad to see it opened. I could open it myself if—if I could only remember. I've tried. When I saw a paragraph in the paper about Moropulos, it made me shiver—because I knew I could open the safe. I sat up all one night trying to get the word."

"You're a liar—the same damned liar that you've always been! I want that transfer, Morelle. I'm through with you—after your appearance in the police court. You're a damned fine asset to a company! You and your Lola! You will resign from the boards of my companies. Get that! And whilst I'm dealing with you, I'd like to tell you that if you attack my stocks, I'll attack you in a way that will make hell a cosy corner, huh?"

His hand shot out and he gripped Ronnie.

"Come here—you! D'ye hear me. I'll—"

Ronnie took the hand that grasped his collar and pried loose the fingers; he did this without apparent effort. The fingers had to release their hold or be broken. Then with a twist of his wrist he flung the hand away.

"Don't do that, please," he said calmly.

Steppe stood panting, grimacing—afraid. Merville felt the fear before he saw its evidence.

"How did you do that?" panted Steppe. It was the resentful curiosity of the beaten animal.

Ronnie opened his mouth and laughed long and joyously. He was, thought the doctor, like a boy conjuror who had mystified his elders and was enjoying the joke of it. Then, without warning, he became serious again and pressed a bell on his table.

"François, open the door—must you go, Bertram? I wanted to see you rather pressingly. Steppe can find his way home, can't you, Steppe? One can't imagine him getting lost—and he can ask a policeman."

"I'll settle with you later, Morelle. Come on, Merville."

The doctor vacillated.

"Come on!" roared Steppe.

"I'll see you this afternoon. I have an engagement now."

Merville went hastily after the big man. Ronnie followed, overtaking them as they were getting into the elevator.

"Will you tell Beryl that I am coming to see her tonight?"

"She'll not see you!" exploded Steppe, "no decent woman would see you—"

"What an ape you are!" said Ronnie reproachfully, "don't you realize that I'm not talking to you?"

XII

Jan Steppe's solitary lunch was served at midday, an hour which ensured his solitude, for he was a man who liked his meals alone. He was nearing the finish of his repast, his enormous appetite unimpaired by his unhappy experience of the morning, when two men mounted the steps of his Berkeley Square residence. They were unknown to one another; one had walked, the other had descended from a taxi, and they stood aside politely.

"You are first, sir," said the taller and healthier of the two.

Their cards went in to Jan Steppe together. He saw the tall man first, jumping up from the table and wiping his fingers on his serviette.

"In the library, huh?"

He looked at himself in the glass, pulled his cravat straight, and smoothed his black hair before he made his way to where the tall man, hat in hand, was waiting his pleasure.

"Well, inspector, what do you want?"

Steppe jerked open the lid of a box and presented its contents for approval.

"Thank you, sir." The inspector of police chose a cigar with care. "It is about this Traction Company of your friend's—I think I remember you saying that you were not in the flotation yourself?"

"No—I bought shares. I have a large number. What about it?"

"Well, sir," said the inspector, speaking slowly, "I am afraid that matters are very serious—very serious indeed. The Public Prosecutor has taken action and a warrant has been issued."

Steppe was prepared for this.

"Have you the warrant?"

The officer nodded.

"Can it be put off until tomorrow?"

"Absolutely impossible, sir. The best I can do is to defer its execution until late tonight. Even then I am taking a risk."

Steppe tugged at his little beard.

"Make it tonight," he said, "I'll undertake that he doesn't leave the country—you won't let him know, of course?"

"No, sir."

If Steppe had offered as much money as he could command to secure the escape of his victim, the bribe would have been rejected. But a postponement of arrest—that was another matter.

"Thank you, inspector."

"Thank *you*, sir; I shall put a couple of men on to watch him. I must do that, he will never know."

Steppe went back to the dining room very much occupied.

"No, I can't see anybody else—order the car. Who is he?"

He took up the second card.

"Mr. Jeremiah Talbot."

The man who was concerned in the case where Ronald Morelle had figured so ingloriously. Perhaps he could tell him something about Ronnie? Something to his further discredit.

"Bring him in," and when the dapper Mr. Talbot appeared: "I can give you two minutes, Mr.—er—Talbot."

"I've come from a sense of duty," began the injured Jeremiah. "I'm certainly not going to be intimidated by threats from a beast like Ronald Morelle—"

Steppe cut him short.

"Is it about Ronald Morelle? I haven't time to go into your quarrels."

"It is about Ronnie—and Beryl Merville."

Jan Steppe gazed at the man moodily, then into the fire—then back to Jeremiah Talbot.

"Sit down," he said. "Now—"

Talbot told his story plainly and without trimmings, save that his hatred of Ronnie led him to digress from time to time.

"You saw; you are certain?"

"Absolutely, I ran down the stairs. There was a fellow taking photographs outside, a man with a brown beard—"

Moropulos! And the photograph was that of Beryl Merville!

"Go on."

"That is all. I felt it my duty to tell you. If Ronald Morelle attempts to browbeat me, I'll give him in charge—"

"All right—you can go. Thank you."

Jan Steppe had his own peculiar views on women in general, the relationship of Beryl with Ronnie Morelle in particular. Things of that kind happened. He had thought some such affair was possible, and was neither shocked nor outraged. Beryl did not love him, he knew: she loved Morelle. He grinned wickedly.

"The car, sir."

His first call was at the registrar's office. The special license had been secured a week before.

"I can marry you at half-past two," said the registrar. "We like a day's notice, but in an exceptional case—"

Steppe paid.

The Mervilles had not gone in to lunch when he arrived. Beryl was in her room, the doctor working in his study. Steppe wondered what he was working at.

"I want to see Miss Merville—don't disturb the doctor."

She came down, a listless, hopeless girl. Intuitively she knew that he had been told. What would he do: she stopped at the door of her father's study, fighting her fear. Should she tell him first? In the end she came to Steppe.

"Well, Beryl. What is this I hear about Ronald Morelle and you, huh?"

"What have you heard?"

"That you've been his mistress—that's what I've heard. Damned fine news for a bridegroom, huh? Does your father know?"

She shook her head.

"Do you want him to know?"

"I don't care."

"You don't care, huh? Got that way now, so that you don't care. You'll marry me this afternoon."

She looked up.

"This afternoon?"

"Yuh. You'd better tell the doctor; you can tell him anything else you like about Morelle—but if you don't tell, I won't."

Her hand had gone up to her cheek.

"This afternoon—I can't—give me a day—you said it would be tomorrow. I'm not ready."

"This afternoon at half past two. Will you tell the doctor, or shall I?"

She was trying to think.

"I'll tell him. As you wish. This afternoon."

Lunch went into the dining room. Nobody touched food. Steppe had to return to the house to get the wedding ring, send telegrams changing the date of his arrival in Paris, settle such minor details of household management as the change necessitated.

He was at the registrar's office when they came, Dr. Merville and the white-faced girl. In a cab behind the doctor's car travelled two Scotland Yard detectives.

The ceremony was simple. The repetition of a few sentences and Beryl Merville became Beryl Van Steppe. She did not know that his name was Van Steppe until she saw the marriage certificate.

"You can go home with your father. Be ready to leave by the boat train tonight."

So he dismissed her. All the way back to the house the doctor was talking, cheerfully, helpfully. She did not hear him. She was looking at the broad gold ring on her finger.

As they were entering the house her father leaned back, and scrutinized the street.

"I'm sure I've seen those two men before—weren't they waiting outside the registrar's, Beryl?"

Beryl had seen only one man. A man with a black beard, a broad, swarthy face and two eyes wherein burned the fires of hell.

XIII

Evie brought the news at a run. She had been shopping with Teddy—the store had given her a holiday, and there was some talk of subscribing for a wedding present.

"I said to Teddy, 'let's stop and see who it is'—we knew it was somebody swaggering by the two cars and the cab outside the door. And then I thought that I knew one of the cars. I said, 'Teddy, I'll bet it is Beryl Merville'—and it was!"

Christina was pale.

"She wasn't to be married until tomorrow," she insisted.

"Well, she's married. My dear, she looked awful. Teddy says—"

"Oh, damn Teddy!" snapped Christina and was sorry. "I don't mean that, but I'm so used to damning your young men that I can't get out of the habit. Did they go away together—Steppe and she?"

"No—she's gone back to the house with her father. Steppe—is he a man with black whiskers—well, he went alone."

Christina kicked off her slippers determinedly. "I'm going to see her," she said.

"What do you think *you* can do?" asked the scornful Evie. "Take my advice, Christina, never interfere between man and wife. Teddy says—"

"I repeat anything I have already said about Teddy," remarked Christina. "Chuck over my shoes, Evie."

She could not tell Beryl. She could tell nobody. Ronnie Morelle must be interpreted by those who saw.

She strode out thanking God for life, and Ambrose Sault for the tingle of her soles upon the pavement. Spring was in the air, the park trees were studded with emerald buttons; some impatient bushes had even come fully into leaf before the season had begun. The sky was blue and carried white and majestic clouds; the birds were chattering noisily above her as she came through the park and the earth smelled good, as it only smells in spring when the awakening of life within its bosom releases a million peculiar odors that combine in one fragrant nidor.

To Beryl's eyes the girl, with her peaked face and her flaming hair, was a vision of radiance.

"So good of you—" Beryl was on the verge of a breakdown as Christina Colebrook put her arms about her shoulders. "So lovely of you, Christina—I wanted to see you. I hadn't the energy to move—or the heart."

"Why today?"

"Steppe knows everything. He insisted upon today. As well today as tomorrow. I am troubled about father. I feel that something dreadful is going to happen. He is so restless and he has asked John Maxton to come; John was a great friend of my mother's. In a way I'm almost glad that there is this other trouble hanging over us—that sounds cruel to poor daddy, but it does distract me from—thoughts."

"What is this other trouble?"

But Beryl shook her head.

"I don't know. There has been some unpleasantness about a company father floated. Jan Steppe did it really, father is only a figurehead. He has had people to see him, people from the Public Prosecutor's office. He doesn't talk much about it to me, but I have a premonition that all is not well. But, Christina, I'm just whining and whining at you, poor girl!"

"Whine," said Christina. "Go on whining. *I* should scream! Beryl, my love, you have to do something for me, something to relieve my heart of a great unhappiness. I intended seeing you today—you had my letter?—well, I'm too late to stop you marrying. I thought I would be in time; but not too late to save your immortal soul."

"What—?"

"Wait. I want you to promise me, by the man we hold mutually sacred, that you will do as I ask. No matter at what inconvenience or danger."

"I will do anything you ask," said Beryl quietly.

"What time do you meet this Steppe?"

"I call for him at eight o'clock. The boat train leaves at nine-thirty."

"At eight o'clock you will go to Ronnie Morelle." \

"No, no! I can't do that—"

"You promised. You will see him: go to his flat and see him. Tell him you are married. Tell him the truth, that you are going away with a man you hate. Tell him that Steppe knows."

"I can't! You don't know what you're asking, Christina, I've—begged Ronnie before—begged him to run away with me. I can't do that again. It is impossible."

"You need beg nothing—nothing. Just tell him."

She caught the girl to her.

"Beryl, you're going to do what I ask you, dear?"

"Yes—you wouldn't ask me—"

"Out of caprice," finished Christina, "or cussedness, or a wish to try experiments. No. But you must go, Beryl. I—I think I should kill myself if you didn't."

"Christina! What do you mean?"

"I mean it is life to go and death not to go!" said Christina, with a sort of ferocity that staggered her companion. "That is what I mean." In a quieter tone: "Have you seen Ronald lately?"

Beryl shook her head.

"No. I saw him that night—the night they killed Ambrose—oh—"

"Don't gulp," warned Christina.

"I'm not gulping. I'm yearning. I saw him yearning once, the dear, I am trying to find some of his strength now. It is a little difficult."

On the way home Christina dropped into a telephone booth and paid three precious pennies.

"Ronnie! Christina speaking. Beryl is coming to see you tonight. At eight. Wait for her—don't dare to be out."

She cut off before he could ask questions.

XIV

Sir John Maxton stayed to dinner. Beryl did not put in an appearance until just before eight.

"Already, Beryl?"

Dr. Merville scrambled up. His face was gray, his eyes sunken, the hands that took her by the shoulders shook.

"My dear—I hope I have done right. I hope I have done right, my little girl."
She tried to smile as she kissed him.

"Can't I take you to Berkeley Square, Beryl?" asked Sir John.

She shook her head.

"No, thank you, John—goodbye."

They stood together, bareheaded, on the pavement, and saw her go. A drizzle of rain was falling, the dull red furnace glow of London was in the sky.

Together they walked back to the dining room and Maxton did not break in upon the doctor's thoughts.

"Thank God she's gone," he whispered at last. "John, I'm at the end, I know it. Perhaps he'll help after—I'll be satisfied if he makes Beryl happy."

"He could help now," said John Maxton. "Why do you deceive yourself? How can you hope for anything from Steppe? I wish to God I had known that this infernal marriage was for today."

"She wished it," said the doctor. "I should not have insisted, but she wished it. Steppe isn't a bad fellow—"

"Steppe is a scoundrel and nobody knows that better than yourself. Why are you in any danger from the law? Because you copied a draft prospectus which Steppe drew up and issued it in your own name. Steppe has only to appear as a witness and tell the truth, and he would find himself in your place—supposing this comes to a prosecution. But he won't. He could have saved—"

He stopped.

"Ambrose Sault?"

"He could have saved the body of Ambrose Sault from annihilation by a word! The draft of the prospectus is in existence. It is in the safe that Sault made. Steppe could open it and ninety-nine hundredths of your responsibility would be wiped out. But he won't risk his own skin."

"You think they will prosecute, John?"

Maxton considered. There was nothing to be gained by evasion.

"I am sure they will," he said quietly. "If I were the Public Prosecutor I should apply for a warrant on the facts as I know them."

The door opened.

"Will you see two gentlemen from Whitehall?" the maid asked.

It was Maxton who nodded.

"Bertram—you have to meet this ordeal—courageously."

The doctor got up as the detectives entered.

"I am Detective Inspector Lord, from Scotland Yard," said the first of them. "You are Dr. Bertram Merville? I have to take you into custody on a charge of misrepresentation under the Companies Act."

"Very good," said Dr. Merville, "may I go to my room for a moment?"

"No sir," said the inspector. "I understand you keep a medicine chest in your room."

Maxton nodded approvingly.

He did not go to the police station with the prisoner. He went in search of Beryl—and Jan Steppe.

XV

Ronald Morelle on the hearthrug before his electric radiator watched the fiery little wave that moved along the surface of the element.

In such moments of complete detachment, when his mind was free from the encumbrance of active thought, he received strange impressions. They were not memories, he told himself, any more than are those faces which grow and fade in the darkness just between sleeping and waking. They were whisps of dreams that were born and dissolved in a fraction of time. He had seen such clouds grow instantly above the lake of Geneva, and watching them from the terraces of Caux, had of a sudden missed them, even as he watched.

So these impressions appeared and vanished. There was one that was distinct and more frequent than any other. It was of a hut, long and narrow. Two broad sloping benches ran down each side and these, at night, were packed with sleeping men. The door to the hut was very solid and was locked by a soldier—he could sometimes hear the swish of the soldier's boots as he paced the gravel path surrounding the hut. Once a man had died—Ronnie helped to carry him out. It was a plague that had struck the island—island? Yes, it was an island, in the tropics, for the nights were very hot and the plants luxurious.

"There is a ring—will M'sieur require me?"

"Yes, stay, François."

Ronnie jumped up and dusted his trousers. Another second, and he was halfway across the room.

"I'm so glad that I came, Ronnie: it wasn't that Christina insisted: I wanted to see you, dear."

How pale, how ill she looked, he thought, with a sinking heart. She was going away somewhere, for she was dressed for travelling.

"Beryl, my dear, you are not well?"

"Oh, I'm well enough, Ronnie," she glanced back at the door. She expected that any moment Steppe would come—he would guess. There was a train to be caught too—the madness of this visit!

He held both her hands in his.

"Beryl, they tell me you are going to be married—that isn't right, Beryl, is it?"
She nodded.

"But Beryl—" he stopped. "I saw you once and I was cruel, wasn't I?"

"What is the use of talking about it? Ronnie, I hope you are going to be a better man than you have been. I admire you so much for defending that poor girl. You are trying to be different now."

"I think so."

"And—I'm believing you, Ronnie. It is not easy to give up that life? Won't you want to go back to it again?"

He smiled.

"I will take away from thee the desire of thine eyes, with a stroke, yet neither shalt thou mourn nor weep."

She looked at him fearfully.

"Ronnie, how solemn you are—and you are so strong too—I feel it. Ronnie, I am married!"

He bent his head as though he had not heard her.

"I was married today to Steppe. Oh God, it is awful, Ronnie, awful!"

He put his arm about her and kissed the tearful face, and then—

Crash!

The door shook again.

"I think that is your husband," said Ronnie gently, "will you go into my room?"

He opened the door for her and said "yes" with his eyes to the alarmed François.

Steppe flung himself into the room. In his great fur-collared coat he looked a giant of a man.

"Well?" said Ronnie.

"Where's my wife!" The man's voice vibrated. "You swine! Where is my wife—she's come here—I know, to her damned paramour. Where is she?" he bellowed.

"She is in my room—" said Ronnie, and Jan Steppe staggered back as if he were shot.

"In your room!" He sounded as if he were being strangled. "Well—now she can come to my room! You called me an ape this morning, I'll show you what kind of an ape I can be! Beryl!" he roared.

She came out, a tragic figure of despair.

"So you had to come and see him, eh—"

François had opened the door again, and a man came in unannounced.

"Steppe!"

It was John Maxton, and Steppe turned with a snarl.

"Merville has been arrested."

"Well?"

"My father! Arrested? Jan, I must go back—"

"You'll go with me, huh! I haven't married your father or your lover, either."

"What are you going to do?" demanded Maxton sternly.

"Catch my train! You can't stop me—"

"Steppe, for God's sake think what you're doing." Sir John Maxton was pleading now with a greater intensity than he had ever pleaded before a tribunal. "You could save Merville—you have the draft of the prospectus—"

"In the safe! In the safe!" roared Steppe his face inflamed with fury. "Come,

Beryl."

He held out his hand, but she shrank back behind Ronnie.

"Then open the safe," demanded Maxton.

"Go to hell! All of you—don't stand up to me, Morelle, or I'll kill you! Beryl—"

"What is the word—this combination word, Steppe? You can get away tonight, they will find nothing until the morning—"

"I won't tell you, damn you! I'll see you—"

"Judas!"

Ronnie Morelle stood, his finger outstretched stiffly pointing at the other.

"Judas—J—U—D—A—S. That is the word!"

Open-mouthed Steppe lurched toward him.

"You—you." He struck, but his blow went wide and then Ronnie had him by the shoulders and they looked into one another's eyes.

Beryl, horrified, sick with fear, saw her husband's face go livid, saw him grimace painfully, monstrously.

"I know you—!" he screamed. "I know you! *You're Sault! Ambrose Sault!*— you're dead! They hanged you, blast you! Ambrose Sault—" He put out his huge hands as to ward off a ghastly sight.

"Come along, Beryl," he mumbled, "you mustn't stay here—it is Sault. Oh, Christ—"

He went down in a heap.

Beryl came forward groping like one blind.

"Ronnie—" She stared into his eyes, and in his agitation he put his knuckle to his chin. "—oh, my dear!"

XVI

"Personally," said Evie, "I think she should have waited six months. After all, Christina, even if her father was acquitted, there is a scandal. I admit she was a wife in name only, as the pictures say, but she was Mrs. Steppe. Teddy quite agrees with me: he says that it isn't decent to marry within a week of your husband's death. Don't think I'm hurt about Ronnie getting married, I wouldn't be so small. It is the principle of the thing."

Christina's mouth was bulging: Ronnie had sent her imposing quantities of candy.

"Pass me that book about Beaulieu that you're sitting on, and don't talk so much," she said. "You're a jealous cat."

"I'm not, I declare I'm not. I like Ronnie I admit, but there was something lacking in him—soul, that's what it was, soul!"

"Did Ambrose Sault have soul?"

"Why—yes, I always thought he had soul."

"Then shut up!" said Christina, opening her book.

THE END

Edgar Wallace Bibliography

Series
Four Just Men
The Four Just Men (1905)
The Council of Justice (1908)
The Just Men of Cordova (1917)
The Law of the Four Just Men
(1921; aka US as Again the Three
Just Men)
The Three Just Men (1926)
Again the Three Just Men (1929;
aka Again the Three & US as The
Law of the Three Just Men)

Commissioner Sanders
Sanders of the River (1911; stories)
The People of the River (1912;
stories)
The River of Stars (1913; novel)
Bosambo of the River (1914; stories)
The Keepers of the King's Peace
(1917; stories)
Sandi the Kingmaker (1922; stories)
Sanders (1926; aka US as Mr.
Commissioner Sanders; stories)
Again Sanders (1928; stories)

Lieutenant Bones
Bones (1915; stories)
Lieutenant Bones (1918; stories)
Bones in London (1921; stories)
Bones of the River (1923; stories)

J. G. Reeder
Room 13 (1924)
The Mind of Mr J. G. Reeder (1925;
aka US as The Murder Book of
J.G. Reeder)
Terror Keep (1927)
Red Aces (1929)
The Guv'nor and Other Stories
(1932; aka US as Mr. Reeder
Returns)

Sergeant Elk
The Nine Bears (1910; aka The
Cheaters & The Other Man;
revised as Silinski—Master
Criminal, 1930)
The Fellowship of the Frog (1925)
The Joker (1926; aka The Park Lane
Mystery & US as The Colossus,
1932)
The Twister (1928)
The India-Rubber Men (1929; aka
The Pool)
White Face (1930)

Educated Evans
Educated Evans (1924; stories)
More Educated Evans (1926;
stories)
Good Evans (1927; stories)

Ringer
The Gaunt Stranger (1925; aka
Police Work, US as The Ringer)
Again The Ringer (1929; aka US as
The Ringer Returns; stories)

Smithy & Nobby
Smithy (1905)
Smithy Abroad (1909)
Smithy and the Hun (1915)
Nobby (1916)

Supt. Minter
Big Foot (1927)
The Lone House Mystery (1929;
aka The Lone House)

Tam of the Scouts
Tam o' the Scoots (1918)
The Fighting Scouts (1919)

Novels
Angel Esquire (1908)
The Duke in the Suburbs (1909)
Captain Tatham of Tatham Island
    (1909; also published as Eve's
    Island; revised as The Island Of
    Galloping Gold 1916)
Private Selby (1912)
The Fourth Plague (1913; aka The
    Red Hand)
Grey Timothy (1913; aka Pallard
    the Punter)
The Man Who Bought London
    (1915)
The Melody of Death (1915)
1925—The Story of a Fatal Peace
    (1915)
A Debt Discharged (1916)
Tomb of T'Sin (1916)
The Secret House (1917)
The Clue of the Twisted Candle
    (1918)
Down-Under Donovan (1918)
The Strange Lapses of Larry Loman
    (1918; serialized only)
Those Folk of Bulboro (1918)
The Adventures of Heine (1919)
The Green Rust (1919)
Kate Plus 10 (1919)
The Man Who Knew (1919)
The Daffodil Mystery (1920; aka
    The Daffodil Murder)
Jack o' Judgment (1920)
The Book of All Power (1921)
The Day of Uniting (1921)
The Angel of Terror (1922; aka The
    Destroying Angel)
The Crimson Circle (1922)

Flying Fifty-five (1922)
Mr. Justice Maxwell (1922; aka
    Take-a-Chance Anderson)
The Valley of Ghosts (1922)
Captains of Souls (1922)
The Clue of the New Pin (1923)
The Green Archer (1923)
The Missing Million (1923)
The Dark Eyes of London (1924;
    aka The Croakers)
Double Dan (1924; US as Diana of
    Kara-Kara)
The Face in the Night (1924; aka
    The Diamond Men & The
    Ragged Princess)
The Sinister Man (1924)
The Three Oak Mystery (1924)
The Blue Hand (1925; aka Beyond
    Recall)
The Daughters of the Night (1925)
King by Night (1925)
The Strange Countess (1925)
The Avenger (1926; aka The Hairy
    Arm)
Barbara on Her Own (1926)
The Black Abbot (1926)
A Debt Discharged (1926)
The Door with Seven Locks (1926)
The Man from Morocco (1926; aka
    Soul in Shadows & US as The
    Black)
The Million Dollar Story (1926)
The Northing Tramp (1926; aka
    The Tramp)
Penelope of the "Polyantha" (1926)
The Square Emerald (1926; aka The
    Woman)
The Terrible People (1926; aka The
    Gallows' Hand)
We Shall See! (1926; US as The
    Gaol-Breakers)
The Yellow Snake (1926; aka The
    Black Tenth)

Flat 2 (1927)

The Feathered Serpent (1927; aka Inspector Wade & Inspector Wade and the Feathered Serpent)

The Forger (1927; aka The Counterfeiter)

Hand of Power (1927; aka The Proud Sons of Ragusa)

The Man Who Was Nobody (1927)

The Mixer (1927)

Mr Justice Maxwell (1927)

Number Six (1927; novella)

The Squeaker (1927; aka The Sign of the Leopard & US as The Squealer)

The Traitor's Gate (1927)

The Brigand (1928)

The Double (1928)

The Flying Squad (1928)

The Gunner (1928; aka Gunman's Bluff)

A King by Night (1928)

Four Square Jane (1929; aka The Fourth Square)

The Golden Hades (1929; aka Stamped in Gold & The Sinister Yellow Sign)

The Green Ribbon (1929)

The Iron Grip (1929)

Planetoid 127 (1929)

The Calendar (1930)

The Clue of the Silver Key (1930; aka The Silver Key)

The Day of Uniting (1930)

Down Under Donovan (1930)

The Feathered Serpent (1930)

The Hand of Power (1930)

John Flack (1930)

The Lady of Ascot (1930)

The Thief in the Night (1930)

The Coat of Arms (1931; aka The Arranways Mystery)

The Devil Man (1931; aka Sinister Street, Silver Steel & The Life and Death of Charles Peace)

The Man at the Carlton (1931; aka The Mystery of Mary Grier)

On the Spot: Violence and Murder in Chicago (1931)

The Frightened Lady (1932; aka The Mystery of the Frightened Lady)

When the Gangs Came to London (1932; aka Scotland Yard's Yankee Dick & The Gangsters Come to London)

The Green Pack (1933; play novelization by Robert George Curtis)

The Man Who Changed His Name (1935; play novelization by Robert George Curtis)

The Mouthpiece (1935; screenplay novelization by Robert George Curtis)

Sanctuary Island (1936; screenplay novelization by Robert George Curtis)

Smoky Cell (1936; play novelization by Robert George Curtis)

The Table (1936; screenplay novelization by Robert George Curtis)

The Road to London (1986)

Story Collections

Admirable Carfew (1914)

Adventures of Heine (1919)

The Books of Bart (1923)

Chick (1923)

The Black Avons (1925)

The Brigand (1927)

The Mixer (1927)

Elegant Edward (1928)

The Orator (1928)

Thief in the Night (1928)
The Big Four (1929; aka Crooks of
    Society)
The Black (1929; aka Blackmailers I
    Have Foiled)
The Cat Burglar (1929)
Circumstantial Evidence (1929)
Fighting Snub Reilly (1929)
For Information Received (1929)
The Ghost of Down Hill & The
    Queen of Sheba's Belt (1929)
The Governor of Chi-Foo (1929)
The Iron Grip (1929)
The Lady of Little Hell (1929)
The Little Green Man (1929)
The Lone House Mystery (1929)
The Prison-Breakers (1929)
The Reporter (1929)
The Terror (1929)
Killer Kay (1930)
The Lady Called Nita (1930)
Mrs William Jones and Bill (1930)
The Stretelli Case and Other
    Mystery Stories (1930)
Sergeant Sir Peter (1932; aka
    Sergeant Dunn, C.I.D.)
The Steward (1932)
The Last Adventure (1934)
Nig-nog and Other Humorous
    Stories (1934)
Woman from the East (1934)
The Edgar Wallace Reader of
    Mystery and Adventure (1943)
The Undisclosed Client (1963)
The Man Who Married His Cook
    (1976)
The Sooper and Others (1984)
The Death Room: Strange and
    Startling Stories (1986)
Winning Colors: The Racing Stories
    of Edgar Wallace (1991)

Omnibus Editions

The New Mammoth Mystery Book
    (1920)
Four Complete Novels (1925)
Three Complete Novels by Edgar
    Wallace (1925)
Fourty-Eight Short Stories (1929)
The Scotland Yard Book of Edgar
    Wallace (1932)
Edgar Wallace Foursome (1933)
The Edgar Wallace Reader of
    Mystery and Adventure (1943)
The Edgar Wallace Souvenir Book:
    Four Complete Novels (1950)
Selected Novels (1985)

Plays and Screenplays

African Millionaire (1904; play, pub
    1972)
Forest of Happy Dreams (1910;
    play, pub 1935)
Dolly Cutting Herself (1911; play,
    unpublished)
The Manager's Dream (1914;
    musical play)
Nurse and Martyr (1915; play,
    filmed same year)
The Four Just Men (1921; filmed
    screenplay)
M'Lady (1921; play, unpublished)
Double Dan (1926; play,
    unpublished)
The Mystery of Room 45 (1926;
    play, unpublished)
A Perfect Gentleman (1927; play,
    unpublished)
The Terror (1927; play, filmed 1928)
The Traitor's Gate (1927; play,
    filmed as The Yellow Mask, 1930)
The Man Who Changed His Name
    (1928; play, screenplay 1934)
The Mark of the Frog (1928; filmed
    screenplay)

The Ringer (1928; filmed screenplay 1928 & 1931; play, 1929)

The Squeaker (1928; play, filmed screenplay, 1930)

The Valley of the Ghosts (1928; filmed screenplay)

Persons Unknown (1929; play, novelized as White Face, filmed 1932)

Prince Gabby (1929; filmed screenplay)

Red Aces (1929; filmed screenplay)

The Calendar (1929; play, pub 1932)

Criminal at Large (1930; filmed screenplay, pub 1934)

The Mouthpiece (1930: play, novelized by Robert George Curtis, 1935)

Should a Doctor Tell? (1930; filmed screenplay)

Smoky Cell (1930; play, novelized by Robert George Curtis, 1936)

To Oblige a Lady (1930; play, filmed 1931)

The Case of the Frightened Lady (1931; play, pub 1932)

The Old Man (1931; play, filmed screenplay)

The Green Pack (1932; play, filmed 1934)

Hound of the Baskervilles (1932; filmed screenplay)

King Kong (1932; filmed screenplay, though only parts of it were used; novelization by Delos W. Lovelace, 1932)

The Lad (1932; play, filmed 1935)

Sanctuary Island (date unknown; screenplay novelized by Robert George Curtis, 1936)

The Table (date unknown; screenplay novelized by Robert George Curtis, 1936)

Poetry

The Mission That Failed (1898)

War and Other Poems (1900)

Writ in Barracks (1900)

Non fiction

Unofficial Despatches (1901)

Famous Scottish Regiments (1914)

Field Marshall Sir John French and His Campaigns (1914)

Heroes All: Gallant Deeds of the War (1914)

The Standard History of the War 4 Vols. (1914-1916)

The War of the Nations (1914; with William le Queux)

Kitchener's Army and the Territorial Forces: The Full Story of a Great Achievement (1915)

Famous Men and Battles of the British Empire (1917)

Real Shell-Man: The Story of Chetwynd of Chilwell (1919)

This England (1927; stories)

People: Autobiography (1926)

The Trial of Patrick Herbert Mahon (1928)

Great Stories of Real Life (1930; with William le Queux)

The Trial of the Seddons and Other True Tales of Suspense (1930)

My Hollywood Diary (1932)

Other Stark House books you may enjoy...

Clifton Adams Death's Sweet Song /
Whom Gods Destroy $19.95
Benjamin Appel Brain Guy / Plunder $19.95
Benjamin Appel Sweet Money Girl /
Life and Death of a Tough Guy $21.95
Malcolm Braly Shake Him Till He Rattles /
It's Cold Out There $19.95
Gil Brewer Wild to Possess / A Taste for Sin $19.95
Gil Brewer A Devil for O'Shaugnessy /
The Three-Way Split $14.95
Gil Brewer Nude on Thin Ice /
Memory of Passion $19.95
W. R. Burnett It's Always Four O'Clock /
Iron Man $19.95
W. R. Burnett Little Men, Big World /
Vanity Row $19.95
Catherine Butzen Thief of Midnight $15.95
James Hadley Chase Come Easy—Go Easy /
In a Vain Shadow $19.95
Andrew Coburn Spouses & Other Crimes $15.95
Jada M. Davis One for Hell $19.95
Jada M. Davis Midnight Road $19.95
Bruce Elliott One is a Lonely Number /
Elliott Chaze Black Wings Has My Angel $19.95
Don Elliott/Robert Silverberg
Gang Girl / Sex Bum $19.95
Don Elliott/Robert Silverberg
Lust Queen / Lust Victim $19.95
Feldman & Gartenberg (ed)
The Beat Generation & the Angry Young Men $19.95
A. S. Fleischman Look Behind You Lady /
The Venetian Blonde $19.95
A. S. Fleischman Danger in Paradise /
Malay Woman $19.95
A. S. Fleischman The Sun Worshippers /
Yellowleg $19.95
Ed Gorman The Autumn Dead /
The Night Remembers $19.95
Arnold Hano So I'm a Heel / Flint /
The Big Out $23.95
Orrie Hitt The Cheaters / Dial "M" for Man $19.95
Elisabeth Sanxay Holding Lady Killer /
Miasma $19.95
Elisabeth Sanxay Holding The Death Wish /
Net of Cobwebs $19.95
Elisabeth Sanxay Holding Strange Crime in Bermuda /
Too Many Bottles $19.95
Elisabeth Sanxay Holding The Old Battle-Ax /
Dark Power $19.95
Elisabeth Sanxay Holding The Unfinished Crime /
The Girl Who Had to Die $19.95
Elisabeth Sanxay Holding Speak of the Devil /
The Obstinate Murderer $19.95
Russell James Underground / Collected Stories $14.95
Day Keene Framed in Guilt / My Flesh is Sweet $19.95

Day Keene Dead Men Don't Talk / Hunt the Killer /
Too Hot to Hold $23.95
Mercedes Lambert Dogtown / Soultown $14.95
Dan J. Marlowe/Fletcher Flora/Charles Runyon
Trio of Gold Medals $15.95
Dan J. Marlowe The Name of the Game is Death /
One Endless Hour $19.95
Stephen Marlowe Violence is My Business /
Turn Left for Murder $19.95
Wade Miller The Killer / Devil on Two Sticks $19.95
Wade Miller Kitten With a Whip /
Kiss Her Goodbye $19.95
Rick Ollerman Turnabout / Shallow Secrets $19.95
Vin Packer Something in the Shadows /
Intimate Victims $19.95
Vin Packer The Damnation of Adam Blessing /
Alone at Night $19.95
Vin Packer Whisper His Sin /
The Evil Friendship $19.95
Richard Powell A Shot in the Dark /
Shell Game $14.95
Bill Pronzini Snowbound / Games $14.95
Peter Rabe The Box / Journey Into Terror $19.95
Peter Rabe Murder Me for Nickels /
Benny Muscles In $19.95
Peter Rabe Blood on the Desert /
A House in Naples $19.95
Peter Rabe My Lovely Executioner /
Agreement to Kill $19.95
Peter Rabe Anatomy of a Killer /
A Shroud for Jesso $14.95
Peter Rabe The Silent Wall /
The Return of Marvin Palaver $19.95
Peter Rabe Kill the Boss Good-By /
Mission for Vengeance $19.95
Peter Rabe Dig My Grave Deep / The Out is Death /
It's My Funeral $21.95
Brian Ritt Paperback Confidential:
Crime Writers $19.95
Sax Rohmer Bat Wing / Fire-Tongue $19.95
Douglas Sanderson Pure Sweet Hell /
Catch a Fallen Starlet $19.95
Douglas Sanderson The Deadly Dames /
A Dum-Dum for the President $19.95
Charlie Stella Johnny Porno $15.95
Charlie Stella Rough Riders $15.95
John Trinian North Beach Girl /
Scandal on the Sand $19.95
Harry Whittington A Night for Screaming /
Any Woman He Wanted $19.95
Harry Whittington To Find Cora /
Like Mink Like Murder / Body and Passion $23.95
Harry Whittington Rapture Alley / Winter Girl /
Strictly for the Boys $23.95
Charles Williams Nothing in Her Way /
River Girl $19.95

Stark House Press, 1315 H Street, Eureka, CA 95501
707-498-3135 www.StarkHousePress.com

Retail customers: freight-free, payment accepted by check or paypal via website. Wholesale: 40%, freight-free on
10 mixed copies or more, returns accepted. All books available direct from publisher or Baker & Taylor Books.